THE HORUS HERESY

Graham McNeill

A THOUSAND
SONS

To Evan. One down, nine hundred and ninety-nine to go.

A BLACK LIBRARY PUBLICATION

First published in Great Britain in 2010 by
The Black Library,
Games Workshop Ltd.,
Willow Road, Nottingham,
NG7 2WS, UK.

10 9 8 7 6 5 4 3 2 1

Cover and page 1 illustration by Neil Roberts.

A CIP record for this book is available from the British Library.

UK ISBN13: 978 1 84416 808 8
US ISBN13: 978 1 84416 809 5

See the Black Library on the internet at
www.blacklibrary.com

Find out more about Games Workshop
and the world of Warhammer 40,000 at
www.games-workshop.com

Printed and bound in the UK.

THE HORUS HERESY

It is a time of legend.

Mighty heroes battle for the right to rule the galaxy. The vast armies of the Emperor of Earth have conquered the galaxy in a Great Crusade – the myriad alien races have been smashed by the Emperor's elite warriors and wiped from the face of history.

The dawn of a new age of supremacy for humanity beckons.

Gleaming citadels of marble and gold celebrate the many victories of the Emperor. Triumphs are raised on a million worlds to record the epic deeds of his most powerful and deadly warriors.

First and foremost amongst these are the primarchs, superheroic beings who have led the Emperor's armies of Space Marines in victory after victory. They are unstoppable and magnificent, the pinnacle of the Emperor's genetic experimentation. The Space Marines are the mightiest human warriors the galaxy has ever known, each capable of besting a hundred normal men or more in combat.

Organised into vast armies of tens of thousands called Legions, the Space Marines and their primarch leaders conquer the galaxy in the name of the Emperor.

Chief amongst the primarchs is Horus, called the Glorious, the Brightest Star, favourite of the Emperor, and like a son unto him. He is the Warmaster, the commander-in-chief of the Emperor's military might, subjugator of a thousand thousand worlds and conqueror of the galaxy. He is a warrior without peer, a diplomat supreme.

As the flames of war spread through the Imperium, mankind's champions will all be put to the ultimate test.

~ DRAMATIS PERSONAE ~

The Thousand Sons

MAGNUS THE RED   Primarch of the Thousand Sons Legion

The Corvidae

AHZEK AHRIMAN   Chief Librarian of the Thousand Sons

ANKHU ANEN   Guardian of the Great Library

AMON   Captain of the 9th Fellowship, Equerry to the Primarch

The Pyrae

KHALOPHIS   Captain of the 6th Fellowship

AURAMAGMA   Captain of the 8th Fellowship

The Pavoni

HATHOR MAAT   Captain of the 3rd Fellowship

The Athanaeans

BALEQ UTHIZAAR   Captain of the 5th Fellowship

The Raptora

PHOSIS T'KAR   Captain of the 2nd Fellowship

PHAEL TORON   Captain of the 7th Fellowship

'The ancient knights' quest for the grail, the alchemist's search for the Stone of the Philosophers, all were part of the Great Work and are therefore endless. Success only opens up new avenues of brilliant possibility. Such a task is eternal and its joys without bounds; for the whole universe, and all its wonders... what is it but the infinite playground of the Crowned and Conquering Child, of the insatiable, the innocent, the ever-rejoicing heirs of the galaxy and eternity, whose name is Mankind?'

– The Book of Magnus

'The only good is knowledge and the only evil is ignorance.'

– Ahzek Ahriman

'The cloud-capped towers, the gorgeous palaces, the solemn temples, the great globe itself: ye, all which it inherits shall dissolve, and like this insubstantial pageant faded, leave not a rack behind.'

– The Prophecy of Amon

All is dust…

How prophetic those words seem now.

A wise man from ancient Terra said them, or words just like them. I wonder if he was gifted as I am. I say gifted, but with every passing day, I come to regard my powers as a curse.

I look out from the top of my tower, over a landscape of madness and storms of impossible energies, and I remember reading those words in a crumbling book on Terra. Over the centuries, I read every one of the texts from the forgotten ages that filled the great libraries of Prospero, but I do not think I really understood them until today.

I can feel him drawing near with every breath, every heartbeat.

That I still have either is a miracle, especially now.

He is coming to kill me, of course. I can feel his anger, his hurt pride and his great regret. The power he now has was unlooked for, unwanted and unnatural. Power is fleeting, some say, but not this power.

Once acquired it can never be given back.

His abilities are like nothing else wielded by man. He could kill me from the other side of the galaxy, but he will not. He needs to look me in the eye as he destroys me. It is his flaw, one of them at least, that he is honourable.

He behaves to others as he expects to be treated.

That was his undoing.

I know what he thinks I have done. He thinks I have betrayed him, but I have not. Truly, I have not. None of our cabal betrayed him; we did everything we could to save our brothers.

It has come to this, a father set to kill his favoured son.

That is the greatest tragedy of the Thousand Sons. They will call us traitors, but such an irony will go unrecorded, even in the lost books of Kallimakus. We remain loyal, as we have always been.

No one will believe that, not the Emperor, not our brothers, and especially not the wolves that are not wolves.

History will say they unleashed the Wolves of Russ on us, but history will be wrong. They unleashed something far worse.

I can hear him climbing the steps of my tower.

He will think I have done this because of Ohrmuzd, and in a way he is right. But it is so much more than that.

I have destroyed my Legion: The Legion I loved, the Legion that saved me. I have destroyed the Legion he tried to save, and when he kills me he will be right to do so.

I deserve no less, and perhaps much more.

Ah, but before he destroys me, I must tell you of our doom. Yet where to begin?

There are no beginnings and no endings, especially upon worlds of the Great Ocean. Past, present and future are one, and time is a meaningless.

So it must be arbitrary, this place where I begin.

I will start with a mountain.

The Mountain that Eats Men.

BOOK ONE

IN THE KINGDOM OF THE BLIND

CHAPTER ONE

The Mountain that Eats Men/Captains/Observers

THE MOUNTAIN HAD existed for tens of thousands of years, a rearing landmass of rock that had been willed into existence by forces greater than any living inhabitant of Aghoru could imagine. Though its people had no knowledge of geology, the titanic forces of orogenic movement, compressional energies and isostatic uplift, they knew enough to know that the Mountain was too vast, too monumental, to be a natural formation.

Set in the heart of an undulating salt plain the ancients of the Aghoru claimed had once been at the bottom of an ocean, the Mountain rose to a height of nearly thirty kilometres, taller even than Olympus Mons, the great Fabricator's forge on Mars.

It dominated the blazing, umber sky, a graceful, soaring peak shaped like an incredible tomb, crafted for some ancient king, of magnificent, cyclopean scale. No regular lines formed the mountain, and no artifice of mankind had shaped its rugged flanks, but one look at the Mountain was enough to convince even the most diehard sceptic that it had been crafted by unnatural means.

Nothing grew on its rocky sides, no plants, gorse or even the thinnest of prairie grasses. The earth surrounding the Mountain shimmered in the baking heat of the planet's sun, which hung low on the horizon like an overripe fruit.

Despite the heat, the rocks of the Mountain were cold to the touch, smooth and slick as though freshly raised from the depths of a black ocean. Sunlight abhorred its sides, its shadowed valleys, sunken grabens and sheared clefts dark and cold, as though it had been built atop some frozen geyser that seeped its icy chill into the rock by some strange, geological osmosis.

Surrounding the rumpled skirts of the Mountain, scattered collections of raised stones, each taller than three men, were gathered in loose circles. Such monuments should have been towering achievements, incredible feats of engineering by a culture without access to mechanical lifting equipment, mass-reducing suspensor gear or the titanic engines of the Mechanicum. But in the face of the Mountain's artificial origins they were primitive afterthoughts, specks against the stark, brooding immensity of its impossibility. On a world such as this, what force could raise a mountain?

None of the many people gathered on Aghoru could answer that question, though some of the greatest, most inquisitive and brilliant minds bent their every faculty to answer it.

To the Aghoru, the Mountain was the *Axis Mundi* of their world, a place of pilgrimage.

To the warrior-scholars of the Thousand Sons, the Mountain and its people were a curiosity, a puzzle to be solved and, potentially, the solution to a riddle their glorious leader had sought to unlock for nearly two centuries.

On one thing, both cultures agreed wholeheartedly. The Mountain was a place of the dead.

'Can you see him?' asked the voice, distant and dreamlike.

'No.'

'He should be back by now,' pressed the voice, stronger now. 'Why isn't he back?'

Ahriman descended through the Enumerations, feeling the psychic presence of the three Astartes gathered beneath the scarlet canopy of his pavilion with senses beyond the rudimentary ones nature had seen fit to gift him. Their potent psyches hummed through their flesh like chained thunder, that of Phosis T'kar tense and choleric, Hathor Maat's lugubrious and rigidly controlled.

Sobek's aetheric field was a tiny candle next to the blazing suns they carried within them.

Ahriman felt his subtle body mesh with his physical form, and opened his eyes. He broke the link with his Tutelary and looked up at Phosis T'kar. The sun was low, yet still powerfully bright, and he squinted against it, shielding his eyes from the reflected glare of sunlight from the salt flats.

'Well?' demanded Phosis T'kar.

'I don't know,' he said. 'Aaetpio can see no farther than the deadstones.'

'Nor can Utipa,' said Phosis T'kar, squatting on his haunches and flicking up puffs of salt dust with irritated thoughts. Ahriman felt each one like an electric spark in his mind. 'Why can't the Tutelaries see beyond them?'

'Who knows?' asked Ahriman, more troubled than he cared to admit.

'I thought you'd be able to see further. You're Corvidae after all.'

'That wouldn't help here,' said Ahriman, rising smoothly from a cross-legged position, and dusting glittering salt crystals from the inscribed crimson plates of his armour. His body felt stiff, and it took a moment for muscle memory to reassert control of his limbs after a flight in the aether.

'In any case,' he said, 'I don't think it would be wise to try on this world. The walls between us and the Great Ocean are thin, and there's a lot of unchannelled energy here.'

'You're probably right,' agreed Phosis T'kar, sweat dripping down his shaven scalp along the line of an elliptical scar that ran from his crown to the nape of his neck. 'You think that's why we linger on this planet?'

'Entirely likely,' said Ahriman. 'There is power here, but the Aghoru have lived in balance for centuries without suffering any ill-effects or mutations. That has to be worth investigating.'

'Indeed it is,' said Hathor Maat, apparently unaffected by the furnace heat. 'There's precious little else of interest on this parched rock. And I don't trust the Aghoru. I think they're hiding something. How does anyone live in a place like this for so long without any signs of mutation?'

Ahriman noted the venom with which his fellow captain spat the last word. Unlike Ahriman or Phosis T'kar, Hathor Maat's skin was pale, like the smoothest marble, his golden hair like that painted on the heroic mosaics of the Athenaeum. Not a bead of sweat befouled Maat's sculpted features.

'I don't care how they've done it,' said Phosis T'kar. 'This place bores me. It's been six months, and we should be making war in the Ark Reach Cluster. Lorgar's 47th are expecting us, Russ too. And trust me, you don't want to keep the Wolves waiting any longer than you must.'

'The primarch says we stay, so we stay,' said Ahriman.

Sobek, his dutiful Practicus, stepped forward and offered him a goblet of water. Ahriman drained the cool liquid in a single swallow. He shook his head when Sobek held a bronze hes out to refill it.

'No, take it to remembrancer Eris,' he commanded. 'She is at the deadstones and has more need of it than I.'

Sobek nodded and left the shade of the canopy without another word. Ahriman's battle-plate cooled him, recycling the moisture of his body and turning aside the worst of the searing heat. The remembrancers that had come to the planet's surface were not so fortunately equipped, and dozens had already been returned to the *Photep's* Medicae decks suffering from heatstroke and dehydration.

'You indulge the woman, Ahzek,' said Hathor Maat. 'It's not *that* hot.'

'Easy for you to say,' replied Phosis T'kar, wiping sweat from his skull with a cleaning rag. 'We can't all be Pavoni. Some of us have to deal with this heat on our own.'

'With further study, meditation and mental discipline you might one day achieve a mastery equal to mine,' replied Maat, and though his tone was jovial, Ahriman knew he wasn't joking. 'You Raptora are belligerent sorts, but eventually you might be able to master the necessary Enumerations.'

Phosis T'kar scowled, and a dense cluster of salt crystals flew from the ground beside him, aimed at Hathor Maat's head. Before it reached its target, the warrior's hand flashed, quick as lightning, and caught it.

Maat crushed the mass of crystals, letting it spill from his hand like dust.

'Surely you can muster something better than that?'

'Enough,' said Ahriman. 'Hold your powers in check, both of you. They are not for vulgar displays, especially when there are mortals nearby.'

'Then why keep them around?' asked Maat. 'Simply send her on her way with the others.'

'That's what I keep telling him,' said Phosis T'kar. 'If she's so damn keen to learn of the Crusade, send her to a Legion that cares about being immortalised, the Ultramarines or Word Bearers; she doesn't belong with us.'

It was a familiar sentiment, and Ahriman had heard it a hundred times from all his fellow captains. T'kar was not the most vocal; that honour belonged to Khalophis of the 6th Fellowship. Whichever viewpoint T'kar took, Khalophis would emulate more vociferously.

'Should we not be remembered?' countered Ahriman. 'The writings of Kallista Eris are among the most insightful I have read from the Remembrancer Order. Why should we be left out of the annals of the Great Crusade?'

'You know why,' said Phosis T'kar angrily. 'Half the Imperium wished us dead not so long ago. They fear us.'

'They fear what they do not understand,' said Ahriman. 'The primarch tells us their fear comes from ignorance. Knowledge will be our illumination to banish that fear.'

Phosis T'kar grunted and carved spirals in the salt with his thoughts.

'The more they know, the more they'll fear us. You mark my words,' he said.

Ahriman ignored Phosis T'kar and stepped out from the shelter of the canopy. The sensations of travelling in his subtle body were all but gone, and the mundane nature of the material world returned to him: the searing heat that had turned his skin the colour of mahogany within an hour of the Stormbird touching down, the oily sweat coating his iron hard flesh and the crisp scent of the air, a mixture of burnt salt and rich spices.

And the swirling aetheric winds that swept the surface of this world.

Ahriman felt power coursing through his body; glittering comet trails of psychic potential aching to be moulded into something tangible. Over a century of training kept that power fluid, washing through his flesh like a gentle tide, preventing dangerous levels of aetheric energy from building. It would be too easy to give in and allow it free rein, but Ahriman knew only too well the danger that represented. He reached up and touched the silver oakleaf worked into his right shoulder-guard, and calmed his aetheric field with a deep breath and a whispered recitation of the Enumerations.

Ahriman looked up at the towering mountain, wondering at the vast power of its makers and what the primarch was doing inside it. Until the power to far-see was taken away, he had not realised how blind he was.

'Where *is* he?' hissed Phosis T'kar, echoing his thoughts.

It had been four hours since Magnus the Red had followed Yatiri and his tribe into the Mountain, and the tension had been gnawing at their nerves ever since.

'You're worried about him, aren't you?' asked Hathor Maat.

'Since when could you master the powers of the Athanaean?' asked Ahriman.

'I don't need to. I can see you're both worried,' countered Maat. 'It's obvious.'

'Aren't you?' asked Phosis T'kar.

'Magnus can look out for himself,' said Hathor Maat. 'He told us to wait for him.'

The Primarch of the Thousand Sons had indeed told them to await his return, but Ahriman had a sick feeling that something was terribly wrong.

'Did you see something?' asked Phosis T'kar, noting Ahriman's expression. 'When you travelled the Great Ocean, you saw something, didn't you? Tell me.'

'I saw nothing,' said Ahriman bitterly. He turned and marched back into his pavilion, retrieving his weapons from a long footlocker of acacia and jade. He holstered a pistol that was as fine an example of the armourer's art as any crafted by the artificers of Vulkan's Salamanders, its flanks plated with golden backswept hawk wings and its grip textured with stippled hide.

As well as his pistol, he also bore a long heqa staff of ivory with a hooked blade at its end, its length gold-plated and reinforced with blue copper bands.

'What are you doing?' asked Hathor Maat when he emerged, accoutred for war.

'I'm taking the Sekhmet into that mountain,' said Ahriman. 'Are you coming?'

LEMUEL GAUMON RECLINED against one of the deadstones in the foothills of the enormous mountain, trying to keep within its shadow and wishing his frame was rather less fulsome. Growing up in the mid-continental drift-hives of the Nordafrik enclaves, he was used to heat, but this world was something else entirely.

He wore a long banyan of lightweight linen, colour-fully embroidered with interlocking motifs of lightning bolts, bulls, spirals and numerous other less easily identifiable symbols. It had been woven by a blind tailor in the Sangha commercia-subsid to his design, the imagery taken from the scrolls collected in the secret library of his villa in Mobayi. Dark-skinned and shaven-headed, his deep-set eyes carefully watched the encampment of the Thousand Sons, while he occasionally made notes in a pad balanced on his thigh.

Perhaps a hundred scarlet pavilions dotted the salt plains, their sides tied up, each home to a band of Thousand Sons warriors. He'd noted which Fellowships were represented: Ahriman's Scarab Occult, Ankhu

Anen's 4th, Khalophis's 6th, Hathor Maat's 3rd and Phosis T'kar's 2nd.

A sizeable war-host of Astartes warriors was encamped before the mountain, the atmosphere strangely tense, though Lemuel could see no cause for it. It was clear they weren't expecting trouble, but it was equally clear something was troubling them.

Lemuel closed his eyes and let his consciousness drift on the invisible currents of power that rippled in the air like a heat haze. Though his eyes were shut, he could feel the energy of this world like a vivid canvas of colour, brighter than the greatest works of Serena d'Angelus or Kelan Roget. Beyond the deadstones, the mountain was a black wall of nothingness, a cliff of utter darkness as solid and as impenetrable as adamantium.

But further out into the salt flats, the world was alive with colour.

The Thousand Sons encampment was a blazing inferno of shifting colours and light, like an atomic explosion frozen at the instant of detonation. Even amid that blazing illumination, some lights shone brighter than others, and three such minds were gathered beneath where Lemuel knew Captain Ahriman's pavilion was pitched. Something preyed upon these minds, and he dearly wished he was strong enough to venture closer. A bright mind, a supernova amongst guttering candles, normally burned at the heart of the encampment, but not today.

Perhaps that was the source of the Thousand Sons' tension.

Their great leader was *in absentia*.

Frustrated, Lemuel's mind drifted away from the Thousand Sons, and he let it approach the sunken dwellings of the Aghoru. Cut into the dry earth, they were as dark and lifeless as the Thousand Sons were bright and vital. The Aghoru people were as barren as the salt plain, without the slightest spark of a presence within them.

He opened his eyes, exhaling and reciting the Mantra of the Sangoma to calm his racing heartbeat. Lemuel took a drink from his canvas-wrapped canteen, the water warm and gritty but deliciously welcome. Three more canteens lay in the pack next to him, but they would only last the rest of the afternoon. By nightfall, he would need to refill them, for the remorseless heat let up only marginally during the hours of darkness.

'How can anyone live in this heat?' he wondered aloud for the hundredth time.

'They don't,' said a woman's voice behind him, and he smiled at the sound. 'They mostly live in the fertile river deltas further north or on the western coast.'

'So you said, my dear Camille,' he said, 'but to willingly trek from there to this desolate place seems to defy all logic.'

The speaker moved into view, and he squinted through the sun's glare at a young woman dressed in a tight-fitting vest, lightweight cut-off fatigues and dusty sandals. She carried a combination vox-recorder and picter in a sling around her neck, and a canvas shoulder bag stuffed with notebooks and sketchpads.

Camille Shivani cut an impressive figure with her sun-browned skin, long dark hair bound up beneath a loose turban of wrapped silk and dark glare-shields. Her skin was ruddy brown, her manner forthright, and Lemuel liked her immensely. She smiled down at him, and he gave her his best, most winning smile in return. It was a wasted effort; Camille's appetites did not include the likes of him, but it never hurt to be courteous.

'Lemuel, when it comes to humanity, even lost strands of it, you should know that logic has precious little to do with how people behave,' said Camille Shivani, brushing her hands together to clear dust from the thin gloves she always wore.

'So very true. Why else would we linger here when there's nothing worth remembering?'

'Nothing worth remembering? Nonsense, there's lots to learn here,' she said.

'For an archaeohistorian, maybe,' he said.

'I spent a week living with the Aghoru, exploring the ruins their villages are built upon. It's fascinating; you should come with me next time I make a trip.'

'Me? What would I learn there?' he asked. 'I study how societies form *after* compliance, not the ruins of dead ones.'

'Yes, but what was there before has an impact on what'll follow. You know as well as I do that you can't just stamp one civilisation on top of another without taking into account the previous culture's history.'

'True, but the Aghoru don't seem to have much history to supplant,' he said sadly. 'I don't think what they have will long survive the coming of the Imperium.'

'You might be right, but that just makes studying them while we can even more important.'

Lemuel clambered to his feet, the effort causing him to break out in torrents of sweat.

'Not a good climate for a fat man,' he said.

'You're not fat,' said Camille. 'You're generously portioned.'

'And you are very kind, but I know what I am,' said Lemuel, brushing his banyan free of salt crystals. He looked around the circle of towering stones. 'Where are your companions?'

'Ankhu Anen returned to the *Photep* an hour ago to consult his Rosetta scrolls.'

'And Mistress Eris?' he asked.

Camille grinned. 'Kalli's returning from taking rubbings from the deadstones on the eastern slope of the mountain. She should be back soon.'

Kallista Eris, Camille and Ankhu Anen had spent hundreds of fruitless hours attempting to translate the graceful, flowing runes that wove around the deadstones. So far, they had met with limited success, but if anyone could decipher their meaning it would be this triumvirate.

'Are you any closer to translating the script on the stones?' asked Lemuel, waving a hand at the ancient menhirs.

'We're getting there,' said Camille, dropping her bag beside his and lifting the picter from around her neck. 'Kalli thinks it's a form of proto-eldar, rendered in a dialect that's ancient even to them, which will make it next to impossible to pin down an exact meaning, but Ankhu Anen knows of some works on Prospero that might shed some light on the runes.'

'On Prospero?' asked Lemuel, suddenly interested.

'Yes, in the Athenaeum, some big library the Thousand Sons have on their home world.'

'Did he say anything about the library?' asked Lemuel.

Camille shrugged, taking off her glare shields and rubbing her gritty eyes. 'No, I don't think so. Why?'

'No reason,' he said, smiling as he saw Kallista Eris approaching the circle of deadstones, and grateful for the distraction.

Wrapped in a flowing white jellabiya, Kallista was a beautiful, olive-skinned young woman who, did she but desire it, had the pick of the male remembrancers attached to the 28th Expedition Fleet. Not that there were many remembrancers attached; the Thousand Sons were ruthlessly selective in choosing those allowed to accompany their campaigns and record their exploits.

In any case, Kallista declined every offer of companionship, spending most of her time with Lemuel and Camille. He had no interest in a liaison with either woman, content simply to spend time with two fellow students of the unknown.

'Welcome back, my dear,' he said, moving past Camille to take Kallista's hand. Her skin was hot, the fingers charcoal stained. She carried a drawstring bag over one shoulder, rolled up sheets of rubbing paper protruding from its neck.

Kallista Eris was a student of history, one whose field of expertise was the manner in which knowledge of the past was obtained and transmitted. Once, in the library aboard the *Photep*, she had shown Lemuel holo-picts of a crumbling text known as the *Shiji*, a record of the ancient emperors of a vanished culture of Terra. Kallista explained how its factual accuracy had to be questioned, given that its author's intent appeared to be the vilification of the emperor previous to the one he now served. The veracity of any historical text, she explained, could only be interpreted by understanding the writer's intent, style and bias.

'Lemuel, Camille,' said Kallista. 'Do you have any water? I forgot to take extra.'

Lemuel chuckled. 'Only you would forget to take enough water on a world like this.'

Kallista nodded, running a hand through her auburn hair, her skin reddening even beneath her sunburn. Her green eyes sparkled with amused embarrassment, and Lemuel saw why so many desired her. She had a vulnerability that made men alternately want to protect or deflower her. Strangely, she seemed oblivious to this fact.

Lemuel knelt beside his pack to retrieve a canteen, but Camille tapped him on the shoulder and said, 'Save it, looks like we're getting some brought to us.'

He turned and lifted a hand to shade his eyes, seeing one of the Astartes walking towards them with a bronze, oval-shaped vase held out before him. The warrior's head was bare, apart from a trailing topknot of black hair, and his golden-skinned features were curiously flat, his eyes dark and hooded like a cobra's. Despite the heat, Lemuel shivered, catching a flicker of cold power hazing the warrior's outline.

'Sobek,' said Lemuel.

'You know him?' asked Camille.

'Of him. He's one of the Scarab Occult, the Legion veterans. He's also Captain Ahriman's Practicus,' he said. Seeing Kallista's look of incomprehension, he added. 'I think it's a rank of proficiency of some sort, like a gifted apprentice or something.'

'Ah.'

The Astartes warrior halted, towering over them like a solid slab of ceramite. His battle armour was gloriously intricate, the crimson plates engraved with geometric forms and sigils that Lemuel recognised as similar to those woven into his banyan. Sobek's right shoulder-guard was stamped with a golden scarab, while the left bore the serpentine star icon of the Thousand Sons.

In the centre of the star was a black raven's head, smaller than the scarab, yet subtly given more relevance thanks to its positioning within the Legion's symbol. This was the symbol of the Corvidae, one of the cults of the Thousand Sons, though he had been able to glean precious little of is tenets during his time with the 28th Expedition.

'Lord Ahriman sends this hes of water,' said Sobek. His voice was sonorous and fulsome, as though produced in a deep well within his chest. Lemuel supposed the peculiar Astartes tone was due to the sheer volume of biological hardware within his body.

'That's very gracious of him,' said Camille, holding her hands out to receive the hes.

'Lord Ahriman instructed me go give the water to Remembrancer Eris,' said Sobek.

Camille frowned and said, 'Oh, right. Well, here she is.'

Kallista took the proffered hes with a grateful smile.

'Please send Lord Ahriman my thanks,' she said, placing the heavy vase on the ground. 'It's most considerate of him to think of me.'

'I shall pass your message to him when he returns,' said Sobek.

'Returns?' asked Lemuel. 'Where's he gone?'

Sobek glared down at him, and then marched back towards his encampment. The Astartes had not answered his question, but Lemuel caught an upward flicker of Sobek's eyes towards the mountain.

'Friendly sort, isn't he?' remarked Camille. 'Makes you wonder why we bother, eh?'

'I know what you mean; none of them are exactly welcoming, are they?' said Lemuel.

'Some are,' pointed out Kallista, emptying water into her canteen, and managing to spill more than she transferred. 'Ankhu Anen has helped us, hasn't he? And Captain Ahriman is quite forthcoming in his remembrances. I've learned a lot from him about the Great Crusade.'

'Here, let me help you,' said Lemuel, kneeling beside her and holding the vase steady. Like most things designed for or by Astartes, it was oversized and heavy in mortal hands, more so now that it was filled with water.

'I'd be fascinated to read what you've accumulated so far,' he said.

'Of course, Lemuel,' said Kallista. She smiled at him, and he felt his soul shine.

'So where do you think Ahriman's gone?' asked Camille.

'I think I know,' said Lemuel with a conspiratorial grin. 'Want to go look?'

THE SEKHMET, THE Scarab Occult, Magnus's Veterans, whichever name they bore, it was one of fierce pride and devotion. None of lower grade than a Philosophus, the last cult rank a warrior could hold before facing the Dominus Liminus, these veterans were the best and brightest of the Legion. Having transcended their likes and dislikes, defied their mortality and broken down their idea of self, these warriors fought from a place of perfect calm.

The Khan had called them automatons, Russ decried their fighting spirit and Ferrus Manus had likened them to robots. Having heard his primarch's tales of the master of the Iron Hands, Ahriman suspected the latter comment was intended as a compliment.

Clad in hulking suits of burnished crimson Terminator armour, the Sekhmet crunched out over the salt plains and onto the lower slopes of the Mountain. Ahriman felt the presence of his Tutelary above him, sensing its unease as the psychic void beyond the deadstones loomed ever closer.

Phosis T'kar and Hathor Maat marched alongside him, their strides sure and eager. The shimmering forms of Tutelaries darted thorough the air like wary shoals of fish in the presence of pack predators. Like Aaetpio, the Tutelaries of his fellow warriors and captains were fearful in the face of the Mountain's emptiness.

To those without aether-sight, Tutelaries were invisible, but to the Thousand Sons with power they were bright visions of exquisite beauty. Aaetpio had served Ahriman faithfully for nearly a century, its form inconstant and beautiful, a vision of eyes and ever turning wheels of light. Utipa was a bullish entity of formless energy, as bellicose as Phosis T'kar, where

Paeoc resembled an eagle fashioned from a million golden suns, as vain and proud as Hathor Maat.

Ahriman had thought them angels at first, but that was an old word, a word cast aside by those who studied the mysteries of the aether as too emotive, too loaded with connotations of the divine. Tutelaries were simply fragments of the Primordial Creator given form and function by those with the power to bend them to their will.

He linked his thoughts briefly with Aaetpio's. If Magnus *was* in trouble, then they would need to find out without the sight or aid of their Tutelaries.

Though he had seen nothing tangible in any of his divinations, Ahriman's intuition told him something was amiss. As Magister Templi of all Prospero's cults, Magnus taught that intuition was just as important a tool for sifting meaning from the currents of the Great Ocean as direct vision.

Ahriman suspected trouble, but Phosis T'kar and Hathor Maat longed for it.

The 28th Expedition had come to Aghoru three months ago. Its official designation in the War Council Records was Twenty-Eight Sixteen, though no one in the XV Legion ever called it that. Following the successful compliance of Twenty-Eight Fifteen, the sixty-three ships of the 28th Expedition translated from the Great Ocean to find a system of dead worlds, empty of life and desolate.

Indications were that life had once existed here, but now did not. What had caused such a system-wide cataclysm was unknown, but as the fleet made its way towards the sun, it became clear that life on the fifth planet had somehow survived the disaster.

How Magnus had known this insignificant shoal of the galaxy had included a planet inhabited by a severed offshoot of humanity was a mystery, for there were no residual electomagnetics or long-dead emissions to suggest anything lived here.

The Rehahti urged Magnus to order the fleet onwards, for the Crusade was at its height and the Thousand Sons had their share of plaudits yet to earn. Nearly two centuries had passed since the Crusade was launched in glory and fanfare, two centuries of exploration and war that had seen world after world folded into the body of the resurgent Imperium of Man.

Of those two centuries, the Thousand Sons had fought for less than a hundred years.

In the early years of the Crusade, prior to the coming of Magnus, the Astartes of the Thousand Sons had proven especially susceptible to unstable genes, resulting in spontaneous tissue rejection, vastly increased psychic potential and numerous other variations from the norm. Labels like 'mutants' and 'freaks' were hung upon the Thousand Sons, and for a time it seemed as though they would suffer an ignoble ending as a footnote in the history of the Great Crusade.

Then the Emperor's fleet had discovered Magnus the Red in a forgotten backwater of the galaxy, on the remote world of Prospero, and everything changed.

'As I am your son, they shall become mine,' were Magnus's words to the Emperor, words that had changed the destiny of the Thousand Sons forever.

United with the Legion that carried his genetic legacy, Magnus bent every shred of his towering intellect to undoing the damage their aberrant genes had done.

And he had succeeded.

Magnus saved his Legion, but the Crusade had progressed in the time it had taken him to do it, and his warriors were eager to share in the glory their brothers were earning with every passing day.

The Expedition Fleets of the Legions pushed ever outwards from the cradle of humanity to reunify the

Emperor's realm. Like squabbling brothers, each of the primarchs vied for a place at their father's side, but only one was ever good enough to fight alongside the saviour of humanity: Horus Lupercal, Primarch of the Luna Wolves and beloved son of the Emperor.

The Emperor stood at the head of the Luna Wolves and Guilliman's Ultramarines, ready to unleash his terrible thunder against the greenskin of Ullanor, a war that promised to be gruelling and punishing. Who better than the favoured son of the Emperor to stand at his side as they throttled the life from this barbarian foe?

Ullanor would be a war to end all wars, but there was fighting closer to hand that demanded the attention of the Thousand Sons. Lorgar's Word Bearers and the Space Wolves of Leman Russ fought in the Ark Reach Cluster, a group of binary stars occupied by a number of belligerent planetary empires that rejected the Imperium's offer to become part of something greater.

The Wolf King had sent repeated calls for the XV Legion to join the fighting, but Magnus ignored them all.

He had found something of greater interest on Aghoru.

He had found the Mountain.

CHAPTER TWO

Drums of the Mountain/Temple of the Syrbotae/
A Place of the Dead

THEY HAD ONLY been climbing for twenty minutes, but already Lemuel was beginning to regret his hasty idea to spy upon the Thousand Sons. He'd discovered the steps hidden in the rocks on one of his frequent solitary walks in the lower reaches of the titanic mountain. Set in a cunningly concealed cleft a hundred metres from the deadstones, the steps wound through the rock of the Mountain, climbing a steep, but far more direct path than the Astartes would be following.

It might be more direct, but it certainly wasn't easier. His banyan was stained with sweat, and he imagined he didn't smell too pleasant. The sound of his heart was like the pounding kettledrums of a triumphal band welcoming the Emperor himself.

'How much further is it?' asked Camille. She was relishing this chance to venture deeper into the Mountain, though Kallista appeared rather less enthusiastic. The Astartes awed and scared her, but the idea of spying on them had sent a delicious thrill through her when he had suggested it. He couldn't read her aura, but her expression said she was regretting her decision to come along.

Lemuel paused, looking up at the metal yellow of the sky to catch his breath and slow his racing heartbeat.

'Another ten minutes, maybe,' he said.

'You sure you'll last that long?' asked Camille, only half-joking.

'I'll be fine,' he assured her, taking a swig of water from his canteen. 'I've climbed this way before. It's not much higher. I think.'

'Just don't collapse on me,' said Camille. 'I don't want to have to carry you back down.'

'You can always roll me back down,' replied Lemuel, attempting some levity.

'Seriously,' said Camille, 'are you sure you're up to this climb?'

'I'm fine,' he insisted, with more conviction than he felt. 'Trust me, it's worth the effort.'

Back at the deadstones it had seemed like a grand adventure for the three of them to undertake, but the numbness of the senses he felt was like having his ears stoppered and his eyes sewn shut. From below, the mountain had been a black wall of nothingness, but climbing deeper into the rocks, Lemuel felt as if that nothingness was swallowing him whole.

He passed the canteen around, grateful that Kallista and Camille indulged his desire to stop for a rest. It was early evening, but the day's heat hadn't let up. Still, at least there was some shade here. They could afford a brief stop, for the only other route he knew would take at least an hour to traverse, even for Astartes.

Lemuel took the bandanna from around his neck and mopped his face. The cloth was soaked by the time he was done, and he wrung it out with a grimace. Camille looked up the steps, craning her neck to try to see the top.

'So where does this lead exactly?' she asked.

'There's a plateau a bit higher up,' he said. 'It's like a viewing platform of some sort.'

'A viewing platform?' asked Kallista. 'For what?'

'It looks out over a wide valley I call the Temple of the Syrbotae.'

'Syrbotae?' asked Camille. 'What's that?'

'A very old legend of my homeland,' replied Lemuel. 'The Syrbotae were a race of giants from the Aethiopian kingdom of Meroe.'

'Why do you call it that, a temple I mean?' asked Kallista, horrified at the word.

'You'll understand when we get there.'

'You have a way of choosing words that could get you into trouble,' said Camille.

'Not at all, my dear,' said Lemuel. 'The Thousand Sons are nothing if not rebels. I think they would appreciate the irony.'

'Rebels? What are you talking about?' asked Kallista angrily.

'Nothing,' said Lemuel, realising he had said too much. Stripped of his ability to read auras, he was being careless. 'Just a bad joke.'

He smiled to reassure Kallista he had been joking, and she smiled back.

'Come on,' he said. 'We should get going. I want to show you something spectacular.'

IT TOOK THEM another thirty minutes to reach the plateau, by which time Lemuel swore never to climb the mountain again, no matter how spectacular the views or what the enticement. The sound of his drumming heartbeat seemed louder than ever, and Lemuel vowed to shed some weight before it killed him.

The sky was a darker shade of yellow brown. The light would never really fade, so he wasn't worried about negotiating the descent.

'This is amazing,' said Kallista, looking back the way they had climbed. 'You were so right, Lemuel.'

'Yeah,' agreed Camille, taking out her picter. 'Not bad at all.'

Lemuel shook his head.

'No, not the salt flats. Over there,' he said, waving towards a row of spiked rocks that looked like slender stalagmites at the edge of the plateau. If the artificiality of the Mountain had ever been in doubt, the sight of the stalagmites, which were clearly the remains of fluted balustrades, would have dispelled it.

'Over there,' he said between gulps of air. 'Look over there.'

Camille and Kallista walked over to the stalagmites, and he saw the amazement in their body language. He smiled, pleased that he hadn't let them down with his talk of a spectacular view. He stood up and stretched his back. His breath was returning to normal, but the drumming in his ears hadn't let up one bit.

'You weren't wrong to call it a temple,' said Camille, looking down into the valley.

'Yes, it's quite a view, isn't it?' said Lemuel, regaining some of his composure.

'It is, but that's not what I mean.'

'It's not?' he asked, finally realising that the drumming he was hearing wasn't in his head. It was coming from the valley, a haunting, relentless beat that was hypnotic and threatening at the same time. The percussive booms of scores of drums interleaved with brutal disharmony, plucking at Lemuel's nerves and sending tremors of unease down his spine.

Intrigued, he walked stiffly on tired legs to join the two women at the edge of the plateau.

He put a hand on Camille's shoulder and looked down into the valley.

His eyes widened and his jaw hung open in surprise.

'Throne of Terra!' he said.

AHRIMAN HEARD THE drums, recognising the dissonant notes echoing from the Mountain as those once declared forbidden in an ancient age. Nothing good could come of such a sound, and Ahriman felt certain that something unnatural was being orchestrated within the valley. The Sekhmet matched his pace, their heavy suits driven on by uncompromising will and strength.

'This bodes ill,' said Phosis T'kar, as the drums grew louder. 'Damn, but I do not like this place. I am blind here.'

'We all are,' replied Hathor Maat, looking towards the upper reaches of the valley.

Ahriman shared Phosis T'kar's hatred of the blindness. As one of the Legion's Adept Exemptus, he had attained supreme summits of mastery, aetheric flight, connection with a Tutelary, and the rites of evocation and invocation. The Sekhmet were powerful warrior-mages, and could call forth powers mortal men could never dream of wielding. On his own, each warrior was capable of subduing worlds, but in this place, with their powers denied them, they were simply Astartes.

Simply Astartes, thought Ahriman with a smile. How arrogant that sounds.

Even as he scanned the valley ahead, Ahriman began forming the basis of a treatise for his grimoire, a discourse on the perils of dependence and overweening pride.

'There is a lesson here,' he said. 'It will do us good to face this without our powers. We have become lax in making war as it was once made.'

'Always the teacher, eh?' said Phosis T'kar.

'Always,' agreed Ahriman, 'and always the student. Every experience is an opportunity to learn.'

'So what lesson can I possibly learn here?' demanded Hathor Maat. Of them all, Maat had the greatest dread of powerlessness, and the walk into the Mountain had tested his courage in ways beyond what they had faced before.

'We depend on our abilities to define us,' said Ahriman, feeling the bass vibration of the drums through the soles of his armoured boots. 'We must learn to fight as Astartes again.'

'Why?' demanded Hathor Maat. 'We have been gifted with power. The power of the Primordial Creator is in all of us, so why should we not use it?'

Ahriman shook his head. Like him, Hathor Maat had faced the Dominus Liminus, but his mastery of the Enumerations was that of Adept Major. He had achieved self-reliance, but he had yet to achieve the oneness of self and ego-extinction that would allow him to reach the higher Enumerations. Few Pavoni could, and Ahriman suspected Hathor Maat was no exception.

'You might as well send us in unarmed and say we should fight with our bare hands,' continued Hathor Maat.

'Someday you may have to do just that,' said Ahriman.

THE GROUND, WHICH had been steadily rising for the last hour, began to climb ever more steeply, and the sound of drums grew louder, as though amplified by the soaring walls of the valley. As it always was, Ahriman's gaze was drawn up the incredible height of the mountain. The summit was hidden from view by its sheer mass, an endless slope rearing into a cloudless, yellow sky that was darkening to burnt orange.

It seemed inconceivable that this towering peak had been raised by natural means. Its proportions were too perfect, its form too pleasing to the eye, and its curves and lines flowed with a grace that was wholly unnatural. Ahriman had seen such perfect artifice before.

On Prospero.

The Vitruvian pyramids and cult temples of Tizca were constructed using golden means and the numerical series of the *Liber Abaci*. Their work had been distilled and refined by Magnus the Red to fashion the City of Light with such beauty that all who beheld it were rendered speechless with delight.

Everywhere Ahriman looked he saw evidence of geometric perfection, as though the mountain's creator had studied the divine proportions of the ancients and crafted the landmass to their design. Spiral patterns on the ground described perfect curves, pillars of rock were equally spaced, and each angle of cliff and cleft was artfully arranged with mathematical exactitude. Ahriman wondered what cause could be so great as to require such magnificent feats of geomorphic sculpting.

The mouth of the valley funnelled the sound of drums towards them, the beats rising and falling in what, at first, seemed a random pattern, but which Ahriman's enhanced cognitive processes quickly discerned was not random at all.

'Prime armaments,' he ordered, and fifty weapons snapped up in unison, a mix of storm bolters, flamers and newly issued rotary cannons capable of unleashing thousands of shells per minute. Their official designation was assault cannon, but such a graceless name had none of the power of its former incarnation, and numerological study had led the Thousand Sons to keep its previous title: the reaper cannon.

The Mechanicum had not the wit or understanding to recognise the power of names or the mastery and fear a well chosen one could instil. With six letters, three vowels and three consonants, the reaper's number was nine. Given the organisation of the Thousand Sons into a *Pesedjet* of nine Fellowships, it was a natural fit and the name had remained.

Ahriman recited the mantras that lifted his mind into the lower Enumerations and calmed his supra-enhanced physiology, allowing him to better process information and react without fear in a hostile environment. Normally this process would enhance his awareness of his surroundings, the essential nature of the world around him laid bare to his senses, but on this mountain the landscape was dead and lifeless to him.

Ahriman saw the diffuse glow of torches and fires ahead. The vibration of the ground was like the heartbeat of the mountain. Was he an ant crawling on the body of some larger organism, insignificant and easily swatted aside?

'Zagaya,' said Ahriman, and the Sekhmet formed a staggered arrowhead, with him at its point. Other Legions knew this formation as the speartip, and though Ahriman appreciated the robust, forceful nature of the term, he preferred the ancient name taught to him by the Emperor on Terra at the island fortress of Diemenslandt.

Phosis T'kar moved alongside him, and Ahriman recognised the urge for violence that filled his fellow captain. In his detached state, Ahriman wondered why he always called Phosis T'kar his 'fellow' and never his 'friend'.

'What are our orders?' asked Hathor Maat, tense and on edge.

'No violence unless I order it,' said Ahriman, opening the vox to the Sekhmet. 'This is a march of investigation, not of war.'

'But be ready for it to become a war,' added Phosis T'kar with relish.

'Sekhmet, align your humours,' ordered Ahriman, using his mastery of the Enumerations to alter his body's internal alchemy. 'Temper the choleric with the phlegmatic, and bring the sanguine to the fore.'

Ahriman heard Hathor Maat muttering under his breath. Normally a Pavoni could balance his humours with a thought, but without access to the aether, Hathor Maat had to do it like the rest of them: with discipline, concentration and self-will.

The valley widened, and Ahriman saw a host of figures standing at the crest of the slope, like the legendary warriors of Leonidas who fought and died at Thermopylae. Ahriman felt nothing for them, no hatred and no fear. In the lower Enumerations he was beyond such considerations.

With their sunset-coloured robes, baked leather breastplates and long falarica, the Aghoru warriors were the very image of the barbarian tribes of ancient Terra. The warriors were not facing down the valley to repel invaders, but were instead focussed on something deeper in the valley and beyond his sight.

Ahriman's fingers flexed on the hide grip of his bolter. The warriors above turned at the sound of the Sekhmet's advance, and Ahriman saw they were all wearing masks of polished glass. Expressionless and without life, they resembled the gold leaf corpse masks placed upon the faces of ancient Mycenaean kings to conceal the decay of their features.

At the most recent conclave of the Rehahti, Magnus had had invited Yatiri, the leader of the Aghoru tribes gathered at the Mountain, to speak with them. The proud chieftain stood in the centre of Magnus's austere pavilion, clad in saffron robes and wearing the ceremonial mirrormask of his people. Yatiri carried a black-bladed falarica and a heqa staff, not unlike those carried by the captains of the Thousand Sons. Though centuries of isolation had separated his people from the Imperium, the regal Yatiri spoke with clarity and fluency as he requested they refrain from entering the valley, explaining that it was a holy place to his people.

Holy. That was the word he had used.

Such a provocative word would have raised the hackles of many Astartes Legions, but the Thousand Sons understood the original meaning of the term – uninjured, sound, healthy – and rose above its connotations of divinity to recognise it for what it truly meant: a place free of imperfection. Yatiri's request had roused some suspicion among the Legion, but Magnus had given his oath that the Thousand Sons would respect his wishes.

That request had been honoured until this moment.

The Aghoru parted as the Sekhmet approached the crest of the valley, the sharpened blades of their falarica glittering in firelight. Ahriman had no fear of such weapons, but he had no wish to start a fight he didn't need to.

Ahriman marched towards the Aghoru, keeping his pace steady, and his gaze was lifted upwards in awed amazement as the titanic guardians of the valley were revealed to his sight.

On Prospero, the cult temple of the Pyrae was a vast pyramid of silvered glass with an eternally burning finial at its peak. Where the other cult temples of Tizca raised golden idols of their cult symbols before their gates, the Pyrae boasted a battle-engine of the Titan legions.

Supplicants to the pyromancers approached along a brazier-lit processional of red marble towards a mighty warlord Titan. Bearing the proud name *Canis Vertex*, the engine had once walked beneath the banners of Legio

Astorum, its carapace emblazoned with a faded black disc haloed by a flaming blue corona.

Its princeps was killed and its moderati crushed when the engine fell during the bloody campaigns of extermination waged in the middle years of the Great Crusade against the barbaric greenskin of the Kamenka Troika. The Emperor had issued the writs of war, commanding the Thousand Sons, Legio Astorum and a Lifehost of PanPac Eugenians to drive that savage race of xenos from the three satellite planets of Kamenka Ulizarna, a world claimed by the Mechanicum of Mars.

Ahriman remembered well the savagery of that war, the slaughter and relentless, grinding attrition that left tens of thousands dead in its wake. Imperial forces had been victorious after two years of fighting and earned a score of honours for the war banners.

Victory had been won, but the cost had been high. Eight hundred and seventy-three warriors of the Thousand Sons had died, forcing Magnus so reduce his Legion from ten fellowships to the *Pesedjet*, the nine fellowships of antiquity.

Of greater sorrow to Ahriman was the death of Apophis, Captain of the 5th Fellowship and his oldest friend. Only now that Apophis was dead, was Ahriman able to use that word.

Canis Vertex had been brought down on the killing fields of Coriovallum in the last days of the war by a gargantuan war machine of the greenskin, crudely built in the image of their warlike gods. Defeat seemed inevitable until Magnus stood before the enemy colossus, wielding the power of the aether like an ancient god of war.

Two giants, one mechanical, one a flesh and blood progeny of the Emperor, they had faced each other across the burning ruins, and it seemed the battle's conclusion could not have been more foregone.

But Magnus raised his arms, his feathered cloak billowed by unseen storms, and the full fury of the aether unmade the enemy war-engine in a hurricane of immaterial fire that tore the flesh of reality asunder and shook the world to its very foundations.

All those who saw the giant primarch that day would take the sight of his battle with that bloated, hateful, war machine to their graves, his power and majesty indelibly etched on their memories like a scar. Ten thousand warriors bowed their heads to their saviour as he returned to them across a field of the dead.

The Legio Astorum contingent had been destroyed, and Khalophis of the 6th Fellowship had 'honoured' their sacrifice by transporting *Canis Vertex* back to Prospero and setting it as a silent guardian to the temple of the Pyrae. The raising of such a colossal sentinel was typical Pyrae showmanship, but there was no doubting the impact made by the sight of the dead engine sheened in the orange firelight of the temple.

Ahriman was no stranger to the impossible scale of the Mechanicum war engines, but he had never seen anything to compare with the guardians of the valley.

TALLER THAN CANIS *Vertex*, the identical colossi that stood at the end of the valley were, like the mountain they inhabited, enormous beyond imagining. Soaring, graceful and threatening, they were mighty bipedal constructions that resembled an impossibly slender humanoid form. Crafted from something that resembled porcelain or ceramic the colour of bone, they were manufactured as though moulded from one enormous block.

Their heads were like sinuous helmets studded with glittering gems, and graceful spines flared from their shoulders like angelic wings. These guardians were prepared for war. One arm ended in a mighty fist, the other in an elongated, lance-like weapon, its slim barrel gracefully fluted and hung with faded banners.

'Sweet Mother of the Abyss,' said Phosis T'kar at the sight of them.

Ahriman felt the calm he had established within him crumble when confronted by such powerful icons of war. Like gods of battle, the towering creations rendered everything in the valley inconsequential. He saw the same grace and aesthetic in these guardians as he had seen in the valley's formation. Whoever had willed this mountain into existence had also crafted these guardians to watch over it.

'What are they?' asked Hathor Maat.

'I don't know,' said Ahriman. 'Xenos Titans?'

'They have the look of eldar about them,' said Phosis T'kar.

Ahriman agreed. Two decades ago, the Thousand Sons had detected a fleet of eldar vessels on the edge of the Perdus Anomaly. The encounter had been cordial, both forces passing on their way without violence, but Ahriman had never forgotten the elegance of the eldar ships and the ease with which they navigated the stars.

'They must be war engines,' said Hathor Maat. 'Khalophis would kill to see this.'

That was certainly true. Khalophis was Pyrae, and a warmongering student of conflict in all its most brutal forms. If an enemy was to be wiped from the battlefield with overwhelming firepower, it was to Khalophis the Thousand Sons turned.

'I'm sure he would,' said Ahriman, dragging his eyes from the titanic war machines. The valley was filled with Aghoru tribesmen, all bearing burning brands or battering their palms bloody on tribal drums.

Phosis T'kar held his bolt pistol at his side, but Ahriman could see his urge to use it was strong. Hathor Maat held his heqa staff at the ready. Warriors who had faced the Dominus Liminus and achieved the rank of adept could release devastating bursts of aetheric energy through their staffs, but here it was no more than a symbol of rank.

'Hold to the Enumerations,' he whispered. 'There is to be no killing unless I give the word.'

Perhaps a thousand men and women in hooded robes and reflective masks filled the valley, surrounding a great altar of basalt that stood before a yawning cave mouth set in the cliff between the towering guardians.

Ahriman immediately saw that this cave was no deliberately crafted entrance to the mountain. An earthquake had ripped it open and the blackness of it seemed darker than the depths of space.

'What's going on here?' demanded Phosis T'kar.

'I do not know,' said Ahriman, advancing cautiously through the Aghoru, seeing the crimson plates of the Sekhmet's armour reflected in their masks. The chanting ceased and the drumming diminished until the valley was utterly silent.

'Why are they watching?' hissed Hathor Maat. 'Why don't they move?'

'They're waiting to see what we do,' replied Ahriman.

It was impossible to read the Aghoru behind their masks, but he didn't think there was any hostile intent. The mirror-masked tribesmen simply watched as Ahriman led the Sekhmet through the crowds towards the basalt altar. Its smooth black surface gleamed in the last of the day's light, like the still waters of a motionless black pool.

Tokens lay strewn across the altar's surface, bracelets, earrings, dolls of woven reeds and bead necklaces; the personal effects of scores of people. Ahriman saw footprints in the dust leading from the altar to the black tear in the mountainside. Whoever had made them had gone back and forth many times.

He knelt beside the tracks as Phosis T'kar and Hathor Maat approached the altar.

'What are these?' wondered Phosis T'kar.

'Offerings?' ventured Hathor Maat, lifting a neck torque of copper and onyx, and examining the workmanship with disdain.

'To what?' asked Phosis T'kar 'I didn't read of any practices of the Aghoru like this.'

'Nor I, but how else do you explain it?'

'Yatiri told us the Mountain is a place of the dead,' said Ahriman, tracing the outline of a print clearly made by someone of far greater stature than any mortal or Astartes.

'Perhaps this is a rite of memorial,' said Phosis T'kar.

'You could be right,' conceded Hathor Maat, 'but then where are the dead?'

'They're in the Mountain,' said Ahriman, backing away from the cave as the drums began once again. He rejoined his warriors, planting his staff in the dusty ground.

As one, the Aghoru turned their mirrored masks towards the end of the valley, chanting in unison and moving forwards with short, shuffling steps, the butts of their falarica thumping on the ground in time with every beat of the drums.

'Mandala,' ordered Ahriman, and the Sekhmet formed a circle around the altar. Auto-loaders clattered and power fists crackled as energy fields engaged.

'Permission to open fire?' requested Hathor Maat, aiming his bolt pistol at the mask of the nearest Aghoru tribesman.

'No,' said Ahriman, turning to face the darkness of the cave mouth as wind-blown ash gusted from the depths of the mountain. 'This isn't for us.'

Bleak despair tainted the wind, the dust and memory of a billion corpses decayed to powder and forgotten in the lightless depths of the world.

A shape emerged from the cave, wreathed in swirling ash: hulking, crimson and gold and monstrous.

CHAPTER THREE

Magnus/The Sanctum/You Must Teach Him

HE COULDN'T FOCUS on it. Impressions were all Lemuel could make out: skin that shone as though fire flowed in its veins, mighty wings of feathers and golden plates. A mane of copper hair, ash-stained and wild, billowed around the being's head, its face appearing as an inconstant swirl of liquid light and flesh, as though no bone formed the basis for its foundations, but something altogether more dynamic and vital.

Lemuel felt sick to his stomach at the sight, yet was unable to tear his gaze from this towering being.

Wait… *Was* it towering?

With each second, it seemed as though the apparition's shape changed without him even being aware of it. Without seeming to vary from one second to the next, the being was alternately a giant, a man, a god, or a being of radiant light and a million eyes.

'What is it?' asked Lemuel, the words little more than a whisper. 'What have they done?'

He couldn't look away, knowing on some primal level that the fire that burned in this being's heart was dangerous, perhaps the most dangerous thing in the world. Lemuel wanted to touch it, though he knew he would be burned to ashes were he to get too close.

Kallista screamed, and the spell was broken.

Lemuel dropped to his knees and vomited, the contents of his stomach spilling down the rockface. His heaving breath flowed like milky smoke from his mouth, and he stared in amazement at his stomach's contents, the spattered mass glittering as though the potential of what it had once been longed to reconstitute itself. The air seethed with ambition, as though a power that not even the dead-stones could contain flexed its muscles.

The moment passed and Lemuel's vomit was just vomit, his breath invisible and without form. He could not take his eyes from the inchoate being below, his previously overwhelmed senses now firmly rooted in the mundane reality of the world. Tears spilled down his cheeks, and he wiped his face with his sleeve.

Kallista sobbed uncontrollably, shaking as though in the midst of a seizure. Her hands clawed the ground, scratching her nails bloody as though she were desperately writing something in the dust.

'Must come out,' she wept. 'Can't stay inside. Fire must come out or it'll burn me up.'

She looked up at Lemuel, silently imploring him to help. Before he could move, her eyes rolled back in their sockets and she slumped forward. Lemuel wanted to go to her aid, but his limbs were useless. Beside Kallista, Camille remained upright, her face blanched beneath her tan. Her entire body shook, and her jaw hung open in awed wonder.

'He's beautiful... So very beautiful,' she said, hesitantly lifting her picter and clicking off shots of the monstrous being.

Lemuel spat a mouthful of acrid bile and shook his head.

'No,' he said. 'He's a monster.'

She turned, and Lemuel was shocked at her anger. 'How can you say that? Look at him.'

Lemuel screwed his eyes shut, only gradually opening them once again to look upon this incredible figure. He still saw the light shining in its heart, but where before it had been beguilingly dangerous, it was now soothing and hypnotic.

Like a badly tuned picter suddenly brought into focus, the being's true form was revealed: a broad-shouldered giant in exquisite battle-plate of gold, bronze and leather. Sheathed at his side were his weapons, a curved sword with an obsidian haft and golden blade, and a heavy pistol of terrifying proportions.

Though the warrior was hundreds of metres below him, Lemuel saw him as clearly as a vivid memory or the brightest image conjured by his imagination.

He smiled, now seeing the beauty Camille saw.

'You're right,' he said. 'I don't know how I didn't see it before.'

A billowing mantle of golden feathers floated at the being's shoulders, hung with thuribles and trailing parchments fixed with wax seals. Great ebony horns curled up from his breastplate, matching the two that sprang from his shoulders. A pale tabard decorated with a blazing sun motif hung at his belt, and a heavy book, bound in thick red hide, was strung about his armour on golden chains.

Lemuel's eyes were drawn to the book, its unknown contents rich with the promise of knowledge and the secret workings of the universe. A golden hasp was secured with a lock fashioned from lead. Lemuel would have traded his entire wealth and even his very soul to open that book and peer into its depths.

He felt a hand on his arm and allowed himself to be pulled to his feet. Camille hugged him, overcome with wonder and love, and Lemuel took pleasure in the embrace.

'I never thought to see him this close,' said Camille.

Lemuel didn't answer, watching as two figures followed the being from the cave. One was an Aghoru tribesman in a glittering mask and orange robe, the other a thin man wearing an ash-stained robe of a remembrancer. They were irrelevant. The majestic being of light was all that mattered.

As though hearing his thoughts, the warrior looked up at him.

He wore a golden helmet, plumed with a mane of scarlet hair, his face wise beyond understanding, like a tribal elder or venerable sage.

Camille was right. He was beautiful, perfect and beautiful.

Still embracing, Lemuel and Camille sank to their knees.

Lemuel stared back at the magnificent being, only now seeing that a single flaw marred his perfection. A golden eye, flecked with iridescent colours without name, blinked and Lemuel saw that the warrior looked out at the world through this eye alone. Where his other eye should have been was smooth and unblemished, as if no eye had ever sat there.

'Magnus the Red,' said Lemuel. 'The Crimson King.'

AGHORU'S SUN HAD finally set, though the sky still glowed faintly with its light. Night did not last long here, but it provided a merciful respite from the intense heat of the day. Ahriman carried his golden deshret helmet in the crook of his arm as he made his way towards his primarch's pavilion. His connection to the secret powers of the universe had established itself the moment he had led the Sekhmet past the deadstones. Aaetpio's light had welcomed him, and the presence of the Tutelary was as refreshing as a cool glass of water in the desert.

Ahriman's relief at the sight of Magnus emerging from the cave was matched only by the recognition of the disappointment in his eyes. The magnificent primarch glared down at the circle of warriors gathered around the altar, and then shook his head. Even denied the use of his enhanced acuity in the Mountain, Ahriman had felt his master's enormous presence, a power that transcended whatever wards were woven into the stones of the mountain.

Magnus marched past them, not even bothering to further acknowledge their presence. The masked tribesman, who Ahriman knew must be Yatiri, walked alongside the primarch, and Mahavastu Kallimakus, Magnus's personal scribe, trotted after them, whispering words into a slender wand that were then transcribed by a clattering quill unit attached to his belt.

'This was a mistake,' said Hathor Maat. 'We shouldn't have come here.'

Ahriman rounded angrily on him, saying, 'You were only too keen to march when I suggested it.'

'It was better than sitting about doing nothing, but I did say that the primarch told us to wait,' Maat said with a shrug.

Ahriman had wanted to lash out at Hathor Maat, feeling his self-control faltering in the face of the Pavoni's smug arrogance. That he was right only made it worse.

He knew he should have trusted Magnus's judgement, but he had doubted. At best it would probably mean a public apology to Yatiri, at worst potential exclusion from the Rehahti, the inner coven of the Thousand Sons chosen by Magnus to address whatever issues were currently concerning the Legion.

Its members were ever-changing, and inclusion within the Rehahti was dependent on many things, not least an Astartes's standing within the Legion. The cults of the Thousand Sons vied for prominence and a place in the primarch's inner circle, knowing that to bask in his radiance would only enhance their powers.

As the power of the aether waxed and waned, so too did the mystical abilities of the cults. Invisible currents inimical to one discipline would boost the powers of another, and portents of the Great Ocean's ever-changing tides were read and interpreted by the Legion's geomancers with obsessive detail. At present the Pyrae was in the ascendance, while Ahriman's cult, the Corvidae, was at its lowest ebb for nearly fifty years. For centuries, the Corvidae had been pre-eminent within the ranks of the Thousand Sons, but over the last few decades, their power to read the twisting paths of the future had diminished until their seers could barely penetrate the shallows of things to come.

The currents of the Great Ocean were swelling and boisterous, the geomancers warning of a great storm building within its depths, though they could see nothing of its source. The subtle currents were obscured by the raging tides that empowered the more bellicose disciplines, ringing in the blood of those whose mastery only stretched to the lower echelons.

It was galling that reckless firebrands like Khalophis and Auramagma strutted like lords while the hidden seers and sorcerers who had guided the Thousand Sons since their inception were forced to the sidelines. Yet there was nothing Ahriman could do, save try every day to re-establish his connection to the distant shores of the future.

He put such thoughts aside, rising through the Enumerations to calm himself and enter a contemplative state. The pavilion of Magnus loomed ahead of him, a grand, three-cornered pyramid of polarised glass and gold that shimmered in the evening's glow like a half-buried diamond. Opaque from the outside, transparent on the inside, it was the perfect embodiment of the leader of the Thousand Sons.

Three Terminators of the Scarab Occult stood at each corner. Each carried a bladed sekhem staff, and their storm bolters were held tightly across the jade and amber scarab design on their breastplates.

Brother Amsu stood at the entrance to the pavilion, holding a rippling banner of scarlet and ivory. Ahriman's pride at the sight of the banner was tempered by the fact that he had incurred his primarch's displeasure by taking the Sekhmet into the Mountain.

Ahriman stopped before Amsu and allowed him to read his aetheric aura, confirming his identity more completely than any gene-scanner or molecular-reader ever could.

'Brother Ahriman,' said Amsu, 'welcome to the Rehahti. Lord Magnus is expecting you.'

THE INSIDE OF the pavilion would have surprised most people with its austerity. Given the suspicions that had surrounded the Thousand Sons since their earliest days, those mortals lucky enough to be granted an audience with Magnus the Red always expected his chambers to be hung with esoteric symbols, arcane apparatus and paraphernalia of the occult.

Instead, the walls were rippling glass, the floor pale marble quarried from the ventral mountains of Prospero. Carefully positioned black tiles veined with gold formed a repeating geometric spiral that coiled out from the centre.

The Captains of Fellowship stood upon the spiral, their distance from the centre but one indication of their standing within the Rehahti. Ahriman walked calmly along the dark portions, past the assembled warriors, to his place upon it. Beneath the crystal apex of the pyramid a golden disc in the shape of a radiating sun met the terminations of both black and white tiles, the heart of the gathering.

Magnus the Red stood upon the golden sun.

The Primarch of the Thousand Sons was a magnificent warrior and scholar beyond compare, yet his outward mien was that of a man faintly embarrassed by his pre-eminence amongst equals. Ahriman knew it was a façade, albeit a necessary one, for who could stand face to face with a being whose intellect and treasury of knowledge rendered all other accomplishments meaningless?

His skin was the colour of molten copper, the plates of his armour beaten gold and hard-baked leather, his mail a fine mesh of blackened adamant. The magisterial scarlet plume of his helmet spilled around the curling horns of his armour, and his mighty cloak of feathers was like a waterfall of bright plumage belonging to some vainglorious bird of prey. Partially hidden within that cloak was a thick tome, bound in the same, stipple-textured hide as that on Ahriman's pistol grip. It came from the body of a psychneuein, a vicious psychic predator of Prospero that had all but wiped out the planet's previous civilisation in ages past.

The primarch's expression was impossible to read, but Ahriman took solace in the fact that his position had not yet fallen to the outer reaches of the spiral. Magnus's eye glittered with colour, its hue never fixed and always changing, though for this gathering it had assumed an emerald aspect with flecks of violet in its iris.

Phosis T'kar stood near Ahriman to his right, with Khalophis on the spiral across from him. Hathor Maat was behind him and to his left, while Uthizzar was to his right and at the furthest extent of the spiral. A warrior's standing was not simply measured by his proximity to the centre of the spiral, but by myriad other indicators: the position of the warrior next to him, behind him and across from him. Who was obscured, who was visible, the arc of distance between his position and the sun disc, all played their part in the dance of supremacy. Each member's position interacted subtly with the other, creating a web of hierarchy that only Magnus could fathom.

Ahriman could not read the aetheric auras of his fellow captains, and he felt Aaetpio's absence keenly. He had not summoned Aaetpio to the meeting, for it would be overwhelmed in the face of the primarch's power. Magnus himself had no Tutelary, for what could a fragment of the Primordial Creator teach one who had stared into its depths and mastered its every nuance?

Magnus nodded as Ahriman took his place on the spiral and Brother Amon stepped from the shadows of the pyramid to pull the golden doors shut. Ahriman had not seen or sensed Amon's presence, but few ever did. Equerry to Magnus and Captain of the 9th Fellowship, Amon trained the 'Hidden Ones', the Scout Auxilia of the Thousand Sons.

'The Sanctum awaits the Symbol of Thothmes,' announced Amon, the crimson of his armour seeming to blend with the shadows that gathered around the edges of the pyramid.

Magnus nodded and lifted his golden khopesh from his belt. A flick of his thumb, and the haft extended with a smooth hiss, transforming the sickle-sword into a long-bladed polearm. Magnus rapped the staff on the sun disc, tracing an intricate, twisting shape on the ground.

Ahriman pursed his lips together as the world went dim and the interior of the pyramid was shielded from outside eyes. To be cut off from the aether was unpleasant, but now no one could eavesdrop within the pyramid by any means, be they technological or psychic.

Magnus had once boasted that not even the Emperor himself could penetrate the invisible veil cast around the Rehahti by the Symbol of Thothmes.

'Are we all assembled?' demanded Ahriman, speaking as the Legion's Chief Librarian. On Prospero, gatherings of the Rehahti would be conducted in aetheric speech, but here the Thousand Sons were forced to rely on the crudity of language.

'I am Ahzek Ahriman of the Corvidae,' he said. 'If you would be heard, then speak your true name. Who comes to this Rehahti?'

'I come, Phosis T'kar, Magister Templi of the Raptora.'

'I come, Khalophis, Magister Templi of the Pyrae.'

'I come, Hathor Maat, Magister Templi of the Pavoni.'

'I come, Uthizzar, Magister Templi of the Athanaeans.'

Ahriman nodded as the Captains of the Thousand Sons recited their names. Only Uthizzar hesitated. The young Adept Minor had only recently ascended to the role of Magister Templi, and Ahriman could not look at him without feeling the sorrow of Aphophis's death.

'We are all assembled,' he said.

'We are alone,' confirmed Amon.

Magnus nodded and looked each of his captains in the eye before speaking.

'I am disappointed in you, my sons,' he said, his voice a rich baritone laden with subtle layers of meaning. These were the first words Ahriman had heard from his primarch since leaving the mountain, and though they were of censure, they were still welcome.

'This world has much to teach us, and you jeopardise that by venturing onto a holy site of the Aghoru. I told you to await my return. Why did you disobey me?'

Ahriman felt the eyes of the captains on him and held himself straighter.

'I ordered it, my lord,' he said. 'The decision to march into the valley was mine.'

'I know,' said Magnus, with the barest hint of a smile. 'If anyone was going to defy me, it would be you, eh, Ahzek?'

Ahriman nodded, unsure whether he was to be reprimanded or lauded.

'Well, you set foot on the Mountain,' said Magnus. 'What did you make of it?'

'My lord?'

'What did you *feel*?'

'Nothing, my lord,' said Ahriman. 'I felt nothing.'

'Exactly,' said Magnus, stepping from the sun disc and following the white spiral out from the centre of the pyramid. 'You felt nothing. Now you know how mortals feel, trapped in their silent, dull world, disconnected from their birthright as an evolving race.'

'Birthright?' asked Hathor Maat. 'What birthright?'

Magnus rounded on him, his eye transformed into a flickering blue orb, alive with motion.

'The right to explore this brilliant, dazzling galaxy and all its wonders with their eyes open to its glory,' said Magnus. 'What is a life lived in the shadows, a life where all the shining wonders of the world are half-glimpsed phantasms?'

Magnus stopped next to Ahriman and placed a hand on his shoulder. The hand was that of a giant, yet he looked up at a face that was only slightly larger than his own, the features sculpted as if from molten metal, the single eye green once more. Ahriman felt the immense, unknowable power of his primarch, understanding that he stood before a living sun, the power of creation and destruction bound within its beauteous form.

Magnus's body was not so much flesh and blood, but energy and will bound together by the ancient science of the Emperor. Ahriman had studied the substance of the Great Ocean with the aid of some of the Legion's foremost seers, yet the power that filled his primarch was as alien to him as a starship was to a primitive savage.

'The Aghoru live on a world swept by aetheric winds, yet they remain untouched by its presence,' said Magnus, walking back towards the sun disc at the centre of the pyramid. His khopesh staff spun in his grip, tracing patterns Ahriman recognised as sigils of evocation that would summon a host of Tutelaries if made beyond the inert air of the Sanctum.

'They come to this Mountain every year, this place of pilgrimage, to bring the bodies of their dead to their final rest. They carry them into the holy valley and place them in the mouth of the mountain, and each time they return, the bodies of the previous year are gone, "eaten" by the Mountain. We all feel that the walls that separate this world from the aether are thin here. The essence of the Great Ocean presses in, yet the Aghoru remain unaffected by its presence. Why should that be? I do not know, but when I solve that mystery we will be one step closer to helping our brothers draw closer to the light at the heart of the universe. There is power in that mountain, great power, yet it is somehow contained, and the Aghoru are oblivious to it except as energy that devours the dead. I only hope that Yatiri forgives your trespass into their holy place, for without his peoples' help we may never unlock the secrets of this world.'

The primarch's enthusiasm for the task was infectious, and the shame Ahriman felt at jeopardising Magnus's great work was like a crushing weight upon his shoulders.

'I will make whatever reparations need to be made, my lord,' said Ahriman. 'The Sekhmet marched at my order and I will explain that to Yatiri.'

'That will not be necessary,' said Magnus, once again taking his place at the centre of the pyramid. 'I have another task for you all.'

'Anything, my lord,' said Phosis T'kar, and the rest joined his affirmation.

Magnus smiled and said, 'As always, my sons, you are a delight to me. The Aghoru are not the only ones who can feel that this world is special. The remembrancers we selected to join our expedition, they know it too, even if they do not consciously realise it. You are to make them welcome, befriend them and study them. We have kept them at a distance long enough; it is time for them to see that we have mellowed to their presence. In any case, I believe the Emperor will soon make their presence mandatory and send thousands more out to join the fleets. Before such an edict becomes law, don the mask of friend, of grudging admirer, whatever it takes to gain their confidence. Study the effects of this world on them and record your findings in your grimoires. As we study this world, we must also study its effect on mortals *and* ourselves. Do you understand this task?'

'Yes, my lord,' said Hathor Maat, the words echoed by the rest of the captains until only Ahriman was left to speak.

He felt the primarch's eyes upon him, and offered a curt bow, saying, 'I understand, my lord.'

'Then this Rehahti is over,' said Magnus, rapping his staff on the sun disc. Light streamed out from the centre, bathing the assembled captains in radiance. The Symbol of Thothmes was undone, and Ahriman felt the wellspring of the aether wash through his flesh.

Amon opened the pyramid's doors, and Ahriman bowed to the primarch. As the captains made their way outside, Magnus said, 'Ahzek, a moment if you please.'

Ahriman paused, and then walked to the centre of the pyramid, ready to face his punishment. The primarch sheathed his khopesh, the haft now returned to its original proportions. Magnus looked down at him, and his glittering green eye narrowed as he appraised his Chief Librarian.

'Something troubles you, my friend. What is it?'

'The story of the men in the cave,' said Ahriman. 'The one you told me when I was your Neophyte.'

'I know the one,' said Magnus. 'What of it?'

'If I remember correctly, that story shows that it is futile to share the truth of what we know with those who have too narrow a view of the horizon. How are we to illuminate our fellows when their vision is so limited?'

'We do not,' said Magnus, turning Ahriman and walking him across the spiral towards the pyramid's open doors. 'At least not at first.'

'I do not understand.'

'We do not bring the light to humanity; we bring *them* to the light,' said Magnus. 'We learn how to lift mankind's consciousness to a higher state of being so that he can recognise the light for himself.'

Ahriman felt the force of the primarch's passion, and wished he felt it too. 'Trying to explain the truth of the aether to mortals is like trying to describe the meaning of the colour yellow to a blind man. They do not *want* to see it. They fear it.'

'Small steps, Ahzek, small steps,' said Magnus patiently. 'Mankind is already crawling towards psychic awareness, but he must walk before he can run. We will help him.'

'You have great faith in humanity,' said Ahriman as they reached the doors. 'They wanted to destroy us once. They may again.'

Magnus shook his head. 'Trust them a little more, my son. Trust *me*.'

'I trust you, my lord,' promised Ahriman. 'My life is yours.'

'And I value that, my son, believe me,' said Magnus, 'but I am set on this course, and I need you with me, Ahzek. The others look up to you, and where you lead, others will follow.'

'As you wish, my lord,' said Ahriman with a respectful bow.

'Now, as far as studying the remembrancers goes, I want you to pay close attention to Lemuel Gaumon, he interests me.'

'Gaumon? The aetheric reader?'

'Yes, that's the one. He has some power, learned from the writings of the Nordafrik Sangoma by the feel of it,' said Magnus. 'He believes he hides this power from us, and has taken his first, faltering steps towards its proper use. I wish you to mentor him. Draw out his abilities and determine how best he may use them without danger to himself or others. If we can do it for him, we can do it for others.'

'That will not be easy; he does not have the mastery of the Enumerations.'

'That is why you must teach him,' said Magnus.

CHAPTER FOUR

The Sound of Judgement/
Shadow Dancers/Summoned

Fires seared the horizon as the planet burned. The skies bucked and heaved with pressure, kaleidoscopic lighting blazing across the heavens with unnatural fire. Screaming shards of glass fell in glittering torrents, the streets ran with molten gold, and once proud avenues of glorious statuary were brought to ruin by the thunder of explosions and the howls of killers.

Predators stalked the ruins of the beautiful city, a glorious representation of paradise rendered on earthly soil. Towering wonders of glass and silver and gold burned around her, the air filled with a billion fluttering scraps of scorched papers like grotesque confetti. The taste of blood filled her senses, and though she had never seen this place before she mourned its destruction.

Such perfect geometry, such pleasing aesthetics... who could ever wish harm to so perfect a refuge? Soaring silver towers sagged in the heat of the fires, broken glass falling from their high windows and pyramidion-capped summits like shimmering tears. Firelight danced in the glass, each reflecting a great, golden eye that wept tears of red.

She wanted to stop the madness, to halt the bloodletting before it was too late to save the city from complete destruction. It was already too late. Its fate had been sealed long before the first bomb had landed or the first invader set foot within its gilded palaces, marble-flagged processionals or glorious parks.

The city was doomed, and nothing could change its fate.

Yet even as the thought formed, she knew that wasn't true.

The city could be saved.

With that thought, the clouds dispersed and the wondrous blue of the sky was revealed. Glorious sunbeams painted the mountains in gold, and the scent of wildflowers replaced the stink of ash and scorched meat and metal. Once again, the silver towers reached up to the heavens, and shimmering, monumental pyramids of glass loomed over her, glittering with the promise of a bright and incredible future.

She walked the streets of the city, alone and without form, relishing the chance to savour its beauty without interruption. Hot spices, rich fragrances and exotic scents were carried on a soft breeze, suggestive of human life, but no matter how hard she looked, there was no sign of the city's inhabitants.

Undaunted, she continued her exploration, finding new wonders and raptures at every turn. Golden statues of hawk-headed figures lined one boulevard of marble libraries and museums, a thousand scented date palms another. Silver lions, hundreds of metres tall, reared at the entrance to a pyramid so huge it was more mountain than architecture.

Mighty carved columns topped with capitals shaped like curling scrolls formed enormous processional avenues down which entire armies could walk abreast. She wandered parks of incredible beauty nestled alongside the artifice of human hands, the two blending so seamlessly that it was impossible to discern where one began and the other ended.

Everywhere she looked, she saw perfection of line and shape, a harmony that could only have come about by the

*seamless fusion of knowledge and talent. This was perfection;
this was everything humanity aspired to achieve.*

*This was bliss, though she knew it was not real, for noth-
ing created by Man was perfect.*

Everything had a flaw, no matter how small.

As with any paradise, this could not last.

*She heard a mournful cry in the far distance, a sound so
faint as to be almost inaudible.*

*Carried from the frozen bleakness of an ice-locked future,
the cry was joined by another, the sounds echoing from the
sides of the pyramids and lingering like a curse in the
deserted streets. It resonated within a withered, atrophied
part of her mind – a forgotten, primal remnant from a time
when man was prey, simply an upstart hominid with ambi-
tions beyond those of other mammals.*

*It was the sound of fangs like swords, claws and hunters
older than Man.*

It was the sound of judgement.

HER HEART THUDDING in her chest, Kallista Eris jack-
knifed upright in her cot bed, drenched in sweat, the
haunting cries fading from her mind. The dream of the
unknown city faded like mist from her thoughts, fleeting glimpses of shimmering towers, silver-skinned
pyramids and majestic parklands all that remained of
her magnificent vision.

She groaned and lifted a hand to her head, a pounding headache pressing against the inner surfaces of her
skull. She swung her legs from the bed, pressing a palm
to her temple as she felt its intensity grow.

'No,' she moaned. 'Not again. Not now.'

She rose from the bed, moving to the footlocker at its
base on unsteady legs. If she could reach the bottle of
sakau before the fire in her brain erupted, she could
spare herself a night of pain and horror.

A sharp spike of agony lanced into her brain, and she
dropped to her knees, falling against the bed with a

muted cry. Kallista screwed her eyes shut against the pain, white lights bursting like explosions behind her lids. Her stomach lurched and she fought to hold onto its contents as the interior of her tent spun around her. She felt the fire pouring into her, a tide of burning nightmares and blood.

The breath heaved in her lungs as she fought against this latest attack, and her hands clawed knots in her thin sheet. She clenched her teeth, hauling herself along the bed towards the footlocker. The pain felt like a bomb had detonated within her brain, a blooming fire that raced out along her dendrites and synapses to sear through the bone of her skull.

Kallista hauled open the lid of her footlocker, throwing aside items of clothing and personal effects in her desperation. Her bottle of sakau was hidden in a hollowed out copy of *Fanfare to Unity*, a dreadful piece of fawning sycophancy that no one would ask to borrow.

'Please,' she moaned, lifting the dog-eared copy of the book. She opened it and lifted out a green glass bottle, mostly full of a cloudy emulsion.

She pulled herself upright, her vision blurring at the edges with flickering lights, the telltale signs of the fire. Every muscle was trembling as she lurched across the tent to her writing table where the hes vase sat alongside her papers and writing implements.

Her hands spasmed with a spastic jerk, and the bottle fell from her hands.

'Throne, no!' cried Kallista as it bounced on the dirt floor, but, mercifully, didn't break.

She bent down, but a wave of nausea and pain washed over her, and she knew it was too late for the sakau. There was only one way to let the fire out.

Kallista collapsed to the folding chair at the table, and her trembling hand snatched up a knife-sharpened pencil before dragging a sheet of scrap paper towards her.

Scrawled notes regarding yesterday's incredible expedition into the Mountain filled the top of the page.

She turned it over angrily as the fire in her brain blinded her, her eyes rolling back as its white heat seared through her body, its luminous light filling her every molecule with its power. Her mouth opened in a silent scream, jaw locked as her hand scratched across the page in manic, desperate sweeps.

The words poured out of Kallista Eris, but she neither saw nor knew them.

IT WAS THE heat that woke her.

Kallista opened her eyes slowly, the searing brightness of Aghoru's sun filling her tent with yellow light and oppressive heat. She licked her dry lips, her mouth parched as though she hadn't drunk in days.

She was asleep at her desk, a broken pencil still clutched in her hand, a sheaf of papers fanned around her head. Kallista groaned as she lifted her head from the table, dizzy and disoriented by the brightness of the sun and the dislocation of waking.

Gradually, her memory reordered itself, and she dimly recalled the half-remembered city of her dreams and its dreadful ending. The pain in her head was a dull ache, a mental bruise that left her dull and numb.

Kallista reached out and poured some water from the hes vase. It was gritty with wind-blown salt, but served to dispel the gumminess that had collected around her mouth.

Spots of water landed on the pages strewn across the desk, and she saw that they were completely covered in frantic writing. She rose awkwardly to her feet, her limbs still unsteady after their abuse during the night, and backed away from the desk.

Kallista sat on her bed, staring at the desk as though the papers and pencils were dangerous animals instead of the tools of her trade. She rubbed her eyes and ran a hand through her hair, sweeping it over her ears as she pondered what to do next.

Scores of sheets were filled with writing, and she swallowed, unsure whether she even wanted to look and see what this latest fugue state had produced. Most of the time it was illegible nonsense, meaningless doggerel. Kallista never knew what any of them meant, and if she was too late to extinguish the fire before it began with a soporific infusion of sakau, she ripped the papers to pieces.

Not so this time.

Kallista looked at the angular writing that was not hers, and the morning's heat was replaced with a sudden chill.

One phrase was written on the crumpled papers, over and over and over, repeated on every sheet a thousand times.

CAMILLE CLEARED THE dust of ages from the smooth object buried in the earth with delicate sweeps of a fine brush. It was curved and polished, and showed no sign it had been hidden for thousands of years. She slowly chipped around the object, marvelling at its condition as more of it was revealed. It was pale cream and had survived without any corrosion or so much as a blemish.

It could have been buried yesterday.

More careful brushes revealed a bulbous protrusion further along its length, something that looked like a vox-unit. She had never seen such a design, for it appeared it had been moulded as one piece. She chipped away more of the earth, pleased to have found an artefact that was clearly of non-human origin.

She paused, thinking back to the titanic statues, recognising a similarity between the material of this object and the giants. For all she knew, this could be part of something just as vast. A ghost of apprehension made her shiver, though she was still wearing her gloves, and had been careful not to touch the find with her bare hands.

Camille stretched the muscles in her back and wiped her arm across her forehead. Even shaded from the direct rays of the sun, the heat was oppressive.

With more of the object revealed, she lifted her picter unit, clicking off a number of shots from differing angles and ranges. The camera had been a gift from her grandfather, an old Model K Seraph 9 he'd sourced from an Optik in the Byzant markets, who'd looted it from a prospector he'd killed in the Taurus Mountains around the Anatolian plateau, who in turn had purchased it in pre-Unity days from a shift overseer in a manufactory of the Urals, where it had been built by an assembly servitor who had once been a man called Hekton Afaez.

Camille looked around, holding her breath as she listened for sounds of anyone nearby. She could hear the repetitive bite of picks and shovels from her digging team of servitors, the gentle murmur of daily life from the nearby Aghoru settlement, and the ever-present hiss of salt crystals blown by the wind.

Satisfied she was alone, she pulled off one of her gloves, her ivory white hand in stark contrast to the dark tan of her arm. The skin was delicate and smooth, not the hand one might expect to see on someone who spent time digging in the earth.

Camille slowly lowered her hand to the half-buried object, gently laying it on top with a soft sigh of pleasure. A comfortable numbness soon reached her shoulder and chest. The feeling was not unpleasant, and she closed her eyes, surrendering to the new emotions that came to her.

She felt the thread of history that connected all things and the residue left by those who had touched them. The world around her was dark, but the object before her was illuminated as though by some internal light source.

It was a battle helmet, an exquisite artefact of fluid, graceful design, and it was unmistakably alien in the subtle *wrongness* of its proportions. It was old, very old; so old, in fact, that she had difficulty in grasping so distant an age of time.

A shape resolved in the darkness, her touch breathing life into the memory of the helmet's long dead owner. Behind her fluttering eyelids, Camille saw the shadow of a woman, a dancer by the fluidity of her movements. She spun through the void like liquid, her body in constant motion between graceful leaps, her arms and fists sweeping out in what Camille realised were killing blows. This woman was not just a dancer, she was a warrior.

A word came to her, a name perhaps: *Elenaria*.

Camille watched, entranced by the subtle weave of the dancer's body as it twisted like smoke on a windy day. The shadow woman left blurred afterimages in the darkness, as though a phantom sisterhood followed in her wake. The more Camille watched, the more it seemed as though she watched thousands of women, all moving in the same dance, yet separated by fleeting moments in time.

The dancers slid through the air, and Camille was filled with aching sadness. Their every pirouette and graceful somersault gave voice to the sorrow and regret carried in their hearts like poison. She gasped as a potent mix of heightened emotions surged into her from the buried object, supreme pinnacles of ecstasy that were matched only by depths of utter misery.

A pair of glittering swords appeared in the dancer's hands, ghostly blades that Camille had no doubt were as deadly as they were beautiful. The shadow woman spun through the air with a shriek of unimaginable fury, her swords incandescent as she somersaulted towards Camille.

With a gasp of disconnection, Camille snatched her hand from the object, her flesh pale and cold, trembling with the aftereffects of powerful emotions. Her breath came in short hikes, and she looked down at the buried object with a mixture of fear and amazement.

Her flesh crawled with chills, and a feathered breath turned to vapour before her. The incongruous sight of breath on such a hot day made her laugh, the sound nervous and unconvincing.

'So what is it?' asked a man's voice, startling her. She jumped in surprise.

'Throne, Lemuel! Don't sneak up on people like that!'

'Sneak up?' he asked, looking down into the trench. 'Trust me, my dear, a man my size doesn't sneak.'

She forced her face to smile, though the memory of the dancer's sadness and fury was still etched in her features.

'I'm sorry,' she said. 'You startled me.'

'Sorry.'

'It's okay,' said Camille, feeling her heart rate returning to normal. 'I could use a break anyway. Here, help me out.'

Lemuel reached down into the trench with his arm extended, and she took hold of his meaty forearm as he took hold of her slender one.

'Ready?'

'Ready,' she said.

Lemuel hauled her upwards, and she scrambled up the sides of the trench, hooking her knee over the edge and hauling herself the rest of the way.

'Dignified, huh?' said Camille, scooting onto her belly before pushing herself to her feet.

'Like a dancer,' said Lemuel, and Camille flinched.

'So, what is it?' asked Lemuel again, pointing at the buried object.

Camille looked down at the battle helmet, the violence of the woman's shriek still echoing within her skull.

She shook her head.

'I have no idea,' she said.

The pit her servitors had dug on the outskirts of the Aghoru settlement was a hundred metres by sixty-five. Initial excavations had revealed a promising number of artefacts that were not of Aghoru or Imperial origin. Half of those servitors now stood in immobile ranks beneath a wide awning set up at the edge of the pit.

The idea of servitors needing to take breaks had amused Camille no end until Adept Spuler of the Mechanicum told her that he had been forced to decommission six of them due to heat exhaustion. Servitors didn't feel fatigue or hunger or thirst, and so continued to work beyond the limits of endurance.

Still, they had achieved more in one day than Camille could have hoped for.

Her dig site lay to the east of an Aghoru settlement named Acaltepec, three hundred kilometres north of the Mountain, and this landscape was as lush as the salt flats were barren. The settlement's name meant 'water house' in the local tongue, and Camille had come to understand that the term referred to the oval-shaped canoes used to fish the lake alongside which the sunken village was built.

The dwellings of the Aghoru were dug down into the earth, and provided shade from the sun and a near-constant temperature, making them surprisingly comfortable places to live in. Camille had been welcomed into Acaltepec's homes, finding its people quiet and polite, the barrier of language easily crossed by small gestures of kindness and courtesy.

Camille's servitors had dug into a series of structures that had long been abandoned. The best the lexicographers could approximate for the Aghoru's explanation of why they had been abandoned was 'bad dreams'. Adept Spuler had dismissed such claims as primitive superstition or a meaning lost in translation, but having touched the alien battle helm, Camille wasn't so sure.

She had enjoyed her time on this world, relishing the relaxed, unhurried pace of life and the lack of history pressing in from every individual. She had no doubt that life was hard for the people of Aghoru, but for her it was a welcome break from the hectic life of a remembrancer of the 28th Expedition.

Masked tribesmen swatted droning insects in the shade of tall trees hung with bright purple fruit, while the women worked on the shoreline, fashioning long fishing spears. Even the children were masked, a sight that had unsettled Camille at first, but like most things, it became part of the scenery after a while.

Wild plants and fields of sun-ripened crops waved in the breeze, and Camille felt a peace she hadn't known in a long time. There was history to this world, but it was buried deep, far deeper than any world she had set foot on before. She relished the sensation of enjoying a world simply for what she could see of it instead of feeling its history intruding on her every waking moment.

Lemuel knelt beside a long tarpaulin where the day's finds had been laid out, and lifted a broken piece of something that resembled a glazed ceramic disc.

'A regular treasure trove,' said Lemuel dryly. 'I can see why I came now.'

Camille smiled. 'It *is* a treasure trove actually. The artefacts here aren't human, I'm sure of that.'

'Not human?' asked Lemuel, rapping his knuckles against the flat edge of the disc. 'Well, well, how interesting. So what are they then?'

'I don't know, but whoever they were, they died out tens of thousands of years ago.'

'Really? This looks like it was made yesterday.'

'Yeah, whatever it's made of, it doesn't seem to age.'

'Then how do you know how old it is?' asked Lemuel, staring right at her.

Did he know? No, how could he?

Camille hesitated. 'The depth of the find and earned instinct I guess. I've spent long enough digging around the ruins of Terra to get a good instinct for how old things are.'

'I suppose,' he said, turning the disc over in his hands and looking at the edge where it was broken. 'So what do you think this is made of? It's smooth like porcelain, but it looks like an organic internal structure, like crystal or something.'

'Let me see,' she said, and Lemuel handed her the disc. His fingers brushed the skin above her glove and she felt a flicker of something pass between them, seeing a white-walled villa surrounded by sprawling orchards at the foot of a mountain with a wide, flat summit. An ebony-skinned woman with a sorrowful expression waved from a roof veranda.

'Are you all right?' asked Lemuel, and the moment passed.

Camille shook off the sadness of her vision.

'I'm fine; it's just the heat,' she said. 'It doesn't look manufactured, does it?'

'No,' agreed Lemuel, standing up straight and brushing dust from his banyan. 'Look at the lines running through it. They're lines of growth. This wasn't pressed in a mould or stamped by a machine. This material, whatever it is, grew and was shaped into this form. It reminds me of the work of a man I knew in Sangha back on Terra, Babechi his name was. He was a quiet man, but he could work wonders with things that grew, and where I came from, that was a rare gift. He called himself an arbosculptor, and he could grow trees and plants into shapes that were simply beautiful.'

Lemuel smiled, lost in reminiscence. 'With just some pruning shears, timber boards, wire and tape, Babechi could take a sapling and turn it into a chair, a sculpture or an archway. Anything you wanted really. I had an entire orchard of cherry plum, crepe myrtle and poplar grown and shaped to resemble the grand dining chamber of Narthan Dume's Palace of Phan Kaos for a charity dinner.'

Camille eyed Lemuel to see if he was joking, but he seemed completely serious.

'Sounds extravagant,' she said.

'Oh, it was, ridiculously so,' laughed Lemuel. 'My wife pitched a fit when she found out how much it cost. She called me a hypocrite, but it was so very beautiful while it lasted.'

Camille saw a shadow flicker on Lemuel's face at the mention of his wife, and wondered if she had been the woman in her vision. Intuition that had nothing to do with her gift kept her from asking.

'I think it might be made of the same substance those giants are made of,' she said. 'What was it you called them, Syrbotae?'

'Yes, Syrbotae,' he said, 'giants amongst men, like our grand host.'

Camille smiled, remembering that first sight of Magnus the Red as he emerged from the cave on the Mountain. What magnificent visions would fill her head were she to touch the Crimson King? The thought terrified and exhilarated her.

'He was magnificent, wasn't he?'

'Impressive, yes,' agreed Lemuel. 'I think you might be right about that disc. It certainly looks like the same material, but I'd have a hard time believing anything that big could be grown.'

'I suppose,' she said. 'Do you think the Aghoru would allow us to study the giants?'

'I don't know, maybe. You can ask.'

'I think I will,' said Camille. 'I have a feeling there's more to them than meets the eye.'

Camille looked back towards the Aghoru village as a personal speeder in the red and ivory of the Thousand Sons skimmed towards the dig site from the village. Wide and disc-shaped, the speeder floated low to the ground, leaving a puffed trail of ionised dust in its wake. Riding the speeder like a floating chariot of antiquity was a single Astartes warrior.

'A friend of yours?' asked Lemuel.

'Yes, actually,' replied Camille, as the skimmer drifted to a halt beside her and Lemuel.

The warrior removed his golden helmet, a gesture few others of the Legion bothered with, forgetting that mortals could not so easily tell them apart while they were clad in battle-plate.

His hair was a salt and pepper mix of grey and auburn, worn in long braids, and his face was deeply lined, as if his scholarly mien had somehow aged his ageless physiology. His skin had been pale when Camille had first met him, but like the rest of his battle-brothers, he was now the colour of burnt umber.

His armour was dusty from travel in the open, the small raven symbol faded and almost unnoticed in the centre of the serpentine star symbol of the Thousand Sons.

'Good day, Mistress Shivani,' said the Astartes, his voice hoary and brusque. 'How go your excavations?'

'Very well indeed, my Lord Anen,' said Camille. 'There are lots of new artefacts and almost as many wild theories to explain them. I've also found some more writings that might help us with the inscriptions on the dead-stones.'

'I look forward to studying them,' said the warrior, and his sincerity was genuine.

The limited number of remembrancers attached to the 28th Expedition had met with resistance amongst the Legion of Magnus, but Ankhu Anen had been a rare exception. He had willingly travelled with Camille to various sites around the mountain, both near and far, sharing her passion for the past and what could be learned from it.

His eyes moved to Lemuel, and Camille said, 'This is my friend, Lemuel Gaumon, he's helping me out with my wild theorising. Lemuel, this is Ankhu Anen.'

'The Guardian of the Great Library,' said Lemuel, extending his hand. 'It is an honour to meet you at last. I've heard a lot about you.'

The Astartes slowly extended his hand and took Lemuel's. Ankhu Anen's gauntlet easily swallowed Lemuel's hand, and Camille felt a flush of unease prickle her skin. A crackling tension fizzled between Lemuel and Ankhu Anen, as though the air between them had suddenly become charged with electricity.

'Have you indeed?' said Ankhu Anen. 'I have, likewise, heard a great deal of you.'

'You have?' asked Lemuel, and Camille could tell he was surprised. 'I didn't think the Thousand Sons paid us poor remembrancers much mind.'

'Just the ones that interest us,' replied Anen.

'I'm flattered,' replied Lemuel, 'Then might I ask if you have read any of my papers?'

'No,' said Ankhu Anen, as though to have done so would be a waste of time. 'I have not.'

'Oh,' said Lemuel, crestfallen, 'well, perhaps I might offer you a selection of my works to read sometime. Though I claim no great insight, you might find some sections of interest, particularly the passages detailing the growth of society after the compliance of Twenty-Eight Fifteen.'

'Perhaps,' said the Astartes, 'but I am not here to gather reading material, I am here to bring you a summons.'

'A summons? From whom?' asked Lemuel.

Ankhu Anen smiled.

'From Lord Ahriman,' he said.

CHAPTER FIVE
The Probationer/Creation Myths/
Memories of Terra

THE INTERIOR OF Ahriman's pavilion was his place of calm. Spacious and well-aired, it was a refuge from the heat of Aghoru. A walnut bookcase sat beside his bedroll, the books on its shelves like old friends, well-thumbed and read countless times, as much for their familiarity as their words.

A battered copy of *Akkadian Literary Forms* sat alongside a translated copy of the *Voynich Manuscript* and the *Codex Seraphinianus*. The *Turba Philosophorum* jostled for space with five of the seven cryptical *Books of Hzan* and the *Clavis Solomoni*, together with assorted other texts that would not attract unwelcome attention. But had anyone unlocked the hidden compartments secreted within the body of the bookcase, they would have found far more provocative tomes.

Thuribles hung from sandalwood rafters, and a brazier of green flame burned at the heart of the pavilion. Ahriman breathed in the heady mix of aromas, letting their calming influence ease his passage into the lower

Enumerations. He stared into the flames and directed his will along the currents of the aether.

The future was mist and shadow, a blurred fog through which no meaning could penetrate. In decades past, fractured timelines had shone through the veil of the empyrean, and Ahriman had seen the echoes of futures yet to come as easily as a mortal man could guess what might happen were he to step off a cliff.

The tides of the Great Ocean were a mystery to him, as unknowable as the far side of the world was to mariners of old. Ahriman felt his concentration slipping, his frustration at his inability to divine the future threatening to overcome his control. Concentration was the key that unlocked all doors, lying at the heart of every practice of the Thousand Sons, and the means by which the greater mysteries could be unravelled.

Angry with himself, Ahriman shook his head and opened his eyes, uncrossing his legs and rising in one smooth motion. Dressed in crimson robes and a wide leather belt, from which hung a set of bronze keys, he had foregone his armour for this meeting.

Sobek stood by the entrance to his pavilion, clad in his ruby plates of armour, and Ahriman felt his disapproval.

'Speak,' commanded Ahriman. 'Your aura wears at me. Speak and be done with it.'

'May I speak freely, my lord?'

'I just said you could,' snapped Ahriman, forcing himself to calm. 'You are my Practicus, and if there is no candour between us you will never achieve the rank of Philosophus.'

'It galls me to see you punished thus,' said Sobek. 'To be forced to train a mortal in the mysteries is no task for one such as you.'

'Punished?' asked Ahriman. 'Is that what you think this is, punishment?'

'What else could it be?'

'The primarch has entrusted me with a great task, and this is but the first stage of it,' said Ahriman. 'Lemuel Gaumon is mortal and he has a little knowledge and a little power.'

Sobek snorted in derision and said, 'That's nothing unusual in the 28th Expedition.'

Ahriman smiled.

'True,' he said, 'but he is a child taking his first steps, unaware that he walks blindfold along the edge of an abyss. I am to help him to remove that blindfold.'

'But why?'

'Because knowledge is a deadly friend, if no one sets the rules. It is our master's wish that I illuminate this mortal,' said Ahriman. 'Or do you doubt the word of the Crimson King?'

Many of the Emperor's sons had earned honourable names over the decades of war, not least of whom was Horus Lupercal, Primarch of the Luna Wolves, beloved son of the Emperor. Fulgrim's warriors knew their leader as the Phoenician, and the First Legion was led by the Lion. Magnus alone of his brothers had earned a series of less than flattering names over the decades of war: *Sorcerer… Warlock…*

So when Ahriman had heard his primarch was known among the 28th Expedition's remembrancers as the Crimson King, he had allowed the name to stand.

Sobek bowed and said, 'Never, my lord. Lord Magnus is the fountainhead of our Legion, and I will never doubt his course, no matter what.'

Ahriman nodded, sensing the presence of Lemuel Gaumon beyond the canopy of his pavilion. He felt the man's aura, its light dull and unfocussed among the glittering flares of his fellow legionaries. Where they shone with purity and focus, Gaumon's was blurred and raw, like an unshielded lumen globe, bright in its own way, but unpleasant to look upon for more than a moment.

'Gaumon is without, Sobek,' said Ahriman. 'Send him in.'

Sobek nodded and left the pavilion, returning a moment later with a heavyset man dressed in a long crimson robe with loose sleeves and a crest of one of the Nordafrik conclaves stitched on his left breast, Sangha, if Ahriman remembered correctly. Lemuel's skin was dark, though not the dark of those who had been tanned by the Aghoru sun. Ahriman smelled the man's body odour even over the megaleion oil coating his skin.

'Welcome,' said Ahriman, modulating his accent to a more natural, fluid tone and indicating the rug beside the brazier. 'Please, sit.'

Lemuel lowered himself to the rug, clutching a battered notebook to his chest as Sobek withdrew, leaving them alone.

Ahriman sat before Lemuel and said, 'I am Ahzek Ahriman, Chief Librarian of the Thousand Sons.'

Lemuel nodded vigorously.

'I know who you are, my lord,' he said. 'I'm honoured you sent for me.'

'Do you know why I sent for you?'

'I confess I do not.'

'It is because you have power, Lemuel Gaumon,' said Ahriman. 'You can see the currents of the aether that flow through the world from the Great Ocean. You may not know the names, but you know of what I speak.'

Lemuel shook his head, flustered and caught off guard.

'I think you must be mistaken, my lord,' said Lemuel, and Ahriman laughed at the sudden panic in his aura.

Lemuel held up his notebook and said, 'Please, my lord, I am just a humble remembrancer.'

'No,' said Ahriman, leaning forward and projecting a measure of fire into his aura. 'You are far more than that – you are a wielder of sorcery, a witch!'

It was a simple trick, an invisible domination to cow weaker minds. The effect was immediate. Waves of fear and guilt washed from Lemuel in a tide. Ahriman rose through the Enumerations to shield himself from the man's raw terror.

'Please... I do no harm to anyone,' pleaded Lemuel. 'I'm not a witch, I swear, I just read old books. I don't know any spells or anything, please!'

'Be at peace, Lemuel,' chuckled Ahriman, holding up an outstretched hand. 'I am teasing you. I am no fool of a witch hunter, and did not summon you to condemn you. I am going to liberate you.'

'Liberate me?' asked Lemuel, his breathing returning to normal. 'From what?'

'From your blindness and limitations,' said Ahriman. 'You have power, but you do not know how to wield it with any skill. I can show you how you can use what power you have, and I can show you how to use it to see things you cannot imagine.'

Ahriman read the suspicion in Lemuel's aura, and eased it with a nudge of his own powers, as an animal is calmed by soft words and a gentle touch. The man had no barriers whatsoever in his mind, his psyche undefended and open to the tides of the Great Ocean. In that instant of contact, Ahriman knew the man's every secret. He saw the barb of sorrow in the man's heart and mellowed, understanding that the grief driving him echoed his own.

Power was no salve to that grief, and Lemuel Gaumon would realise that in time. That crushing realisation could wait though; there was no need to dash his hopes just yet.

'You are so vulnerable, and you don't even realise it,' said Ahriman softly.

'My lord?'

'Tell me what you know of the Great Ocean.'

'I don't know that term.'

'The warp,' said Ahriman. 'The empyrean.'

'Oh. Not much really,' admitted Lemuel. He took a deep breath before continuing, like a student afraid of giving the wrong answer. 'It's a kind of higher dimension, a psychic realm where starships can travel far faster than normal. It allows astrotelepaths to communicate and, well, that's about it.'

'That is broadly true, but the Great Ocean is so much more than that, Lemuel. It is the home of the Primordial Creator, the energy that drives all things. It is a reflection of our universe and we are a reflection of it. What occurs in one affects the other, and like a planetary ocean, it is not without its predators. Your mind, dull though it is, shines like a beacon in the ocean for the creatures that lurk in its depths. Were I to allow you to use your powers unchecked, you would soon be dead.'

Lemuel swallowed and placed the notebook beside him.

'I had no idea,' he said. 'I just thought… I mean, I don't know what I thought. I figured I was able to tap into parts of my mind others weren't able to. I could see lights around people, their auras, and I learned to read them, to understand what they were feeling. Does that make sense?'

'It makes perfect sense. Those lights, as you call them, are aetheric echoes of a person's emotion, health and power. A shadow self of that person exists in the Great Ocean, a reflection of their psyche that imprints itself in its currents.'

Lemuel shook his head with a wry smile and said, 'This is a lot to take in, my lord.'

'I understand that,' said Ahriman. 'I do not expect you to absorb it all just now. You will become my Probationer, and begin your studies on the morrow.'

'Do I have a choice in this?'

'Not if you want to live.'

'Tomorrow,' said Lemuel. 'Lucky I happened to be selected for the 28th Expedition, eh?'

'If there is one thing I have come to know in my long years of study, it is that there is no such thing as luck when it comes to the positioning of the universe's chess pieces. Your coming here was no accident. I was *meant* to train you. I have seen it,' said Ahriman.

'You saw the future?' asked Lemuel. 'You knew I was going to be here and that this was all going to happen?'

'Many years ago, I saw you standing on the streets of Prospero in the robes of a Neophyte.'

'On Prospero!' said Lemuel, his aura shimmering with his excitement. 'And a Neophyte, that's one of your ranks, isn't it?'

'It is,' confirmed Ahriman, 'a very low one.'

'And you saw this? It's the future? That's amazing!'

Ahriman smiled at how easily mortals were impressed by such powers. How impressed and, more often, how frightened.

'In years past, I could travel the Great Ocean and open my eyes to a world of potential futures,' explained Ahriman. 'To do that is no great trick, even mortals can do it. But to read those currents and sort meaning and truth from the chaos is a skill beyond all but the most gifted of seers.'

'Will I be able read it?'

'No,' said Ahriman, 'not without decades of training by the Corvidae. To read the multi-dimensional patterns of the Great Ocean and lift meaning from the meaningless requires two modalities of thought. Firstly, the rapid, accurate and efficient movement of thought from concept to concept, whereby all ideas become one; and secondly, the halting of thought altogether, were one idea is reduced to nothing. I have an eidetic memory, a mind crafted by the greatest technologists of the forgotten ages that allows me to do this. You do not.'

'Then what *can* I do?'

'First you must learn how to shield your consciousness from danger,' said Ahriman, rising to his feet. 'When you have accomplished that, *then* we will see what you can do.'

THE ALIEN TITANS towered above him, majestic and powerful, but Khalophis wasn't impressed. True, they were bigger than *Canis Vertex*, but they had none of the robust brutality of the Warlord guarding the gates of the Pyrae cult's temple. He stepped back, craning his neck to see the elongated curves of their mighty head sections.

Phosis T'kar had told Khalophis of the giant statues, and he'd wanted to see them for himself, to measure himself against them.

He turned from the towering constructs to face his warriors. A dozen Astartes from the 6th Fellowship stood behind the black altar, an object that reeked of dark rites of sacrifice. He'd listened at the Rehahti as his primarch had explained that the Mountain was a place of remembrance for the dead and was to be treated with respect. That didn't change the fact that Khalophis simply didn't trust the Aghoru.

Their masked leader stood with ten other tribesmen, all with their faces obscured by mirrored masks. Their presence had been a condition of allowing Khalophis and his warriors to come to the valley. That spoke of subterfuge. Why would the Aghoru not want the Legion to come to their valley?

'What do you have to hide?' he whispered, unheard by any save himself.

The masked leader of the Aghoru was looking at him, and Khalophis gestured towards the giant constructs.

'Do you know what these are?' he asked.

'They are the guardians of the Mountain,' said the tribesman.

'Maybe they were once, but now they are just expensive statues.'

'They are the guardians,' repeated the masked tribesman.

'They are Titans,' said Khalophis, slowly, 'giant war machines. In ages past they could level cities and lay waste to entire armies, but now they are dead.'

'Our legends say they will walk again, when the *Daiesthai* break the bonds of their eternal prison.'

'I don't know what that means, but they won't walk again,' said Khalophis. 'They are just machines, dead machines.'

He pointed up towards the giant head of the construct. 'The princeps would sit up there if this was an Imperial Titan, but since it's alien, who knows what's really in there? A giant brain in a jar, a wired-in collective of self-aware robots, it could be anything.'

The Aghoru tribesman said, 'What is a princeps? Is that a god?'

Khalophis laughed uproariously. 'He might as well be. It's not a term in favour, but what else really gets the sense of it across? An Astartes is a god to mortals, a Titan... Well, that's the god of the battlefield. Even the Legions take note when the engines of the Mechanicum walk.'

'These have never walked,' said the tribesman, 'not as long as we have known them. We hope they never do.'

'It's Yatiri, isn't it?' asked Khalophis, bending down.

'Yes, Brother Khalophis, that is my name.'

'I am not your brother,' he hissed. Even cut off from his powers and unable to communicate with his Tutelary, Khalophis felt energised, not with the surging tides of aether that normally empowered him, but by the act of domination.

'We are all brothers,' said Yatiri, calm in the face of his hostility. 'Is that not what your great leader teaches? He tells us that we are all one race, divided by a great catastrophe, but drawing together once more under the watchful eye of the great Sky Emperor.'

'That's true enough,' conceded Khalophis. 'But not all who were divided wish to be drawn together again. Some of them fight us.'

'We are not fighting you,' said Yatiri. 'We welcome your coming.'

'That's your story,' said Khalophis, leaning on the altar and regarding the mortal through the green-hued lenses of his battle helm. Though this was designated a compliant world, Khalophis had his combat senses to the fore. The Aghoru falarica were picked out in white, the tribesmen themselves in red, though the threat indicators were negligible.

'We *are* the story,' said Yatiri. 'From the moment your leader set foot on our lands, we became part of it.'

'That's remembrancer talk,' spat Khalophis. 'And I don't trust people who wear masks, especially masks like mirrors. I ask myself what they're hiding behind them.'

'You wear a mask,' pointed out Yatiri, walking past Khalophis towards the cave mouth.

'This is a helmet.'

'It achieves the same thing, it conceals your features.'

'Why do you wear them?' asked Khalophis, following the tribesman towards the towering guardians of the Mountain.

'Why do you?' countered Yatiri without turning.

'For protection. My helmet is armoured and it has saved my life on more than one occasion.'

'I wear this mask for protection also,' said Yatiri, reaching the foot of the leftmost giant.

'From what? Your tribes do not make war on one another and there are no predators of any great size on this world. Where is the need?' asked Khalophis.

Yatiri turned and rested his hand on the smooth surface of the enormous foot. This close to the giants, the scale of them was truly breathtaking. Khalophis thought back to the fire-blackened ruins of Kamenka Ulizarna and the sight of Magnus the Red standing before the might of the greenskin colossus. That had been a battle to remember, and standing this close to an alien war engine made him fully appreciate the power of his beloved leader.

'Our legends speak of a time when this world belonged to a race of elder beings known as *Elohim*,' said Yatiri, squatting beside the enormous foot, 'a race so beautiful that they fell in love with the wonder of their own form.'

Yatiri turned his gaze towards the cave mouth and said, 'The *Elohim* found a source of great power and used it to walk amongst the stars like gods, shaping worlds in their own image and crafting an empire amongst the heavens to rival the gods. They indulged their every whim, denied themselves nothing and lived an immortal life of desire.'

'Sounds like a good life,' said Khalophis, casting a suspicious glance into the darkness.

'For a time it was,' agreed Yatiri, 'but such hubris cannot long go unpunished. The *Elohim* abused the source of their power, corrupting it with their wanton decadence, and it turned on them. Their entire race was virtually destroyed in a single night of blood. Their worlds fell and the oceans drank the land. But that was not the worst of it.'

'Really? That sounds bad enough,' said Khalophis, bored by Yatiri's tale. Creation and destruction myths were a common feature in most cultures, morality tales used to control emerging generations. This one was little different from a hundred others he had read in the libraries of Prospero.

'The *Elohim* were all but extinct, but among the pitiful survivors, some were twisted by the power that had once served them. They became the *Daiesthai*, a race as cruel as they had once been beautiful. The *Elohim* fought the *Daiesthai*, eventually driving them back to the shadows beneath the world. Their power was broken and they had not the means to destroy the *Daiesthai*, so with the last of their power, they raised the Mountain to seal their prison and set these giants to guard against their return. The *Daiesthai* remain imprisoned beneath the world, but their hunger for death can never be sated, and so we bring them the dead of our tribes at every turning of the world to ensure their eternal slumber continues.'

'That's a pretty tale,' said Khalophis, 'but it doesn't explain why you wear those masks.'

'We are the inheritors of the *Elohim's* world, and their destruction serves as a warning against the temptations of vanity and self-obsession. Our masks are a way of ensuring we do not fall as they fell.'

Khalophis considered that for a moment.

'Do you ever take them off?' he asked.

'For bathing, yes.'

'What about mating?'

Yatiri shook his head and said, 'It is unseemly for you to ask, but you are not Aghoru, so I will answer. No, we do not take them off, even then, as pleasures of the flesh were among the greatest vices of the *Elohim*.'

'That explains why there're so few of you on this world,' said Khalophis, wanting nothing more than to return to the encampment and re-establish his connection to Sioda. With the power of the Pyrae in ascendance, his Tutelary was a winged essence of shimmering fire. His connection with Sioda allowed Khalophis and the 6th Fellowship to burn entire armies to ashes without firing a single shot from their many guns.

The thought empowered him and he snarled, feeling his anger rise to the fore. It was good to feel controlled aggression after so long keeping it in check. This world was nothing to the Thousand Sons, and he railed against their enforced presence here when there were wars to be fought elsewhere. The Wolf King had demanded their presence in battle, and yet they wasted time on a forgotten world that offered nothing of value.

Khalophis reached out and ran his hand across the Titan's foot, feeling the smoothness of its surface. Such a material must surely be brittle, and he longed to destroy it. He clenched his fists and dropped into a boxer's stance.

'What are you doing?' cried Yatiri, leaping to his feet.

Khalophis didn't answer. The strength in his arms built, the strength to shatter steel and buckle the hull of an armoured vehicle. He pictured exactly where his fists would strike.

'Please, Brother Khalophis!' begged Yatiri, putting himself between Khalophis and the enormous, splay-clawed foot. 'Stop this, please!'

Khalophis distilled his focus into his clenched fists, but the blows did not land. His consciousness rooted itself in the eighth sphere of the Enumerations, but he forced his thoughts into the seventh, calming his aggression and shackling it to that more contemplative state of being.

'Your strength would be wasted,' cried Yatiri. 'The guardians are impervious to harm!'

Khalophis lowered his arms and stepped back from the target of his violence.

'Is that what you think?' he asked. 'Then what's that?'

Rising from the ground and spreading into the foot of the towering construct like cracks in stonework, thin black lines oozed upwards like malevolent, poisoned veins.

'*Daiesthai*!' hissed Yatiri.

KNEELING ON THE sun disc of his glittering pyramid, Magnus closed his first eye and unshackled his body of light from his flesh. His captains and warriors required the Enumerations to achieve the separation from flesh, but Magnus had mastered spirit travel in the aether without being aware that such a thing might be considered difficult.

The Enumerations were philosophical and conceptual tools to allow a practitioner of the mysteries to sift through the myriad complexities involved in bending the universe to his will. Such was his gift, the ability to achieve the impossible without knowing it was beyond comprehension.

On a world such as Aghoru, that process was eased by the aetheric winds that blew invisibly across the planet's surface. The Great Ocean pressed in, as though around a precious and delicate bubble. Magnus plucked a thought from the third Enumeration to express the concept; this world was a perfect sphere, structurally impossible to improve upon, yet the Mountain was a flaw, a means by which that perfect balance might be upset. When he had entered the cave with Yatiri, he had observed all the formalities of the Aghoru ritual of the dead, but the pointless chanting and somatic posturing had amused him with its naivety.

The Aghoru truly believed they placated some dormant race of devils imprisoned beneath the earth, but the time was not yet right to disabuse them of that notion. Standing in the dark of the cave, he could feel the vast pressure of the Great Ocean far beneath his feet, leeching up through wards worn thin by uncounted aeons.

There were no devils beneath the Mountain, only the promise of something so incredible that it took Magnus's breath away. It was too early to be certain, but if he was right, the benefit to the human race would be beyond imaging.

What lay beneath the Mountain was a gateway, an entrance to an indescribably vast and complex network of pathways through the Great Ocean, as though an unseen network of veins threaded the flesh of the universe. To gain control of that network would allow humanity free rein over the stars, the chance to step from one side of the galaxy to the other in the blink of an eye.

There was danger, of course there was. He could not simply open this gate without the Great Ocean spilling out with disastrous consequences. The secret to unlocking this world's great potential would be in careful study, meticulous research and gradual experimentation. As Yatiri intoned the meaningless rituals for the dead, Magnus had drawn a filament of that power upwards, and had tasted the vast potential of it. It was raw, this power, raw and vital. His flesh ached for its touch again.

The things he could do with such power.

Magnus rose up, leaving his corporeal body kneeling upon the sun disc. Freed from the limitations of flesh, his body truly came alive, a lattice of senses beyond the paltry few understood by those whose only life was that lived on the mundane realms of existence.

'I will free you all from the cave,' said Magnus, his voice unheard beyond the walls of the pyramid. His body of light shot through the pyramid's peak, rising into the night sky of Aghoru, and Magnus relished this chance to soar without company or protection.

The Mountain reared over him, its immense presence towering in its majesty.

He rose up thousands of metres, and still it dwarfed his presence.

Magnus shot higher into the sky, a brilliant missile that twisted, spun and wove glittering traceries of light in the sky. His dizzying flight was invisible to all, for Magnus desired to remain alone, and masked his presence from even his captains.

He flew as close to the Mountain as he could, feeling the black wall of null energy radiating from artfully fashioned rocks and peaks designed with but a single purpose: to contain the roiling, unpredictable energies trapped beneath it.

Magnus spun around the mountain, relishing the aetheric winds whipping around his body of light. Ancient mystics had known the body of light as the *linga sarira*, a double of the physical body they believed could be conjured into existence with time, effort and will, essentially creating a means to live forever. Though untrue, it was a noble belief.

Onwards and upwards he flew. The atmosphere grew thin, yet the subtle body needed no oxygen or heat or light to sustain it. Will and energy were its currency, and Magnus had a limitless supply of both.

The sun was a fading disc of light above him, and he flew ever upwards, spreading his arms like wings as he bathed in the warmth of the invisible currents of energy that permeated every corner of this world. The world below was a distant memory, the encampment of the Thousand Sons a pinprick of light in the darkness.

He saw the vast swathe of the galaxy, the misty whiteness of the Milky Way, the gleam of distant stars and the impossible gulfs that separated them. Throughout history, men and women had looked up at these stars and dreamed of one day travelling between them. They had balked at distances so vast the human mind was incapable of conceiving them, and then bent their minds to overcoming the difficulties in doing so.

Now the chance to take those stars, to master the galaxy once and for all, was in their grasp. Magnus would be the architect of that mastery. The ships of the Thousand Sons hung motionless in the void above him, the *Photep*, the *Scion of Prospero* and the *Ankhtowë*. Together with Mechanicum forge vessels, Administratum craft and a host of bulk cruisers bearing army soldiers of the Prospero Spireguard, they made up this portion of the 28th Expedition.

Up here, bathed in light and energy, Magnus was free of his earthly limitations, self-imposed though many of them were. Here, he saw with perfect clarity, his form unbound by the laws and bargains made by both him and his creator. Unlike his brothers, Magnus remembered his conception and growth, recalling with perfect clarity the bond that existed between him and his father.

Even as he was forged in the white heat of genius, he spoke with his father, listening to his grand dreams, the colossal scale of his vision and his own place within it. As a mother might talk to the unborn babe in her womb, so did the Emperor speak with Magnus.

But where a growing child knows nothing of the world outside, Magnus knew everything.

He remembered, decades later, returning to the world of his birth to travel its forgotten highways and explore its lost mysteries with his father. The Emperor had taught him more of the secret powers of the universe, imparting his wisdom while little realising that the student was on the verge of outstripping the teacher. They had walked the searing red deserts of Meganesia, travelling the invisible pathways once known as songlines by the first people to walk that land.

Other cultures knew them as ley lines or lung-mei, believing them to be the blood of the gods, the magnetic flow of mystical energy that circulated in the planet's veins. His father told him how the ancient shamans of Old Earth could tap into these currents and wield power beyond that of other mortals. Many had sought to become gods, raising empires and enslaving all men before them.

The Emperor spoke of how these men had brought ruin upon themselves and their people by trafficking with powers beyond their comprehension. Seeing Magnus's interest, his father warned him against flying too long and too high in the aether for selfish gain.

Magnus listened attentively, but in his secret heart he had dreamed of controlling the powers these mortals could not. He was a being of light so far removed from humanity that he barely considered himself related to his primordial ancestors. He was far above them, yes, but he did not allow himself to forget the legacy of evolution and sacrifice that had elevated him. It was his duty and his honour to speed the ascension of those who would come after him, to show them the light as his father had shown him.

In those early days, Terra was a changing world, a planet reborn in the image of its new master as shining cities and grand wonders were raised to mark this turn in humanity's fortunes. The crowning glory of this new age was his father's palace, a continent-sized monument to the unimaginable achievement of Unity. It took shape on the highest reaches of the world, a landmass of architecture to serve as an undeniable symbol of Terra's new role as a lodestar for humanity. It would be a shining beacon in a galaxy starved of illumination during the lightless ages.

Magnus had studied the ancient texts his father had assembled within the Librarius Terra, devouring them all with a hunger that bordered on obsession. He stared into the heavens from the Great Observatory, toppled mountaintops with his brothers upon the Martial Spires and, greatest of all, soared upon the aether with his father.

He had watched in amusement as Fulgrim and Ferrus Manus vied for supremacy in the Terrawatt forges beneath Mount Narodnya, debated the nature of the universe with Lorgar in the Hall of Leng, and met ever more of his brothers as they travelled to the world that had birthed them.

He had felt a kinship with some, a brotherhood he had not known he craved until it was right in front of him. With others, he felt nothing; hostility even, but he had not returned that hostility. The future would vindicate him.

When the time had come to make his way in the stars, it was bittersweet. It had seen him parted from his beloved father, but could not have come soon enough for his warriors, as the gene-defects that plagued them were growing ever more severe.

Magnus had led his Legion to Prospero, and there he had…

There he had done what needed to be done to save his sons.

Thinking of his Legion, he turned his gaze from the stars and remembered his father's warning of flying too high and too far on the aether. He turned his flight back to earth, dropping like a comet towards the surface of Aghoru. The dark ground raced up to meet him, the encampment of the Thousand Sons like a lone campfire on an empty prairie. The minds of his warriors were the flames, some gently wavering, others blazing with ambition.

Magnus slowed his descent, feeling the heat of one flame in particular.

Ahriman. Always it was Ahriman who burned brighter than the others.

His Chief Librarian stood before his pavilion with Sobek at his side. He was speaking with three mortals whose minds were little more than faded embers.

Magnus read them in an instant and knew them better than they knew themselves.

One was Lemuel Gaumon, Ahriman's new Probationer. The taller of the two women was Camille Shivani, a psychometric, while the slighter one was Kallista Eris, an asemic writer.

She carried a handful of papers, though her aura told Magnus she was unhappy to be holding them. Shivani stood behind Gaumon, who spoke with some force to Ahriman.

Ahriman stared at the page he had been handed.

Magnus floated closer to Ahriman, reading what was written.

Over and over and over again, the same phrase.

The Wolves are coming.

CHAPTER SIX

Skarssen/The Demands of War/Wyrdmake

IT WAS A day like any other. The sun beat down on the salt plains of Aghoru, the shimmer haze and dryness of the air as punishing as it always had been. A hot wind blew from the Mountain, snapping at the scores of scarab and hawk banners of the Thousand Sons as they formed up into two lines on either side of a processional a kilometre long.

Five Fellowships of the Legion, nearly six thousand Astartes, stood resplendent in crimson and ivory battle armour, jade scarabs gleaming on breastplates, golden crests rearing from the atef helmets of the Scarab Occult. The deshrets of the rest of the Legion were polished and plumed with gold and amethyst.

It was a day like any other, but for one thing.

The Wolves were coming.

Word had come down from the *Photep* that a small fleet of Astartes vessels had translated from the Great Ocean and was closing with Aghoru with frightening speed. Like a blade through water, the fleet had sliced through the outer reaches of the system on the swiftest route towards the 28th Expedition's anchorage. Auspex interrogation protocols revealed them to be ships of the Space Wolves, but the Thousand Sons already knew who they were.

Magnus had shown no surprise when Ahriman had presented Kallista Eris's words, merely ordering his captains to have the Legion ready to parade at dawn. To sense the arrival of a fleet of ships through the warp should have been no great feat for the Thousand Sons, but, save for Magnus, none of its warriors had any inkling of the imminent arrival of the Space Wolves. Ahriman had broached this with Magnus, but the primarch had dismissed his concerns, saying that while their understanding of the currents of the fluid medium in which starships travelled was second to none, it was not infallible.

That hadn't reassured Ahriman.

Thousands of Legion serfs gathered to witness this reunion of brothers, though they watched proceedings from afar. The remembrancers too were kept at a distance, including Magnus's personal scribe, Mahavastu Kallimakus. Ahriman sensed Lemuel, Camille and Kallista among them, sharing their sense of foreboding. He feared there was more to Kallista Eris's message than he understood, yet a night spent in contemplation trying to divine the echoes of the future from the Great Ocean had once again met with failure.

The frustration of the remembrancers at being excluded from today's proceedings was palpable, but this was a meeting of Astartes, a private thing. As auspicious as this day was, there was no mistaking the martial atmosphere, or the tension in the too rigid, too precise postures of the Thousand Sons.

This was not simply an honour guard to welcome a brother Legion: this was a show of force, a warning, and a declaration of purpose all in one.

The primarch stood beneath a glorious canopy of white silk held aloft by sixty bronze-skinned Legion eunuchs and attended by eighty-one Terminators of the Scarab Occult. Dressed in his full battle-plate, Magnus had eschewed many of the more intricate accoutrements of his armour in favour of a simpler aesthetic, one more suited to the directness of the Wolves. A cloak of dark mail hung from the golden pauldrons of his armour and his plumed helmet rose like a glorious cockade. His great book was absent, secreted within his pavilion behind locks that none save him could open.

Ahriman glanced at the sky, a searing white plate of metal ready to press its great weight down upon them. He would not see the iron-grey drop-ships until they were almost upon them, but kept looking anyway. The inconstant forms of the Tutelaries shimmered above their heads, barely visible against the glare of the sunlight on armour plates. Aaetpio flickered in and out of sight, its nervousness matching his wariness. Utipa and Paeoc held close to their masters, while Sioda pulsed in time with Khalophis's heartbeat, red as blood.

Uthizzar's Tutelary, Ephra, was almost invisible, a hidden skein of timid luminosity that shrank from proximity to the others of its kind.

'They spend all this time racing to get here, and then can't hurry up now that we're ready for them,' complained Phosis T'kar.

'Vintage Space Wolves,' said Hathor Maat, and Ahriman saw that his brother had shaped his flesh into a less sculpted cast, no longer the porcelain features of ancient statue, more the rugged warrior. 'Isn't that right, Uthizzar?'

Uthizzar nodded without looking at Maat.

'The warriors of Russ are unpredictable. Except in matters of war,' he said.

'You should know,' said Phosis T'kar. 'You served with them for a time.'

'For a short time only,' said Uthizzar softly. 'They are… not fond of outsiders.'

'Ha!' barked Phosis T'kar. 'They sound just like us. I almost like them already.'

'The Wolves? They're barbarians,' said Khalophis, surprising them all. He bristled like the alpha male of a hunting pack. The Captain of the 6th Fellowship was a brutal man, but Ahriman understood his sentiment. As much as he relished destruction, Khalophis was never imprecise or needless with his violence.

'Kindred spirits for you, Khalophis,' said Hathor Maat. 'You should get on famously.'

'Say what you will, Pavoni, but don't think I can't see your newly-fleshed features.'

'Merely adapting to the circumstances,' replied Hathor Maat archly, his Tutelary flickering with irritation.

'Why do you call them barbarians?' asked Phosis T'kar. 'No disrespect, but you are not a subtle man.'

'I know what you're thinking, but I have studied their campaigns and they are a blunt instrument of war. There is no subtlety or precision to their fights, simply swathes of destruction without control. When the Emperor unleashes them, be sure not to get in their way, for when the Wolves slip their leash, nothing will stop them until only ashes remain. Perturabo's warriors, now that's controlled aggression. We could all learn a lot from them. Precise force delivered exactly where it is needed.'

'For once I feel myself in agreement with Khalophis,' said Ahriman. 'I must be ill.'

They laughed, though Ahriman saw Uthizzar's grimace.

As part of their training, all Captains of Fellowship undertook a secondment to another Legion to learn its ways and further the Thousand Sons' understanding of the galaxy. Khalophis had served with the Iron Warriors, a Legion he admired and ranked second only to the Thousand Sons. Phosis T'kar fought alongside the Luna Wolves, and never tired of regaling his brothers with tales of meeting Horus Lupercal, or boasting of his close friendship with Hastur Sejanus and Ezekyle Abaddon, the First Primarch's closest lieutenants.

Hathor Maat's secondment had seen him serving with the Emperor's Children in their earliest days as they fought alongside the Luna Wolves. As Hathor Maat told it, he had caught the Phoenician's eye with his perfectly moulded features, and had fought within his sight on many an occasion. Maat's proudest possession was an Oath of Moment carved by Fulgrim, and fixed to his breastplate as he took his leave to return to Prospero.

Uthizzar's secondment had been amongst the shortest ever served, lasting a little less than a Terran year. Ahriman was never sure whether the Wolves or Uthizzar had ended the exchange. Athanaeans shunned large gatherings or those whose thoughts were too loud, too brutal, too jagged and too raucous.

Ahriman had spent five years with the Word Bearers, learning much of their Legion and methods of war. It had been an unhappy time for Ahriman, for the scions of Lorgar were a zealous Legion, their devotion to the Master of Mankind bordering on the fanatical. All the Legions were devoted to their lord and his cause, but the Word Bearers lived and fought with the passion of those who claimed to carry the fire of the divine before them.

Their auras had been blazing pillars of certainty; certainty Ahriman felt was unwarranted, for it was unsupported by foundations of knowledge. Some called it faith, Ahriman called it hopeful ignorance. Save for a warrior named Erebus, he had made few friends in the

XVII Legion, for their fervour left no room for those who did not share its passion.

Lorgar's Legion bore an inauspicious number, for in the traditions of ancient Tali, the number seventeen was one of ill-fortune. XVII was considered as the anagram and numerical value for the ancient Gothic expression VIXI, which meant, 'I lived', and whose logical extension was, therefore, 'I am dead'.

Ahriman's thoughts were dragged back to the present by a wordless expression of unease from Aaetpio. He looked up to see a pair of angular grey aircraft plunging down through the hard yellow sky, dropping as though their engines had failed. They screamed down, flaming contrails blazing from the leading edges of their wings.

'They're in a hurry,' said Phosis T'kar.

'Is that a good thing?' asked Ahriman.

'No,' said Uthizzar, his face pale beneath the darkness of his browned skin. 'It is never good when the Wolves race towards you.'

'You can read them?' asked Hathor Maat. 'Even from here?'

'I could read their thoughts from orbit,' said Uthizzar, fighting to keep his tone even.

Ahriman watched as the drop-ships fell, plotting their approach vectors and realising they would miss the landing fields.

'Something's wrong,' he said. 'They are off target. Way off.'

The drop-ships fell like meteors that would impact on the salt flats and leave nothing behind save devastation and a giant crater. The image fixed in Ahriman's mind for a moment, and he wondered if it was imagination or a fragmentary glimpse of the future.

The drop-ships fired their engines just as Ahriman was sure it was too late to arrest their descent, the roar of retros like the howls of a thousand wolves as they slammed down, off to the side of Magnus's silk canopy. Gritty clouds of exhaust roared out from the landing site, a hurricane of hot air and burned salt crystals. The gene-bulked eunuchs fought to hold the wind-blown canopy down in the face of the drop-ships' jetwash.

Even before the obscuring clouds had begun to dissipate, the assault ramps of the drop-ships slammed down. Grey-armoured figures emerged from the swirling, stinging smoke; their lithe power wolf-clad, sure and honed to a lethal edge, a pack of voracious predators who relish the fight at bay. Leading them was a figure in grey, a leather-masked warrior of pure, streamlined aggression.

Amlodhi Skarssen Skarssensson, Lord of the 5th Company of the Space Wolves.

AHRIMAN HADN'T KNOWN what to expect from the Space Wolves. Uthizzar had not exactly been forthcoming after his secondment had ended. They were not friends enough for him to press for details, but he had assumed the grand tales and hyperbolic praise heaped upon the sons of Russ was the exaggeration of storytellers.

Now he knew that was not so.

A pack of slavering wolves, dappled grey and white, with powerful, muscular shoulders, ranged ahead of the Astartes. Their eyes, slitted yellow, were locked on Magnus, and their jaws drew back to expose masses of long, overdeveloped fangs like ivory daggers.

The wolves snapped and snarled, and their monstrous, shaggy heads swung from side to side, as though deciding what to attack first.

Behind the wolves came hulking warriors in steeldust Terminator armour, with Amlodhi Skarssen Skarssensson at their head. He marched through the smoke and dust towards the ruin of Magnus's pavilion, shoulders down as though he were advancing into the teeth of a blizzard. His armour was the battered grey of a thundercloud, and a blackened wolf pelt was secured around his neck on a bone clasp, the slain beast's enormous skull and teeth forming his right shoulder guard.

Instead of a helmet, Skarssen wore a tight-fitting leather mask fashioned in the form of some hideous amalgam of wolf and demon, lacquered and pierced with fragments of stone. His eyes shone through the mask, cold flint to match the grey of his armour, and a black-bladed axe with an edge like napped obsidian was sheathed across his back.

His warriors were no less feral, their weapons and armour festooned with talismans and fetishes torn from the corpses of wolves. They followed in their leader's wake, carried along in the slipstream of his march, juggernauts of ceramite that Ahriman wasn't sure were going to stop.

He rose through the Enumerations, outraged at this blatantly challenging behaviour. Aaetpio squalled in fear, and Ahriman's concentration slipped as his Tutelary fled to the sanctuary of the Great Ocean. He looked back at the snarling wolves, their form blurring for a moment as they stared at him with intelligent eyes that were chilling in their perception.

It took him a moment to realise that all the Tutelaries had fled. Anger turned to momentary confusion, and all eyes turned to Magnus.

Ahriman felt his primarch's soothing presence in his mind, the words unspoken, but heard by all the Captains of Fellowship.

Hold, my sons, this is posturing, nothing more.

The giant wolves halted, forming a rough semi-circle around them and the terrified eunuchs. The wolves lowered their heads, teeth bared. The urge to send a pulse of destructive energy along the length of his heqa staff was almost overwhelming.

'Magnus the Red,' said Skarssen, as though there might be some doubt. His voice was booming and harsh, the voice of a killer. 'I am called Amlodhi Skarssen Skarssensson, Lord of the 5th Company of the Space Wolves, and I bring a call to arms from Leman Russ, Great Wolf of the Legions of Fenris. You are to muster your forces and make all haste to the Ark Reach Cluster. This the Wolf King commands.'

To stand before a being so mighty as a primarch and deliver such a baldly aggressive demand beggared belief. Without being aware of it moving, he realised his hand was on the butt of his gun, and seething waves of outrage shone in the auras of his fellow captains.

His limbs trembled with aetheric energies, the gently lapping tide within roiling into a series of roaring breakers that demanded release. The influence of the Corvidae was at its lowest ebb, but Ahriman could still draw on the power of the Great Ocean to unleash phenomenal powers of destruction.

The aether swelled around him as he built energy in his flesh. This was what it meant to be alive, to tap into the wellspring of the Primordial Creator and wield that power as deftly as a swordsman wields a blade.

That energy swirled around Skarssen and his warriors, yet where it easily passed through the Astartes of the Thousand Sons, the Space Wolves were anathema to it. Skarssen's aura was little more than a dulled haze, like winter sunrise through thick fog.

Was Skarssen veiled?

That seemed unlikely, though perhaps the many fetishes hanging from his armour were shielding him. The protection offered by such talismans was largely illusory, but belief in such things could be a potent force. Even as he formed the thought, Ahriman caught a flash of a bearded warrior in a leather skull-cap in the midst of the Terminators, like a shadow amongst the deeper darkness or a whisper in a thunderstorm.

He sensed kindred power, but in the instant of its recognition, it vanished.

'Show some damned respect!' snarled Phosis T'kar, and the moment passed.

The captain of the 2nd Fellowship stepped forward with his heqa staff planted in the ground before him and said, 'Speak thusly again and I swear by the Great Ocean I will end you.'

To his credit, Skarssen didn't flinch, which was impressive considering the bludgeoning force of Phosis T'kar's choler hammering his aura.

Skarssen kept his attention fixed solely on Magnus.

'Do you understand my message as I have spoken it to you?' he asked.

'I understand it,' said Magnus, coolly. 'Take off your mask.'

The Space Wolf flinched as though slapped, and Ahriman sensed a ferocious build up of power. He gasped as the energy filling him was drained in an instant, siphoned off by a mind infinitely greater than his.

With painful deliberation, his limbs shaking with the effort of resistance, Skarssen reached up and unfastened the buckles securing his mask. He pulled it from his face to reveal features that were craggy and worn like a storm-carved cliff. Clean-shaven, with high cheekbones and a brow pierced with jutting canine fangs like a crown, his lower jaw was tattooed to mimic the toothed jawbone of a wolf.

Throbbing veins pulsed at Skarssen's temple.

'That's better,' said Magnus. 'I never like to kill a man without first seeing his face.'

Magnus seemed to swell, growing in stature, while simultaneously remaining as he had always appeared. The wolves yelped, lowering their heads and backing away from the mighty primarch, and Ahriman saw the beginnings of... not fear exactly, but the wariness of prey.

Skarssen had come with one purpose, to bring the Thousand Sons to the Ark Reach Cluster. He had delivered his message in the most unequivocal way possible, but Magnus could not be so easily dominated by the brute force of the Space Wolves.

'Kill me and you will suffer the wrath of the Great Wolf,' hissed Skarssen.

'Be silent!' thundered Magnus, and the world stilled. All sound died as the wind ceased its moaning and salt crystals hung motionless on the hardpan. 'You are nothing to me, Amlodhi Skarssen Skarssensson. I can kill you where you stand, before you or any of your savage brethren could lift a hand to stop me. I can smash your ships to debris with a thought. Know this and choose your next words carefully.'

Ahriman saw that Skarssen was not a warrior without courage, his aura instinctively rebelling at the challenge in Magnus's words, but nor was he without the wit to understand that he was a mote in the face of the primarch's power. He looked to his left and right, seeing the world frozen around him, every banner hanging motionless and every observer save the Thousand Sons like statues lining a triumphal roadway.

Skarssen lifted his head to expose the corded muscles of his thick neck, and Ahriman recognised the symbolism of the gesture.

Magnus nodded and the world snapped back into its natural rhythms. The wind blew once more and the silk banners flapped in the haze of dancing salt crystals.

'Wolf Lord Skarssen,' said Magnus, 'I understand your message, but there is much to do on Aghoru before we can fight alongside your father's Legion.'

'This world is compliant, is it not?' asked Skarssen, and Ahriman sensed the confusion amongst the Space Wolves at his newly subservient tone.

'It is,' agreed Magnus.

'Then what is left to do?' he asked. 'There are worlds yet to be brought to heel, and your Legion's strength is required. Your brothers-in-arms call for you, and it is a warrior's duty to fight when called.'

'On your world perhaps,' said Magnus, 'but this is not Fenris. Where and when the Thousand Sons fight is for me to decide, not the Wolf King, and certainly not you. Do I make myself clear?'

'You do, Lord Magnus, but I swore a blood oath not to return without your warriors.'

'That is none of my concern, and this is not a matter for discussion,' said Magnus, an unmistakeable edge of impatience in his tone.

'Then we are at an impasse.'

'I fear that we are,' said Magnus.

AHRIMAN CONCENTRATED ON the words before him, his quill scratching at the heavy paper as he committed the morning's events to his grimoire. There would be other records, of course, but none that told of events with a true understanding of what had really happened. His words flowed from him without conscious thought as he rose through the Enumerations and let the natural rhythm of memory and intuition guide him.

He closed his eyes, freeing his body of light and letting it rise up from his flesh. The currents of the Great Ocean bore him into the darkness, and Ahriman hoped to catch a glimpse of things to come. He quashed the thought. To focus on the desires of the ego in this place of emotion would only diminish the probability of success.

His connection with the material world faded, and the Great Ocean swelled around him, a maelstrom of non-existent colours, nameless emotions and meaning-less dimensions.

Occasional ripples ushered him onwards, powerful minds, intense emotions and primal urges. The anger of the Space Wolves was a red reef of raw directness, the gasping lust of two remembrancers as they coupled a purple swirl of conflicting desire. The fear of a Legion serf as he rubbed a salve into an infected rash was a splash of vivid green, the scheming of yet another as she plotted how to further her career, a dull ochre yellow.

They rose around him like temple smoke, though concepts such as up and down had no meaning here. A swirling fog surrounded him, an impenetrable mist of emotion, feeling and possibility. His mere proximity wrought potential existences within the fog, his pres-ence an imprint in the warp and weft of the Great Ocean, shaping and shaped by the immaterial unmatter that made up this alternate dimension.

This was the very essence of the Primordial Creator, the wellspring from which all things came. Nothing was impossible here, for this was the foundry of creation, the origin of all things, past, present and future.

Ahriman flew onwards, revelling in the aetheric ener-gies, bathing in them and refreshed by them. When he returned to his body, he would be energised as a mortal would be by a good night's rest.

The kaleidoscopic world around him stretched out to infinite realms of possibility. Ahriman let his con-sciousness be borne along by the currents, hoping to chance upon a rich seam of things yet to pass. He focussed his mind on the teachings of the Corvidae even as he opened his mind to the vast emptiness of thought. Such apparently contradictory states of mind were essential to the reading of the future, difficult for one such as him, near impossible for anyone less gifted.

He felt the first nibblings of other presences in the Great Ocean, formless creatures of insensate appetite, little more than mewling scraps of energy drawn to his mind as students flock to a great master. They thought to feed on him, but Ahriman dismissed them with a flicker of thought.

Such whelp creatures were no threat to an Adept Exemptus of his skill, but older, hungrier things swam the depths, malevolent predators that fed on the hot, life-rich energies of mortal travellers. Ahriman was protected, but he was not invulnerable.

It began softly, a faint hiss, like rain on glass.

He felt its feather-light pull, and he drifted towards it without apparent interest. Too quick, and he would disturb the fabric of the Great Ocean, overwhelming the skittish trickle of future events with the swells of his eagerness.

Ahriman controlled his excitement, letting his course and that of the thin stream come together, opening his mind's eye to the bracing cold of unwritten events.

He saw a mountain of glass, tall and hollowed out, yet a stripling compared to the Mountain of Aghoru. A great space within was filled with yellow light, a spiking cauldron of conflicting emotions and hurt, a gathering thundercloud, shot through with golden lightning, filled the sky.

Ahriman knew this was important; visions in the aether were shaped as much by the viewer as they were by the Great Ocean. This mountain and thunderstorm could be a true vision, or could be allegory, each aspect symbolic of something greater. It was the skill of the adept to sort one from the other.

Hot excitement ghosted through his immaterial form. It had been years since any Corvidae had been able to peel back the skin of the aeather to reveal the future. Might this mean the eternal waxing and waning of the tides of power were shifting once more in his cult's favour?

The intensity of the thought rippled outwards, disturbing the liquid nothingness enfolding him. The vision fractured, like the surface of a lake in a rainstorm. Ahriman fought for calm, but his tenuous grasp on the stream was slipping. The glass mountain vanished, breaking into millions of pieces and falling like tears. A weeping eye was reflected in every shard, red and raw with pain.

He fought to hold on to the jagged, painful images, but the aether surged, and it was gone, swept away in the angry swells of his own desire. Like the onset of a sudden storm, the substance of the Great Ocean turned violent. His own frustration was turning against him. Red waves broke against him as his mind was wrenched from thoughts of the future.

His perception of the immediate returned to him, and he sensed the vibrant hunger of nearby void hunters, rapacious conceptual predators that followed the spoor of travellers' emotions to devour their bodies of light. Dozens of them circled him like sharks with the scent of blood. He had remained longer than was safe, far longer.

The first emerged from the blood red mist, all appetite and instinct. It came at him directly, its glittering teeth forming in the instant it took to think of them.

Ahriman flew out of its path, its crimson form twisting around to follow him as another predator emerged from the mists. His mental analogy of sharks had given them form, and its body was sleek and evolved to be the consummate killer. He forced his mind to empty, discarding all metaphor and vocabulary, for they were the weapons his enemies would use against him.

He flew from them, but they had his scent now. Half a dozen more followed, their forms blurred and protean, borrowed from those whose bodies of light had been given shape by his careless simile. A void hunter surged towards him, massive and powerful, its jaws opened wide to swallow him whole.

Ahriman gathered the energy of the aether to him, feeding on the red mists and unleashing a torrent of will at the hunter. Its body exploded into shards of fire, each one snapped up and devoured by one of the other predators. Twin heqa staffs appeared in Ahriman's hands, blazing with aetheric fire. Such weapons were necessary and dangerous at the same time. To burn so brightly would attract other beasts, yet without them he would surely perish here, leaving his mortal body a dead, soulless husk on the floor of his pavilion.

They circled him, darting in to bite and snap, each time deterred by a sweep of his fiery staffs. Ahriman rose into the eighth Enumeration. He would need the focus of its aggression to stay alive, but it would only inflame the hunger of the beasts. The creatures came at him in a rush. Ahriman had seen their gathering fury, and lashed out with his blazing weapons.

The closest beast billowed out of existence at his blow, the second with a violent burst of thought that overwhelmed its hunger and dispersed its essence. Another snapped at him. He swayed aside, its immaterial teeth snapping shut an instant from tearing his insubstantial existence apart. He thrust his heqa staff into his head, feeling its primal hunger and rage as its essence was obliterated.

The pack broke off its attack, wary of him, but unable to halt their pursuit. The instincts of the void hunter were murderously sharp, but they demanded satisfaction. They would attack again, soon.

They came at him three more times. Each time they retreated to a pack that grew larger with every passing moment, while he grew weaker and bled irresistible morsels of energy into the void.

He could not long keep up this pace of battle. Combat in the aetheric realms was more draining than battling in the physical. In the material realm, an Astartes could fight for weeks on end without rest, but here such endurance was measured in minutes. A high-ranking warrior of the Thousand Sons could travel the Great Ocean far longer than most, but the strain of this fight was pushing Ahriman to the limits of his endurance.

A great maw raced up at him from below, a thought-shaped need of monstrous proportions. Its teeth closed on his leg, tearing into his light, and his pain bled out like glittering diamonds, brilliant white and impossible to resist. His staff carved into the beast, and it vanished in its moment of triumph.

He could not fight them much longer, and it seemed they knew his resistance was almost at an end. Their eagerness for him had them jostling one another, each beast desperate to make the kill and secure the choicest cuts.

His energy was fading and one of the fiery heqa staffs winked out of existence.

How galling to die after such a tantalising glimpse of the future.

Then came a howling cry that split the Great Ocean, a furious sound that scattered the hunters as a wild darkness rose out of the swelling tides and currents. Fangs like swords of ice snapped and bit through the void-hunters. This was form and will honed to a knife-edge, a force streamlined for destruction and utterly without mercy. Yellow eyes, a shaggy pelt of black fur and slavering jaws roiled amid the frenzy.

Even before Ahriman's mind formed the image, he saw the phantasmal outline of the wolf, a beast larger and more powerful than any living animal could ever be. It tore through the void-predators, howling as it destroyed them with brutal swipes of thunderous claws and bites that swallowed each enemy whole.

Within the dark of the wolf's body, Ahriman caught fleeting glimpses of the furious will that drove it: a distant shadow in dark armour, not black but deep, metallic grey. The wolf howled, and waves of untrammelled fury spread into the Great Ocean with the force of a boulder dropped into a millpond. The predators scattered, cowed by this apex predator.

And, like fading inkspots on a blotter, they melted into the darkness.

The wolf turned towards Ahriman, its form turning in on itself and folding like the pieces of an origami puzzle until all that was left was the shadow at its heart, the subtle body of an Astartes in the hard grey of the Space Wolves.

He drifted towards Ahriman, and it took no special skills to feel the primal, bruising energy that suffused this traveller's flesh. His sheer vitality was incredible. Ahriman was a controlled reactor, but this warrior was a violent supernova. Both were deadly, both burned as bright, but where Ahriman could pluck a single soul out of a horde of millions, this warrior would destroy a million to kill the one.

The wolf was gone, but Ahriman saw it tightly leashed within the warrior's heart.

'We should go, brother,' said the wolf warrior, with a voice like colliding glaciers. 'The longer we tarry, the more our presence will draw fouler beasts.'

'I saw you,' said Ahriman. 'You came with Skarssen.'

'*Lord* Skarssen,' corrected the warrior. 'But, aye, you speak true, brother. My name is Ohthere Wyrdmake, Rune Priest to Amlodhi Skarssen Skarssensson of the 5th Company of Space Wolves.'

'Ahzek Ahriman, Chief Librarian of the Thousand Sons.'

'I know well your name, Ahzek Ahriman,' said Wyrdmake, with a feral grin, 'for I have long desired to meet you.'

CHAPTER SEVEN

**The Wolves of Fenris/A Meeting of Minds/
The Dam Breaks**

THERE ARE NO wolves on Fenris.

Ahriman had heard that before, a nugget of scandalous rumour passed down from nameless source to nameless source. Such contention was, of course, ridiculous; the evidence padded alongside the Thousand Sons as they marched into the Mountain once again. A score of iron-furred wolves roamed at will along the length of the column of warriors, like herding dogs watching over a flock.

Six hundred Astartes marched into the Mountain, the Thousand Sons and Space Wolves together. At the head of the column, Magnus the Red led the way, surrounded by Terminators of the Scarab Occult and flanked by his captains. Lord Skarssen and his retinue of Wolf Guard marched alongside the towering primarch. Ohthere Wyrdmake walked at his master's side, and the Rune Priest inclined his head as he caught Ahriman's eye.

They had spoken last night, yet Ahriman still did not know quite what to make of him.

Land Raiders crunched their way uphill alongside the Astartes, the war footing at the behest of Yatiri.

The tribal elder had come down from the Mountain with Khalophis prior to the arrival of Lord Skarssen and begged to see the Crimson King. The Space Wolves were en route, and he had been forced to wait until after their arrival. As important as the Aghoru were to the Thousand Sons, mortal business took second place to Astartes business.

Ahriman had watched as Yatiri was shown into the glittering pyramid of Magnus, seeing the fear in his body language. Like all the masked tribesfolk of the Aghoru, Yatiri cast no shadow in the aether, his life-energies somehow hidden from the sight of the Thousand Sons. He came with his fellow elders, and Ahriman saw their anger, no matter that they were masked and unreadable.

Whatever passed between Yatiri and Magnus had been serious enough for the primarch to order Ahriman to gather warriors from every Fellowship and assemble a battle march.

Seeing the Thousand Sons preparations, a warrior calling himself Varangr Ragnulf Ragnulfssen, herald of Lord Skarssen, had come to Magnus to request an audience.

And so the Space Wolves marched with the Thousand Sons.

They had marched past the deadstones, the rocks streaked with oily black tendrils like rotten veins. Upon seeing the condition of the deadstones, the Aghoru dropped to their knees and wept in fear. Ahriman paused to examine the stones, knowing only one thing that could have had so dramatic an effect on such impervious stone.

'What do you think?' asked Phosis T'kar.

'The same as you,' he had replied, and walked on.

Ahriman watched the warriors of Lord Skarssen as the march continued. They set a brutal pace, and the Thousand Sons matched it. What was a fast walk for the Astartes was a punishing run for the Aghoru. Despite that, the tribesmen kept pace with the armoured warriors, fear lending their limbs strength to endure the exhausting temperature of the day.

'They don't feel the heat,' said Phosis T'kar as the march continued.

'Who?'

'The beasts Skarssen brought with him,' clarified T'kar. 'They come from a world of ice and snow, yet they seem untroubled by this heat.'

Ahriman watched as a wolf that reached to his waist padded by. Its fur was a patchwork of grey and white, thick and shaggy around its forequarters, sleek and smooth at its rear. As though sensing his scrutiny, it swung towards him, baring its fangs and narrowing its yellow eyes in a blatant challenge.

'I do not know for sure,' said Ahriman, 'but all that lives on the surface of Fenris does so because it can adapt to changing circumstances. These wolves are no exception.'

'Then I wish I could adapt like them. I am sick of this damned heat,' said Phosis T'kar angrily. 'My body is gene-wrought to withstand all extremes, but the fire of this sun saps us all of life. Even Hathor Maat struggles with it.'

'Speak for yourself, T'kar,' retorted Hathor Maat. 'I am quite comfortable.'

Despite his bluster, Maat suffered as the rest of them did. Without the powers of the Pavoni to call on, he was unable to regulate his body as efficiently as would normally be the case. Yet the wolves of Fenris marched as though through a balmy summer's day, the heat as untroubling to them as the frozen tundra of their home world.

'It is thanks to their engineering,' said Magnus, joining their conversation. The primarch had said nothing since the march had begun, content to let his captains do the talking.

'They were engineered?' asked Ahriman. 'By whom?'

'By the first colonists of Fenris,' said Magnus with a smile. 'Can't you see the dance of helices within them? The ballet of genes and the remarkable feats of splicing the earliest scientists achieved?'

Ahriman shared a glance with his fellow captains, and Magnus laughed.

'No, of course you do not,' said Magnus, shaking his head. 'Uthizzar, you have travelled to Fenris, have you not?'

It was a rhetorical question, for Magnus knew everything about their secondments and legacies of honour.

Uthizzar nodded.

'Briefly, my lord,' he said. 'It was not a pleasant experience.'

'I imagine it was not. Fenris does not welcome visitors, nor is it a gracious host,' said Magnus with a hidden smile. 'It is a world like no other, unforgiving and pernicious. The ice waits to kill those who travel its frozen seas and snow-locked cliffs at the first signs of complacency. A mortal man, even a well-prepared one, would freeze to death on Fenris within minutes of setting foot on its surface.'

'Yet the tribes survive there well enough,' said Ahriman. 'Apparently, they are little more than feral savages, endlessly waging war for the few scraps of land that survive the upheaval of the Great Year.'

'That they are,' said Magnus. 'But also so much more.'

'What makes them so special?' asked Hathor Maat, unwilling to believe that such barbarous mortals could earn the primarchs's approbation.

'Were you not listening? Fenris is a death world, a planet so hostile it would test even your powers of bio-manipulation. Yet these mortals carve themselves land, home and families on a world most right-thinking men would avoid.'

'So how do they do it?'

Magnus smiled, and Ahriman saw he was enjoying the role of teacher once more.

'First, tell me what you know of the Canis Helix?'

'It's a genetic primer,' said Hathor Maat, 'a precursor gene that allows the remainder of the Space Wolf gene-seed to take root in an aspirant's body.'

Magnus shook his head. His great eye glittered with green and gold as he regarded his captains.

'That is part of its function, yes, but it was never intended to be used so... obviously,' he said.

'Then how was it supposed to be used?' asked Ahriman. He looked over at Skarssen, the warrior once more wearing his leather mask, and wondered if the Apothecaries of the Fang knew as much as Magnus. The Wolf Lord walked warily around Magnus, having tasted a measure of his power. Ahriman suspected his primarch's boast that he could destroy the Space Wolf ships in orbit was a calculated bluff. Clearly Skarssen wasn't so sure.

'Imagine the time when mankind first discovered Fenris,' continued Magnus, 'a world so utterly inimical to life that humans simply could not survive. Everything about Fenris was death, from the blood-freezing cold to the sinking lands to the howling winds that suck the life from your lungs. Back then, of course, geneticists saw impossibility as a challenge, and daily wrought new codes within the chromosomes of human and animal genomes as easily as the Mechanicum punch data-wafers for servitors.'

'So you're saying that these colonists brought gene-bred wolves with them to Fenris?' said Phosis T'kar.

'Perhaps they did,' allowed Magnus, 'but more likely they adapted, imperfectly at times and without thought to the consequences. Or perhaps there were other, older races living on Fenris.'

Ahriman watched Magnus as he spoke, feeling that there was more to the origins of Fenris than he was telling. Magnus was a traveller who had ventured deeper into the hidden reaches of the Great Ocean than any living soul. Perhaps he had actually witnessed the earliest days of the Wolf King's world.

Magnus gave a studied shrug and said, 'You look at those beasts and you see wolves, but is that only because it is what you expect to see?'

'What else would we see?' asked Hathor Maat. 'They *are* wolves.'

'When you have travelled as far as I have, and seen as I have seen, you will learn that it is possible to look beyond the expected and into the true heart of a thing.'

Magnus gestured towards a wolf loping alongside the column, its powerful muscles driving it uphill through the heat without pause.

'I can look past the flesh and muscle of that beast, paring back the bone into the heart of its marrow to read every scar and twist in its genetic code. I can unravel the millennia of change back to the logos of its origins,' said Magnus. Ahriman was surprised to hear sadness in his voice, as though he had seen things he would rather not have seen. 'The thing it is, what it wished to be, and all the stages of that long evolutionary road.'

The wolf stopped beside Magnus and he nodded towards it. An unspoken discourse seemed to pass between them. Ahriman caught a knowing glance from Ohthere Wyrdmake. Despite his reservations, he felt the urge to nurture the nascent kinship between them.

'Away with you!' shouted Phosis T'kar, shooing it. 'Damned wolves.'

Magnus smiled. 'I told you, there *are* no wolves on Fenris.'

THEY HAD MET the previous evening, after Ahriman returned to his corporeal body. Opening his eyes, he groaned as his flesh ached with the stress of his body of light's reintegration. His leg flared painfully, his entire body a mass of discomfort.

With careful slowness, Ahriman uncrossed his legs and used his heqa staff to push himself to his feet. His right thigh felt numb, like it belonged to someone else, and cold pain burned the muscles and sinews the length of his leg. He opened his robe gingerly, pressing his fingertips to the bulked musculature of his smooth torso and grimacing in pain.

Repercussions covered his flesh where the void-hunters had wounded him, blackened patches of skin drained of their vitality. More completely than any wound dealt with blade or bullet, injuries to the subtle body damaged the very essence of a traveller's flesh.

An Astartes could rise above pain, his body designed to allow him to function without loss of effectiveness, but nothing save rest and meditation could undo the damage of repercussions.

He saw his grimoire lying open on the ground of his pavilion and knelt to retrieve it, wincing as the dead areas of his body pulled tight. He felt like he had fought for a month without rest, his body pushed nearly to the limits of its endurance.

Ahriman secreted his grimoire and changed from his robe into a hooded tunic of crimson, edged with ivory and sable. Though his body ached for sleep, he had one last meeting to attend, one he had not anticipated until his near-fatal flight into the Great Ocean.

The flap at his pavilion's entrance pushed open and Sobek entered, his face a mask of concern. Cooler night air gusted in with him.

'My lord, is everything all right?'

'Everything is fine, Sobek,' said Ahriman.

'I heard you calling out.'

'An interesting flight in the aether, Sobek, that is all,' said Ahriman, lifting the hood over his head. 'Some predatory creatures thought to make me a morsel.'

'And yet you are venturing out?' asked Sobek. 'You should be resting, my lord.'

Ahriman shook his head.

'No,' he said, 'there is someone I need to see.'

THE LAIR OF the Wolves was on the edge of the mountain, in the shadow of the deadstones. Skarssen had set his warriors' shelters in concentric rings, with his at its heart. Ahriman saw a great wolf-skull totem planted in the crystalline hardpan, hung with wolf tails as long as a mortal man's leg and teeth like blades.

As he drew near, shadows bled from the twilight, sleek killers that put Ahriman in mind of the predators that had almost ended him earlier. Six of them padded towards him, their forms indistinct against the darkness, their hackles raised.

They halted and he saw the gleam of stars on their fangs. Their muscles were tensed and ready, like pistons ready to fire on the launch rails of an embarkation deck.

'I have come to see Ohthere Wyrdmake,' said Ahriman, feeling foolish at addressing beasts. The largest of the wolves threw back its head and loosed an almighty howl that split the faded evening.

Ahriman waited for the wolves to back away, but they remained where they were, barring him entry to their master's domain. He stepped forward, and the wolf that had announced his presence bared its iron fangs with a threatening growl.

Another shadow moved behind the wolves, a tall warrior in granite grey armour who walked with a tall staff topped with an eagle of gold and silver. His beard was waxed, and he wore a plain leather skullcap over his shaven scalp. Ahriman recognised him immediately.

'Ohthere Wyrdmake,' he said.

'Aye,' replied the Space Wolf, tilting his head and regarding him carefully. 'You are hurt, mistflesh hurt.'

'I was careless,' he said, not knowing the word, but understanding the meaning.

Wyrdmake nodded and said, 'That you were. I watched you chase the wyrd, blind to the hunting packs gathering for the murder-make. How came you to miss them?'

'As I said, I was careless,' repeated Ahriman. 'How did you find me?'

Wyrdmake laughed, the sound rich with genuine humour.

'That took no great skill,' he said. 'I am a son of the Storm and I know the ocean of souls like the seas around Asaheim. When the Wolf's Eye swells in the sky, the world forge turns and the dowsers seek the silent places, those places that are still amid the turmoil. I looked for stillness, and I found you.'

Much of what Wyrdmake said made no sense to Ahriman, the terms too archaic, the vocabulary expressing parochial understandings beyond one not of Fenris.

'That begs the question, why were you looking for me?'

'Come,' said Wyrdmake. 'Walk with me.'

The Rune Priest set off towards the deadstones without waiting to see if Ahriman obeyed. The wolves parted to allow him through their ranks. Keeping a wary eye on the beasts, Ahriman followed Wyrdmake towards the deadstones, the menhirs like black teeth growing up from the ground.

The warrior walked the circumference of the stones, careful not to touch them as he passed. He turned as Ahriman approached.

'Anchors in the world,' said Wyrdmake. 'Places of still-ness. The Storm rages across this world, but all is still here. Like Asaheim, immovable and unchanging.'

'The Aghoru call them deadstones,' said Ahriman, as the wolves padded softly around the edge of the circle, each one with its eyes locked on him.

'A fitting name.'

'So, are you going to tell me why you were looking for me?'

'To know you,' said Wyrdmake. 'Amlodhi came with a summons for your master, but I came for you. Your name is known to the Rune Priests of the Space Wolves, Ahzek Ahriman. You are star-cunning. Like me, you are a Son of the Storm, and I know of your affinity with the wyrd.'

'The wyrd? I don't know that term,' said Ahriman.

'You are not of Fenris,' said Wyrdmake, as though that explained everything.

'Then enlighten me,' said Ahriman, losing patience.

'You would have me share the secrets of my calling?'

'We will have precious little else to talk about if you do not.'

Wyrdmake smiled, exposing teeth honed to sharp points. 'You cut to the heart of the meat, friend. Very well. At its simplest, wyrd is fate, destiny.'

'The future,' said Ahriman.

'At times,' agreed Wyrdmake. 'On Fenris we ken it as the turning of the world forge that continually reshapes the face of the land. As one land rises, another sinks to its doom. Wyrd shows us how past and present shape the future, but also how the future affects the past. The storms of time flow, weave together and burst apart, forever entwined within the great saga of the universe.'

Ahriman began to understand the words of the Rune Priest, hearing in them a debased echo of the teachings of the Corvidae.

'Fate goes ever as she shall,' quoted Ahriman, and Wyrdmake laughed.

'Aye, she does indeed. The Geatlander knew his business when he said that line.'

Ahriman looked up at the Mountain, feeling his hostility to Wyrdmake easing in the face of their shared understanding of the mysteries. As different as his teachings were, the Space Wolf had an insight Ahriman found refreshing. That didn't mean he trusted him, not by a long way, but it was a start.

'So you have found me,' he said. 'What do you intend now?'

'You and I are brothers of the Storm,' said Wyrdmake, echoing Ahriman's earlier thought. 'Brothers should not be strangers. I know the saga of your Legion's past, and I know that nothing gets men's murder-urge pumping like fear of what they do not understand.'

Ahriman hesitated before asking, 'What is it you think you know?'

Wyrdmake stepped towards him, saying, 'I know that a flaw in your heritage almost destroyed your Legion, and that you have a terror of its return. I know, for my Legion is the same. The curse of the Wulfen haunts us, and we keep watch over our brothers for wolf-sign.'

Wyrdmake reached up to touch the silver oakleaf worked into Ahriman's shoulder guard.

'Just as you watch your fellow legionaries for the flesh change.'

Ahriman flinched as though struck, backing away from Wyrdmake.

'Never touch that again,' he said, fighting to keep his voice even.

'Ohrmuzd?' asked Wyrdmake. 'That was his name, was it not?'

Ahriman wanted to be angry, wanted to lash out at this unwarranted picking of an old wound. He forced his mind into the lower Enumerations, casting off the shed skin of grief and regret.

'Yes,' he said at last. 'That was his name. That was my twin brother's name.'

AHRIMAN FELT THE sickness from the valley long before they crossed the ridge where he had first seen its titanic guardians. Only when he felt the bitter, metallic taste in the back of his throat did he realise that he could feel the ripple of aetheric energies along his limbs. It was faint, barely more than a whisper, but it was there.

How was that possible when it had been so conspicuously absent before?

As the ridge of the valley came into sight he felt that sickness more strongly, like the taste of wind blowing over a mass grave. Something foul had taken root in the valley.

Ahriman looked over at Magnus, seeing his enormous form as a haze of indistinct images, like a thousand pict negatives placed on top of one another: Magnus the giant, Magnus the man, Magnus the monster, a thousand permutations on the theme of Magnus.

He blinked away the afterimages, feeling sick at the sight of them. The sensation was unknown to him and he shook off his momentary dizziness.

'You feel it too, don't you?' asked Phosis T'kar.

'I do,' he said. 'What is happening?'

'The sleepers are waking,' hissed Uthizzar, one hand pressed to his temple.

'Sleepers?' asked Hathor Maat. 'What are you talking about?'

'The sleeping souls, bound to crystal immortality, left behind to watch,' gasped Uthizzar, 'trapped and corrupted, dragged to a slow doom that is worse than death.'

'What in the Emperor's name is he talking about?' demanded Khalophis.

'The Aghoru call them *Daiesthai*,' said Magnus, 'void beasts given form by the nightmares of mortals since the dawn of time. Men, in their ignorance, call them daemons.'

Ahriman almost smiled. Daemons, indeed...

'You will feel the call of the Great Ocean, my sons,' said Magnus, his eye red and angry. 'It will be strong, but rise to the ninth Enumeration. Enter the sphere of inner determination and close your minds off from its power, for it will call to you like nothing you have ever known.'

'My lord?' asked Ahriman. 'What is going on?'

'Do it, Ahzek!' snapped Magnus. 'This is not power as you know it. It is stagnant and dead. It will try to force its way into your mind, but you must not let it, not for a moment.'

It felt alien to Ahriman to close himself off from the power of the aether, but he did as his primarch ordered, focusing his will and lifting his consciousness to the essence of his higher self, where he became an observer in his own flesh.

Magnus set off towards the mouth of the valley without another word, almost outpacing them all. The tempo of the march picked up, and Ahriman saw confusion in the Space Wolves at this sudden urgency. But the wolves... they understood. Ohthere Wyrdmake spoke to Amlodhi Skarssen, and the masked warrior cast a furious glare towards Magnus the Red.

In his objective state of being, he saw the familiar fear of the unknown, the hatred engendered by the strange and unfamiliar. The Space Wolves did not trust his Legion, but perhaps the tentatively established cooperation of Ohthere Wyrdmake might change that.

The valley climbed towards the ridge, and Ahriman noticed a change in the very character of the landscape. The perfection he had seen in its flawless geometries had subtly altered, as though the world had been shifted a fraction of a degree. Angles that once complemented one another were now horribly dissonant, like a musical instrument a hair's-breadth out of tune.

Golden ratios were upset and the graceful dance of intersecting lines became a tangle of discordant shapes that violated the perfect order that had existed before. The valley was a place of threat, its every angle hostile. The throaty rumbles of the Land Raiders' engines echoed strangely from the valley sides, thrown back as if from a hundred different sources.

At last they came to the mouth of the valley, and Ahriman stared in detached horror at what had become of its mighty guardians.

'I CAN HEAR them screaming,' hissed Uthizzar, and Ahriman saw why that should be so.

The titanic constructs stood as they always had, towering and immense, but the smooth, clean lines of their limbs were no longer graceful and pristine. Once they had been the colour of sun-bleached bone, but a loathsome network of poisonous, greenish-black veins threaded their limbs, a necrotic plague that poured from the cave in thick, oily ropes and filled the colossal statues with sickness.

Their splay-clawed feet were rank with the stuff, like rotted vegetable matter that heaved and writhed with foul growth. Blackened legs supported torsos webbed with thin lines of dark matter that absorbed any light that fell upon it. Their slender arms were slick with black veins, polluted conduits carrying the foulness of some nameless corruption. The graceful curve of their enormous heads remained pale and untouched, but even as Ahriman watched, the questing black tendrils oozed around the huge gems set in the surfaces.

Ahriman felt the insistent pressure of their Great Ocean breaking against his barriers of self-control. There was power here, rising up from somewhere far below. Yet what he felt was a fraction of what lay beneath, the trickle that becomes the stream that becomes the torrent. A dam had cracked, and inexorable pressure would soon break it wide open.

He ached to taste that power, to feel it flowing through his body, but he kept it shut out as Magnus had ordered, forcing his gaze away from the great statues.

'What's happening to them?' he asked.

Magnus looked down at him.

'Something evil, Ahzek,' he said, 'something I fear my presence on this world may have hastened. A balance has been upset, and I must restore it.'

Yatiri and his tribal elders, men who had managed to keep pace with the Astartes despite their advanced years, finally reached the edge of the valley.

'*Daiesthai!*' he cried, holding his falarica in a tight, white-knuckled, grip. 'They return!'

'What in the name of the Wolf's Eye is he talking about?' demanded Skarssen, marching over with Ohthere Wyrdmake. 'What are these things?'

Magnus glared at the Wolf Lord, and Ahriman saw his primarch's frustration at having a brother Legion's warriors present. What needed to be done here was best done hidden from inquisitive eyes.

Yatiri turned to Magnus and said, 'They crave the dead. We must give them what they desire.'

'No,' said Magnus. 'That is the last thing you should do.'

Yatiri shook his head, and Ahriman saw his anger.

'This is our world,' he said, 'and we will save it from the *Daiesthai*, not you.'

The mirror-masked elder turned from the primarch and led his tribesmen into the valley, making his way towards the altar before the cave mouth.

'Lord Magnus,' pressed Skarssen, 'what does he mean?'

'Superstition, Lord Skarssen,' said Magnus, 'nothing more.'

'That looks like a damn sight more than superstition,' said Skarssen, gripping his bolter tight to his chest. 'Speak true now, Magnus of the Thousand Sons, what is going on here?'

'Hel,' said Ohthere Wyrdmake, staring at the titanic constructs with a mixture of horror and fascination, 'the Father Kraken of the deep, the keeper of the dead!'

'*This* is what keeps you from the Wolf King's side?' cried Skarssen. 'Consorting with sorcerers!'

Magnus rounded on the Space Wolf.

'Did you not learn your lesson before, whelp?' he said.

Skarssen recoiled at Magnus's anger, and Ahriman felt the wash of his fury as it spread like the shockwaves of an explosion. Deeper in the valley, Yatiri and his tribesmen surrounded the altar, chanting a mantra of supplication to non-existent gods. They stood in pairs, facing one another. Ahriman watched Yatiri lift his falarica, and knew what would happen the instant before it was too late to prevent it.

'No!' cried Magnus, seeing what Ahriman saw. 'Stop!'

Yatiri turned to the tribesman next to him and rammed his falarica through his chest. His fellow elders stepped together; one man the victim, the other his killer. Spears flashed, blades bit flesh and bone. Blood was spilled.

Ahriman would never know for sure whether it was the death of the tribesmen, the blood splashing the altar or some unknown catalyst, but no sooner had the dead men fallen than the power building in the valley surged like a tidal flood.

The dam holding it back had no chance of stopping it.

With a titanic rumble of cracking stone, the guardians of the valley began to move.

CHAPTER EIGHT

Slayer of Giants

THE GIANTS WERE moving. The fact was as undeniable as it was inconceivable. The ground shook with the force of it. The cliff face cracked and broke, vast boulders falling like dust from the side of the Mountain. Straining with the effort of breaking the shackles of their ancient bindings, the behemoths tore free of the rock.

Ahriman felt the howling shriek of something primal roar from the mouth of the cave with insensate hunger, a force of mindless destruction given free rein after uncounted aeons trapped in the darkness. Rank winds roared from the depths of the Mountain.

He dropped to his knees, hands pressed to his helmet as the Great Ocean tried to force its way inside his skull. He remembered his primarch's warning and fought to keep it out.

Even in the desolation of Prospero, amid the ruined cities depopulated by the psychneuein, there was not this ferocity of psychic assault. Through tear-blurred eyes, he saw Astartes scatter, those without a connection to the aether spared the worst of the keening knife blade that gouged at his mind.

The ground shook as the first of the great machines took a ponderous step, its foot slamming down with seismic force. Lord Skarssen shouted at his warriors, but the words were lost to Ahriman. Ohthere Wyrdmake sagged against his staff, its haft swirling with coruscating arcs of black lightning. Beside him, Phosis T'kar and Hathor Maat fought against the corrupt power Magnus had warned them against. He couldn't see Uthizzar or Khalophis.

Another shockwave shook the valley as the second giant tore free, the thunderous crashing of hundreds of tonnes of rock slamming down a forceful reminder of the physical world. Slabs of roaring red metal ground past Ahriman, churning the dusty ground with their passage; Land Raiders, their hull-mounted guns crackling with furious energies as they swept towards the Titans.

Ahriman felt a presence beside him and looked up to see Khalophis bellowing at his warriors. Astartes bearing the symbol of the scarlet phoenix moved to obey his orders, rushing to optimum firing positions and bringing their weapons to bear.

Ahriman wanted to laugh. What use would their weapons be against such war machines?

He tried to stand, but the pressure battering down his mind's defences held him like a moth pinned to a slide. His resistance was locking his limbs together, fusing his joints with a stubborn refusal of the power that could be his were he only to let it in.

Ahriman recognised these temptation as the insidious whisperings that lured void travellers to their doom, as corpse lights had once ensnared those lost in ancient marshes.

That recognition alone was not enough to keep him from wanting to heed their siren song.

All he had to do was let it in and his powers would be restored: the power to smite these war machines, the power to read the currents of the future. The last of his will began to erode.

No, brother… Hold to my voice.

The words were an anchor in the madness, a lodestar back to self-control. He latched onto them as a drowning man holds fast to a rescuer's hand.

Ahriman felt someone touch his shoulder guard, and saw Uthizzar standing above him like a priest offering benediction. The Athanaean pulled him around so that they were face to face. They gripped each other's arms tightly, as though locked in a test of strength.

Rebuild your barriers, brother. I can protect you for a time, but only for a time.

Ahriman heard Uthizzar's voice in his mind, the telepath's measured tones stark against the raging torrents that threatened to overwhelm him. He felt a blessed quiet in his psyche as Uthizzar shouldered his burden.

Rise through the ranks, brother. Remember your first principles!

One by one, Ahriman repeated the mantras that allowed a Neophyte to control the powers of his being, easing into the energy-building meditations of the Zealator. Then came the control of the mind of the Practicus, the achievement of the perfectly equanimous perspective of the Philosophus. With every advance, the barriers protecting his mind were restored, and the furious howling of the aether abated.

Hurry, brother. I cannot shield you much longer.

'No need,' said Ahriman, as the world snapped back into focus. 'I have control.'

Uthizzar sagged and released his hold on him.

'Good,' he said. 'I could not have kept that up.'

Ahriman pushed himself upright, the world around him chaotic as the Astartes aligned themselves to face the gigantic war machines. Both were free of the cliff, the black tendrils enveloping them pulsating like newly filled arteries pumping strength around their bodies.

His situational awareness was complete. The Space Wolves had found cover in the huge piles of debris at the side of the valley. Ahriman was impressed. The Sons of Russ had a reputation for wild recklessness, but that didn't make them stupid. To charge headlong into this battle would see them all dead, and Skarssen knew it.

The Thousand Sons had assumed the formation of the Nine Bows, an aggressive configuration of three warrior groupings named for the ancient Gyptus kings' representation of all their enemies.

'He has gathered them all into his fist, and his mace has crashed upon their heads,' said Ahriman in recognition. Khalophis stood at the centre of the first block, Phosis T'kar commanded the second, Hathor Maat the third.

Geysers of fire spiralled around Khalophis, pillars of white flame enveloping him with searing light. Ahriman felt the enormous power surrounding the captain of the 6th Fellowship, its incredible potential bleeding into the warriors who followed him.

'Trust Khalophis not to take heed,' said Uthizzar, his voice scornful.

'He was not the only one,' said Ahriman, seeing blooms of aetheric energy centered on Phosis T'kar and Hathor Maat.

'Fools,' snapped Uthizzar, his stoic manner faltering in the face of such power. 'They were warned!'

In the midst of the chaos, Ahriman saw Yatiri standing on the basalt altar, its gleaming surface splashed with the blood of his fellow elders. He held his falarica above his head and he was screaming. The winds from the cave mouth howled around him in a hurricane of corrupt matter, a blizzard of unnatural energy revelling in its freedom.

At the centre of the hurricane stood Magnus the Red.

Magnificent and proud, the Primarch of the Thousand Sons was the eye of the storm, a quantum moment of utter stillness. Though a giant amongst men, the soaring Titans dwarfed him, their towering forms still trailing thick tarry ropes of glistening black.

The first Titan inclined its enormous head towards Magnus, its alien mind picking out the primarch like a golden treasure in a junkyard. Its body shook with what might have been disgust, regarding him as a man might view a loathsome insect. It took a step towards Magnus, its stride unsteady and hesitant, as though it were unused to controlling its limbs after so long inert. The Mountain shook with the reverberative weight of its tread, yet still Magnus did not move. His cloak of feathers billowed about his body, the violence of the Titans' awakening seeming not to concern him at all.

The machine's enormous fist flexed and its arm swung down, the movement so unlike the monstrous, clanking machine noise of Imperial engines. A haze of electromagnetic fire vented along the length of its smooth gauntlet.

Then it fired.

A blizzard of slicing projectiles shredded the space between its fist and Magnus, a thunderous storm of razor-edged death. Magnus didn't move, but the storm broke above him, shunted aside by an invisible barrier to shred the ground and fill the air with whistling, spinning fragments of rock and metal.

The enormous, lance-like weapon in its other arm swung around, and Ahriman was again struck by the fluid, living grace of the Titan. It moved as if its every

molecule was part of its essence, a living whole as
opposed to a distant mind imperfectly meshed to a
mechanical body with invasive mind impulse units and
haptic receptors.

Before it could unleash the destructive fire of the
weapon, a storm of energy blistered its limbs. The
Thousand Sons Land Raiders stabbed it with bright
spears of laserfire, like ancient hunters surrounding a
towering prey-beast.

The Astartes of the 6th Fellowship let fly with explosive warheads and storms of gunfire. Ceramic plates
cracked and spalled. Fires rippled across the surface of
the Titan's armour. Imperial engines marched to war
protected by shimmer-shields of ablative energy – not
so this behemoth. Whatever protection it had relied on
in life was denied it in this incarnation.

Magnus stood firm before the Titan, a child before a
towering monster. He lifted his arm, palm upward, as
though to offer the giant some morsel to sate its
appetite. Ahriman saw a thin smile play around his primarch's face as he drew his fingers back to make a fist.

The enormous gauntlet that had spat such venom
upon Magnus was crushed utterly as an invisible force
compressed it. Fire bloomed from the shattered hand,
black tendrils like dead veins hanging from the ruin of
its shoulder as Magnus coolly crushed the entire length
of its arm. The giant war machine shook, the movement
unnatural and hideous in its imitation of pain. Land
Raiders swept in to press the advantage, furious, rippling bolts of laser energy smacking the Titan's legs and
torso.

The second machine rotated its lance, and the air
grew thin, as though the Mountain had sucked in a
great breath. An impossibly bright pinpoint of light
grew at the end of the weapon before a pulsing storm
erupted in a blaze of streaming fire.

Three Land Raiders exploded, instantly vaporised in the blast, and a fireball of burnt metal mushroomed skyward. The surging beam of liquid light swept on, carving a glassy trench across the valley and immolating everything in its path. A group of Hathor Maat's warriors on the periphery of the seething fire burst into flames, their armour running like melted rubber. Ahriman could hear their screams. The heat wash of their death was a rancid flesh stink that threatened to break his concentration.

'Ahzek!' cried a voice, almost lost amid the shriek of the Titans' weapons fire. His anger fled, the rigid mental discipline of the Enumerations reasserting itself. He turned to the source of the cry, seeing Ohthere Wyrdmake frantically beckoning him from behind the cover of a spit of red rock. Gunfire streamed from the Space Wolves position.

Logic took hold, the measured calm of mental acuity honed over a century of study.

'Uthizzar,' he said, 'let's go.'

Uthizzar nodded and together they ran through the deafening, blazing crescendo of weapons fire that filled the valley. Firepower to end entire regiments surged back and forth: heatwash, ricochets and shrieking intakes of breath from guns capable of mass murder. The shape of the battle was fluid and its tempo was increasing.

The Astartes were fighting back, filling the valley with disciplined volleys, but save for the augmented fire of Khalophis's warriors, it was having little effect. There were too many targets for the Titans to effectively engage them all, but that wouldn't last long. Fifty more Astartes died as the second Titan's fist spat a shrieking hail of death, the impacts sounding like a thousand mirrors shattering at once.

Ahriman ducked into cover with Uthizzar, feeling strange at taking refuge with warriors in midnight-grey armour instead of crimson and ivory. A shaggy wolf snapped its jaws at him, thick saliva drooling between its fangs.

'What were you doing out there?' shouted Wyrdmake over the din of gunfire.

'Nothing,' replied Ahriman, unwilling to speak of the mental ordeal he and Uthizzar had endured, 'just picking our moment to run for cover.'

'What I would not give for a Mechanicum engine right now,' hissed Wyrdmake as a rolling wall of boiling air washed over their position. The Rune Priest's staff crackled with miniature lightning bolts. The power filling the valley had almost overwhelmed Ahriman with the urge to wield it, but Wyrdmake appeared oblivious to its temptations.

Space Wolves shouldered missile launchers, sighting on the undamaged Titan. Skarssen shouted an order, lost in the din, pointing towards the Titan's head. Spiralling contrails zoomed upwards, detonating against the surface of the giant's head, rocking it back, but doing little obvious damage.

'Again!' shouted Skarssen.

'That won't bring it down!' cried Ahriman over the booming cough of missile fire.

'Never hunted a Fenrisian Kraken, have you?' cried Skarssen.

'How perceptive,' snapped Ahriman, ducking down as the rocks around him exploded in pinging fragments. A Space Wolf went down, but picked himself back up again. 'What has that got do with anything?'

'A single wolfship will be smashed to kindling and its crew devoured,' said the Wolf Lord, as though enjoying this fight immensely, 'but put a dozen in the water and then it becomes a hunt worth undertaking. Shield scales buckle, flesh tears and blood flows, the beast weakens and then it dies. Every harpoon matters, from the first to the last.'

Then all thought was obliterated as a world-shaking scream of ancient loss and pain ripped through the mind of every warrior.

It was the sound of worlds ending. It was the birth shout of a vile and terrible god, and the death scream of glory that died when the race of Man was young. Ahriman collapsed as pain like nothing he had ever known wracked his body with a torturer's skill, finding the secret parts of him and driving itself home without mercy. His fragile control crumbled in the face of it, his mind ablaze with images of a civilisation overturned, worlds consumed and an empire that had spanned the stars brought low by its own weakness.

No one was spared the scream's violence, not the Space Wolves and certainly not the Thousand Sons, who suffered worst of all. The pain drove Ahriman to the edge of sanity in the blink of an eye.

Then it was over. The echoes of the scream retreated, its power like a breaker upon a seawall, forceful and spectacular, but quick to fade. Ahriman blinked away tears of pain, surprised to find he was lying flat on his back.

'What in the name of the Great Wolf was that?' demanded Skarssen, towering over him as though nothing had happened. Once again, Ahriman was impressed by the Space Wolves.

'I'm not sure,' he gasped, blinding spots of light sparkling behind his eyes from burst blood vessels, 'a psychic scream of some sort.'

'Can you block it?' asked Skarssen, holding his hand out to Ahriman.

'No, it's too powerful.'

'We will not need to,' said Uthizzar.

Ahriman took Skarssen's hand and hauled himself upright, his head still aching from the pressure of the unexpected war shout. Uthizzar nodded at him and pointed out into the valley.

He glanced over the white-hot rocks he and the Space Wolves sheltered behind. The searing fire of the Titan's weapons had vitrified them, the solid stone now smooth and translucent. Razor-edged discs the width of a man were embedded in the glass, caught by the molten rock before it hardened and singing with the vibration of their impacts.

Blinking away bright afterimages, Ahriman looked down the valley. The elongated head sections of the war machines were burned black, their previously impervious armour cracked and their bejewelled heads split open. Ahriman smelled the burnt metal taste of an incredibly powerful aetheric discharge. Whips of wild lightning lashed from the broken armour, and he watched with fierce pride as Magnus the Red stalked through the storm of fire and death towards the towering machines with twin fists of fire.

Ghostly light rippled across the Titans. Explosions bit chunks out of their ceramic skin, and viscous black liquid, like boiling oil, slithered from the wounds.

'You see!' roared Skarssen. 'They bleed!'

'It won't be nearly enough,' returned Ahriman, 'no matter how many harpoons you bring to bear!'

'Just watch,' promised Skarssen, throwing himself flat as a shrieking wall of light broke against their cover. Superheated air hissed and greedily sucked oxygen from the air with a thunderclap.

'The Storm breaks!' roared Wyrdmake. 'The Tempest gives its sign!'

Magnus faced the giant machines alone, his feathered cloak spread behind him like an eagle's wings. His flesh swelled with power, and for a brief moment it seemed that he matched the Titan in stature. His unbound hair was a stiffened mane of red, and his limbs ran with electric light. The Primarch of the Thousand Sons drew back his arm and loosed a stream of blue fire that struck the nearest Titan square in the chest.

The alien engine was an artfully designed war machine from an age long-forgotten, the ancient craft of its makers wondrous to behold, but it could not resist such incredible, awe-inspiring power. Its torso exploded, vast ribs of unknown manufacture shattering like brittle china and falling in fire-blackened splinters. The pendulous head toppled from its neck and crashed to the rocks far below.

The war machine fell with infinite majesty, slamming down in pieces upon the rocky ground over which it had stood sentinel for longer than humans could comprehend. Blinding clouds of dust swept out from its fall, obscuring the fate of the second Titan.

A strange silence fell over the battlefield, as though no one could really believe they had seen the incredible war machine die. The silence was uncanny, but it did not last long.

A triumphant howl erupted from the throats of the Wolves, an ululating victory roar, but Ahriman took no pleasure at such destruction.

'A terrible thing to see something so magnificent brought low,' said Ahriman.

'You pity it?' asked Wyrdmake. 'Does not the hunter feel the joy at the moment of the kill?'

'I feel nothing but sorrow,' said Ahriman.

Wyrdmake looked at him with genuine confusion, affronted that Ahriman sought to sour this moment of great victory. 'The beast killed entire packs of your warriors. Vengeance demanded its death. It is right to honour your foe, but to mourn its death is pointless.'

'Maybe so, but what secrets and knowledge have been lost in its destruction?'

'What secrets worth knowing does such a beast keep?' said Skarssen. 'Better it dies and its secrets are lost than to ken such alien witchery.'

The smoke of the mighty construct's death parted, and a keening roar built from within the depths of the ashen clouds, a wail of sorrow and anger entwined. A mighty shadow moved in the depths of the billowing dust, and the surviving Titan emerged. It was wounded and bled black rivers of glistening liquid, but like a cornered animal it was still horribly dangerous.

Its lance arm slid around, the barrel aimed squarely at Magnus, and Ahriman saw that the enormous power the primarch had wielded had cost him dearly. Magnus's skin was pale, the fiery copper lustre dimmed to a faded brass. He was down on one knee, as though offering servitude to a bellicose god of war.

The ground shook as the giant moved forward. It lowered its head to study the insignificant creature ranged against it. The remnants of its ruined arm spat flames and smoke. Its sweeping shoulder wings were aflame, sagging and useless at its shoulders, like a broken angel of destruction come to rid Aghoru of all life.

Killing light built along the length of its weapon, and a shriek of violated air built as it drew breath.

And a blazing lance of sunfire stabbed out, searing Magnus from the face of the world.

THE THOUSAND SONS screamed.

The heat of a million stars wreathed their primarch, and no matter that he was one of twenty towering pinnacles of gene-wrought superhuman warriors, even he could not survive such an attack. A surge tide of liquid fire swept out, turning the rock of the Mountain to glass.

Ahriman's grip on the Enumerations collapsed in the face of such visceral horror; grief, anger and hatred jammed a twisting knife in his guts. The Titan poured its deadly fire upon Magnus, and Ahriman knew he would never live to see so hideous a sight.

Beside him, Uthizzar clutched his head in agony. Even in the midst of his grief, Ahriman pitied Uthizzar. How terrible must it be for a telepath to feel the death of his father?

Moments passed in utter silence, as though the world itself could not quite believe what had happened. One of the Emperor's favoured sons had been struck down. It was inconceivable. What force could end the life of a primarch? The stubborn reality of it could not yet penetrate their legends, could not break the unassailable fact of their immortality.

That fact was fiction, and Ahriman felt his world crumble.

The Thousand Sons screamed.

The Space Wolves howled.

The vox exploded with it, an atavistic declaration of fury.

'With me!' shouted Skarssen.

And the Wolves were unleashed.

They poured from the rocks, bolters spitting fire and missiles launched on the run as they swept towards the Titan. The Terminators led the charge, a wall of armoured fury that would eviscerate any normal foe, but which would be next to useless against this enemy. Ahriman and Uthizzar went with them, knowing it was madness for infantry to move in the presence of so powerful and terrible a war machine. The Titan was king of the battlefield, a towering killing machine that crushed foot-soldiers without even registering their presence.

Yet there was an undeniable thrill in risking everything like this, a noble heroism and vitality he normally never felt in combat. The Enumerations gave a warrior focus, prevented his emotions from overwhelming him, and kept his mind free of distractions that could get him killed. The business of war was more deadly than it had ever been in any of the violent ages of Man, the surety of death or injury a warrior's constant companion. The Enumerations helped the Thousand Sons face such thoughts objectively, and allowed them to fight on regardless.

To do otherwise was inconceivable, and Ahriman was always amazed that mortals ever dared to step onto a battlefield. Yet here he was, raw grief and the vicarious energy of the Space Wolves carrying him forward without the protection of emotional detachment.

As the Space Wolves came, so too did the Thousand Sons.

The last surviving Land Raiders, both black and belching smoke, darted like pack predators as they fired on the Titan. Desperate to avenge their primarch, the red-armoured warriors of Magnus charged with the same boundless energy as the Space Wolves, their cool detachment cast aside in this one, headlong charge.

It was reckless and futile, but also brave and heroic.

The seething fire began to fade, and Ahriman's charge faltered at the sight before him. A vitrified bowl of a crater spread out at the mighty war engine's clawed feet, yet at its centre was a sight that lifted his heart and filled him with awe.

A shimmering dome of golden-hued energy rippled in the heat haze, and within it, two armoured figures. Atop a crooked pillar of rock at the heart of the crater, all that had survived the Titan's fire, were Phosis T'kar and Magnus the Red. The captain of the 2nd Fellowship was bent almost double, his arms raised to his shoulders like *Atlas Telamon* of Old Earth, the rebellious titan doomed to bear the celestial sphere upon his shoulders for all eternity.

'A kine shield,' breathed Uthizzar. 'Who knew T'kar was so strong?'

Ahriman laughed in desperate relief. Magnus was alive! He was on his knees, weakened and all but exhausted by his destruction of the first Titan, but he was alive, and that simple fact pulsed through every warrior of the Thousand Sons in a connected instant of joy and wonder.

In that moment of relief, the Astartes of both Legions let fly their anger and hurt pride.

The Space Wolves unleashed the fangs of their every weapon, bolts, missiles and armour-cracking shells seeking out the Titan's wounds and tearing them wider. In the midst of the Sons of Russ, Ahriman and Uthizzar did likewise, unloading magazine after magazine of explosive rounds at the object of their hatred. Skarssen exhorted his warriors with bellowed howls without meaning, but with a power all their own. Ohthere Wyrdmake prowled the length of the Space Wolf advance, surrounded by pack wolves as a frozen wind and the echo of a distant winter storm swirled around him.

The Wolves of Fenris attacked with all their weapons, and so too did the scions of Prospero fight with all of theirs.

Hundreds of waving streams of fire licked up at the Titan, but this was no ordinary barrage. Warriors bearing the phoenix symbol of the Pyrae were firing on the move, hurling aetheric flames from their gauntlets. In the midst of the 6th Fellowship, Khalophis threw his fists like a pugilist, each jab sending a stream of coruscating fire against the enormous Titan. Where it struck, it burned away the Titan's armour, exposing its crystalline structure and unmaking the bone-like material of its construction.

'Merciful fates!' cried Uthizzar at the sight of Khalophis. 'What is he doing?'

'Rescuing our primarch!' yelled Ahriman. 'As we should!'

The strength of the Pyrae was ascendant, but this was incredible. Within the cult temples of Prospero, such art could be wielded without fear, but to do so with outsiders present was reckless beyond imagining.

Nor were Khalophis and Phosis T'kar alone in their brazen displays.

Hathor Maat whipped his hands back and forth, each time casting traceries of purple lightning towards the towering machine. Explosions and dancing balls of fire crackled like electric chains around its body, burning its armour open. Arcs of lightning flashed between the warriors of the Pavoni as their captain drank deep of their energies and channelled it through his flesh.

Uthizzar grabbed his arm, and Ahriman read the fear in his aura.

'They have to stop!' hissed Uthizzar. 'All of them! To tap into the Great Ocean is intoxicating, you know that all too well, but only the most disciplined and powerful dare wield power such as this!'

'Our brother-captains are powerful and disciplined practitioners of the hidden arts,' said Ahriman, shrugging off Uthizzar's hold.

'But are they disciplined *enough*? That is the real question.'

Ahriman had no answer for him and returned his attention to killing the Titan.

The Titan was dying, but it didn't die easily. Its limbs thrashed in its death throes, spitting incandescent pulses of energy that tore down the valley walls and obliterated dozens of Astartes with every fiery sweep.

Its defiance was finally ended when Khalophis and Hathor Maat combined a hurricane of fire and a spear of lightning that struck the war machine's head with a killing blow. The curved skull exploded and the towering machine collapsed, plummeting straight down like dead wood hewn by a woodsman's axe.

The noise was deafening: breaking plates, shattering glass and snapping bone all in one. It fell hard, breaking into a billion pieces, none larger than the size of a man's fist, and a glittering rain of splintered ceramic fell upon the victorious Astartes like musical notes. The Astartes lowered their weapons, and took a collective breath as the dust and smoke of battle began to settle.

The golden dome shielding Phosis T'kar and the primarch collapsed with a squalling shriek. Phosis T'kar fell, utterly drained by the act of protecting his primarch, as Magnus the Red rose to his feet once more. Though the toll taken upon him was great, he remained as magnificent as ever. Magnus lifted the stricken body of Phosis T'kar, and stepped from the pillar of rock.

He did not fall. Instead, Magnus floated across the crater like a battle-weary angel, borne aloft by his incredible power through a billowing mist of shimmering crystal.

The Thousand Sons were there to greet him, ecstatic beyond words that their primarch had survived. Ahriman and Uthizzar pushed through the scrum of Astartes, their warriors only reluctantly parting to allow them through. Ahriman reached the edge of the crater as Magnus set foot on the glassy floor of the valley and gently laid Phosis T'kar before him.

'Hathor Maat,' said Magnus, his voice weary and thin. 'See to him. Bend all the power of the Pavoni to his survival. You will not allow him to die.'

The captain of the 3rd Fellowship nodded. He knelt beside Phosis T'kar and swiftly removed his helmet. T'kar's face was deathly pale. Hathor Maat placed his hands on either side of his neck, and almost instantaneously colour returned to his face.

'My lord,' said Ahriman, his voice almost too choked with emotion to speak. 'We thought... We thought you lost to us.'

Magnus smiled weakly, dabbing at a trickle of blood that ran from the corner of his mouth. His eye shone a bruised violet and red. Never had Ahriman seen his beloved leader so battered.

'I will live,' said Magnus. 'But this is not over yet. These guardians were perverted by the corruption imprisoned beneath this peak. It has lain dormant for an age, but it has awoken. Unless we stop it, everything we have learned here will be lost.'

'What would you have us do, lord?' demanded Khalophis.

Magnus turned to the cave mouth. It was thick with growths, like blackened roots from some parasitic weed burrowed into the meat of the Mountain.

'Walk with me into the depths, my sons,' said Magnus. 'We will finish this together.'

CHAPTER NINE

Abilities/Beneath the Mountain/
The Language of Angels

THE SUN WAS at its zenith, and the idea of moving from beneath the canopy of his tent didn't appeal to Lemuel one bit. Camille wanted to travel the secret path through the Mountain again, eager to know what had drawn the Thousand Sons and Space Wolves into its high valley with such speed. The climb had almost ended Lemuel in the cool of sunset. He didn't want to think what it would do to him at noon.

'Aren't you in the least bit curious?' asked Camille, reclining on a canvas chair and drinking water from a battered leather canteen. 'I mean, what's got them all riled up that they needed to take battle tanks? Land Raiders no less. Did you see?'

'I saw,' said Lemuel, dabbing his brow with his bandanna. 'They were impressive.'

'Impressive?' said Camille, incredulously. 'They were more than impressive, they were amazing.'

'Okay, they were amazing, but no, I'm not that curious as to what's happening in the Mountain. I'm sure
whatever is going on, we'll find out in due course.'

'Easy for you to say,' noted Camille. '*You* have a direct
line to the Thousand Sons now.'

'It's not like that,' said Lemuel.

'Then what *is* it like?' asked Kallista.

The three of them had taken to meeting each night
since the arrival of the Space Wolves, their shared dis-
cussions of what Kallista had written bonding them like
conspirators with a dark secret. The more time Lemuel
spent with Kallista and Camille, the more he began to
realise they shared more than one.

'Lord Ahriman sees potential in me,' he said, knowing
his words were wholly insufficient to explain why the
Chief Librarian of the Thousand Sons had sent for him.

'What sort of potential?' asked Kallista.

Lemuel shrugged and said, 'I'm not really sure yet.'

'Come on, that's no answer,' pressed Camille.

Lemuel's fear when Ahriman had told him he knew of
his ability, had quickly faded, replaced with a simmering pride in his powers. He had long suspected that his
ability to read people marked him out as special, and
now he knew that was true. After spending time with
Camille and Kallista, he realised he wasn't the only one.
He hesitated before answering, knowing he could be
wrong, but wanting to be sure.

'After the other night, we know Kallista has a talent
for, what would the word be? Channeling, I suppose.
Channeling a power that allows her to write things that
haven't happened yet.'

'Talent's hardly the word I'd use,' said Kallista bitterly.

'No, I suppose you wouldn't,' agreed Lemuel, 'not if
it's as painful as you say, but the physical manifestation
of your ability aside, you can do things most people
cannot, yes?'

'Yes,' said Kallista, nodding, and he could read how uncomfortable talk of her power made her.

'Well, I also have an ability,' he said.

'What kind of ability?' asked Camille.

'An ability to see things that other people cannot.'

Kallista leaned forward, her aura revealing her interest.

'What sort of things?' she asked.

'Auras, I suppose you'd call them. It's like a glowing haze surrounding a person. I can see when someone's lying, read their feelings and moods. That sort of thing.'

'So what am I feeling right now?' asked Camille.

Lemuel smiled.

'You are overcome with feelings of unbridled lust for me, my dear,' he said. 'You want to leap on me and ravish me to within an inch of my life. Were it not for the presence of Mistress Eris, you would be astride me right now.'

Camille laughed.

'Okay, I'm convinced,' she said.

'Seriously?' asked Kallista.

'*No!*' squealed Camille. 'I'm fond of Lemuel, but I prefer partners of a different flavour.'

'Oh,' said Kallista, looking away with a guilty flush. She looked at Lemuel. 'Can you really do that?'

'Yes, I can,' he said. 'Right now you're embarrassed and wishing Camille wouldn't refer to her sexuality in front of you. You believe me, and you're relieved that you're not the only one with a secret.'

'You don't need special powers to see that, Lemuel,' said Camille. 'Even I can see that.'

'Yes, but you believe me as well, and you have a power too, don't you?'

Camille's smile froze.

'I don't know what you're talking about,' she said.

'Now *that's* a lie,' said Lemuel, rising from his chair and fetching himself a drink. 'You touch things and you know where they've come from, who owned them and everything about their history going all the way back to when they were made. That's why you always wear those gloves and why you never borrow anything from other people. I don't blame you. It must be hard learning all of a person's secrets like that.'

Camille looked away, her eyes downcast, and Lemuel smiled, trying to put her at ease.

'I watched you touch that object buried in the ruins of the Aghoru house the other day,' he said. 'You knew what it was the moment you laid your hand on it, didn't you?'

Camille kept her eyes on the floor and said, 'I did, yes. I haven't always been able to do it. I was about thirteen when it started.'

'Don't worry, my dear,' said Lemuel gently. 'We all have something special about us. And I don't think it's an accident we're here.'

'I don't follow.'

'Think about it. What are the chances that the three of us, people with talents beyond the understanding of most ordinary people, would find ourselves together like this? I'm no mathematician, but I suspect the odds are pretty much against it.'

'So what are you saying, that we're here deliberately? Why?'

Lemuel sat down again, sweating and breathless thanks to the heat.

'I think our hosts may have something to do with it,' he said. 'Look around. How few remembrancers are there with the XV Legion? Forty-two spread throughout the Fellowships. A number like that makes me think there was a great deal more to our selection than our talents as remembrancers.'

'So you're saying we were all selected by the Thousand Sons *because* we have these abilities?'

'Almost certainly,' said Lemuel.

'Why?' asked Kallista.

'That, I don't know,' confessed Lemuel, 'but if there's one thing I've come to know about the Thousand Sons, it's that they don't do anything without good reason.'

THE INSIDE OF the Mountain was alive with sound and colour. Not any sound the Space Wolves could hear, despite their legendarily heightened senses, nor any colour they could name, for these were hues of the aether, rippling like smoke and radiating from the smooth walls of the cave like bioluminescence.

The armour worn by the Astartes was equipped with sensors that could penetrate darkness, but to those without aether-sight, the view would be a sea-green monochrome, a poor rendition of the true light saturating the rock.

A hundred warriors delved the innards of the Mountain, all that could be spared from the business of harvesting the gene-seed of the fallen.

Magnus led the way down, following a twisting path only he could see. Lord Skarssen and Ohthere Wyrdmake marched with him, and Ahriman took a moment to study the Wolf Lord. Skarssen's aura was a keen blade, a focussed edge of single-minded determination. Here was a warrior who never let up, never stopped to question, and would never, ever, falter in his duty.

Such surety of purpose reminded Ahriman of the golem legends written in the ancient Qabalah. The golem was a creature shaped from clay, raised by an ancient priest to defend his people from persecution. It was a powerful, unstoppable force, a creature that obeyed its master's instructions absolutely literally, never deviating from its task, no matter what.

It was a perfect representation for the Space Wolves, for Ahriman had read accounts of the war they made. The sons of Russ were weapons, a consummate force for destruction that absolutely would not stop until the job was done.

Of course, the legends of the golem were also cautionary tales of hubris, with later tales depicting golems that had to be undone through trickery, whereupon they more often than not turned on their creators. The Golem of Ingolstadt was one such beast, a monster that wreaked havoc on its creator and all he loved before destroying itself upon a polar funeral pyre.

The comparison made Ahriman uneasy, and he put the thought from his mind as the tunnel sloped ever downwards. Normally he could retrace any route, no matter how complex, but within moments of entering the Mountain he was utterly lost. Only the primarch seemed to know where he was going, but how he knew which passage to take and which junction to follow was a mystery to Ahriman.

Of the captains of Fellowship, only Uthizzar had come into the Mountain. Phosis T'kar was too weak, and Hathor Maat was restoring him with the healing arts of the Pavoni. Khalophis too had remained on the surface to secure the battlefield. The alien Titans were no more, but who knew what other horrors might yet lurk in hidden valleys and caves?

As a result, the Thousand Sons beneath the Mountain were a mix of Astartes from different Fellowships, and Ahriman saw ghostly flickers of power rising from each of them, subtly different, revealing their cult affiliations by the tempers of their auras.

He noted that most of them were Pyrae.

'I know,' said Uthizzar. 'Together with the Space Wolves, there will be no room for subtlety here.'

Ahriman was about to nod, when he realised he hadn't spoken the thought aloud.

'Did you just read me?' he asked.

'It is hard not to at the moment,' replied Uthizzar. 'Everyone's thoughts are so heightened, with the level of aetheric energy here. It is as if you are all shouting. I find it quite uncomfortable.'

Ahriman bristled at the idea of his thoughts being read.

'Be careful,' he warned. 'That could get you into trouble some day. People do not like their innermost secrets revealed.'

'My power is no different from yours,' said Uthizzar.

'How do you reach that conclusion?' said Ahriman. 'The powers of the Corvidae and the Athanaeans are nothing alike.'

'I read what people are thinking *now*. You read what they are going to be doing in the future. All that is different is the timing.'

'I hadn't thought of it in that way,' conceded Ahriman. 'Perhaps this can form a debate for another day? This is probably not the best time.'

'No,' said Uthizzar with an amused chuckle.

They marched in silence for a while longer, following the crooked path deeper and deeper into the darkness. To feel the touch of the aether in the Mountain, after its chronic absence, was both exhilarating and worrying. Nothing happed without reason, and only something of great magnitude could force the state of a thing to change with such extreme polarity.

What lurked in the depths of the Mountain that could effect such change?

THE GROUP LAPSED into silence, each person pondering the implications of their shared abilities. Kallista and Camille were relieved to share their burdens with others, yet wary of discarding a lifetime of secrecy in so short a time.

It had bonded them. Whatever else might happen, whatever other journeys they might take, this shared secret had forged a link between them. For now it was a fragile thing, but with careful nurturing, it might prove to be enduring.

'So what do we do with this then?' asked Camille at last.

'What do you mean?' asked Lemuel.

'I mean, what do we do?' said Camille, throwing her hands up as though he were being obtuse. 'If you're saying that we're part of the 28th Expedition because of our abilities, are we supposed to know that's why we were selected? Can we use our abilities openly?'

Lemuel considered the question before saying, 'I would caution against that, my dear. Powers like ours are still considered witchery in some circles.'

'Do you think we are we in danger?' asked Kallista, picking at a fold in her jellabiya. 'Is that why they've gathered us together? To get rid of us?'

'No, I don't believe so,' said Lemuel hurriedly. He stood and went over to her chair, taking her hand and looking her straight in the eye. 'I don't believe the Thousand Sons would go to such lengths just to have us burned at the stake.'

'Then why do they want us?'

'I confess I do not know for sure,' he said. 'Lord Ahriman says he wants to teach me how best to use my powers. I think we are here to learn.'

'Why would the Thousand Sons care about teaching us anything?' asked Camille.

'Lord Ahriman said that by using our powers we make ourselves vulnerable,' said Lemuel, grasping for concepts he didn't know how to articulate. 'I don't understand it really, but I got the impression that we're all part of something larger, and that we're on the cusp of something wonderful. We could be the first of a new breed of people, people who can use their abilities safely and teach other to do the same.'

Kallista snatched her hand back, and Lemuel was shocked at the fear he saw in her face. Her aura shifted hue, turning from a soft yellow to an angry red.

'I don't want to be a new breed of anything,' she said, pushing her chair back and rising to her feet. 'I don't want this ability. If I could get rid of it I would!'

Lemuel stood and raised his hands in a placating gesture.

'I'm sorry,' he said. 'I didn't mean to push you.'

'It hurts so much,' she said, haltingly, pressing her hands to her temples and holding back tears with an effort of will. 'Every time the fire comes, it burns part of me away with it. Unless I stop it, I'm afraid it's going to burn me away entirely one day.'

Camille pushed herself from her chair and took Kallista in her arms.

'Don't be silly,' she said. 'We'll look out for you, won't we, Lemuel?'

'Of course,' he said, 'without question. People like us need to stick together.'

'People like what?' said a voice behind them.

Lemuel jumped as though struck, and turned to see a frail old man in the beige robe of a remembrancer with a long mane of frizzy white hair, only reluctantly contained in a wiry ponytail. Thin and stooped, he carried a slim, leatherbound book under his arm, and his walnut coloured skin was ancient and deeply creased with great age.

'I'm not interrupting anything, am I?' asked Mahavastu Kallimakus, Scrivener Extraordinary to Magnus the Red.

Lemuel was first to recover. 'Mahavastu! No, no, you're always welcome. Come in, won't you? I rarely see you these days. Magnus got you so busy writing his memoirs you don't have time for your old friend?'

Kallimakus looked uncomfortable, and Lemuel read the unease permeating his aura.

'Is something the matter, my friend?' asked Lemuel, steering Kallimakus into the tent.

'I rather fear it might be,' said Mahavastu.

'What is it?' asked Camille, getting up and allowing the old man to take her seat.

'It is the primarch,' said Mahavastu, placing the leatherbound book in his lap with a guilty shudder. 'I fear he and his warriors are in great danger.'

'What kind of danger?' asked Kallista.

The gravest danger,' said Mahavastu. 'The gravest danger imaginable.'

THEY CAME AT last to a great chasm in the heart of the Mountain, a perfectly circular sinkhole, hundreds of metres in diameter. The roof above the enormous pit was a crystalline temple dome, formed from the same substance as the Titans. The dome was pale cream, threaded with veins of crimson like the finest marble. And, like the Titans, its substance had been invaded with the black ropes of corruption.

Thousands of glistening, pulsing black pillars rose from the pit like the roots of some unnatural weed. They pulsed with liquid motion, obscene mockeries of life-giving veins that fed on life instead of sustaining it.

'Great bones of Fenris,' hissed Skarssen. 'What manner of beast is this?'

No one had an answer for him, their horror at the sight too visceral to put into words.

Ahriman moved through the stunned Astartes to the edge of the pit. A ledge ran around the circumference of the chasm, easily wide enough to drive a pair of Land Raiders abreast. Gold and silver symbols were worked into the bones of the rock, as the though they had always existed and the Mountain had simply grown up around them.

Magnus stood at the edge of the chasm, looking in wonder at the impenetrable forest of oozing black tentacles rising from the pit. The lustre had returned to his skin, as though he were refreshed by the journey closer to the source of the power beneath the Mountain. Ohthere Wyrdmake and Lord Skarssen followed Ahriman, joining the primarch at the edge.

'What are they?' asked Skarssen, kneeling beside the nearest symbol, a gold serpent entwined with a silver eye.

'Warding symbols?' suggested Wyrdmake, 'Like the wolf talismans we bear.'

Skarssen touched the wolf pelt at his shoulder, and Ahriman watched as all the Space Wolves superstitiously reached for various fetishes hanging from their armour. Those closest to Wyrdmake touched the eagle-topped staff he carried, and Ahriman smiled.

'Superstition?' he said. 'The Emperor would not approve.'

'An Astartes of the Thousand Sons telling us what the Emperor would not approve of?' laughed Wyrdmake. 'Ironic, wouldn't you say?'

'No, I just find the gestures quaint,' smiled Ahriman, 'almost primitive. I mean no offence of course.'

'None taken,' replied Wyrdmake. 'But you too reached for a talismanic device.'

The smile froze on Ahriman's lips as he realised the Rune Priest was right. Without even being aware of it, he had pressed his fingers to the silver oakleaf cluster on his shoulder guard, the icon that had once belonged to Ohrmuzd.

'Perhaps we are not so different after all,' said Wyrdmake.

'Perhaps not,' allowed Ahriman, turning his attention back to the thick ropes of black matter rising from the pit.

Magnus stood immobile, as though in silent communion, and Ahriman stood next to him.

'My lord?' he asked. 'What is it?'

'It's incredible, Ahzek,' said Magnus. 'It's raw matter, the very stuff of the Primordial Creator given form.'

'It's rank is what it is,' hissed Skarssen. 'Any fool can see that.'

'It's alive,' hissed Uthizzar, walking to the edge of the pit with sleepwalker's strides.

'Oh, it is alive, all right,' nodded Magnus. 'I have never felt anything quite so alive, not for a long time. Not for a very long time indeed.'

Ahriman felt a thrill of warning along the length of his spine. Previously, the primarch had labelled this power stagnant and dead.

'It's calling us,' said Uthizzar, and Ahriman heard the dream-like quality of his voice. 'I need to go to it.'

'What's calling to you?' said Ahriman, but no sooner had he spoken than he heard it, a soft whisper, like a distant friend calling from afar. It was not an unwelcome sound. It was gentle, a beguiling whisper redolent with the promise of raptures beyond measure.

Magnus turned to his captains and shook his head. Ahriman saw that Magnus's eye was deep black, the pupil massively enlarged and swollen, as though filled with the same dark substance as the glistening pillars.

'My sons,' said Magnus, and Ahriman felt the barely constrained power laden in every syllable. 'Concentrate. Rise to the tenth Enumeration and shut out the voices. You are not strong enough to resist them. I have dealt with power like this before. I mastered it then, and I will master it now.'

Uthizzar nodded, and Ahriman felt his consciousness rise into the uppermost Enumeration, a place of inner solitude where a warrior could find peace, untroubled by the concerns of the world around them.. It was an effort to reach such a state of mind, especially here, but Uthizzar was master of his own psyche. Ahriman rose alongside him, and the voices ceased, shut off as surely as a vox-caster with the power cell removed.

With the clarity imparted by the tenth sphere, Ahriman saw movement within the heart of the mass of tentacles, a flash of saffron and a glitter of something reflective.

'No,' he whispered, his grip on the tenth sphere slipping as a flash of recognition surfaced. 'Please don't let it be so.'

As though in response to his words, the tentacles shivered, and a repulsive slithering sound, as of a thousand greasy limbs moving together, filled the chamber. The Space Wolves were instantly alert, their guns snapping upright, though there were no obvious targets for their wrath beyond the black tentacles.

'What is going on?' demanded Skarssen.

Wyrdmake's staff crackled with power, but the Rune Priest regarded it with horror, as though it had transformed into a poisonous snake.

'Spread out,' ordered Magnus, 'and stay away from the edge.'

The gelatinous mass of plant-like growths rippled, and a number of thick stems detached themselves from the domed roof of the chamber. Like disease-ridden fronds in a polluted pool, the nearest tentacles sagged and spread as something moved through them, on a course angled towards the Thousand Sons.

A black veil parted, and Ahriman's control of the spheres collapsed completely as he saw a wretched figure drift through the tar-black tentacles.

Scraps of orange fabric clung to its naked body, which hung limp with its head down like a puppet bereft of a puppeteer. The figure was borne aloft by a host of slender tentacles, one a gleaming noose around his neck, another around his temple like a crown of obsidian.

These tentacles were not like the others. Their vile substance was alive with gaping mouths and seething eyes that bubbled into existence before dissolving into nothingness.

The figure drew nearer, and he lifted his head. His eyes were oil-dark and reflective, and fine black lines threaded his skin as though the black tentacles had filled him with their corrupt substance. A cracked mirrormask hung at his throat.

The man's mouth was moving, as though he were screaming in unimaginable torment, but no sounds emerged, only a sopping gurgle of fluid-filled lungs.

'Is that…?' asked Uthizzar.

'It is,' said Magnus sadly. 'Yatiri.'

MAHAVASTU KALLIMAKUS HAILED from the subcontinent of Indoi, and was a meticulous recorder of data and a fastidious observer of details. He had scribed much of the earliest days of the Great Crusade and had been one of the first remembrancers to be chosen by the Thousand Sons. His reputation had preceded him, and he was immediately assigned to Magnus the Red.

He had been at Magnus's side since the restored Legion had departed Prospero in a fanfare of triumph, cheering crowds and billowing clouds of rose petals. He had recorded the primarch's every thought and deed in a great tome that many called the Book of Magnus.

Those remembrancers who found it difficult to collect any first-hand accounts of the Great Crusade from the Thousand Sons looked upon Mahavastu Kallimakus with no small amount of jealousy. Lemuel had met

Mahavastu Kallimakus on the *Photep* during a symposium on the best form of data collation, and their friendship had been borne of a mutual love of detail.

'God is in the details,' Mahavastu would say as they pored over one of the many manuscripts in the vessel's fascinating library.

'You mean the devil is in the details,' Lemuel would reply.

'That, my dear Lemuel, depends entirely on the detail in question.'

Kallimakus was energetic, with the vigour of a man half his chronological age, which was somewhere in the region of a hundred and thirty standard.

Right now, Mahavastu Kallimakus looked every one of those years.

The aged remembrancer opened his book, and Lemuel looked over his shoulder.

'An artist's notebook,' he said, seeing the charcoal and pencil marks of an artist's preliminary outlines. 'I never had you pegged as a sketcher. All seems a bit woolly for a man like you, none of the precision of language.'

Kallimakus shook his head.

'And you would be right, Lemuel,' he said. 'I am not an artist. In truth, I am no longer sure what I am.'

'I'm sorry, Mahavastu, I don't follow.'

'I do not remember drawing them,' said Mahavastu in exasperation. 'I do not remember anything in this book, neither pictures nor words. I look back over every entry I have made and they are a mystery to me.'

Tears glistened in the old man's eyes, and Lemuel saw the anxiety in his aura replaced with aching sorrow.

'Everything I have written… I remember none of it.'

'Have you had someone from the medicae corps check you out?' asked Camille. 'I had an uncle who got old and his mind turned on him. He couldn't remember anything, even things you just told him. Soon he forgot who he was and couldn't remember his wife or children. It was sad, watching him die by degrees in front of us.'

Mahavastu shook his head.

'I am familiar with such progressive patterns of cognitive and functional impairment, Mistress Shivani, so I had a medicae scan my brain this morning,' he said. 'The neuron and synapse counts in my cerebral and subcortical regions are quite normal, and he found no atrophy or degeneration in my temporal and prietal lobes. The only anomaly was a minor shadow in the cingulate gyrus, but there was nothing that might explain all this.'

Lemuel looked more closely at the drawings, trying to sort out some meaning from the ragged sketches and scrawled notations.

'Are you sure you did all this?' he asked, studying the strange symbols that filled every page. He could not read the words, but he recognised the language, and knew that this was no ordinary book of remembrance.

This was a grimoire.

'I am sure,' said Mahavastu. 'It is my handwriting.'

'How do you know?' asked Kallista. 'You use a scrivener harness.'

'Yes, my dear, but in order to calibrate such a device for use, one must first attune it to one's own penmanship. There is not a graphologist alive who could tell the machine's work from mine.'

'What is it? I can't read it,' said Camille.

'I do not know. It is in a language I have never seen.'

'It's Enochian,' said Lemuel, 'the so-called language of angels.'

'Angels?' asked Camille. 'How do you know that?'

'I have an incomplete copy of the *Liber Loagaeth* in my library back on Terra,' explained Lemuel. Seeing their confusion, Lemuel said, 'It's supposed to be a list of prayers from heaven channelled through an ancient magician of Old Earth. It's written in this language, though I've only ever been able to translate tiny fragments of it. Apparently there was once a twin book, the *Claves Angelicae*, which had the letter tables, but I never found a copy.'

'Enochian,' mused Mahavastu. 'Interesting, you must tell me more of it.'

'In case anyone's forgotten, didn't you say that Magnus the Red was in grave danger?' asked Kallista. 'Shouldn't we focus on that?'

'Oh, of course, yes!' exclaimed Mahavastu, flicking through the book to the last page, which bore a charcoal sketch rendered with quick, passionate strokes. The image seemed to depict a naked figure emerging from a giant forest, though as Lemuel looked closer he saw that it wasn't a forest at all.

It was a nest of sinuous, snake-like tentacles emerging from a giant chasm, and before it was the unmistakable form of Magnus the Red, ensnared by half a dozen of them. His warriors were also under attack, fighting for their lives in a giant cave.

Within a mountain...

'What is it?' asked Camille. 'I can't make head nor tail of it.'

'I have no idea,' said Mahavastu. 'Lemuel?'

'I can't say for sure, but I agree it looks bad.'

'What's that word below the picture?' asked Kallista.

Scrawled beneath the image was a single word, and Lemuel's blood froze in his veins as he realised it was one of the few Enochian words he understood.

'Panphage,' he translated, and Mahavastu flinched.

'What?' asked Kallista. 'What does that mean?'

'It means "the thing that devours all",' said Lemuel.

CHAPTER TEN

The Hydra/Belly of the Beast/Time will Tell

THE THING THAT had once been Yatiri drifted towards the Thousand Sons, borne aloft by the supporting black tentacles. The darkness of his eyes was absolute, as though they were gateways into a realm where endless night held sway. Magnus drew his curved sword, and Ahriman felt his master's enormous power swell to the fore.

The vox spat with Fenrisian oaths and muttered catechisms of the Enumerations, but Ahriman heard only the sibilant whispers drifting from the black mass that rose from the pit.

Magnussss… Magnusss…

It seemed to be repeating his primarch's name, but it was impossible to be certain.

Magnus the Red stepped towards Yatiri, and the tentacle around the Aghoru's neck tightened. Veins bulged on Yatiri's face, his skin pale and discoloured, calloused where his enforced wearing of the mask had hardened the skin.

Yatiri's features were blunt and wide-spaced across the skull, a heavy brow and high forehead suggestive of thick bone protecting the brain. Ahriman realised that he had never seen the Aghoru without their masks, not even the children.

Questing tentacles that had detached from the domed roof descended towards the Astartes, and Ahriman drew his pistol, fingers tightening on his heqa staff.

'If those tentacles get too close, destroy them,' he ordered.

The cavern echoed with the sound of the saw-toothed edges of chainblades revving up.

Yatiri's body drifted towards Magnus, and Ahriman felt his finger twitch on the trigger. Great power filled the tribesman's body, a dark tide that Ahriman sensed was but the merest fraction of the power leaking up from beneath the world.

'My lord?' he said.

'I know,' said Magnus. 'I can contain it. This is no mystery to me.'

Uthizzar moved alongside Ahriman, his heqa staff alive with internal lines of power. Though he could not see Uthizzar's face, he saw the strain he was under in every forced movement.

Ahriman kept one eye on Magnus and the other on the waving pseudopods approaching from above. They were smooth and oily, quite unnatural, and Ahriman sensed a monstrous intelligence in their sinuous movements, like snakes poised to strike at helpless prey.

'My lord,' said Ahriman once more. 'What are your orders?'

Magnus did not reply, meeting Yatiri's gaze. Ahriman felt the power flowing between them, sensing immense energies struggling for supremacy. A silent battle of the soul was being fought, and Ahriman could do nothing to help his primarch.

Then two things happened at once.

Yatiri's body suddenly rushed forward, and his arms closed around Magnus in a hideous parody of a brotherly embrace, his black eyes ablaze with inner fire.

And the black serpent-like tentacles poised above the Astartes attacked.

No sooner had they moved than Ahriman opened fire.

The deafening crack of bolters filled the cavern with echoing bursts and strobing muzzle flashes. Black ichor splashed armour as the tentacles exploded with each impact. Yet there were scores of them, and for each one obliterated, a dozen more remained.

Ahriman emptied his magazine in four controlled bursts.

He felt Uthizzar next to him, the telepath forced to fight with combat moves drawn from muscle memory rather than skill. The crushing pressure of dreadful power seeking entry to his mind was almost unbearable, and he could only imagine what it must feel like to a telepath.

'They keep coming!' yelled Uthizzar.

'Like the hydra of Lerna,' said Ahriman between swings of his staff.

Each time a bolt found a target, a tentacle exploded in a mass of tarry black blood, hissing fiercely as it evaporated. They were insubstantial, but their threat was in quantity, not quality. Ropes of matter enfolded Ahriman, wrapping around him like constrictor lizards.

He released controlled bursts of energy, and they melted from his body. More reached for him, but his heqa staff swept out, its copper and gold bands rippling with fire. Uthizzar stepped back, and Ahriman braced his mind's defences, knowing what would come next.

A blistering surge of invisible aether erupted from Uthizzar in a deafening shriek, burning through the air like the shockwave of a magma bomb. It went unheard by the Space Wolves, but the tentacles around them dissolved into black fog at its touch, and others drew back, recognising his power and wary of him. Uthizzar dropped to his knees, head bowed, and bleeding aetheric light from every joint in his armour.

In the few moments' space Uthizzar had created, Ahriman pushed towards where he had last seen Magnus. The primarch's body was still held in Yatiri's loathsome embrace, but his flesh was all but obscured by a mass of writhing tentacles. More were slithering around his body with every second that passed.

'Go!' cried Uthizzar, and Ahriman saw how much the unleashed storm had drained him. To loose such power while under so fierce an attack was nothing short of a miracle.

Ahriman nodded to Uthizzar and pushed onwards as fresh enemies flailed from the pit, blocking him from reaching the primarch. It was a living wall of snaking darkness, but his staff cleaved through them like a threshing scythe.

An unstoppable mass of tentacles boiled from the chasm, thousands of blind monsters empowered by some hideous perversion of the Great Ocean's energy. His power was anathema to these creatures, the pure fire of the aether a nemesis touch to such corruption.

The Space Wolves fought with immovable fury, blades hacking with relentless force and implacable resolve. Their guns fired in a non-stop crescendo, yet they were hideously outnumbered by their foes and had not the power of the aether to aid them.

Ahriman saw one of the Space Wolves lifted from his feet by a host of tentacles, his armour buckling under the awful pressure. He kept firing and howling until his armour finally gave way with a horrid crack of ceramite and bone. Blood fountained from the shorn halves of his body, but he continued shooting, even as his remains were drawn into the pit. Nor was he alone in his fate. Everywhere Ahriman looked, warriors were being torn apart. Dozens were dying with every passing minute, yet still they fought on.

Lord Skarssen laid about himself with a sword that glittered with cold light, a blade that legend would say was fashioned from ice hewn from the heart of a glacier and tempered in the breath of the mightiest kraken. Like Ahriman's staff, the blade was the bane of the darkness, destroying it with the merest touch.

Ohthere Wyrdmake fought at his side, his eagle-topped staff spinning around his body in a glowing arc, leaving glittering traceries on the retina with its impossible brightness. Like Ahriman, Wyrdmake had power, and the darkness was wary of him.

The Rune Priest saw him, and Ahriman forged a path towards him.

Lord Skarssen looked up at his approach, and the cold flint of his eyes was even colder. There was no hatred, no battle fury, simply the implacable will to destroy his foe. The methodical, clinical nature of Skarssen's battle surprised Ahriman, but he had no time to dwell upon it.

'We need to reach my primarch,' he yelled over the barking gunfire and ripping sound of chainblades. 'And then we need to get out of here.'

'Never!' shouted Skarssen. 'The foe is yet to die. We leave when it is dead, and not before.'

Ahriman could see there was no use in arguing with the Wolf Lord; his course was set and nothing he could say would sway him. He nodded and turned back towards the battle, a writhing, heaving mass of dark tentacles and struggling warriors.

The Thousand Sons enjoyed the best of the fight, their heqa staffs and innate powers having a greater effect on the enemy than the Space Wolves' guns and blades. The Astartes were holding, but against an unstoppable, numberless enemy, it would take more than simple determination to win.

'Very well,' he said. 'You will fight at my side?'

'Wyrdmake will,' snarled Skarssen. 'I fight with the warriors of my blood.'

Ahriman nodded. He had expected no more. Without another word, he set off towards the edge of the chasm, forging a path with blazing swipes of his staff and bursts of aether-fire from his gauntlets. Wyrdmake matched him step for step, two warriors of enormous strength fighting side by side with powers beyond the ken of mortal men.

A black snake lashed at Wyrdmake's helmet, and Ahriman severed it. Another wrapped around Ahriman's waist, and Wyrdmake burned it to ash with a gesture. Their thoughts were weapons as much as their staffs, but they were forced to fight for every step, destroying the tentacles with killing blows and violent impulses. Bred of different gene-fathers, they nevertheless fought as one, each warrior's fighting style complementing the other. Where Ahriman fought with rigidly controlled discipline, each blow precisely measured and weighted, Ohthere fought with intuitive fluidity, invented on the move and owing more to innate ability than to any imposed training.

It was a combination that was lethally effective, with both warriors fighting as though they had trained with one another since birth. They fought through a dense thicket of black limbs to reach the edge of the chasm, the sinuous matter parting before their every blow. Only when Ahriman felt the faded symbols underfoot did he realise they had reached the edge.

The bodies of Thousand Sons and Space Wolves were being dragged into the pit, their limbs wrapped in glistening black ropes. Ahriman reached out with his aetheric senses, and turned as he felt the spiking, awesome presence of Magnus.

'The primarch!' cried Ahriman, looking deep into the heaving mass.

Magnus and Yatiri, locked together like lovers, were carried away by the tentacles, and drawn deeper into the beating heart of the mass.

The darkness closed around Magnus.

And he was gone.

IT WAS NOT unpleasant, not in the slightest.

Magnus felt the impotent rage of the seething enemy as it sought to twist him and overpower him the way it had overpowered Yatiri. The elder was gone, his mind a broken thing shattered by such exposure, his body degenerating with every passing second. Magnus had a mind crafted and honed by the greatest cognitive architect in the galaxy, and remained aloof from such brute displays.

He felt its manifestations writhing around his corporeal body, but shut himself off from physical sensations, turning his perceptions inwards as it bore him down into its depths. It amused him to see how its substance had been shaped, its form a reflection of the nightmares and legends of the Aghoru.

So simple and yet so dreadful.

What culture did not have a dread of slimy, wriggling things that lived in the dark? These creatures were shaped by the tortured mind of Yatiri, filtered through the lens of his darkest terrors and ancient legends. Magnus was fortunate indeed that the people of Aghoru had so limited a palette from which to paint its existence.

The inchoate energy pouring into the world had its source far below him, and he shrugged off Yatiri's embrace with a thought. His flesh burned as hot as a forge, and he blasted the elder's body to ash as he plunged into the chasm with the first words of the Enumerations on his lips.

His warriors used the Enumerations to rise to states of mind where they could function with optimum mental efficiency, but they were like stepping-stones across a tiny stream to a being such as Magnus. He had mastered them before he had left Terra for the first time, his father's words of warning still ringing in his mind.

He had heeded the warning, enduring Amon's tutorials and sermons regarding the power of the Great Ocean on Prospero, while knowing that greater power lay within his reach. Amon had been kind to him, and had accepted the knowledge of his growing obsolescence with good grace, for Magnus outstripped him in learning and power at an early age. Yet he too had warned of peering too deeply into the Ocean's depths.

The desolation of Prospero was warning enough of the consequences of reaching too far and too heedlessly.

Only when the Emperor had brought the survivors of his Legion to Prospero had Magnus known he would have to disregard the warnings and delve further into the mysteries. His gene-sons were dying, their bodies mutating and turning against them as uncontrolled tides wrought ever more hideous changes in their flesh. Nor were such horrific transformations limited to their bodies. Their minds were like pulsing flares in the Great Ocean, drawing predators, hunters and malign creatures that sought to cross into the material universe.

Unchecked, his Legion would be dead within a generation.

The power to save them was there, just waiting to be used, and he had given long thought and contemplation to breaking his father's first command. He had not done so heedlessly, but only after much introspection and an honest appraisal of his abilities. Magnus knew he was a superlative manipulator of the aether, but was he strong enough?

He knew the answer to that now, for he had saved his warriors. He had seized control of their destinies from the talons of a malevolent shadow in the Great Ocean that held their fates in its grasp. The Emperor knew of such creatures, and had bargained with them in ages past, but he had never dared face one. Magnus's victory was not won without cost, and he reached up to touch the smooth skin where his right eye had once been, feeling the pain and vindication of that sacrifice once more.

This power was a pale echo of that, a degenerate pool of trapped energy that had stagnated in this backwater region of space. He could sense the billionfold pathways that spread out from this place, the infinite possibilities of space linked together by a web-like network of conceptual conduits burrowed through the angles between worlds. This region was corrupt, but there were regions of glittering gold in the ocean that threaded the galaxy, binding it as roads of stone had once bound the empires of the Romanii Emperors together.

To memorise the entire labyrinthine network was beyond even one as gifted as him, but in a moment of connection beyond the darkness, he imprinted a million paths, conduits and access points in his mind. He might not know the entire network, but he would remember enough to find other ways in and other paths. His father would be pleased to learn of this network, pleased enough to overlook Magnus's transgression at least.

It still amazed him that he had not known of these pathways, for he and his father had flown the farthest reaches of the Great Ocean and seen sights that would have reduced any other minds to gibbering madness. They had explored the forsaken reefs of entropy, and

flown across the depthless chasms of fire that burned
with light of every colour. They had fought the nameless, formless predators of the deep, and felt the gelid
shadows of entities so vast as to be beyond comprehension.

He realised he had not seen these paths because they
were not there to be seen. Only this break in the network on Aghoru had allowed him to see it.

Concerns of the material world intruded on his intro-
spective plunge, and Magnus looked out on a world of
shadows and deceit. He had passed from the realm of
flesh to the realm of spirit without even thinking of it,
and floated in a place without form and dimensions
save any he desired to impose upon it. This was the
entrance to the network, the nexus point that led into
the labyrinth. *This* was what he had come to Aghoru to
find.

He stood upon a broken landscape of upthrust crags
and tormented geometry, a world of madness and desolation. Multi-coloured storms lashed the ground with
black rain, and blistering lightning scored the heavens
with burning zigzag lines. A golden line filled the horizon, a flame that encircled him and seethed with
wounded power.

Jagged mountains reared up in the distance, only to
be overturned within moments of their creation.
Oceans surged with new tides, drying up in a heartbeat
to become ashen deserts of dust and memory. Everywhere, the land was in flux, an inconstant whirl of
creation and destruction without end and without
beginning. Ash and despair billowed from cracks in the
rock, and it was as perfect a vision of hell, as Magnus
had seen.

'Is this the best you can do?' he said, the words dripping with scorn. 'The mindless void-predators can
conjure this much.'

The darkness before Magnus coalesced, wrapping itself in black spirals until a glistening snake with scales of obsidian coiled before him, weightless and disembodied from any notions of gravity. Its eyes were whirlpools of pink and blue, and a pair of brightly coloured wings ripped from its back. Its jaw peeled back, revealing fangs that dripped with venom.

Its forked tongue glittered, and its maw was an abyss of infinite possibility.

'This?' said the serpent, its voice dry as the desert. 'This is not of my making. You brought this with you. This is Mekhenty-er-irty's doing.'

Magnus laughed at such a blatant lie, though the name was unknown to him. The sound was a glittering rain. The very air was saturated with potential. With a thought, Magnus conjured a cage of fire for the serpent.

'This ends now,' said Magnus. 'Your falsehoods are wasted on me.'

'I know,' hissed the serpent. 'That is why I do not need any. I told you this was no invention of mine. It is simply a re-creation of a future that waits on you like a patient hunter.'

The cage of fire vanished, and the serpent slithered through the air towards Magnus, its wings shimmering through a spectrum of a million colours in the time it took to notice.

'I am here to end this,' said Magnus. 'This portal was sealed once and I will seal it again.'

'Craft older than your master's tried and failed. What makes you think you will do better?'

'No one has a craft better than mine,' laughed Magnus. 'I have looked into the abyss and wrestled with its darkest powers. I overcame them, and I know the secrets of this world better than you.'

'Such arrogant certainty,' said the serpent with relish. 'How pleasing that is to me. All the very worst sins are accomplished with such certainty: gluttony, wrath, lust... pride. No force in existence can compete with mortals in the grip of certainty.'

'What are you? Do you have a name?' asked Magnus.

'If I did, what makes you think I would be foolish enough to tell it to you?'

'Pride,' said Magnus. 'If I am guilty of sin, then I am not the only one. You *want* me to know who you are. Why else manifest like this?'

'If you will forgive the cliché, I have many names,' said the serpent, with a dry laugh. 'To you, I shall be Choronzon, Dweller in the Abyss and the Daemon of Dispersion.'

'Daemon is a meaningless word, a name to give power to fear.'

'I know, isn't it wonderful?' smiled the serpent, coiling around Magnus's legs and slithering up his body. Magnus did not fear the serpent. He could destroy it without effort.

The serpent lifted its head until they were face to face, the length of its glossy body still coiled around his torso. Magnus felt the pressure as it tightened, but simply expanded his own form to match it. As its form enlarged, so too did his until they were two titans towering over the landscape of discord.

'You cannot intimidate me,' he told the serpent. 'In this place I am more powerful than you. You exist only because I have not yet destroyed you.'

'And why is that? Your warriors are dying above. Do you not care for the lives of mortals, you who are so removed from mortality?'

'Time has no meaning here, and when I return it will be as if I was gone for mere moments,' said Magnus. 'Besides, much can be learned from a talkative foe.'

'Indeed.'

'I grow weary of these games,' said Magnus, returning to his mortal size once more. The rearing mountains took on a glassy, silvery hue, and he was struck by a momentary flash of sickening recognition. 'This ends now.'

'Truly?' asked the snake, its vast bulk shrinking until it was only a little longer than Magnus's arm. 'I have not even tempted you yet. Don't you want to hear what I can offer you?'

'You have nothing I want,' Magnus promised the snake.

'Are you so sure? I can give you great power, greater than you wield already.'

'I have power,' said Magnus. 'I do not need yours.'

The snake hissed in amusement, and its fanged maw parted with a serpentine approximation of a smile.

'You have already supped from a poisoned chalice, Magnus of Terra,' it said. 'Yours is a borrowed power, nothing more. You are a puppet given life and animation by an unseen master. Even now you dance a merry jig to another's tune.'

'And I should believe you?'

'I have no reason to lie,' said the snake.

'You have *every* reason to lie.'

'True, but not here, not now,' said the snake, slithering free of Magnus and turning lazy circles in the air. 'There is no need. No lie can match the horror of the truth that awaits you. You have bargained with powers far greater and more terrible than you can possibly imagine. You are their pawn now, a plaything to be used and discarded.'

Magnus shook his head.

'Spare me your theatrics. I bested powers greater than you, with your tawdry vision of hell,' said Magnus with contempt. 'I travelled the farthest reaches of the Great Ocean to save my Legion, unwound the strands of fate that bound them to their destruction and wove them anew. What makes you think your paltry blandishments will appeal to one such as I?'

'Arrogance too,' hissed the snake, 'matched with your towering conceit and certainty… Such a sweet prize you will make.'

Magnus had heard enough, content that the alien intelligence behind this vision was no more than a petty dynast of the Great Ocean, a malevolent entity with nothing to offer him but empty boasts and false promises. With a gesture, he drew the snake to him and took its struggling, whipping form in an unbreakable grip.

It squirmed, but he held it fast with no more effort than he might hold a lifeless rope. Magnus squeezed and the scales peeled from its body, the coloured feathers of its wings becoming lustreless and dull. Its eyes dimmed and its fangs melted from its jaws. The landscape began to break apart, its cohesion faltering in the face of the serpent's unmaking.

'You bested nothing,' said the snake as Magnus broke its neck.

AHRIMAN SWEPT HIS heqa staff in a wide arc, clearing a space in which he and Wyrdmake could fight. It was a hopeless task. No sooner was one mass of writhing tentacles severed, than hundreds more would slither from the pit to take their places. His control of the Enumerations was lost, his concentration broken in the face of the primarch's disappearance into the pit. Ahriman would normally fight divorced from the concerns of emotion that compromised his clarity of combat, but his mind was swamped with the competing fires of anger and hate.

With control stripped from his mind, Ahriman knew fear once more.

Only when he had watched Ohrmuzd die had he felt such a void in his soul.

He had vowed never to feel that way again, but this was even worse.

Ahriman fought to reconnect with his higher states, but his primarch's fate was too near to be salved with the Enumerations. Instead, he focussed on the fight for survival, letting his consciousness stretch no further than the next enemy to be slain. Such a state of being was unfamiliar, but cathartic.

The air was thick with foes, making it impossible to tell in which direction the exit lay. The dark power that energised the tentacles bloated the chamber, a seething corruption that pressed on the surface of his mind like a lead weight.

He could no longer see Uthizzar, and did not know whether the warrior still lived. The Thousand Sons and Space Wolves fought in isolation, small groups cut off from one another in the midst of the black morass. Diametric opposites, they were united as one force as they battled not for victory, but for survival.

Ahriman's pistol had long since run dry, and he swung his staff in a two-handed grip, laying about himself with crushing strokes. His every movement was leaden, his thoughts dull and slow. The Great Ocean was a potent force in combat, but the toll it took upon a warrior was equally potent.

Ahriman's mastery of his battle powers was second to none, but even he had nothing left to give, his spirit exhausted and his body pushed to the very limits of endurance. He fought as a mortal must fight, with courage, heart and brute strength, but he already knew that alone would not be enough. He needed power, but all he could feel was the energy boiling from the chasm that had taken the primarch. Even in despair, he knew that would be the first step on a road that had but one destination.

He would face what was left of this fight without the aether.

That made it an alien fight to make, and he was reminded of his words to Hathor Maat when he had glibly told him he might one day need to go to war without his powers. How prophetic those words now seemed, though he had said them without any expectation of facing such a situation himself.

Ahriman's concentration slipped, and a whipping mass of tentacles enfolded his arm, dragging his heqa staff aside. He struggled against its strength, but it was too late, and his other arm was entangled. His legs and torso were enveloped, and he was lifted from the ground, the joints of his armour creaking at the abominable pressure.

Wyrdmake tried to pull him down, but even the Rune Priest's strength could not equal the alien power matched against him. Over the hideous slithering of the deathly tentacles, he could hear the sounds of warriors dying, the shouted oaths of the Space Wolves, and the bitter curses of the Thousand Sons.

Then the pressure eased and the tentacles around his body began crumbling and flaking to nothingness. Even in his exhausted state, he felt the rampant energies of the pit suddenly vanish, as surely as if a spigot had been shut off.

The sound of gunfire and chopping blades was replaced by heaving breaths and sudden silence. Ahriman tore himself free of the desiccating tentacles that bound him, bracing himself as he fell back to the ground. He landed lightly, and looked up into the towering mass of writhing blackness as its substance unravelled before his eyes. What had been dark and glossy was now ashen and bleached of colour. The liquid solidity of the tentacles was now as insubstantial as mist, and they fell in a powdered rain.

Floating in the haze of their ending was a blood-red figure, a blazing giant in dusty armour, who descended with his arms outstretched, his single eye shimmering with a golden light. His hair was matted and wild, like an ancient war god come to earth to scour the unbelievers with his divine fire.

'My lord!' cried Ahriman, dropping to one knee.

The Thousand Sons followed his example, as did many of the Space Wolves. Fewer than twenty had survived the battle, but the bodies of the fallen were nowhere to be seen.

Magnus set foot on the ground, and the gold and silver symbols worked into the rock at the edge of the chasm shone with renewed vigour, as though freshly energised. Ahriman felt the deadening effect immediately, a force like that which had once filled the deadstones, but cleaner, fresher and stronger.

'My sons,' said Magnus, his flesh invigorated and vital. 'The danger is passed. I have destroyed the evil at the heart of this world.'

Ahriman drew in a cleansing breath, closing his eyes and rising into the first of the Enumerations. His thoughts cleared and his emotional peaks were planed smooth. He heard footsteps behind him and opened his eyes. Lord Skarssen of the Space Wolves' 5th Company and Ohthere Wyrdmake stood beside him. The Rune Priest gave him a weary nod of respect.

'The battle is won?' asked Skarssen.

'It is,' confirmed Magnus, and Ahriman heard fierce pride in his voice. 'The wound in the world is no more. I have sealed it for all time. Not even its makers could undo my wards.'

'Then you are done with this world,' said Skarssen, and Ahriman could not tell whether it was a question or a statement.

'Yes,' said Magnus. 'There is nothing more to learn here.'

'You owe the Wolf King your presence.'

'Indeed I do,' said Magnus, and Ahriman caught a wry grin at the very corner of his primarch's mouth, as though he were privy to a jest that eluded the rest of them.

'I will inform Lord Russ of our departure,' said Skarssen. The Wolf Lord turned away, gathering his warriors in readiness for the march to the surface.

'Direct, without fuss or unnecessary formality,' said Uthizzar, appearing at Ahriman's side, 'that is the Space Wolf way. Maddening at times.'

'Agreed, though there is much to admire in its simplicity,' said Ahriman, pleased that Uthizzar had survived the battle. The telepath was on the verge of collapse. Ahriman was impressed by his fortitude.

'It is not simplicity, Ahzek,' said Magnus as the surviving Thousand Sons gathered around him. 'It is clarity of purpose.'

'Is there a difference?'

'Time will tell,' said Magnus.

'Then we are truly finished here?' asked Uthizzar.

'We are,' confirmed Magnus. 'What drew us here is no more, but I have uncovered the existence of a prize beyond measure.'

'What manner of prize?' asked Ahriman.

'All in good time, Ahzek,' said Magnus with a knowing smile. 'All in good time.'

BOOK TWO

MUTATIS MUTANDIS

CHAPTER ELEVEN

Shrike/A Good War/The Wolf King

DAWN WAS ONLY a few hours old and the battle for Raven's Aerie 93 was won. The slender, feather-cloaked bodies of its defenders lay strewn around its craggy ramparts. Thanks to the foresight of the Corvidae, the battle to take the hidden crag had been a massacre.

Six months of flying the Great Ocean on the hunt for strands of the future and constant war had drained those warriors of the Thousand Sons Magnus had led to answer Russ's summons. They had been bled white matching the war pace of the Space Wolves.

The air in the southern polar mountains was thin and lung-bitingly cold, but it was a welcome change from the heat of Aghoru. Ahriman did not feel the cold, but the soldiers of the Prospero Spireguard were not so fortunate. To survive the sub-zero temperatures, they wore thick crimson greatcoats, heavy boots and silver shakoes, lined with fur cut from the wings of the snow-shrikes used by the Avenians as brutally effective line-breakers.

Ahriman, Hathor Maat and Phosis T'kar sat with three hundred Astartes attending to their wargear in the ruins of the mountain fortress. They cleaned their bolters and repaired chips in their armour while Apothecaries tended to the few wounded.

Dead Avenians littered the toppled battlements and shattered redoubts, a drop in the ocean compared to how many had died since the invasion of Heliosa had begun. Ahriman estimated they had killed close to three million of their warriors.

'Five thousand,' said Sobek, returning from tallying the dead.

'Five thousand,' repeated Phosis T'kar. 'Hardly any. I told you there wasn't as much of a fight in this one as the last.'

Phosis T'kar's bolter floated in the air in front of him, the weapon disassembled and looking like a three-dimensional diagram in an armourer's manual. A cleaning cloth and a vial of lubricating oil moved of their own accord through its parts, guided by Phosis T'kar's Tutelary. The faint glow of Utipa formed a haze around the components, as if a ghostly Techmarine attended the gun.

Hathor Maat's weapon sat next to him, gleaming as though lifted fresh from the sterile wrapping of a packing crate. He had no need to even strip down his weapon, and simply disassembled the molecular structure of the grease, dirt and foreign particles from the weapon's moving parts with the power of his mind.

Ahriman worked a wide-bore brush down the barrel of his bolter, enjoying the tactile, hands-on approach to weapon maintenance. Aaetpio hovered at his shoulder, but he had no wish to employ his Tutelary for so menial a task as cleaning his bolt gun. It was too easy to forget that while ensconced in one of the expedition fleet's many libraries or meditating alone in an invocation chamber.

In the six-week journey to the Ark Reach Cluster, Ahriman had spent much of his time with Ohthere Wyrdmake, the Rune Priest proving to be an entertaining companion. Though the terms they used for their abilities were very different, they found they had more in common than either of them had imagined.

Wyrdmake taught Ahriman the casting of the runes, and how to use them to answer vexing questions and gain insight into matters of inner turmoil. As a means of reading the future, they were a less precise method than those taught by the Corvidae, for their meanings required much in the way of interpretation. Wyrdmake also taught him the secret of bind-runes, whereby the properties of several different runes could be combined to draw similarly-attuned aetheric energies towards an object or person.

Wyrdmake's chest and arms were tattooed with numerous bind-runes: runes for strength, runes for health and runes for steadfastness. None, Ahriman noticed, were for power. When he asked Wyrdmake about this, the Rune Priest had given him a strange look and said, 'To speak of *possessing* power is as foolish as saying you own the air in your lungs.'

In return, Ahriman taught the Space Wolf more subtle means of manipulating the energies of the Great Ocean. Wyrdmake was skilled, but his Legion's teachings were tribal and violent in the drama of their effect. The calling of the tempest, the sundering of the earth and the rising of the seas were the currency of the Rune Priests. Ahriman honed Wyrdmake's abilities, inducting him into the outer mysteries of the Corvidae and the rites of Prospero.

The first part of this was introducing him to the concept of Tutelaries.

At first, Wyrdmake had been shocked that the Thousand Sons employed such creatures, but Ahriman believed he had come to accept that they were little different from the wolves that accompanied the Space Wolves. Wyrdmake's companion, a silver-furred beast named Ymir, had been less accepting, and whenever Ahriman summoned Aaetpio, the wolf howled furiously and bared its fangs in expectation of a fight.

Such secrets had never before been taught to an outsider, but Magnus himself had sanctioned Ahriman's work with Wyrdmake, reasoning that if a Legion such as the Space Wolves could be turned into allies through understanding and careful education, then other Legions would surely present few problems.

Though Ohthere Wyrdmake was a frequent visitor to the *Photep*, Lord Skarssen preferred to keep to his own vessel, a lean, predatory blade named the *Spear of Fenris*.

'Do you want me to help you with that?' grinned Hathor Maat, displaying a perfect smile of brilliantly white teeth. His hair was dark today, his eyes a deep brown. Though his features were still recognisably his own, they had taken on a rugged look, as if mirroring the terrain they had so recently fought over.

'No,' said Ahriman. 'I do not use my powers to accomplish things I can do without them. You should not either. When was the last time either of you used your hands to clean a bolter?'

Phosis T'kar looked up and shrugged.

'A long time ago,' he said. 'Why?'

'Do you even remember how to do it?'

'Of course,' said Phosis T'kar, 'How do you think I do this?'

'Spare us yet another "we shouldn't rely too much on our powers" lecture,' groaned Hathor Maat. 'Look at what would have happened to us on Aghoru if we had followed your teachings. The primarch might have died without Phosis T'kar's kine shield. And without my mastery of biomancy, T'kar certainly *would* be dead.'

'As you've never let me forget,' grumbled Phosis T'kar.

'Astartes first, psykers second,' said Ahriman. 'We forget *that* at our peril.'

'Fine,' said Phosis T'kar, dismissing Utipa and bringing the components of his weapon to his hands. He slotted the gun back together with a pleasing series of metallic clicks and snaps. 'Happy now?'

'Much happier,' said Ahriman, reassembling his own bolter.

'What's the matter?' asked Hathor Maat. 'Are you afraid your new friend will disapprove?'

Phosis T'kar spat over the edge of the rampart, his spit falling thousands of feet.

'That damned Wyrdmake shadows us like a psychneuein with the taste of an unguarded psyker in its mandibles,' he hissed, his anger fierce and sudden. 'We could have won this war months ago but for the shackles you put on us.'

Phosis T'kar jabbed an accusing fist at the smoking remnants of the tallest peak of the mountain aerie.

'The primarch shows no such restraint, Ahzek, why should we?' he asked. 'Are you so afraid of what we can do?'

'Maybe I am,' said Ahriman. 'Maybe we all should be. Not so long ago, we hid our powers from the world. Now you use them like mere cantrips to save you getting your hands dirty. Sometimes it is necessary to climb down into the mud.'

'Climb down into the mud, and all you will get is muddy,' said Hathor Maat.

'Not much in the way of mud on this world,' said Phosis T'kar. 'These aeries put up little fight. How this planet has held out for so long is a mystery to me.'

'The bird-warriors are stretched thinly now,' Hathor Maat pointed out. 'The Wolves have seen to that. And what Russ and his warriors haven't savaged, the Word

Bearers have put to the flame. An entire mountain range was burned out with a saturation promethium bombing three days ago to cleanse the aeries that Ahzek and Ankhu Anen found.'

'Cleanse?'

'Kor Phaeron's word,' said Hathor Maat with a shrug. 'It seemed appropriate.'

Kor Phaeron was one of Lorgar's chief lieutenants, and epitomised all that Ahriman disliked about the Word Bearers. The man's mind was filled with zealous certainties that could not be shaken by logic, reason or debate.

'A waste of lives,' said Ahriman, looking at the bodies the Spireguard were carrying from the broken fortress and arranging in neat lines for incineration.

'An unavoidable one,' responded Hathor Maat.

'Was it?' said Ahriman. 'I am not so sure.'

'Lorgar led negotiations with the Phoenix Court,' said Phosis T'kar. 'A primarch no less, yet every attempt was rejected. What more proof do you need that these cultures are degenerate?'

Ahriman did not answer, having renewed his acquaintance with the Word Bearers' gold-skinned primarch at the greeting ceremony held to honour the arrival of the Thousand Sons. It had been a glittering day of overblown ritual and proselytising, as pointless as it was time-consuming.

Leman Russ had not attended the ceremony, nor even bothered to send representatives. He and his huscarls were at war in the soaring peaks of the east, and did not waste time with ceremony when there was fighting to be done.

For once, Ahriman found himself in complete accord with the Wolf King.

He put thoughts of the XVII Legion from his mind and turned his gaze upwards. A too-wide, too-blue sky yawned above him, and omnipresent clouds of birds filled the air: wheeling, black-winged corvus, long-legged migratory birds and circling carrion eaters.

Ahriman had seen altogether too many of the latter in the past six months.

THE THOUSAND SONS had proven to be instrumental in breaking open the defences of the Ark Reach Cluster, their additional weight of force tipping the balance of war in favour of the Imperium.

First contact with the disparate cultures of the binary cluster had been made two years previously, when scout ships of the Word Bearers' 47th Expeditionary Fleet discovered six systems linked together by trade and mutually supporting defence networks.

Four of those systems had fallen to the combined forces of the Word Bearers and the Space Wolves, the fifth soon after the arrival of the Thousand Sons. Only the Avenians remained to be conquered.

The defeated empires all stemmed from an incredibly diverse genetic baseline, far removed from the archetypal human genome by millennia of separation from the world of their birth. Mechanicum geneticists confirmed such variances were within tolerable parameters, and thus Magnus had arrived in expectation of acquiring treasure troves of accumulated knowledge in the wake of compliance.

He was to be sorely disappointed.

Ahriman had seen a taste of the war the Space Wolves made on Aghoru, but the scale of what Russ's Legion left in their wake was nothing short of genocide. Their single-minded savagery left no room for anything other than the foe's complete and utter destruction.

Nor were the Word Bearers any more forgiving. In the wake of their triumphs, great monuments were carved in the flanks of the mountains, ten-thousand metre high representations of the Emperor and his conquests. Such a blatant challenge to the Emperor's edict on such things set a dangerous precedent, and Ahriman was uncomfortable with such behaviour.

Kor Phaeron had declared vast swathes of the indigenous culture unwholesome, resulting in virtually every repository of knowledge, art, literature and history being burned to ashes.

From Ahriman's perusal of the encounter logs, it appeared that Lorgar and Kor Phaeron had met with the Phoenix Court, a polyarchal leadership of the various worlds' kings and system lords, offering numerous overtures to entice them into the fold of the Imperium. Despite his best efforts, Ahriman could find no record of what these overtures had comprised.

In any event, all had been rejected, and thus the war of compliance had been unavoidable.

The histories of the Great Crusade would record it as a just war, a good war.

The subjugation of the Avenians had begun well, with the outer worlds falling quickly to the combined Imperial forces, but Heliosa, the cardinal world of their empire, had proven a tougher nut to crack.

Violent tectonic forces in ages past had shaped its landscape into three enormous continents almost entirely composed of jagged, mountainous terrain separated by wide expanses of azure seas. Its people lived in silver towers that clung to the flanks of the tallest peaks, with glittering, feather-light bridges spanning the chasms between them, while their people soared on billowing thermals on the backs of graceful aerial beasts.

As well as this lost strand of humanity, Helios was a world that belonged to the creatures of the air. The skies were alive with flocks of every description, from tiny, insect-sized creatures that fed on guano to rabid pterosaurs that hunted from lairs in hollowed-out peaks. More than one Imperial craft had been lost to bird strikes before weapon systems were modified to provide continuous clearance fire.

Its air was clean and its skies boundless. It reminded Ahriman of Prospero.

Ark Reach Secundus was the Imperial Cartographe designation for this world, a convenient label that began the process of assimilation before envoys were even despatched or shots fired in anger. Its people called it Heliosa, but the Imperial Army had another name for it, a name synonymous with the razor-beaked killers that were the bane of soldiers forced to assault the aerie fortresses.

They called it Shrike.

SINCE AGHORU, THE power of Ahriman's cult had risen, buoyed by unexpected swells in the Great Ocean, and the Corvidae were saving Imperial lives. They had seen echoes of future events, returning to their bodies with the locations of their enemies' hidden aeries and fore-knowledge of their ambush tactics.

Armed with such vital intelligence, the Thousand Sons and the Prospero Spireguard had launched a campaign of coordinated assaults on the aeries housing the fighter aircraft protecting the principal strongpoints of the Avenian defence network.

Magnus himself led many of the assaults, wielding the power of the Great Ocean like weapons that could be drawn or sheathed at any time. No force could stand against him, his mastery of time and space, force and matter beyond the reach of even his most gifted followers.

While the Word Bearers quelled the civilian population of outlying mountain cities, the Thousand Sons cleared a path for the Space Wolves to deliver the deathblow to the heart of the Avenian Empire. With the fall of Raven's Aerie 93, that battle was days away at most.

Ahriman walked the line of dead bodies, stopping to examine one of the Avenian warriors whose body had not been too brutally destroyed in the fighting. Aaetpio flickered at his shoulder, flitting down to the dead body to enhance the fading patterns of the soldier's aura.

Fear, anger and confusion were all that remained of the man's imprint on the world: fear that he was going to die here, anger at these inhuman invaders for defiling their homeland, and confusion... confusion born of not knowing why. Ahriman was surprised at this last emotion. How could he not know why the Imperium's forces were making war against his world?

The dead man wore thin black armour, form-fitting and gracefully proportioned to match his tall, overly slender form. A two-headed shrike with outstretched wings was moulded into the chest piece, an icon so similar to the Imperial bird of union that it was almost inconceivable that these warriors were enemies.

The Avenians were graceful and fine-boned, their facial features sharp and angular, like the mountains in which they lived. Their bodies appeared weak and fragile, but that was a lie. Autopsies had discovered bones that were flexible and strong, and their armour was augmented with fibre-bundle muscles not dissimilar to those within Astartes battle armour.

Ahriman smelled hot animal sweat, recognising the sharp, bitter tang of ice and claw that were the hallmarks of a Fenrisian wolf. The wolf barked, and Aaetpio fled to the aether. Ahriman turned to find himself face to face with a fang-filled maw and amber eyes that wanted nothing more than to devour him. Behind the wolf stood Ohthere Wyrdmake, wrapped in a wolf-pelt cloak. He looked past Ahriman to the dead bodies.

'A strange form to take on a world of mountains,' said Wyrdmake.

'Proof that life can sometimes buck the odds,' agreed
Ahriman.

'Aye, you have the truth of it. Just look at Fenris. What
sane form of life would choose to evolve on a world so
hostile? Yet it teems with life: drakes, kraken and
wolves.'

'There are no wolves on Fenris,' said Ahriman
absently, remembering Magnus's words on the subject.

'What did you say?'

'Nothing,' said Ahriman, hearing the warning tone in
the Rune Priest's voice. 'Just a scurrilous rumour I
heard.'

'I know the one. I have heard it myself, but the proof
is here to see,' said Wyrdmake, running a gloved hand
down the wire-stiff fur of the wolf's back. 'Ymir is a wolf
of Fenris, born and raised.'

'Indeed,' said Ahriman. 'As you say, it is there to see.'

'Why do you attend upon the enemy?' asked Wyrdmake, rapping the base of his staff against the corpse.
'They can offer you nothing, or do you now talk to the
dead?'

'I am no necromancer,' said Ahriman, seeing the mischief in Wyrdmake's eyes. 'The dead keep their secrets. It
is the living who will expand our understanding of
these worlds.'

'What is there to understand? If they fight, we kill
them. If they bend to our will, we spare them. There is
no more to be said. You overcomplicate things, my
friend.'

Ahriman smiled and rose to his full height. He was a
shade taller than Wyrdmake, though the Rune Priest
was broader and more powerful in the shoulders.

'Or perhaps you see things too starkly.'

The Rune Priest's face hardened.

'You are melancholic,' said Wyrdmake coldly.

'Perhaps,' agreed Ahriman. He looked out over the mountains, his gaze flying to the horizon and the silver cities that lay beyond it. 'It galls me to imagine what is being lost here, the chance to learn of these people. What will we leave behind us but ashes and hate?'

'What happens here after we leave is not our concern.'

Ahriman shook his head.

'But it *should* be,' he said. 'Guilliman has the way of it. The worlds his Legion wins venerate his name and are said to be utopias. Their inhabitants work tirelessly for the good of the Imperium as its most loyal subjects. The people of these worlds will be reluctant citizens of the Imperium at best, rebels-in-waiting at worst.'

'Then we will return and show them what happens to oathbreakers,' snarled Wyrdmake.

'Sometimes I think we are alike,' said Ahriman, irritated by Ohthere's black and white morality, 'And other times I remember that we are very different.'

'Aye, we are different, brother,' agreed Wyrdmake, his tone softening, 'but we are united in war. Only Phoenix Crag remains, and when it falls our enemies must surrender or face extermination. Shrike will be ours within the week, and you and I will mingle our blood in the victory cup.'

'Heliosa,' corrected Ahriman. 'Its people call this world Heliosa.'

'Not for long they won't,' said Wyrdmake, looking up as a thunderous howl of engines exploded over the highest peak. 'The Wolf King is here.'

LEMAN RUSS: THE Wolf King, the Great Wolf, Wolf Lord of Fenris, the Feral One, the Foebane, Slayer of Greenskins.

Ahriman had heard all those titles and more for the master of the Space Wolves, but none of them came close to capturing the sheer dynamism of the towering

wolf in human form that set foot on the cracked stones
of Raven's Aerie 93. The jetwash of his Stormcrow had
scorched the pale mountain stone and smelled of burnt
rock.

A pack of wolf-clad Terminators armed with glittering
harpoon spears followed the Primarch of the Space
Wolves, a towering warrior forged from the ice of Fenris
and tempered in its freezing oceans. Magnificent and
savage, Leman Russ was the power and violence of the
Space Wolves distilled and sharpened to the keenest
edge. A black-furred wolf pelt encircled his broad shoulders, and clawed fetishes adorned a wolf-stamped
breastplate and hung about his neck. His battle-plate
was the grey of a thunderstorm's heart, its every surface
scratched and gouged as though he had recently
wrestled the two mighty, blade-shouldered wolves that
prowled at his side, one silver and one dark as night.

Ahriman's skin shivered at the presence of Leman
Russ, as though an icy wind whistled through his
armour. The primarch's hair was a resin-stiffened mane
of molten copper, his piercing grey eyes cold and unforgiving, forever moving and on the hunt. A mighty
blade, fully a metre and a half long, was sheathed at his
side, and Ahriman saw its hilt had been rune-bound
with symbols to draw the frozen ice of winter to its
edge.

It seemed impossible that any foe could stand against
this warrior. Ahriman saw wild, unchecked power in
Russ, a recklessness of spirit that jarred with his own
strict discipline and dedication to duty. Leman Russ
blazed with incandescent white fire, his aura filled with
unnameable colours. So forceful was it that Ahriman
shut himself off from the aether, the primarch's searing
presence in the Great Ocean like the first instant of a
supernova. He blinked away the glittering afterimages,
feeling a nauseous surge of dislocation before his

mortal senses adjusted to the sudden absence of extra
sensory information.

Ohthere Wyrdmake dropped to one knee, and his
lupine companion prostrated itself before the wolves of
Russ.

Ahriman felt his body move of its own accord, and
the mighty primarch seemed to stretch towards the sky
as he knelt before his primal glory. The cold of the
mountain air intensified as Russ approached, striding
with the easy confidence of a warrior who knows he has
no equal. Russ's swagger was arrogant, but it was well-
earned.

Ahriman was used to being in the presence of his primarch; they shared a bond of brotherhood attained
through their scholarly mien, but this was something
else entirely. Where Magnus valued understanding, perception and knowledge acquired for its own sake, Russ
cared only for knowledge that helped him better anni-
hilate his foes.

Ahriman was not intimidated, but being so close to
Russ immediately made him feel acutely vulnerable, as
though an unknown nemesis had revealed its true face.

'You are the star-cunning one?' asked Russ, his voice
coarse and heavily accented. The guttural bark of his
voice was like Wyrdmake's, yet Ahriman's keen ear
detected a studied edge to it. It was almost as though he
was *trying* to sound like a feral savage from one of the
regressed worlds whose people had forgotten their technological heritage and reverted to barbarism.

Ahriman hid his surprise. Was the impression a true
one? An ancient Strategos of Old Earth had once
claimed that all war was deception. Was the Wolf King's
noble savage a mask to hide his true cunning from
those he considered outsiders?

Russ met his gaze, his eyes brimming with barely controlled aggression. The urge to do harm was wrought in

every line on Russ's face, a constant presence that could be loosed in a moment.

'Ahzek Ahriman, my lord,' he said finally. 'You honour us with your presence.'

Russ brushed off the compliment, turning his attention to the fire-blackened ruin of the Avenian's mountain fortress and the smouldering wreckage of those few aircraft that had reached the launch pads.

'Ohthere Wyrdmake,' said Russ, reaching out to tousle the dappled fur of the Rune Priest's wolf. 'Once again I find you in the company of a fellow wyrd.'

'That you do, my king,' laughed Wyrdmake, rising from bended knee and taking his primarch's outstretched hand. 'He's no Son of the Storm, but I'll make a decent rune-caster out of him yet.'

The words were spoken lightly, yet Ahriman again sensed a hollow ring to them, as though this were a pantomime for his benefit.

'Aye, well see you keep some of our secrets, Wyrdmake,' growled Russ. 'Some things of Fenris are for its sons and no others.'

'Of course, my king,' agreed Wyrdmake.

Russ returned his attention to Ahriman. The Wolf King was not looking at him as an individual, but as a target for his aggression. The primarch's eyes darted over Ahriman's armour, identifying weakened joints, areas of damage and points of entry for a blade. In an instant, Russ knew his physique better than he knew it himself, where his bones could most easily be broken, where a sword might best penetrate or where a fist would break open a protective plate and sunder internal organs

'Where is your liege lord?' demanded Russ. 'He should be here.'

'I am here,' said the deeply resonant voice of Magnus, and the force of Russ's presence diminished, like a storm kept at bay by one of Phosis T'kar's kine shields.

The Wolf King's natural state of aggression slackened, the hostility he'd displayed towards Ahriman mitigated. Such was only to be expected, for Magnus was Russ's brother, a genetic kinsman who shared a connection to the Emperor few other beings could claim.

Decades ago, Magnus had attempted to tell the tale of his creation to a gathering of the Rehahti. 'Creation', deliberately chosen instead of 'birth'. Magnus had not been born as mortals were born, but had been willed into life by the designs of the Emperor. As philosophically advanced as his captains were, the concepts were too alien, too beyond mortal comprehension for any of them to understand.

To be conscious of your body growing around you, to have awareness of your brain taking shape as architecture instead of organism, and to have discourse with your creator even as your existence moved from conceptual possibility to tangible reality had proved too complex to explain to those who had not experienced such a uniquely hastened evolution.

And these were the simplest of concepts to absorb. To know these things and to not be driven insane required a singular mind, a mind advanced enough to grasp the ungraspable, to conceive the inconceivable: a primarch's mind.

To have shared that moment of creation with another being, to know that amongst all the galaxy's aeons of creation there had never existed beings like you and your brothers, had bonded the primarchs in ways unattainable by mortals.

Yet despite that shared heritage, there was no love lost between Magnus and Russ. The legendary brotherhood of primarchs, so beloved of the iterators orations was utterly absent.

'Brother Russ,' said Magnus the Red, moving past Ahriman to stand before the Wolf King. Magnus wore his horned armour of gold and leather, his feathered cloak snatched and fluttered by the winds. The two primarchs had served in the same war for just over six months and this was the first time they had met in thirty years.

Ahriman wasn't sure what he had expected of two primarchs meeting after decades apart, but it certainly wasn't this stilted display of forced friendship. Russ's wolves snarled and bared their fangs. Magnus shook his head slowly, and they stepped back, pressing close to their master's legs with their ears pressed flat to their skulls.

'Magnus,' said Leman Russ, the fraternal shake perfunctory and lacking any warmth. Russ looked Magnus up and down. 'That cloak makes you look like the enemy. It's the feathers.'

'Or perhaps, their cloaks make them look like me?'

'Either way, I don't like it. You should get rid of it. A cloak is a liability in battle.'

'I could say the same of that mangy wolf pelt.'

'You could, but then I'd have to kill you,' replied Russ.

'You could try,' said Magnus, 'but you wouldn't succeed.'

'Is that what you think?'

'It's what I know.'

Ahriman was horrified by this exchange. Then he saw the faintest smirk on Russ's lips, and a glint of mischief in his primarch's glittering amber eye.

He let out a tense breath, sensing a familiar pattern to their argumentative banter. Ahriman had often observed that soldiers who exchanged the most vulgar comments were often steadfast brothers-in-arms, where the level of friendship could be judged by how foul their greetings were to one another. Might this be something similar?

Despite his realisation, there was an edge to this exchange, as though cruel barbs neither primarch was aware of were concealed in the jests.

Or perhaps they *were* aware of them. It was impossible to tell.

'What brings you to Raven's Aerie 93, brother? I had not thought to see you until the assault on Phoenix Crag.'

'That time is upon us,' said Leman Russ, all levity absent from his icy tone. 'My forces are poised to unleash the murder-make at our foe's kings.'

'And the Urizen?' asked Magnus, using the Word Bearers devotional name for their primarch. 'Is he also ready to strike?'

'Do not call him that,' said Leman Russ. 'His name is Lorgar.'

'Why do you dislike that name so much?'

'I don't know,' said Russ. 'Do I need a reason?'

'No, I was simply curious.'

'Not everything needs an explanation, Magnus,' said Russ. 'Some things just *are*. Now gather your warriors, it is time to finish this.'

CHAPTER TWELVE

Phoenix Crag

EXPLOSIONS PAINTED THE sky, burning wrecks spiralled down to destruction, and streaking blasts of anti-aircraft fire stitched bright traceries across the heavens. Ahriman felt them all moments before they happened, flinching in anticipation of shells that hadn't burst or zipping lines of flak that hadn't been fired.

He reclined in a converted gravity harness built into the crew compartment of a heavily modified Stormhawk transporter designated *Scarab Prime*. Flying behind the main body of the aerial assault, the tempo of Ahriman's pulse increased as the jerking images of the future blazed like miniature suns in his mind.

A dozen warriors of the Scarab Occult stood behind him in vertical restraints, bolters clamped to their chests, looking like reliquary statues at the entrance to an ancient king's tomb. Lemuel Gaumon was dwarfed by their bulk, his ebony features pale and sweat-streaked as he kept his eyes screwed tightly shut.

To bring mortals on combat missions was a new development for the Thousand Sons, but in response to their repeated requests, Magnus had decreed that any remembrancers that desired to witness the full fury of an Astartes assault would be permitted to do so.

Surprisingly, only a few had accepted. Ahriman knew Lemuel was beginning to regret his hasty decision, but as a Neophyte it was only right that he be here. Camille Shivani travelled on a Thunderhawk of the 6th Fellowship, her mind relishing the chance to get close to the front lines of war. Her normal line of research dealt with civilisations long gone.

Now she might see one vanish before her very eyes.

Kallista Eris had chosen not to fly into harm's way. Another attack of what she called the fire had left her drained and exhausted. Mahavastu Kallimakus travelled with Magnus, though compared to the panicked and exhilarated thoughts of his fellow remembrancers, his mind was dull, like a fire all but smothered by suffocating foam.

Within Ahriman's Stormhawk, internal spaces normally reserved for troops and heavy equipment were filled with banks of surveyor gear and crystalline receptors. Heavy cables snaked across the armoured floor of the compartment, plugging into the elevated harness upon which he sat.

Ahriman's head was encased in a gleaming hood of shimmering light, a gossamer-thin matrix of precisely cut crystals hewn from the Reflecting Caves beneath Tizca. His mind floated in a meditative state, unbound from his mortal flesh and occupying a detached state in the higher Enumerations.

Fine copper wires trailed from this crystal hood, their nickel-jacketed ends immersed in psi-reactive gels that amplified Ahriman's thoughts and allowed others to receive them. His mind skimmed the surface of the

Great Ocean, allowing Aaetpio to guide the currents of potential futures his way. This close to the present, such echoes were easy to find, and it was a simple matter for a Tutelary of a Master of the Corvidae to pluck them from the aether.

His heightened sensitivity to the immediate future gave him an unmatched situational awareness. He could read the flow of thermoclines across the mountains, see every aircraft, and feel the fears of their crews as they surged towards Phoenix Crag. His awareness floated above the unfolding assault, reading its ebbs and flows as surely as if it were a slow-moving battle simulation.

The flame-crowned city of the Avenian kings lay ten kilometres east of the tightening noose of aircraft. It was a silver-sheathed mountain with an eternally burning plume of blue fire at its highest tower, a majestic creation of glass spires and soaring bridges that appeared as fragile as spun silk. Graceful minarets and pyramids of glass capped the mountain peaks, and sprawling habitation towers glittered like pillars of ice in the bright sunlight. Columned processionals marched their way into the mountains from the shadowed valleys below, their lengths wreathed in explosions and smoke as artillery brigades and the heavy armour of the Prospero Spireguard, Lacunan Lifewatch and Ouranti Draks laid siege to its lower levels.

As Phoenix Crag was battered from below, so too was it assaulted from the air.

'As above, so below,' whispered Ahriman.

Three thousand aircraft streaked towards the last bastion of the Avenians, roaring through a storm of defensive gunfire and the last squadrons of enemy fighters. Impulsive Space Wolf Thunderhawks raced for the crown of the mountain, while heavier Word Bearer Stormbirds and Imperial Army bulk landers dived towards its sprawling base. Thousand Sons aircraft speared towards its guts, a mixture of darting Lotus fighters, Apis bombers and Stormhawk transports.

Ahriman likened the Thousand Sons assault to a living organism, with the awesome force of Magnus the Red as its unimaginably powerful mind. Magnus directed the assault, but the Athanaens were his thoughts, the Raptora his shield, and the Pyrae and Pavoni his fists.

The Corvidae were his eyes and ears.

Ahriman saw a flickering image of an armour-piercing shell punch through the belly of *Eagle's Talon*, a roaring Stormbird of the 6th Fellowship, and sent a pulse of warning into the matrix. He felt the brief moment of connection with the impossibly complex lattice of Magnus's mind, the brightest sun at the heart of a golden web that eclipsed all others with its brilliance.

No sooner had his warning been sent than *Eagle's Talon* banked sharply. Seconds later, a stream of shells tore empty air and exploded harmlessly above it. This was one of a score of warnings pulsing from Ahriman's enhanced awareness, the vessels of the Thousand Sons dancing to his directions to evade harm. Each permutation altered the schemata of the future, each consequence rippling outwards, interacting with others in fiendishly complex patterns that only the enhanced mental structure of a specially trained Astartes could process.

On another modified Stormhawk, Ankhu Anen, a fellow disciple of the Corvidae, undertook similar duties. It was not an exact science, and they could not see every danger. Some aircraft were going to be hit, no matter how much the Corvidae sought to prevent it.

To mitigate against such immovable futures, every assault craft carried a mix of covens from each cult.

High ranking cultists of the Pavoni and Pyrae filled the air around the aircraft with crackling arcs of lightning and fire to detonate incoming shells before impact, while the Raptora maintained kine shields to deflect those shells that penetrated the fire screen. Athanaeans scanned the thoughts of enemy fighter pilots, skimming the manoeuvres and intercepts they planned from the surfaces of their minds.

It was a dance of potential futures, a whirlwind of the possible and the real, each one moving in and out of existence with every passing moment.

It was as close as Ahriman ever felt to perfection.

A nearby explosion rocked the Stormhawk, the shell that had been destined to blow it from the sky detonating harmlessly off its starboard wing.

'Two minutes to skids down,' shouted the pilot.

Ahriman smiled.

The dance continued.

CAMILLE FELT SICK to her stomach, but relished the feeling as the aircraft hurled itself to the side and an explosion thumped their underside with a deafening clang of metal. The helmet she wore was dented and uncomfortable, but had saved her skull from being smashed open on the fuselage several times already.

'Not like you read about, is it?' shouted Khalophis from the far end of the compartment.

'No!' shouted Camille with a forced laugh. 'It's better.'

She wasn't lying. Though her skin prickled with fear and her heart was thudding against her chest, she had never felt more alive. The prospect of seeing up close what the Expeditionary fleets were doing in humanity's name was a unique opportunity.

Phoenix Crag was a combat zone, and nothing was certain in a place like that. A chance ricochet, a stray artillery round, anything could snuff out her life in a moment, but what was the point of being alive if you weren't willing to come out of your comfort zone and see what was being done on the bloody knife-edge of history?

'How long until we land?' she called.

'One minute,' said Khalophis, walking down the centreline of the aircraft's ready line with his Practicus, a warrior called Yaotl, ensuring the Thunderhawk's cargo was ready for deployment. 'Are you sure you want to see this? Astartes war is not pretty for those unused to such sights. Mine is certainly not.'

'I'm ready,' Camille assured him. 'And I want to see it. I'm a remembrancer, I need to see things first hand if my accounts are to be worth anything.'

'Fair enough,' said Khalophis. 'Just keep behind the maniples. Stay out of my way, for it's not my duty to protect you if you get into trouble. Keep close to Yaotl, he will shield you with a fire cloak, so be careful not to touch anything of value you might find – it will burn like promethium-soaked paper.'

'Don't worry,' said Camille holding up her gloved hands. 'I won't.'

Khalophis nodded and turned to the muttering Techmarine following him. The Techmarine consulted a data-slate and made last minute adjustments to the weapon systems of the Thunderhawk's silent passengers.

Ranked up in three lines were nine automatons, bulky machines in the shapes of humanoids, but twice as tall as an Astartes. Khalophis had called them Cataphracts, battle robots that reeked of grease and a hybrid electric fuel smell. Their bodies were exaggerated and armoured on the torsos and thighs, heavy plates of armaplas bolted to piston legs and cog-driven arms.

Coloured a vivid blue and gold, their heads were hunched down in the centres of their chests like peaked crowns, their carved faces like expressionless masks of long-dead emperors. Each was armed with a long cannon on one arm and a grossly oversized fist on the other. A huge, belt-fed weapon was slung behind each robot, and from the greased rails on their backs, Camille guessed they would slide up onto the shoulders when the time came for them to fire.

What would she feel from such an inanimate hunk of metal, what purely objective recall might its frame of steel and ceramite yield? She pulled off a glove and tentatively reached out to touch its cold arm.

She closed her eyes as the sensations came: the lightless times between battles, the dark, oil-dripping voids between activation and oblivion. She saw through its unfeeling eyes, a host of foes falling beneath its weapons, an eternity of war waged without thought for the consequences or reasons behind its actions.

Camille followed the coursing energy filling the robot as its power came online and new life flowed through its cabled veins. She followed the trail of power from its source, feeling the swelling sense of purpose as the robot's battle program came alive, its synthetic cortex processing the instructions that would send it to war.

That journey stopped as she sensed a higher consciousness within the machine, a spark of something she hadn't expected to find within its circuits and valves. She sensed a dreadful, aching need to destroy occupying the higher functions of its part-machine, part-organic mind.

Camille saw a shard of mirror-smooth crystal embedded in the robot's cortex, and knew immediately that it had been cut from a place called the Reflecting Cave on Prospero, just as she knew it had been carefully nurtured by an apprentice crystal grower named Estoca, a man who had that day learned he had an inoperable form of lung blight, but who wasn't worried because a

Pavoni healer had been scheduled to come to his home that evening.

Seated in the back of the crystal was a dancing flame, an animating will that overrode the robot's childishly simple doctrina wafer, a consciousness that linked all nine robots together under one supreme authority.

The fire burned brightly, swelling to fill the crystal with potency and the urge to fight. The robots raised their cannons in unison, their shoulder-mounted weapons locking into the upright position with a clatter of gears and a wheeze of hydraulics.

Then the Thunderhawk slammed down with a jarring thud, and the connection was broken as her hand fell from the robot's arm.

The robots turned their faces to her, and a lifeless voice rumbled from the depths of every one of them. The electronically rendered voice of the Khalophis rasped from the mouthpiece of all nine robots, saying, 'Stay out of our way, Mistress Shivani.'

The assault ramp blew open, and a howling wind of grit and acrid propellant smoke was sucked inside. The deafening roar of gunfire and explosions filled the compartment.

The maniples of robots marched from the Thunderhawk in ordered ranks and into battle.

THE DISTINCTIVE SNAP of wings folding tight into a white furred body was the first warning of the attack. Magnus looked up past the ruin of a smoking tower to see a host of snow-shrikes plummeting on an attack run, thirty at least.

'Spread out!' he cried, and the warriors of the Scarab Occult threw themselves into the plentiful cover. With a thought, he sent Mahavastu Kallimakus into the shadow of a toppled lion statue, the venerable scribe glassy eyed and compliant. His scrivener harness recorded Magnus's thoughts, the quill-tipped mechadendrites filling page after page for his grimoire. Shards of glass and twisted metal filled the street, as well as the blazing wrecks of Avenian fighters brought down by the Space Wolves.

The shrikes let loose ululating screams as they dived down through the hail of gunfire. Bolts filled the air, but even Astartes found it hard to hit such fast-moving targets. Mass-reactive shells sparked from toppled spires, but only a few of the diving creatures were hit, tumbling to the street in explosions of bloody fur.

They were agile flyers, their white-furred bodies like feathered serpents. Their wings were long and flexible, capable of incredible feats of manoeuvrability. Raking dewclaws snapped from the leading edges of their wings, turning them into serrated blades, but their long, razor-sharp beaks were their preferred killing tools. Two riders, strapped into flight harnesses, controlled the beasts, one a pilot of sorts, the other a marksman equipped with a lethally accurate longrifle.

Magnus watched in fascination as the Avenian linebreakers swooped low through the maze of debris, their riders controlling them with an ease that spoke of a bond formed over decades of shared experience.

One of the Scarab Occult stepped from cover to take a snap shot, but he had misjudged the speed of the creatures. A shrike flashed down like a glorious chevalier of old Franc, its razored beak like a glittering lance as it skewered the warrior. The blade punched through his chest, and the shrike's gunner fired a repeating pistol into his face. One direct hit punched through the warrior's visor and blew out the back of his helmet.

Magnus blinked and the creature erupted in flames, its piercing shrieks a paltry revenge for the death it had caused. Its riders tried to hurl themselves from their blazing mount, but Magnus pinned them to its back with a thought, and let them burn.

The other shrike-riders swept through their position, but the Scarab Occult were too canny to be caught in the open when they had other weapons to wield.

'Channelling,' ordered Magnus, and glittering shapes unfolded from each warrior, Tutelaries in the forms of birds, eyes, lizards and a myriad other unnameable guises. They darted out into the open, and streams of fire and lightning erupted from their shimmering forms as their masters channelled aetheric powers through their insubstantial bodies. A score of shrikes erupted into blazing torches of screaming flesh and fur. The survivors fled skyward, and Magnus waited until they had reached suitably lethal altitude before crushing their bones to powder.

He heard the beasts' shrill cries of agony, but didn't bother to watch the riders plummet to their deaths. Sporadic gunfire barked towards the Thousand Sons as running Avenian infantry came into view at the end of the street.

'Foolish,' said Magnus. 'Very foolish.'

He clenched his fist, and the guns exploded in the Avenians' hands, felling the entire line at a stroke. Screams of pain quickly followed, but Magnus paid the awful sound no heed, and strode towards the fallen soldiers. Most still blazed with fear and life, but the stamping boots of the Scarab Occult soon doused them.

Mahavastu Kallimakus trotted obediently after him, the continual stream of Magnus's thoughts transcribed faithfully into his journal. When this battle was won, Magnus would cull those thoughts into a more artful text for his great work.

He reached the end of the street, looking into the sky along a glorious, flying buttress-like causeway that arced out into thin air towards the raised entrance of the Phoenix Crag's Great Library.

Corvidae divinations had pinpointed the location of the city's largest repository of knowledge and history, a vast museum housed in a pyramid of silver, six hundred metres high and two kilometres wide that rose from the main body of the mountain. The similarity to the Great Library on Prospero was not lost on Magnus. Dozens of slender bridges led to a plaza before the eagle-wreathed gateway, some shattered in the assault, others on fire and yet more the scenes of furious running battles.

Leman Russ and his Space Wolves were mauling the upper echelons of the city, tearing through its leaders and politicians like ocean predators in a feeding frenzy. Vox reports indicated that the Word Bearers and Imperial Army units had swiftly overcome the defenders of the valley gates, and were pushing up through the lower levels of the city, leaving little but ashes and devastation in their wake.

Nothing would be left of the city if it were not for Magnus's restraining hand.

The primarchs had met the previous evening to discuss how best to assault Phoenix Crag, Leman Russ and Lorgar both eager to utterly eradicate the city, though for very different reasons. Russ simply because it stood against him, Lorgar because its ignorance of the Emperor offended him.

It would be hard to imagine three more different brothers: Russ with the bestial mask he thought fooled everyone with its bellicose savagery, and Lorgar with his altogether subtler mask that hid a face even Magnus could not fully discern. They had spoken long into the night, each of his brothers vying for the upper hand.

Phoenix Crag would not be like the other mountain cities of Heliosa, its records destroyed, its artefacts smashed and its importance forgotten. Magnus would save the history of this isolated outpost of humanity, and reclaim its place in the grand pageant of human endeavour.

This world had survived the nightmare of Old Night, and deserved no less.

'Onwards, my brothers,' said Magnus. 'We have a world's legacy to save.'

THE CITY'S BUILDINGS were graceful structures built into the fabric of the rock, a maze of dwellings, workplaces, recreational spaces and interconnecting streets, boulevards and subterranean passages. To any normal force, this kind of uphill fight would be a brutal, building-to-building brawl, time-consuming and wasteful of lives, but the Thousand Sons were no normal force.

Ahriman maintained his connection to Aaetpio, using his Tutelary's link to the aether to shift his perceptions into the near future. He saw traps before they were sprung, and read the presence of minds alive with anticipation of ambush.

Instead of breaking open each building, the Scarab Occult simply willed their Tutelaries into their enemies' hiding places, and burned them out with invisible fires or crushed them with psychic hammer blows. Methodical and swift, Ahriman's First Fellowship pushed upwards towards Magnus, the primarch calling his warriors to him to defend the city's intellectual heart from destruction. The Thousand Sons fought their way up into the mountain city along marble-flagged boulevards, each Fellowship fighting in the manner of its captain's nature.

Phosis T'kar's 2nd Fellowship bludgeoned their way straight through the middle of the enemy brigades they encountered, smashing their strongholds with barrages of aetheric force while advancing under the protection of invisible mantlets of pure thought. Hathor Maat's

3rd Fellowship burned their enemies alive, boiled the blood in their veins or sucked the air from their lungs, turning their bodies against them in spitefully painful ways.

Khalophis alone was not summoned by the primarch's call, instead tasked with securing the Thousand Sons' rear echelons with his Chapters of Devastators and battalions of robot maniples. Psychically resonant crystals allowed the captain of the 6th Fellowship to direct his mindless charges with complete precision, instead of relying on the doctrina wafers provided by the Legio Cybernetica.

Flocks of shrikes looped in to attack the Thousand Sons at every opportunity. These attacks were so swift and bloody that not even Ahriman's heightened precognitive senses could anticipate them all. The First Fellowship had suffered nearly a hundred casualties so far, and he knew there would be more before the battle was concluded.

Ahriman made his way towards a fallen pillar, behind which Lemuel Gaumon was sheltering. He noticed its fluted length was classically proportioned and the capital was shaped like the leaf-topped columns of the Great Library on Prospero. Ahriman smiled at the incongruous nature of the observation.

Lemuel's hands were pressed to his ears to block out the barking shrieks of the alien birds and the thunderous bangs of Astartes bolt fire. The man's terror flared from his body in streams of greenish yellow energy. Beside him, Sobek returned fire, the percussive reports of his weapon sending up puffs of dust from the top of the column.

'Is it all you hoped for?' asked Ahriman, slamming a fresh magazine into his pistol.

Lemuel looked up, his eyes brimming with tears. He shook his head.

'It's terrible,' he said. 'How can you stand it?'

'It is what I am trained for,' said Ahriman, as a booming volley of bolter fire echoed from the walls. Shrieking wails echoed, and stuttering return fire spanked from the top of the pillar. Lemuel flinched as energy projectiles whined past, curling himself into a tight ball. Sobek kept up his methodical volleys, unfazed by the nearness of the enemy fire-bullets.

A sudden, violent pulse of warning from Aaetpio sent Ahriman to his knees.

The shrike's beak slashed over his head, and he spun his heqa staff up to block a slashing wing. He shot the creature in the face, leaving only a spraying stump as the bolt detonated within its skull. It collapsed, as another flight of shrikes dived in to attack.

A flying killer's claws tore into the column next to him. The stone split apart as the beast slashed its wings at him, dewclaws snapping from leathery chitin-sheaths. Lemuel screamed in terror, and the monster turned its long, stabbing beak towards the remembrancer. Ahriman reached out with an open palm and crushed his hand into a fist.

The shrike standing over Lemuel gave a strangled squawk as its nervous system overloaded with pain impulses. It collapsed into a shivering heap until Ahriman stamped down on its neck, spinning around as his precognitive sense screamed a warning at him. He blocked another bladed beak with a sweep of his staff, sending a pulse of fire along its length.

The creature shrieked as its body caught light, the flames spreading over its furred body with unnatural rapidity. The flames fed on a victim's life-force, and would only extinguish when the creature was dead.

Sobek battled two of the beasts, his left arm held in the beak of a white-furred shrike as it attempted to saw through his shoulder. The second beast's wings boomed as it hovered above his Practicus in a dust-filled whirl-wind, raking Sobek's armour with tearing claws.

Astartes and predatory killers fought in a confused mass of thrashing limbs, blades and claws. Ahriman swung his pistol around and drew on Aaetpio's connec-tion to the Great Ocean, tracing the myriad potential pathways of the future to follow the path his bolt would take in a fraction of a second. He squeezed the trigger twice in quick succession.

The first bolt punched through the skull of the shrike holding Sobek down, the second exploded the heart of the hovering beast, both impact points less than ten centimetres from Sobek's body. Both beasts collapsed, slain instantly by Ahriman's precision kill-shots.

'Thank you, my lord,' said Sobek, freeing his gouged limb from the beak of the shrike. The armour was sliced through, and the meat of Sobek's arm was bloody and torn.

'Are you able to fight?'

'Yes, my lord,' Sobek assured him. 'The wound is already healing.'

Ahriman nodded and knelt beside Lemuel.

'And you, my Neophyte?' he asked.

Lemuel took a deep breath. His skin was ashen, and streaked tears cut through the dust caking his cheeks. Gunfire still rattled further down the boulevard, but none of it was aimed in their direction.

'Are they dead?' asked Lemuel.

'They are,' confirmed Ahriman. 'You were in no dan-ger. Sobek maintained a chameleon field around you, so the birds were probably not even aware of you until you screamed, and Sergeant Xeatan protects you from a chance kill with a kine shield.'

'I thought you were Corvidae?' said Lemuel. 'Divina-tors? Aren't Raptora the telekines?'

'Most of my warriors are Corvidae,' nodded Ahriman, pleased to have this opportunity to teach, even in the midst of a firefight. 'Like all Fellowships of the Thousand Sons, each Chapter and every squad is made up of warriors belonging to a variety of cults. Sobek and I are Corvidae, but Xeatan is Raptora.'

Ahriman pointed to a warrior sheltering in a recessed doorway from the sustained fire of a dozen Avenian soldiers. His shoulder guard was emblazoned with the serpentine star of the Thousand Sons with the image of a long, colourful feather at its centre.

'And Hastar over there is Pavoni. Watch.'

Despite his obvious terror, Lemuel peeked over the edge of the column in time to see Hastar leap out into the street as the Avenian soldiers broke from cover. His bolter was clamped to his thigh, and he braced himself with his back foot at right angles to his out-thrust left leg. The Avenians saw him, and raised their weapons. Before they could fire, sheet lightning leapt from Hastar's outstretched hands, and a deafening thunderclap shattered every pane of glass for five hundred metres in all directions.

Ahriman's autosenses compensated for the sudden brightness, but Lemuel blinked away dazzling afterimages. By the time his vision had cleared, it was all over. The Avenian soldiers were charred columns of blackened flesh, burned statues kept upright by heat-fused bones. Flesh ran from their corpses like melting butter. Lemuel bent over and vomited the contents of his stomach.

Lemuel looked up in horror.

'Sweet Inkosazana, Lady of Heaven save me,' he said.

Ahriman forgave the heathen imprecation as Lemuel took several deep breaths and wiped his mouth clean. He spat and said, 'That's... horrible, I mean to say, incredible... How... how did he know those soldiers were going to move at that moment?'

'Because across the street is an Athanaean captain named Uthizzar,' said Ahriman, indicating a warrior crouched in the cover of another fallen column. 'He read the thoughts of their commander and told Hastar when they were going to move.'

'Incredible,' repeated Lemuel. 'Simply incredible.'

Ahriman smiled, pleased that his Neophyte had so quickly accepted the fundamental powers of the Thousand Sons. The new Imperium's unseemly rush to embrace secularism and reason had encouraged many of its subjects to abandon their sense of wonder. The new creed denied knowledge of the esoteric, condemning those who pursued such science as unclean sorcerers instead of embracing their work as simply a new form of understanding.

'You are a fast study, Lemuel,' said Ahriman, standing and rallying his warriors with a raised fist. 'Now read the auras and tell me what you feel.'

Three hundred warriors, primarily Ahriman's Sekhmet Terminators and veterans of the Scarab Occult, formed up alongside Uthizzar's plate-armoured warriors.

'Pride,' said Lemuel, closing his eyes, 'fierce pride in their abilities.'

'You can do better than that,' said Ahriman. 'A child could tell me that of warriors. Reach out further.'

Lemuel's breathing deepened, and Ahriman read the change in his aura as he forced himself into the lowest of the Enumerations. It was clumsily done and awkward, but it was more than most mortals could do.

How easy it was to forget that Ahriman had once not known how to rise through his states of consciousness. Teaching someone a task he found as natural as breathing made it easy to forget where the difficulties lay.

'Let it come naturally,' said Ahriman. 'Be borne upon its waves and it will guide you to what you seek.'

Lemuel's face eased as he caught the city's emotional pulse, the fearful black of its populace, the angry crimson of its soldiers and the underlying golden pride that beat in every heart.

Ahriman sensed the violent spike of psychic energy a second before it hit.

It swept over them, a sudden, shocking blast of psychic noise that overwhelmed the senses with its sheer violence. Uthizzar cried out and dropped his weapon. Lemuel doubled over in pain, convulsing in spastic fits.

'What in the name of the Great Ocean was that?' cried Sobek. 'A weapon?'

'A psychic shockwave,' gasped Uthizzar. 'One of immense proportions.'

Ahriman forced the pain away and knelt beside Lemuel. The remembrancer's face was a mask of blood. It wept from his eyes and poured in a steady stream from his nose.

'So strong?' asked Ahriman, still blinking away hazy afterimages. 'Are you sure?'

Uthizzar nodded.

'I am,' he said. 'It is a howl of pure rage, cold, jagged and merciless.'

Ahriman trusted Uthizzar's judgement, tasting icy metal and feeling the rage of a hunter's fury denied.

'Such a force of psychic might is too powerful for any normal mind,' said Uthizzar, reliving a painful memory. 'I have felt this before.'

Ahriman read Uthizzar's aura and knew.

'Leman Russ,' he said.

CHAPTER THIRTEEN

The Library/Flesh Change/The Peacemaker

THEY PUSHED HIGHER into the Phoenix Crag. Ahriman's First Fellowship linked with Hathor Maat's 3rd in a gorge of artisans's workshops, and scout elements of the Prospero Spireguard joined them in a region of hollowed out silo peaks. Drop-troops of the Ouranti Draks, with their scale cloaks and reptilian helmets, had seized the districts above Ahriman's position, and parted to allow the purposeful Astartes past.

Reports of the fighting came in a haphazard jumble: a close range firefight in the south-western subsids, a swirling melee involving six thousand soldiers across the lower slopes of a manufacturing region in the mountain's rumpled skirts, artillery duels on the northern residential flanks, dizzying aerial jousts fought between the disc-skimmers of the Thousand Sons and the last of the shrike-riders.

The reports intersected and cut across each other in blurted outbursts. Ahriman was barely able to sift meaning from the chaos. Through all the reports of impending victory and the destruction of enemy forces, two facts were abundantly clear.

The Word Bearers were advancing slowly, much slower than he would have expected.

The same could not be said of the Space Wolves.

Leman Russ and his First Great Company had dropped directly onto the silver mountain's highest peak, extinguishing its eternal flame and toppling the symbols of rulership. The hearthguard of the Phoenix Court valiantly opposed the surging, unstoppable force of the Space Wolves, but they had been torn to scraps and hurled from the mountaintop.

The defeated kings offered terms of surrender, but Leman Russ was deaf to such pleas. He had sworn words of doom upon the Grand Annulus, and the Wolf King would never break an oath for something as trivial as mercy. The Space Wolves tore down through the mountain, an unstoppable force of nature, their blades and bolts gutting the defenders' ranks like a butcher with a fresh carcass.

Nothing was left in their wake, the mountain city a work of art vandalised by thoughtless brutality and wanton savagery. Behind the warriors of Russ was only death, and before them was their next target for destruction: the Great Library of the Phoenix Crag, where Magnus the Red and Phosis T'kar's 2nd Fellowship stood in ordered ranks.

Finally, the Space Wolves rampage was halted.

AHRIMAN LED HIS warriors across a yawning chasm on a slender causeway that arched up towards a wide plaza before an enormous glittering pyramid of glass and silver. Many of its gilded panes had been shattered in the battle, but it was still a magnificent structure, like the pyramid temples of Prospero, albeit on a much smaller scale.

'Russ's warriors made a holy mess of this place,' said Hathor Maat, surveying the damage done to Phoenix Crag. 'I'm inclined to agree with you, Ahzek.'

'About what?'

'That maybe all this was a waste of lives,' said Hathor Maat, surprising Ahriman with the sincerity he heard.

This far up the mountain, Ahriman could see its summit, a sagging silver peak that belched smoke instead of symbolic fire. Fires burned across the mountain's heights, and from his vantage point on the causeway, he saw that the lower reaches fared no better.

Ahead of him, kneeling Astartes in the livery of the 2nd Fellowship defended the end of the causeway. The Astartes had their bolters levelled, and he saw the shimmer of kine shields distorting the air before them.

Lemuel Gaumon caught up with Ahriman. The man's complexion was ruddy, and smears of blood coated his cheeks.

'What's going on?' asked Lemuel, between greedy heaves of thin air. 'Can you see the Wolf King? Are his warriors in trouble?'

'Something like that,' agreed Ahriman. 'They are in trouble. I just do not yet know of whose making.'

Ahriman shared a glance with Uthizzar, but his fellow captain shrugged in bewilderment. That wasn't good. If a telepath couldn't fathom what was going on, then he had little chance.

'Come on,' he said, 'let's find out what's at the heart of this.'

The warriors at the end of the causeway lowered their bolters at his approach, and Ahriman saw wide gouges torn in their shoulder guards. These were not the neat slices of shrike claws, they were the maim-wounds of chainswords.

The grandeur of the Great Library reared above him in a shimmering vitreous slope of polarised glass. A vast golden gateway led inside, and Ahriman took a moment to relish the thought of exploring its farthest depths to unlock this world's secrets.

Bands of Thousand Sons warriors defended the ends of a number of other causeways, each one leading back to the bulk of the mountain. Magnus the Red stood at the edge of the plaza, his armour a blaze of gold and crimson. His curved sword was bared and his entire body crackled with aetheric fire. Behind Magnus stood his ancient scribe, and Ahriman was amazed that the old man had survived the fury of this fight.

Phosis T'kar ran over to Ahriman, his heqa staff alive with hissing lines of energy.

'Ahzek, Hathor, you took your time,' said Phosis T'kar.

'We got here as soon as we could,' snapped Hathor Maat.

'You're both here now, that's what matters I suppose. Any sign of Khalophis?'

'No,' said Ahriman. 'He is crystal-joined with his robots. It is hard to pinpoint his location when his consciousness is so dispersed.'

Phosis T'kar shrugged.

'Fine,' he said. 'We'll need to deal with this situation without him.'

'T'kar,' said Ahriman. 'Tell me what is happening! We heard a psychic shout more powerful than anything I've ever known.'

'It was Leman Russ,' said Uthizzar. 'Wasn't it?'

Phosis T'kar nodded, turning and indicating that they should follow him.

'Most probably,' he spat. 'Killed almost every Athanaean in my Fellowship, and most of the ones that aren't dead are reduced to drooling lackwits.'

'Dead?' cried Uthizzar. These warriors were not of his Fellowship, but as Magister Templi of the Athanaeans, they were as much Uthizzar's as they were Phosis T'kar's.

'Dead,' snapped Phosis T'kar. 'That's what I said. Now stop wasting time. The primarch calls you to his side.'

Ahriman put aside his anger at Phosis T'kar's brusqueness and followed him to where Magnus stood at the end of the widest causeway.

'Where is the Wolf King?' asked Lemuel.

Phosis T'kar looked down at the man with disdain.

'Answer him,' said Ahriman.

'We don't know for sure,' said Phosis T'kar, 'but he is on his way, *that* we do know.'

Magnus turned at their approach, and Ahriman felt the force of the primarch's anger. His flesh seethed with life, pulsing red just beneath the skin, and his eye was a similarly belligerent hue. Magnus's stature had always been one of variable proportions, but his rage had made him huge.

Ahriman felt Lemuel's fear, but was surprised not to feel any from Mahavastu Kallimakus before realising that the man's will was suppressed by a mental connection to the primarch.

'Who would have thought it would come to this?' said Magnus, and Ahriman put thoughts of the primarch's scribe from his mind.

'Come to what?' asked Magnus. 'What is going on?'

'That,' said Phosis T'kar, pointing down the length of the causeway.

A wedge of Space Wolves massed at the end of the causeway, led by a warrior in a leather mask whose eyes were chips of cold, merciless flint. Their blades were bared, and a pack of slavering wolves hauled on thick chains, desperate to rend and tear.

'Amlodhi Skarssen?' said Ahriman. 'I don't understand. Are they attacking us? Why?'

'No time to explain,' said Phosis T'kar. 'Here they come!'

* * *

THE CHARGE OF the Space Wolves was a thing of great and terrible beauty.

They advanced in a great wave of clashing armoured plates, beating shields and waxed beards. They did not run, but came on in a loping jog, their feral grins, exposed fangs and lack of haste speaking of brutal confidence in their abilities.

These warriors didn't need speed to break through their enemies.

Their skill at arms would be enough.

Ahriman's horror mounted with every stride the Space Wolves took towards the Thousand Sons. How had these warriors, so recently their allies, become their enemies? The chains holding the snarling wolves were let slip and the monstrous beasts sprinted along the causeway.

Phosis T'kar took up position in the centre of the Thousand Sons line. His fellow warriors of the Raptora cult knelt to either side of him.

'Kine shields,' ordered Phosis T'kar, extending his hands before him. The air before them hazed as the force shields rippled to life.

'Give those wolves something to think about,' said Hathor Maat, as his Pavoni conjured writhing electrical storms in the path of the bounding wolves. Hastar took up position beside Hathor Maat, his gauntlets crackling with potent lightning.

'There is to be no killing, my sons,' said Magnus. 'We will have no blood on our hands from a fight that is not of our making.'

The crackling webs of lightning paled as Hathor Maat diminished their power, though Ahriman felt his reluctance.

'My lord?' begged Ahriman. 'Why is this happening?'

'I secured the Great Library with the Scarab Occult,' said Magnus, 'but Skarssen's Great Company arrived right on our heels. They sought to destroy the library. I stopped them.'

Ahriman had the sickening feeling of events spiralling beyond control. Pride, ego and the primal urge for war had collided, and such blinding drives almost always had to run their devastating course before they could be halted.

The charge of the Space Wolves was an unstoppable, elemental power.

The Thousand Sons were an implacable and immovable bulwark.

What force in the galaxy could yoke these unleashed forces?

THE BOUNDING WOLVES were the first to feel the fury of the Thousand Sons. They bounded into the flickering web of lightning and their fur instantly caught alight. Howls of agony echoed from the mountainside as fur was seared from their backs. The wolves snapped and rolled in their frenzy to douse the flames. Two fell from the causeway, fiery comets streaking to their deaths far below. Others fled, while a hardy few pushed onwards.

None survived to reach the Thousand Sons.

The Space Wolves jogged through the wall of aetheric fire, their armour hissing and blackening, but keeping them safe from harm. Wolf-painted shields locked together, and swords the colour of ice slid between them. The cries of the beasts had died, replaced with a furious, ululating howl torn from the throats of Amlodhi Skarssen's warriors.

Ten metres separated the two forces.

'Push them back!' ordered Magnus.

Phosis T'kar nodded, and the warriors of the 2nd Fellowship marched onto the causeway, kine shields matched against physical ones.

'We have to stop this!' cried Ahriman. 'This is madness.'

Magnus turned his gaze upon him, and his primarch's towering fury coalesced around him, a crushing rage as primal as anything felt by a Space Wolf.

'We did not start this fight, Ahzek,' said Magnus, 'but if need be we will finish it.'

'Please, my lord!' begged Ahriman. 'If we take arms against the Wolf King's warriors, he will never forgive us.'

'I do not need his forgiveness,' snapped Magnus, 'but I will have his damned respect!'

'This is not the way to get it, my lord. We both know it. The Wolf King never forgets and never forgives. Kill even one of his warriors and he will forever hold you accountable.'

'It is too late, Ahzek,' said Magnus, his voice haunted by some nameless fear. 'It has already begun.'

The shields of the Thousand Sons clashed with those of Amlodhi Skarssen's Space Wolves with a discordant squealing, scraping sound of invisible force meeting ice-forged steel. Space Wolves and Thousand Sons bent their backs to push one another back, a battle of strength against will.

No guns were drawn, as though both forces realised that this struggle needed to be settled with each warrior looking his foe squarely in the eye. They locked together, unmoving and as rigid as carved Astartes in a triumphal battle fresco, but it was a deadlock that couldn't last.

Slowly, metre by metre, the Thousand Sons were being forced back.

'Hathor Maat!' ordered Magnus. 'Take them down!'

The captain of the 3rd Fellowship hammered a fist into his chest and directed his ferocious will to aiding his battle-brothers. Hastar stood next to him as his fellow warriors of the Pavoni unleashed the full force of their bio-manipulation.

Unseen currents of aetheric energy sliced into the Space Wolves, blocking neural transmitters, redirecting electrical impulses in the brain and rapidly deoxygenating the blood flowing from their lungs. The effect was instantaneous.

The Space Wolves' push faltered as their bodies rebelled. Limbs spasmed, heart muscles fibrillated and warriors lost all physical autonomy, jerking like the maddened dolls of a demented puppeteer. Ahriman watched as Amlodhi Skarssen dropped to one knee, his shield falling from nerveless fingers as his body refused to answer his demands.

The Wolf Lord's teeth gnashed together, bloody foam spilling from the mouthpiece of his mask. Space Wolves thrashed in bone-cracking agony as their nervous systems were flooded with conflicting neural impulses. Ahriman despaired of the relish Hathor Maat took in this wanton display of power. The Pavoni had a reputation for venality and spite, but this was sickening.

'Stop this!' cried Ahriman, unable to contain his wrath. He ran forward and gripped Hathor Maat's arm, twisting him around to face him. 'Enough! You are killing them!'

Ahriman sent a blast of white noise into Hathor Maat's aura, and the captain of the 3rd Fellowship flinched.

'What are you doing?' demanded Hathor Maat.

'Stopping this,' said Ahriman. 'Release them.'

Hathor Maat stared at him, and then glanced at Magnus. Ahriman leaned in and gripped him by the edge of his pauldrons.

'Do it!' shouted Ahriman. 'Stop it now!'

'It's done,' snapped Hathor Maat, pushing Ahriman away.

Ahriman turned back to the Space Wolves, letting out a shuddering breath as the energies of the Pavoni diminished. The grey-armoured warriors lay on the causeway, their charge broken, their impetus lost. Amlodhi Skarssen struggled to his feet, battling against rogue impulses tearing through his body. Skarssen's eyes were filled with blood, and his entire body shook with the effort of standing before his enemies.

'I... Know... You,' hissed Skarssen, fighting for every word. 'All... Of... You.'

'I told you to stop this!' cried Ahriman, rounding on Hathor Maat.

'And so I did,' protested Hathor Maat. 'I swear.'

Ahriman felt a ferocious surge of power beside him and saw Hastar shaking as hard as Amlodhi Skarssen. Ahriman reached into his aura and felt a hot pulse of terror mixed with aberrant energies.

With a sickening sense of horrified recognition, he understood what was happening.

Hathor Maat saw it at the same time, and they barrelled into Hastar, knocking him to the ground as he began thrashing in the grip of a violent seizure.

'Hold him down!' shouted Ahriman, tearing at the pressure seals of Hastar's gorget.

'Please, no,' begged Hathor Maat. 'Hold on, Hastar! Fight it!'

Ahriman tore off the warrior's helmet and threw it aside, looking down at something he had hoped and thought never to see again.

Hastar's flesh seethed with ambition, writhing and twisting in unnatural ways, the meat and bone of his skull bulging with fluid growth. The warrior's eyes were terrified, uncomprehending orbs filled with red light, like coals from a smouldering forge.

'Help me,' gasped Hastar.

'Flesh-change!' shouted Ahriman.

He fought to hold Hastar's body down, but the changes wracking his body were as apocalyptic as they were catastrophic. His armour buckled as the body beneath it expanded so furiously and violently that the breastplate cracked down its centreline, the flesh beneath alive with change. Energised veins of electricity threaded his pallid flesh, sheened with glittering hoar-light sweating from the agonised warrior's suddenly malleable flesh.

Hastar screamed, and Ahriman's grip slackened as the horror of Ohrmuzd's death surged from the locked room of his memory. Hastar threw them off, his expanding body swollen with grotesquely misshapen musculature, encrusted growths, mutant appendages and slithering ropes of wet matter.

With the gurgle of wet meat and the crack of malformed bones, Hastar's body was suddenly upright, though any semblance of limbs was impossible to pick out in his erupting flesh. Swelling bulk and crackling energy patterns writhed across his flesh, and his screams turned to bubbling gibbers of maniacal laughter.

'Kill it!' shouted a voice, but Ahriman couldn't tell whose.

'No!' he shouted, though he knew it was futile. 'It's still Hastar. He's one of us!'

The Thousand Sons scattered from Hastar's terrible new form, horrified and terrified in equal measure. This was their greatest fear returned to haunt them, a horror from their past long thought buried.

Unchained energies whipped from Hastar's appendages, his torso and legs fused in a rippling trunk of glowing, protean flesh. Frills of half-formed membranes flapped in unseen winds, and a hateful laughter bubbled up from vestigial mouths that erupted all across his flesh. Hundreds of distended eyes, compound like an insect's, slitted like a reptile's or milky with multiple pupils boiled to life and popped with wet slurps every second. No part of the creature's anatomy was fixed for more than a moment.

A dreadful, wracking sickness seized Ahriman, as though his innards were rebelling against their fixed shapes, his entire body trembling with desire for a new form.

'No!' cried Ahriman through gritted teeth. 'Not again… I will not… succumb! I am Astartes, a loyal servant of the Supreme Master of Mankind. I will not fall.'

All around him, the Thousand Sons were on their knees or backs, fighting the virulent power of transformation as it spread from Hastar with the speed of the Life-Eater virus. Unless this power was dispelled, they would all fall prey to the spontaneous mutations that had once nearly ended their Legion.

'I survived before,' snarled Ahriman, clenching his fists. 'I will survive again.'

Determination gave him strength, and he flexed his mind into the Enumerations, distancing himself from the pain and his trembling flesh. With every sphere he attained, his mastery of his corporeal form increased until he could open his eyes once more.

His every muscle ached, but he was still Ahzek Ahriman, of sound mind and body. He glanced over his shoulder, seeing the Space Wolves coming to their senses on the causeway. Either they were beyond the reach of these transformative energies or they were immune to its effects. The damage the Pavoni had wreaked upon their nervous systems was coming undone, and Amlodhi Skarssen took faltering steps towards the Thousand Sons, his axe unsheathed.

A surging wave of power erupted behind Ahriman and he rolled onto his side in time to see Magnus the Red step towards the hideously transformed Hastar. Unchecked energy had destroyed the warrior of the

Pavoni, but it empowered Magnus. The creature Hastar had become reached out to Magnus, as though to embrace him, and the primarch opened his arms to receive him with forgiveness and mercy.

A thunderous bang sounded and Hastar's body exploded as a single, explosive round detonated within his chest. Silence descended, and Ahriman distinctly heard the heavy *tink* of a monstrous brass casing striking the ground.

Ahriman followed the trajectory the shell had taken, tracing a smoking line back to a giant pistol gripped in the fist of a towering giant clad in grey ceramite and thick wolf pelts.

The Wolf King had come.

A faded poem, last read in a dusty archive in the Merican dustbowl, leapt unbidden to Ahriman's mind. Supposedly transcribed from a commemorative monument, it marked the beginning of an ancient and awesomely destructive war:

> *By the rude bridge that arched the flood,*
> *Their flag to April's breeze unfurled;*
> *Here once the embattled farmers stood,*
> *And fired the shot heard 'round the world.*

Surrounded by a pack of fur- and armour-clad warriors, bearing great axes and bloodied harpoon-like spears, Leman Russ approached the Great Library of Phoenix Crag. Though Ahriman had seen the Wolf King before, Leman Russ at war was an entirely different proposition to Leman Russ at peace. One was brutally fearsome and intimidating, and the other utterly terrifying, an avatar of destruction as monstrous as the bloodiest culture's renditions of their gods of murder, war and death combined.

A living engine of destruction, Ahriman saw Russ clearly for what he was: pure force and will alloyed into a living weapon that could be aimed and loosed, but never called back.

The Wolf King reached the end of the causeway, and Ahriman saw Ohthere Wyrdmake at his side, the Rune Priest's expression impossible to read. Together with his enormous wolves, Leman Russ marched towards the Thousand Sons. Ahriman expected the Wolf King to charge wildly towards them, to confirm every negative caricature his detractors painted, but he came slowly, with infinite patience and infinite fury.

His packwarriors awaited his return, aching to do harm.

All Ahriman could hear was the footsteps of Russ as he marched across the causeway. His stride was sure and measured, his expression set in stone. His frost-shimmer blade leapt to his hand, a weapon to cleave mountains. Magnus went to meet him, his curved golden sword bound with the power of the sun: Two war gods marching to battle, the souls of their Legions carried with them.

Ahriman wanted to say something, to halt this inexorable confrontation, but the sight of the two primarchs drawing together with murder in their hearts robbed him of speech.

Before either one could speak, a blistering sheet of light flashed into existence between them, a coruscating fire that shimmered with the light of the brightest star. Impossible images were thrown out by the light, faraway places and the bitter tang of incense, burned plastic and reeking generators that thrummed with power.

A hard bang of displaced air boomed from the mountainside, and the light was gone.

A broad-shouldered giant in battle armour of granite grey with skin of gleaming gold stood in its place.

'The Urizen,' whispered Ahriman.

* * *

'THIS ENDS NOW,' said the golden-skinned warrior.

He stood between Magnus and Russ like the arbiter of a fistfight. Ahriman's previous impression of Lorgar was utterly dispelled as he looked upon the soulful features of the Word Bearers' Primarch. His eyes were kohl-rimmed and filled with infinite sadness, as though he bore the burden of a sorrowful secret that he could never, ever, share.

Lorgar's armour was dark, the colour of stone that has lain beneath the ocean for aeons, its every perfectly-nuanced plate worked with cuneiform inscriptions taken from the ancient books of Colchis. One shoulder-guard bore a heavy tome, its pages yellowed with age, fluttering in the disturbed air of his teleportation.

A cloak of deepest burgundy hung from his shoulders, and though he appeared unarmed, a primarch was never really without weapons.

Ahriman heard every word that passed between the three primarchs, each indelibly carved on his mind for all time. Their import would haunt him for the rest of his span.

'Get out of the way, Lorgar,' snarled Leman Russ, his veneer of apparent calm slipping for a moment. 'This does not concern you.'

'Two of my brothers about to draw each other's blood?' said Lorgar. 'That concerns me.'

'Get out of my way,' repeated Russ, his fingers flexing on the hide-wound grip of his sword. 'Or so help me–'

'What? You will cut me down too?'

Russ hesitated, and Lorgar stepped towards him.

'Please, brother, think of what you are doing,' he said. 'Think of all the bonds of love and friendship that will be lost if you continue down this path to bloodshed.'

'The Cyclops has gone too far, Lorgar. He has spilled our blood and must pay.'

'Blood spilled through misunderstanding,' said Lorgar. 'You must calm your fury, brother. Anger is no one's friend when hard choices must be made. Let it cloud your mind and all you will have when it is gone are regrets. Remember Dulan?'

'Aye,' said Russ, and his thunderous expression mellowed. 'The war with the Lion.'

'You brawled with Jonson in the throne room of the fallen Tyrant, and yet now you are oath-sworn brothers-in-arms. This is no different.'

Magnus was saying nothing, and Ahriman held his breath. Two such mighty beings facing one another with their aggression simmering so close to the surface was the most dangerous thing he had ever seen.

'Should we do something?' hissed Phosis T'kar, looking to Ahriman for guidance.

'Not if you want to live,' said Ahriman.

Titanic energies were bound within the immortal flesh of these warriors, and the tension crackling between them was razor-taut. Ahriman could feel their awesome psychic presences pressing against the lid of his skull, but dared not open his senses.

'You would stand with the Cyclops, Lorgar?' said Russ. 'A wielder of unclean magicks? Look at the corpse of that... thing over there, the one with my bullet in its heart. Look at that and tell me I'm wrong.'

'An instability of gene-seed is no reason for two brothers to go to war,' cautioned Lorgar.

'That is more than just unstable gene-seed, it is sorcery. You know it as well as I. We all knew Magnus was mired in the black arts, but we turned a blind eye to it because he was our brother. Well, no more, Lorgar, no more. Every warrior of that Legion is tainted, wielders of spellcraft and necromancy.'

'Necromancy?' scoffed Magnus. 'You know nothing.'

'I know enough,' spat Russ. 'You have gone too far, Magnus. This is where it ends.'

Lorgar placed a golden hand upon his breastplate and said, 'All the Legions wield such power, brother. Are your Rune Priests so different?'

Russ threw back his head and laughed, a booming roar of great mirth and riotous amusement.

'You would compare the Sons of the Storm with these warlocks?' he asked. 'Our power is born in the thunder of Fenris and tempered in the heart of the world forge. It comes from the strength of the natural world and is shaped by the courage of our warrior souls. It is untainted by the corruption that befouls the Thousand Sons.'

Now it was Magnus's turn to laugh.

'If you believe that, then you are fool!' he said.

'Magnus! Enough!' barked Lorgar. 'This is not the time for such debate. Two of my dearest brothers are at each other's throats, and it grieves me to know how this shall disappoint our father. Is this what he created us for? Is this why he scoured the heavens looking for us? So we could descend into petty bickering like mortals? We have greater destinies before us, and must be above such lesser concerns. We are our father's avatars of conquest, fiery comets of righteousness set loose to illuminate the cosmos with his glory. We are his emissaries sent out into the galaxy to bear word of his coming. We must be bright, shining examples of all that is good and pure in the Imperium.'

Lorgar's words reached out to all who heard them, the fundamental truth they contained like a soothing balm. Ahriman was ashamed they had allowed things to spin so violently out of control, seeing the true horror of this situation.

Brother against brother. Could there be anything worse?

The golden primarch seemed to shine with inner light, his skin radiant and beatific as he spoke. Hearts once raging were now calmed. The Space Wolves lowered their blades a fraction, and the Thousand Sons' defensive posture relaxed in response.

'I will not stand by and let him destroy this world,' said Magnus, lowering his khopesh.

'It is not yours to save,' snapped Russ. 'My Legion discovered this world. It is mine to do with as I see fit. Its people had a choice: join us and live, fight us and die. They chose to die.'

'Not everything is so black and white, Russ,' retorted Magnus. 'If we destroy everything we encounter, what is the point of this crusade?'

'The point is to win it. Once it is over, we will deal with what is left.'

Magnus shook his head, saying, 'What is left will be in ruins.'

Leman Russ lowered the ice-limned blade of his sword, his killing fury stilled for now.

'I can live with that,' he said, and without another word, marched from the causeway.

When he reached its end, he turned to face Magnus once more.

'This is not over,' he promised. 'Blood of Fenris is on your hands, and there will be a reckoning between us, Magnus. This I swear upon the blade of Mjalnar.'

The Wolf King slashed the blade across his palm, letting brilliant scarlet droplets of blood spill out onto the cracked ground. He threw back his head and howled, and his warriors added their voices to their master's cry until it seemed the whole mountain was howling.

The mournful cry rose to its tallest spires and echoed in its deepest valleys, a lament for the dead and a grim warning of things to come.

CHAPTER FOURTEEN

Compliance

WITH THE FALL of Phoenix Crag, the war on Shrike was as good as over, though, as with any conquest of such scale, isolated pockets of fighters remained. The mountains were rife with hidden aeries that not even the divinations of the Corvidae could uncover, and it was certain more blood would be spilled before compliance became complete.

While the Ouranti Draks garrisoned the city, Khalophis led the Prospero Spireguard and Lacunan Lifewatch in the task of hunting down the rogue aeries. The maniples of crystal-joined robots of the 6th proved invaluable in the work, climbing into the highest crags without fear, exhaustion or complaint. The warriors of the 6th Fellowship employed their Tutelaries to channel the fire of the Pyrae into the heart of the mountains, burning out their enemies and setting the peaks ablaze.

Less than ten hours after the Victory Confirmation, Leman Russ led his warriors from Shrike. Russ's flagship, the *Hrafnkel*, led the Space Wolf Expeditionary

fleet from the Ark Reach Cluster without fanfare or
promises of brotherly camaraderie. Nothing more had
been said of the confrontation before the Great Library,
but the matter was far from settled. Magnus dismissed it
as irrelevant, but those closest to him saw that the
encounter had shaken him, as though it had confirmed
some long-held fear.

Civilians were afforded the opportunity to descend to
the surface, and an army of iterators from the 47th
Expedition began the long process of inculcating the
populace with the enlightened philosophies of the
Imperium. The Word Bearers participated in this
process with the zeal of missionaries, shipping whole
swathes of the populace to vast re-education camps
constructed in the long valleys by follow-on teams of
Mechanicum Pioneers.

Over the course of the three months since the death
of the Phoenix Court, the entire repository of the Great
Library was copied via pict scanners or transcribed by
thousands of quill-servitors under the supervision of
Ankhu Anen. The Primarch of the Thousand Sons
devoured each text, digesting every morsel in the library
faster than even the most advanced data-savant could
process it.

Camille Shivani spent almost every waking minute in
the library, poring over the histories of Heliosa and the
earliest legends regarding the mythical birth rock of
Terra. Immersed in the wealth of information, she studied the texts as any scholar might, but also freely
indulged her talent for reading the imprints of past
owners. Many of the histories were written by men with
no connection to the events they described or by those
who had won the wars they wrote about, and were thus
of little value beyond subjective descriptions.

Tucked away in a neglected chamber near the top of
the pyramid structure, however, Camille found a

flaking, ochre-stained book that changed everything. Many of its pages were illegible thanks to moisture damage, but no sooner had she touched it than she knew she wouldn't need to read the words to unlock its secrets.

This was history written by someone who had lived through it, an authentic account of an alien world as it passed through a turbulent period of change. In an instant, she knew the writer, a young man from the south by the name of Kaleb. She felt his hopes and dreams, his passions and his vices. Through his eyes, Camille lived a lifetime of joys and regrets, learning of his time, nearly two thousand years ago, when the tribal city-states of Heliosa had united under the belief in an ancient thunder god from their earliest days to defeat a marauding race from the stars.

Ankhu Anen was thrilled by Camille's accounts of Kaleb's time, and immediately assigned her an Astartes Zealator from the Athanaean cult to skim the thoughts from her mind and transcribe them via a scrivener harness. From that moment on, any book of unknown provenance was brought to Camille for authentication.

In contrast, Lemuel Gaumon was a stranger in the Great Library. His time belonged to Ahriman, who continued his intensive training in the proper use of his abilities and how to shield his presence from the void-predators that swam the shallows of the Great Ocean.

Only once did Lemuel attempt to broach the subject of what had happened to Hastar upon the causeway before the Great Library. The dreadfully transformed body had been returned to the *Photep* and placed in stasis, but the shadow of his horrific death hung over the Thousand Sons like a guilty secret.

No sooner had he asked than he knew he had touched an exposed nerve.

'He could not control his power,' said Ahriman, with a haunted, reflexive glance towards the silver oakleaf cluster on his shoulder-guard. Lemuel made a mental note to ask about that symbol in quieter times, for it was clear there was a link.

'Could that, what did you call it, flesh change… happen to you?' asked Lemuel, all too aware that he was treading on dangerous ground.

'He promised it would never happen again, to any of us,' said Ahriman, and Lemuel read the hurt betrayal in his aura, its nearness too raw and naked to conceal. Ahriman's words spoke of the cold dread of prey that can sense the nearness of a stalking predator. To know that Astartes could feel such emotion shocked Lemuel.

Ahriman would be drawn no further, and nothing more was said on the matter as Lemuel's teachings continued. He was taught how to free his body of light from his body of flesh, and fly the invisible currents and thermals of the aether. Such voyages were short, for his skill had not yet developed enough to allow him any great time apart from his flesh.

Between such instructional times, Lemuel was in his element, travelling from city to city in the company of a squad of Astartes from Ahriman's First Fellowship to document the reconstruction of a world, first-hand. These warriors were all Philosophus, a rank so far above Lemuel's provisional one of Neophyte that it made him dizzy to think a man could master the mysteries so completely.

Mechanicum forge-vessels, city-sized monoliths bringing vast builder-machines and billions of tonnes of raw materials, dropped into the lower atmosphere like continents set adrift in the sky. The descent of such enormous cities of metal through the atmosphere set off a butterfly effect of clashing tempests that howled and raged across the world before settling into a continuous downpour that lasted two months.

Campfire scuttlebutt had it that the planet's inhabitants believed their world was weeping for its conquered people, but no sooner were the iterators made aware of this morsel than it was spun afresh that the rains were the planet washing away the stains of the old days. In conjunction with this, anonymously sourced tales painting the kings of the Phoenix Court as corrupt despots, who exploited the people for their own selfish ends, were subtly fed into the rumour mill.

As the iterators did their work in the deep-valley re-education camps, public debates and potent examples of the Imperium's majesty were unveiled to the people of Heliosa. Lemuel studied the techniques used by the Imperial speakers, noting the armsmen discreetly placed to drag off hecklers, the native turncoat planted within an audience to reinforce the speaker's message with loud agreement, and the unseen vox-bee that flitted through the crowds to broadcast Imperial-friendly questions to which the answers were already prepared.

Each iterator had a team of investigators, whose task it was to unearth local beliefs and traditions, which were then embellished and finally supplanted with subtly altered versions that reinforced loyalty to the Imperium. The work of the Thousand Sons in the Great Library proved to be an enormous help with this.

Magnus's Legion hardly strayed from the library, but the Word Bearers worked closely with the iterators, providing security for the camps and reinforcing the teachings with their own brand of loyalty. Lemuel found this element of compliance the most distasteful, seeing the indigenous culture of a world gradually overwhelmed by the Imperium's doctrines like a cuckoo invading a nest. The Word Bearers version of the Imperial Truth was particularly hardline, and Lemuel soon grew weary of the hectoring rhetoric that smelled more of indoctrination than it did of education. It was rumoured that the Emperor had chastised Lorgar's Legion in the past for such zeal, but even if that were true, it seemed the lesson hadn't stuck.

The Imperium *was* benign. It *did* bring hope in the form of Unity, but the Word Bearers' argument seemed absurdly petulant, posited along the lines of a school-yard bully's argument.

'We are right because we say we are right,' it said. 'Agree with us and we will be friends. Disagree with us and we will be enemies.'

That was no way to win the hearts and minds of a conquered people, but what other choice was there? It rankled that this new beginning had to be won with linguistic subterfuge and outright intimidation, but Lemuel was not naïve enough to believe that a populace who had fought so hard to resist the Imperium would be brought to compliance without such stratagems. It would shorten the process massively if the populace could be made to believe they were better off now than they were before.

What saddened Lemuel most was that it seemed to be working.

Lemuel was reminded of the ancient text Camille had shown him, the *Shiji*, a meticulous record of a grand historian that glorified the ruling emperor while vilifying the previous dynasty.

In his quieter, darker moments, Lemuel would often wonder if the Imperium was really as enlightened as it claimed.

LIKE AGHORU, AN Imperial Commander was appointed to oversee the Ark Reach Cluster and the long years of reconstruction and integration that lay ahead. Where Aghoru received a civilian administrator, Heliosa required a firmer hand. Major General Hestor Navarre was a senior officer of the Ouranti Draks, a regiment of swarthy-skinned fighters exclusively recruited from the desiccated jungle regions of Sud Merica. A career soldier of Hy Brasil, Navarre had fought his way across a hundred battlefields alongside the Word Bearers, and his appointment was greeted with sage approval.

Unlike Aghoru, scores of regiments were dispersed throughout the conquered Ark Reach Cluster. Imperial administration burrowed its way into every level of society, replacing defunct planetary rulers with Imperial delegates and the infrastructure to allow them to function. Munitorum officials calculated each planet's worth to the Imperium, while storytellers and mythmakers travelled system-wide extolling the glorious history of mankind.

Four months after the collapse of resistance, word came that the last text of the Phoenix Crag library had been copied into the archive stacks of the *Photep*. A day later, the 28th Expeditionary fleet broke orbit, and Magnus the Red gave the order to make best speed for an isolated shoal of spatial debris in the galactic east of the Ark Reach.

The various shipmasters of the 28th Expedition queried the coordinates, as they were far from the calculated system jump point, but Magnus's order was confirmed. This region of space would allow their vessels a calmer entry to the Great Ocean, and only when the fleet had reached this newly declared jump point did Magnus reveal their ultimate destination.

The 28th Expedition had been summoned to the Ullanor system, and excitement spread through the fleet at the prospect of joining the war against the greenskin. More thrilling was the prospect of joining forces with the Emperor himself, who fought in the forefront of the campaign, smiting the savage foe alongside Horus Lupercal.

Hopes of glory to be earned and battles to be fought were dashed, only to be replaced by awe, as it became known that the campaign was already over. The war against the greenskins of Ullanor had been projected to last years, decades even.

The Emperor's summons was not in the name of war, but of victory.

The Thousand Sons were to stand with many of their brother Legions in a Great Triumph honouring the Emperor's victory, a spectacle the likes of which the galaxy would never see again. Under Magnus's expert direction, the fleet Navigators plotted a razor's course for the Ullanor system.

The Expedition fleet of the Word Bearers was deeply enmeshed in the integration of the worlds of the Ark Reach into the Imperium, and Lorgar would pull his warriors out and make for Ullanor when they were able.

Magnus and Lorgar said their goodbyes briefly, the mighty primarchs speaking words that only they could hear. But as Ahriman watched them part, he caught a flicker of Magnus's aura, the faintest whisper of something indefinable, yet disquieting.

The last time he had seen it had been when Magnus and Russ had almost come to blows.

CHAPTER FIFTEEN

Triumph/The Dusk Lord/Old Friends

ULLANOR WAS A world transformed. In the hands of the greenskin it had been reduced to a rough world of reeking lairs and filth-choked encampments. Astartes war had cleansed its surface with scarifying fury that swept all before it. Yet for all its ferocity, it could not compare with the industry of the Mechanicum.

Four Labour Fleets of geoformers went to work on the rugged hinterlands that had housed the feral warlord of the savages, levelling the world's largest continent as a stage befitting the Master of Mankind. Millions of servitors, automatons and penal battalions went to work on its construction, reducing mountains to rubble and using the debris of their grinding down to fill the lightless valleys and even out the undulant wastelands where the greenskin had lit his revel fires and thrown up his ugly fortresses of mud and clay.

What should have taken centuries took months, and as squadron after squadron of Thunderhawks of the Thousand Sons broke through the acrid clouds of smog and dust hanging over Ullanor, it was a sight calculated to take a viewer's breath away.

The ground below was a polished granite mirror, a terrazzo landmass that shone like the angelglass of the ancient court astronomer. Vitrified craters had been melted into the landscape and filled with promethium. Searing flames turned the sky orange and sent towering pillars of smoke into the heavens. A laser-straight road, half a kilometre wide and five hundred long cut through the heart of the craters, its extremities marked by trophy posts bearing the bleached, fleshless skulls of greenskin brutes.

Almost obscured by the smoke, hundreds of enormous vessels hung in low orbit, their engines straining against the pitiless attraction of gravity. The atmosphere clashed with chain lightning from the blistering electromagnetic fields each vessel generated. Flocks of strike cruisers, fighter aircraft and bombers flew formation overhead, the roar of their engines a wordless vocalisation of primal glory.

The vermilion starships of the Blood Angels jostled for position with the fabulously ornamented vessels of the Emperor's Children. *Phalanx*, the mighty golden fortress of the Imperial Fists, dominated its segment of the sky, defying the laws of nature by hanging immobile above the earth.

The battle-scarred flagships of the Khan, Angron, Lorgar and Mortarion flew above the mirrored ground alongside their brother primarch's ships, yet supreme amongst them was a gilded warship that held anchor above the one element of the continent not planed flat by the industrial meltas of the Mechanicum.

This was the *Vengeful Spirit*, command ship of Horus Lupercal, second only to *Phalanx* in its savage power of destruction. Entire worlds had died by its lethal arsenal, and Horus Lupercal had shown no restraint in unleashing its full fury. Fourteen Legions had answered the Emperor's summons, a hundred thousand of the greatest warriors in all human history, and nine of the primarchs were in attendance, the rest too scattered by the demands of the crusade to reach Ullanor in time.

Eight million soldiers of the Imperial Army had come, and a dizzying plethora of banners, battle flags, trophy standards and icon poles were rammed into the ground in the centre of each armed camp. They stood proud alongside thousands of armoured vehicles and hundreds of Titans of the Legio Titanicus. Towering above the mortal soldiers, the treads of the mighty battle engines were like a city of steel on the march.

The Thousand Sons were amongst the last Legion forces to make planetfall. The entire continent sweltered like a blacksmith's forge, the hammer of history ready to beat the soft metal of existence into its new form.

Only an event of galaxy-changing magnitude could warrant such a spectacle.

Only the greatest being in the galaxy could inspire such devotion.

This was to be a gathering like no other.

AHRIMAN FIXED THE primarch's cloak to the pauldrons of his armour, hooking the bone catches on a clasp in the form of an upthrust talon. He settled it around Magnus's shoulders, letting the flowing lines of iridescent feathers mould to his frame.

Magnus stood at the centre of the spiral within his Sanctum, the glass pyramid brought in pieces from the *Photep* and rebuilt upon the perfectly flat surface of Ullanor. The crystalline panels shimmered orange in the light of the giant fires outside, but Magnus's mastery of the arts of the Pavoni kept the temperature within perfectly cool.

Under normal circumstances, Amon would attend upon the primarch, but on this momentous day, Magnus had requested Ahriman prepare him, fastening the plates of his armour to his muscled frame and ensuring he was not outshone by his brothers.

'How do I look?' asked Magnus.

'You will certainly attract attention,' said Ahriman, stepping back from his primarch.

'And why should I not attract attention?' countered Magnus, throwing out his arms in an operatic gesture. 'Am I not worthy of it? Fulgrim and his warriors may quest for perfection, but I embody it.'

The primarch was clad in all his finery, the gold of his armour shimmering bright in the flickering torchlight. His horned breastplate was thrusting and magnificent, his helmet barely able to contain his slicked crimson hair, which was bound in three long scalp-locks. He bore twin blades sheathed across his back and carried a heqa staff of gold and emerald, his chained grimoire partially concealed in a long kilt of leather and mail.

'It's not the sort of attention I think you want,' said Ahriman. 'I have seen the way the other Legions look at us.'

He hesitated before speaking again, giving voice to the fear that had plagued him in the two months since departing the Ark Reach Cluster, 'Like they did when the flesh change was still rife.'

Magnus turned his gaze upon him, the emerald green of his eye matching the gemstones on his heqa staff.

'The Symbol of Thothmes holds within my Sanctum, so none may hear your words, but make no mention of the flesh change beyond these walls,' warned Magnus. 'That curse is behind us. When the Emperor brought you all to Prospero I ended the degradation of the gene-seed and restored biological harmony to the Thousand Sons.'

Magnus reached down and placed a hand on Ahriman's shoulder. 'Too late for your brother, I know, but soon enough to save the Legion.'

'I know, but after seeing what happened to Hastar...'

'An aberrant mutation, a one in a billion fluke,' promised Magnus. 'Trust me, my son, that can never happen again.'

Ahriman looked up into Magnus's eye, seeing the power that lay in his heart.

'I do trust you, my lord,' he said at last.

'Good. Then we will speak no more of this,' said Magnus with finality.

WITH MAGNUS AT their centre, the Sekhmet marched across the mirror-smooth surface of the continent towards the one feature that stood proud of the landscape. The mountain had once served as the greenskin warlord's lair, but it had been erased from the world, its flattened base a steel-skinned dais for the Emperor and his honoured sons.

Magnus would take his place alongside his gene-sire with his brothers: Dorn, the Khan, Angron, Sanguinius, Horus, Fulgrim, Mortarion and Lorgar. The warriors of the Thousand Sons had spent the entire voyage from the Ark Reach Cluster preparing for this moment, for none wished to be found wanting in the eyes of his brothers.

Ahriman had picked only the best and most learned of his Fellowship to accompany Magnus to the dais, and each had been honoured with a cartouche secured to his armour by a wax scarab. Auramagma had joked that they should all put out an eye to mark themselves as the chosen of Magnus. No one laughed, but that was Auramagma's way, to carry the joke too far into tastelessness.

At the head of the thirty-six warriors of the Sekhmet were the captains of Fellowship, the senior warriors of

the *Pesedjet* who bore the title of Magister Templi. Only
Phael Toron of the 7th was absent. His Fellowship
remained on Prospero to protect its people and train
the students who hoped, one day, to be counted
amongst the Thousand Sons.

The flickering embers of the Tutelaries frolicked in the
air above them, basking in the presence of so much raw
aetheric energy. Some of that was the invisible aftertaste
of the xenos species that had once called this rock
home. It was as crude and powerful as a flamethrower,
but its potency was equally short-lived. Aaetpio followed in Magnus's aetheric slipstream, while Utipa
prowled the edge of their group with Paeoc and Ephra,
each one a shifting, formless mass of light and wings
and eyes.

The air of Ullanor still bore traces of the greenskin,
despite the seared reek of the promethium basins and
the lingering aroma of gun oil and Astartes bio-
chemicals. Exhaust fumes hung in low-lying smog
banks, and the burnt metal taste of Mechanicum
machines was a sour reek of exotic oils and unguents.

Thousands of Astartes filled the plain as far as the eye
could see, preparing for their triumphal march. Though
this was perhaps the most heavily-armed planet in the
Imperium, there was tension in the air, a volatile mixture
of martial pride and superiority, common among gatherings of fighting men of different origins. Each group of
warriors measured the others, deciding which was the
strongest, the proudest and the most courageous.

Ahriman marched alongside Magnus, feeling the
wariness of his brother warriors as they stared at his
magnificent primarch.

'I never thought to see so many Astartes gathered
together,' Ahriman said to Magnus.

'Yes, it is impressive,' agreed Magnus. 'My father
always knew the value of the symbolic gesture. They

won't forget this. They'll carry tales of it to the far corners of the galaxy.'

'But why now?' asked Ahriman. 'When the Crusade is in its final stages.'

A shadow crossed Magnus's face, as though Ahriman's question had strayed into a region he disliked.

'Because this in an epochal moment for humanity,' he said, 'a time when great change is upon us. Such times require to be marked in the race memory of the species. Who among us will ever experience a moment like this again?'

Ahriman was forced to agree with that sentiment, but as they drew near to the first checkpoint in the perimeter around the Emperor's dais, he realised that Magnus had neatly diverted his question.

A pair of Warlord Titans stood sentinel on the approaches to the sheared root of the mountain. Clad in gold and bearing the thunderbolt and lightning motif of the Emperor, the Titans had come from Terra to protect their lord and master. His mightiest praetorians, these titanic custodians were the perfect blend of technology and martial spirit.

'Bigger than the one you have propped up outside the Pyrae temple,' said Hathor Maat to Khalophis as they marched between the engines.

'That they are,' agreed Khalophis, missing or ignoring Maat's mocking tone, 'but war isn't always won by the warrior with the biggest gun. *Canis Vertex* is a predator, and would take both these fine fellows with it before it went down. Size is all very well, but experience, that's what counts, and *Canis Vertex* earned its fair share on Coriovallum.'

'We all did,' agreed Phosis T'kar sagely. 'But when you talk about *Canis Vertex*, don't you mean it *was* a predator.'

'We'll see,' said Khalophis with a grin.

'A Titan wouldn't worry me,' said Hathor Maat. 'It's just a machine, a big one, I'll grant you, but without a princeps to command it, a Titan is simply a giant statue. For all their skill, the Mechanicum haven't yet invented a machine that doesn't need a human being to control it. I could agitate the water molecules in the princeps's skull until his head exploded, boil the blood in his veins or send millions of volts through its carapace to electrocute the crew.'

'I could bring it down easily enough,' said Phosis T'kar playfully. 'I did it once before, remember?'

'Yes,' said Uthizzar. 'We all remember. You never tire of telling us how you saved the primarch from a Titan on Aghoru.'

'Exactly' said Phosis T'kar. 'After all, the bigger they are–'

'The bigger mess they make of you when they tread on you,' finished Ahriman. 'We are here to escort the primarch, not indulge your fantasies of how powerful you are.'

Beyond the Titans, hulking golden warriors in the armour of the Custodes protected every approach to the hub of the continent, giant warriors of equal aspect to the Astartes, with plates of brazen gold, inscribed with curling script, bedecked with fluttering oath papers secured with wax seals. Six of them manned the checkpoint, with a trio of Land Raiders growling behind them and a pair of dreadnoughts to further augment their strength.

'First Titans, now this. You think they expect trouble?' asked Hathor Maat with a smile.

'Always,' said Ahriman.

'Surely these security measures are ridiculously overblown and unnecessary? After all, who would dare attempt something hostile on a world crowded with Astartes and the best war machines the Imperium has at its disposal?'

'Have you ever met a Custodes?' asked Phosis T'kar.

'No, what has that got to do with anything?'

'If you had, you would know how stupid that question is.'

'I met one on Terra before setting out for Prospero,' said Ahriman, 'a young, ramrod-straight warrior named Valdor. I believe the primarch knows him.'

Magnus grunted, telling them everything they needed to know about *that* acquaintance.

'What was he like?' asked Uthizzar.

'Can't you tell?' asked Hathor Maat. 'What's the matter, don't you read minds anymore?'

Uthizzar ignored the Captain of the 3rd Fellowship, and Ahriman smiled as Magnus turned to face his officers with a mock-serious expression.

'Enough,' said Magnus. 'Captains or not, you will not be permitted to pass onwards if the Custodes decide you are not of a serious enough mindset. Their word is absolute, and not even a primarch can go against it in matters of the Emperor's safety.'

'Come on, Ahzek,' pressed Hathor Maat. 'What was this Valdor like?'

Magnus nodded indulgently, and Ahriman said, 'He was a grimly efficient praetorian, if rather humourless. I suppose when you are part of the cadre responsible for the safety of the greatest being in the galaxy, there is little room for levity.'

'Little?' said a voice appearing at Ahriman's side. 'There is no room whatsoever.'

How THE CUSTODES had come upon Magnus and the Sekhmet, Ahriman could not fathom.

He had not sensed their nearness or caught the faintest tremor in the aether of their presence. One minute they had been approaching the checkpoint, the next, their Tutelaries had vanished in the blink of an eye and two Custodes warriors were alongside them.

They were tall, as tall as the Astartes, though their armour was nowhere near as bulky. It had a ceremonial look to it, but Ahriman knew that was a misleading interpretation, one calculated to give the warriors encased within the advantage. So like Astartes and yet so different, like distantly-related kin gone their separate ways and evolved into new forms.

They held long Guardian Spears, lethal polearms that could cut through sheet steel with ease and could sever the ogre-like body of an armoured greenskin in two with a single blow. Red horsehair plumes spilled from their tapered helmets like waterfalls of blood, and the green glow of their helmet lenses was eerily similar to that of the Thousand Sons. Gilded carvings snaked from the seals of their neck plates, curling around their shoulders and down the inner facings of their breastplates.

'Halt and be recognised,' said the warrior who had spoken before, and Ahriman focussed all his attention on him. He could sense nothing, not even an echo of his presence in the world, as though he were as insubstantial as a hologram. Ahriman's throat felt dry, and an unpleasantly bitter aftertaste flooded his mouth.

Untouchables, said a voice in his mind with a familiar flavour, *powerful, but not powerful enough.*

Ahriman could not see them, but with the knowledge that there were psychic nulls nearby, he found he could identify them by their very lack of presence.

'Six of them,' he said over his armour's suit-vox.

'Seven,' corrected Magnus. 'One is more subtle than her compatriots in veiling her presence.'

The Custodes crossed their spears, barring their path to the Emperor's dais, and Ahriman's anger flared at the insult implied by the presence of the untouchables. Magnus stood before the Custodes, his physique imposing and threatening, his crested helmet a larger version of those belonging to the warriors before him. For an instant, it looked as though Magnus was one of them, a towering golden-armoured warrior lord.

Magnus leaned down, his eye tracing a path over the inscriptions that flowed across the burnished golden plates of the leftmost warrior.

'Amon Tauromach Xiagaze Lepron Cairn Hedrossa,' said Magnus. 'I would go on, but the rest of your name is hidden within the curve of your armour. And Haedo Venator Urdesh Zhujiajiao Fane Marovia Tra-jen. Fine names indeed, displaying grand heritage and exceptional lineage, but then I would expect nothing less of Constantin's warriors. How is the old man these days?'

'Lord Valdor abides,' said the warrior that Magnus had identified as Amon.

'I expect he does,' said Magnus, reaching out to touch the beginning of the spiralling script on Amon's shoulder. 'You have an old name, Amon, a proud name. It is a name borne by my equerry, a student of poetry and the hidden nature of things. If the name maketh the man, does that mean you are a similar student of the unknown?'

'Defending the Emperor requires a talent for discerning hidden truths,' replied Amon carefully. 'I pride myself on having a certain skill in that regard.'

'Yes, I see you do. You are an exceptional man, Amon, and I believe you will go far within your order. I see great things ahead for you,' said Magnus, before adding, 'and for you also, Haedo.'

Amon inclined his head at the primarch's comment, and the two Guardian Spears were lifted aside, allowing Magnus and the Sekhmet to pass.

'That's it?' asked Ahriman as the Custodes lowered their weapons.

'The Unified Biometric Verification System has identified and logged your genetic markers within its network,' said Haedo. 'You are who you claim to be.'

Magnus laughed, and asked, 'Is anyone ever who they claim to be?'

The Custodes did not answer, but stood aside to allow them past.

The podium was in sight, but one last intercession was to come before Magnus could take his place at the Emperor's side. Even once through all the checkpoints, Ahriman could feel the shadowing presence of the untouchables on the periphery of vision and sense.

From the primarch's comment, he surmised that the watchmen were in fact the Sisters of Silence, the mute sisterhood of untouchables and the guardians of the Black Ships. How typical to see them and the Custodes working hand in hand.

This was the inner circle, metaphorically and literally, for here were gathered the mightiest beings in the cosmos, the brightest sons of the most incandescent sire. Here was where the primarchs gathered before ascending the platform to stand at their father's side.

Ahriman could see the winged, angelic form of Sanguinius, the lusty red of his armour contrasting with pale feathers of his wings. Hung with loops of silver and pearl like glistening tears, the beatific primarch stood with the Khan, a swarthy warrior shawled in furs and lacquered leather plate, with a winged back-banner that echoed those of the Lord of Angels.

The golden-skinned Urizen held intense discourse with Dorn of the Fists and Angron, while the Phoenician and his cadre of lord commanders preened alongside Horus Lupercal and his lieutenants. Fulgrim's white hair shone like a beacon, his perfect features gloriously sculpted. Little wonder the members of his

Legion prided themselves on their aesthetic with such an example to follow.

Magnus swept forward to join his brothers, but before he reached them, a warrior in dusty white armour edged in pale green stepped to meet him. His shoulder-guard bore the image of a skull in the centre of a spiked halo, marking him as Death Guard. His posture was bellicose, and Ahriman read his hostility in an instant.

'I am Ignatius Grulgor, 2nd Company Captain of the Death Guard,' said the warrior, and Ahriman heard the judgemental tone and the arrogant sneer that spoke of a man without humility.

'I do not care who you are, warrior,' said Magnus calmly, though the undercurrent of threat was unmistakable. 'You are in my way.'

Like a living statue, the Astartes stood his ground before Magnus. Two mighty warriors in brass, gold and ash-coloured Terminator armour appeared on either side of Grulgor, long, ebony-hafted scythes held in spiked cestus gauntlets. The harvest blades were dark and heavy with the weight of slaughter they had accumulated. A name leapt to Ahriman's mind:

Manreapers.

'Ah, the nameless Deathshroud,' said Magnus, looking around him. 'Tell your master to show himself. I know he is here, within forty-nine paces, if memory serves.'

Ahriman blinked as a dark outline seemed to flow from a patch of shadow at the foot of one of the Custodes Titans, a tall, gaunt figure in armour of pallid white, bare iron and brass, shrouded in a mantle of stormcloud grey. A bronze rebreather collar obscured the lower part of his hairless skull, and feathers of rancid air gusted from it at regular intervals. The giant figure breathed deeply of these vapours.

'Mortarion,' hissed Hathor Maat.

His sunken cheeks were those of a consumptive, and the deep-set amber eyes those of a man who has seen horrors without number. Glass vials and philtres strung together on Mortarion's breastplate clinked musically as he walked, his strides sepulchral, punctuated by the rap of his enormous scythe's iron base on the polished ground. A long, drum-barrelled pistol hung at his side, and Ahriman recognised the merciless form of the Lantern, the Shenlongi-designed pistol that was said to unleash the fire of a star in every blast.

'Magnus,' said the Primarch of the Death Guard by way of a greeting. 'I wondered if you would show your face.'

Mortarion's words were brazen. These were brothers, warrior gods crafted by the Emperor to conquer the galaxy in his name. Like all brothers, they squabbled and vied to attract the attention of their father, but this... this was distilled anger.

'Brother,' said Magnus, ignoring Mortarion's words. 'A great day is it not? Nine sons of the Emperor gathered together on one world, such a thing has not happened since...'

'I know well when it was, Magnus,' said Mortarion, his voice robust and resolute in contrast to his pallid features. 'And the Emperor forbade us to speak of it again. Do you disobey that command?'

'I disobey nothing, brother,' said Magnus, keeping his tone light, 'but even you must recognise the symbolism of our number. Three times three, the *pesedjet* of ancient gods, the Occidental orders of angels and the nine cosmic spheres of the forgotten ages.'

'There you go again with talk of angels and gods,' sneered Mortarion.

Magnus grinned and moved to take Mortarion's hand, but the Lord of the Death Guard pulled away from him.

'Come on, Mortarion,' said Magnus, 'you are not immune from the music of the spheres. Even you know that numbers are not cast blindly into the world, they come together in orderly balanced systems, like the formation of crystals or musical chords, in accordance with the laws of harmony. Why else would you insist on keeping these bodyguards within seven times seven paces of you?'

Mortarion shook his head and said, 'Truly you are as lost in your mysteries as the Wolf King says.'

'You have spoken with Russ?'

'Many times,' promised Mortarion. 'He has been quite vocal since departing the Ark Reach Cluster. We know all about what you and your warriors have been doing.'

'What is it you think you know?'

'You have crossed a line, Magnus,' hissed Mortarion. 'You hold a snake by the tail and bargain with powers beyond your understanding.'

'No power is beyond my understanding,' countered Magnus. 'You would do well to remember that.'

Mortarion laughed, the sound like mountains collapsing.

'I knew a being like you once before,' he said, 'so sure in his powers, so convinced of his superiority that he could not see his doom until it was upon him. Like you, he wielded dark powers. Our father made him pay with his life for such evil. Have a care you do not suffer the same fate.'

'*Dark* powers?' said Magnus with a shake of the head. 'Power is simply power, it is neither good nor evil. It simply *is*.'

He pointed to the pistol at Mortarion's side.

'Is that weapon evil?' he asked. 'Is that great reaper of yours? They are weapons, nothing more and nothing less. It is the use men put such things to that makes them evil. In your hands, the Lantern is a force for good. In an evil man's hands it is something else entirely.'

'Give a man a gun and he will want to fire it,' said Mortarion.

'So now you are going to give me a lesson in causality and predestination?' snapped Magnus. 'I am sure Ahriman and the Corvidae would welcome your input on the subject. Come to Prospero and you can instruct my warriors.'

Mortarion shook his head.

'No wonder Russ petitioned the Emperor to have you censured,' he said.

'Russ is a superstitious savage,' said Magnus dismissively, but not before Ahriman saw the shock at the Wolf King's action. 'He speaks out of turn about things he does not understand. The Emperor knows I am his most loyal son.'

'We shall see,' promised Mortarion.

The Death Lord turned away and marched towards the Emperor's dais as a thunderous braying erupted from the warhorns of every Titan on Ullanor.

'Now what do you suppose he meant by that?' asked Phosis T'kar.

THE SEKHMET FULFILLED their duty of seeing their primarch to the Emperor's sheared mountain podium, marching in procession alongside the honour guards of the nine primarchs who had come to Ullanor. To move in such elevated circles was a notion Ahriman found himself hard-pressed to comprehend.

The primarchs took their place upon the steel-sheathed dais and their honour guards were dismissed. The chance to parade before the Emperor was a once in a lifetime opportunity for most of the warriors.

To know a primarch was an honour, but to parade before nine of them in the presence of the Emperor was the stuff of dreams. Ahriman would march with his head held high before demi-gods made flesh, the apotheosis of humanity and genetic engineering, wrought from the bones of ancient science.

That twenty such beings could have been created was nothing short of miraculous, and as he surveyed the noble countenances around him, Ahriman suddenly felt very small, the tiniest cog in an ever-expanding machine. The notion of the titanic forces at work struck a powerful chord within him, and he felt the power of the Great Ocean swell in his breast. He saw his metaphor take shape in his mind's eye, a magnificent, planet-sized machine of wondrous artifice working seamlessly in balance with its every cog, gear and piston. Those mighty pistons thundered, powering the greatest industry and causing the worlds around it to swell with new life and new beginnings.

In the midst of the machine he saw a piston stamped with a snarling wolfshead, its amber eyes glinting like gems. It fired up and down in a bank of similarly embossed piston heads, each with an emblematic design stamped upon it, a golden eye, a white eagle, a set of fanged jaws, a crowned skull.

Even as the image formed in his mind, he saw that the wolfshead piston was fractionally out of sync with the other pistons in the machine, working to a different beat, and gradually shifting its direction until it was completely in opposition to its fellows. The machine vibrated in protest, its harmonic balance upset by the rogue piston, and the squeal of metal grinding metal grew in volume.

Ahriman stumbled and let out a gasp of horror as he saw that the machine would soon tear itself apart. To see such an industrious machine destroyed and reduced to little more than wreckage by a previously unseen defect in its design was truly tragic.

He felt a hand on his arm and looked into the face of a startlingly handsome warrior in the pearl-coloured plate of a Luna Wolf. The vision of the machine vanished from his mind, but the lingering sorrow of its imminent destruction creased Ahriman's features with anguish.

'Are you well, brother?' asked the warrior with genuine concern.

'I am,' replied Ahriman, though he felt sick to his stomach.

'He says he's fine,' said a massively shouldered brute behind the warrior. Taller than Ahriman, with a gleaming topknot crowning his skull, he radiated choler and the urge to continually prove himself. 'Leave him be and let's rejoin our companies. The march will begin soon.'

The warrior extended his hand, and Ahriman accepted the proffered grip.

'You will have to excuse Ezekyle,' said the warrior. 'He forgets his manners sometimes, most of the time in fact. I am Hastur Sejanus, pleased to know you.'

'Ahzek Ahriman,' he said. 'Sejanus? Ezekyle? You are Mournival.'

'Guilty as charged,' said Sejanus with a winning smile.

'I said those Custodes didn't know security worth a damn,' said Phosis T'kar, pushing past Ahriman to pull Sejanus into a crushing embrace. 'Damn, but it's good to see you again, Hastur.'

Laughing, Sejanus pulled himself free of Phosis T'kar's embrace and punched him on the shoulder as two more warriors in the livery of the Luna Wolves appeared at his side. 'Good to see you too, brother. Nobody's managed to kill you then?'

'Not for lack of trying,' said Phosis T'kar, standing back to regard the warriors before him. 'Ezekyle Abaddon and Tarik Torgaddon, as I live and breathe, and

Little Horus Aximand too. I still tell my brothers of the foes we faced together. Do you remember the battles in the Slaughterhouses of the Keylekid? Those damn dragons gave us a hard fight, and no mistake. There was one, remember Tarik? The one with the vivid blue hide that almost–'

Little Horus held up a hand to stall Phosis T'kar's reminiscence.

'Perhaps we can gather after the Triumphal March?' he said, adding, 'All of us. I would greatly like to meet your fellows and swap more outrageous tales of battle.'

Sejanus nodded.

'Absolutely,' he said, 'for I have it on good authority that the Emperor has a great announcement to make. I, for one, do not want to miss it.'

'Announcement?' asked Ahriman as a shiver of premonition passed along his spine. 'What sort of announcement?'

'The kind we'll hear when we hear it,' growled Abaddon.

'No one knows,' said Sejanus with a diplomatic chuckle. 'Horus Lupercal has not yet deigned to tell even his most trusted lieutenants.'

Sejanus looked back towards the podium with a grin.

'But whatever it is,' he said, 'I suspect it will be of great import to us all.'

CHAPTER SIXTEEN

New Order/Tuition/Fresh Summons

Stars swam in the glass of the crystal pyramid, faint shimmers of light that winked from the past, the light already thousands or even millions of years old. To be able to look into the past so clearly had always fascinated Ahriman, the notion that what you were seeing in the present was an echo of the past.

The air within the *Photep's* Sanctum was cool, a precisely modulated climate that owed nothing to machine control. The floor was a spiral of black and white crystal, each piece hand-picked from the Reflecting Caves beneath Tizca and shaped by Magnus's own hand.

Starlight glinted on the reflective chips, and gleamed from the silver threads and blood-drop pendants hanging from Magnus's feathered cloak. The primarch stood immobile as a statue beneath the apex of the pyramid, his arms folded across his chest and his head tilted back to allow him to look out into the immensity of space.

When Magnus descended to the surface of a world, his pavilion was a re-creation of this inner sanctum, but it could never hope to capture the rarefied atmosphere that filled this place.

'Welcome, Ahriman,' said Magnus without averting his gaze from the stars. 'You are just in time to watch Mechanicum Borealis with me. Come, join me in the centre.'

Ahriman walked the spiral, following the black chips towards the centre, letting the walk cleanse him of his negative thoughts in readiness for his walk out along the white spiral. He studied Magnus as he walked.

Ever since the conclusion of the Great Triumph, the primarch had been withdrawn and sullen. Hastur Sejanus had been right about the nature of the Emperor's announcement; it had radically changed the universe in which they operated. For close to two hundred years, the Emperor, beloved by all, had led the Great Crusade from the front, fighting in the vanguard of humanity's second expansion to the edges of the galaxy.

Those days were over, for the Emperor had announced his withdrawal from the fighting, telling his faithful warriors that the time had come for him to relinquish control of the Crusade to another. The Astartes had wept to hear that their beloved master was leaving them, but as epochal as this separation was, it was more than matched by the Emperor's next pronouncement.

Before the gathered warriors, the Emperor removed the golden laurels that had been his most iconic accoutrement and bestowed them upon his brightest son. No longer would the Emperor command the armies of the Imperium. That honour, now fell to Horus Lupercal: The Warmaster.

It was an old title, revived from dusty antiquity, yet it was a natural fit and perfectly encapsulated the unique qualities of the Luna Wolves Primarch. From the millions of warriors gathered before the steel-sheened dais, adulation had mixed with sorrow, but Ahriman had felt the conflicting waves of powerful emotions as the other primarchs reacted to Horus's ascension. Perhaps they felt it should have been them, or perhaps they raged at having to take orders from one of their own.

Either way, it made little difference. The decision had been made, and the Emperor was unequivocal in its necessity. Many warriors had expected to renew old acquaintances or swear new bonds of brotherhood on Ullanor, but with the Emperor's pronouncements made, the gathering of Astartes broke up with almost unseemly haste.

The 28th Expedition had left Ullanor and made the two-month journey to Hexium Minora, a Mechanicum outpost world, to resupply. The bulk of the Thousand Sons had borne witness to the beginnings of the galactic new order, while some had been on detached duties elsewhere in the sector. With each passing day, more of Magnus's sons joined their parent Legion to await tasking orders from the Crusade's new master.

Sotekis led a mentor company back from supporting the World Eaters in the Golgothan Deeps, and word came through that the last battle formation to arrive, Kenaphia's Thunder Bringers, had returned after fighting alongside the IV Legion of Perturabo. There were still elements of the Legion scattered throughout the galaxy, but the majority had found its way to Hexium Minora.

For six months, the Thousand Sons fleet suckled at the planet's forges and materiel silos like newborns eager for the teat. Billions of rounds of ammunition, thousands of tonnes of food and water, uniforms, dried goods, pioneer supplies, armoured vehicles, power cells, fuel bladders and the myriad items an expeditionary fleet required in order to function were shipped from the surface in bulk lifters or via impossibly slender Tsiolkovsky towers.

With resupply almost complete, the Legion and its millions of supporting soldiers lay at anchor awaiting orders. The months had not been wasted; Army units conducted battle drills alongside the Astartes, both forces learning much of the other's abilities and limitations.

Each Captain of Fellowship divided his time between battle training and exercises of mental discipline to refresh his powers and his connection to the aether, but the Legion was eager to be in the thick of things again. Nor were the remembrancers idle. Most spent their time honing prose for post-Crusade publication, all the while hoping to learn more of the glorious Triumph on Ullanor.

Others rendered sketches taken over the course of the conquest of Heliosa or during its transitional period en route to compliance, while the lucky few chosen as Neophytes by the Thousand Sons continued their training.

'It's beautiful, is it not?' asked Magnus as Ahriman joined him.

'It is, my lord,' agreed Ahriman.

'I can see so much when I look out from this sanctum, Ahzek, but there is so much more that can be learned. I know much, it is true, but I will know everything one day.'

Magnus smiled and shook his head, as though amused at his own conceit.

'No need to hide your frown, my friend,' he said. 'I am not so arrogant as to have forgotten my studies of the plays of Aristophanes and the dialogues of Plato. "To know, is to know that you know nothing. That is the meaning of true knowledge".'

'I do not look so deeply into the heavens, my lord,' said Ahriman, 'But looking at the stars always gives me a sense of peace, knowing that there is an order to the galaxy. It gives me stability in times of change.'

'You say that as though change is to be feared,' said Magnus, at last looking down at him.

'Change is sometimes necessary,' said Ahriman with a disarming smile, 'but I prefer order. It is more... predictable.'

Magnus chuckled. 'Yes, I can see how that would be pleasant, Ahzek, but the perfect, ordered world is dead and stagnant. The real world is alive *because* it is full of change, disorder and decay. The old order must pass away so the new one may arise.'

'Is that what happened on Ullanor?' ventured Ahriman.

'In a manner of speaking. No order, not even a god-given one, will last forever. After all, the grand principle of creation is that nothing and possibility come in and out of bond infinite times in a finite moment.'

Ahriman kept silent, unsure as to the primarch's exact meaning.

Magnus folded his arms and sighed and said, 'We are alone in the stars, Ahzek.'

'My lord?'

'The Emperor leaving the Crusade,' said Magnus. 'I heard him speak to Horus upon the reviewing stand. My brother desired to know why our father was leaving us, and do you know what he said?'

'No, my lord,' said Ahriman, though he understood the question was rhetorical.

'He said that it was not because he wearied of the fighting, but because a greater destiny called him, one he claimed would ensure the legacy of our conquests will live on until the ending of the stars. Of course Horus wanted to know what that was, but our father did not tell him, which I saw cut him deeply. You see, Horus was the first of us to be reunited with our father after our... scattering. He fought at his side for nearly thirty years, father and only son. Such a bond is unique and not easily relinquished. Truth be told, it is a bond many of my brothers look upon with no small amount of jealousy.'

'But not you?'

'Me? No, I never lost contact with my father. We spoke many times before he ever set foot on Prospero. That is a bond that none of my brothers can claim. As our Legion departed Ullanor, I communed with my father and told him what I found on Aghoru, a hidden labyrinth of tunnels that pierce the immaterium and link all places and all times.'

Magnus returned his eye to the stars, and Ahriman kept silent, sensing that to intrude on Magnus's introspection would be unwise, though the ramifications of his discoveries on Aghoru were staggering.

'Do you know what he said, Ahzek? Do you know how he greeted this momentous discovery, this key to every corner of the galaxy?'

'No, my lord.'

'He knew,' said Magnus simply. 'He already knew of it. I should not have been surprised, I suppose. If any being in the galaxy could know such a thing, it would be my father. Now that he knew I had also discovered this lattice, he told me he had discovered it decades ago and had resolved to become its master. This is why he returns to Terra.'

'That is great news, surely?'

'Absolutely,' said Magnus without enthusiasm. 'I immediately volunteered my services, of course, but my offer of assistance was declined.'

'Declined? Why?'

Magnus's shoulders dropped a fraction as he said, 'Apparently my father's researches are at too delicate a stage to allow another soul to look upon them.'

'That surprises me,' said Ahriman. 'After all, there is no greater student of the esoteric than Magnus the Red. Did the Emperor say why he declined your help?'

'He not only declines my assistance, he warns me to delve no further into my studies. He assures me that he has a vital role for me in the final realisation of his grand designs, but he would tell me no more.'

'Did you ask what Leman Russ had told him?'

Magnus shook his head.

'No,' he said. 'My father knows my lupine brother's ways well enough; he does not to need me to point out how ridiculous and hypocritical they are.'

'Still,' said Ahriman, 'it is a shame to have lost the opportunity to learn more of the Wolves. Ohthere Wyrdmake and I formed a close bond. With Uthizzar's help, I would have learned much of the inner workings of the Wolf King's Legion.'

Magnus nodded and smiled.

'Have no fear, Ahzek,' he said, 'Wyrdmake was not our only source within the Wolves. I have other assets in place, none of whom know they dance to my tune.'

Ahriman waited for Magnus to continue, but the primarch kept his own counsel.

Before he could ask any more, the stars shimmered, as though a layer of gauze had been drawn over the crystal pyramid.

'Look,' said Magnus, 'The Mechanicum Borealis, it begins.'

Like a painting left out in the rain, the image of the stars smeared in the blackness. A fusion of chemical over-spill and atmospheric vapour fires on Hexium Minora caught the arcing light of the system's distant star, refracting a shimmering halo around the world as though it were ablaze from pole to pole with rainbow fires.

The effect was wondrous, despite being born of chronic pollution and rampant industry pursued

without heed of the cost to the planet's ecology. To
Ahriman, it was proof that something wonderful could
come from the most ugly of sources. A side effect of the
Mechanicum Borealis was the thinning of the veil
between the material world and the immaterium, and a
melange of unnameable colours and aetheric tempests
swirled around the planet's corona, a distant seascape
viewed through a glass darkly.

'The Great Ocean,' said Magnus, his voice full of long-
ing. 'How beautiful it is.'

Ahriman kept the lights in his private library low,
claiming that any aid to concentration was of para-
mount importance. Lemuel had been surprised how
small his mentor's sanctum was, a chamber no larger
than that of a Terran bureaucrat. For a room described
as a library, there were precious few books to be found,
merely a single bookcase filled with leather scroll tubes
and loosely bound sheaves of paper.

A large wooden desk of a pale, polished and darkly-
veined wood with an inset blotter of green leather stood
against one wall, and a number of thick books with
spines a half-metre or more in length lay opened across
its length.

An armour-stand bore Ahriman's battle-plate, like a
silent observer of his failures. It reminded Lemuel of
Khalophis's robots, and the thought of those soulless,
mechanised warriors sent a shiver down Lemuel's spine.

'Can you see it yet?' asked Ahriman.

'No.'

'Look again. Drift with the currents. Remember all I
have taught you since Shrike.'

'I'm trying, but there are so many. How can I tell
what's the actual future and what's a potential future?'

'That,' said Ahriman, 'is where the skill of the individual diviner comes into play. Some prognosticators have

an innate connection to the aetheric paths that guide them with unerring accuracy to the truth, while others must sift though a thousand images of meaningless symbolism to reach it.'

'Which are you?' asked Lemuel without opening his eyes and trying to visualise the myriad paths of the falling cards.

'Think less about me, more about the cards,' warned Ahriman. 'Ready?'

'Ready.'

A precisely stacked house of cards sat on the lip of the desk, arranged in a delicately balanced pyramid. Ahriman had produced them from a battered, cloth-wrapped tin, seventy-eight cards of what he called a Visconti-Sforza trionfi deck. Each card was exquisitely detailed and lovingly rendered with vivid colours and expressively wrought images of regal men and women.

'Catch the Seven of Denari,' said Ahriman, and slammed an open palm down on the desk.

The pyramid of cards collapsed, each one fluttering to the floor in a crazed whirlwind of spinning horsemen, kings and princesses. Lemuel snatched his hand out, seizing a card and holding it up before him.

'Show me,' said Ahriman.

Lemuel flipped the card, which showed a female fig-ure reaching up to touch an eight-rayed star.

'The Star,' said Ahriman. 'Try again.'

'It's impossible,' said Lemuel in resignation. He had been trying to catch whichever card Ahriman named from the falling stack for the last three hours without success. 'I can't do it.'

'You can. Lift your mind into the lower Enumerations to clear it of the clutter of material concerns. Let your mind float free of hunger, want and desire. Only then can you follow the correct path to the future echoes.'

'Free my mind from desire? That's hard for me to do,' pointed out Lemuel.

'I never promised this would be easy. Quite the contrary in fact.'

'I know, but it's not easy for a man of my appetites to suppress them,' said Lemuel, patting his ample, but shrinking, gut. Shipboard cuisine was a bland mixture of reconstituted pastes and flash frozen organics grown in ventral hydroponic bays. It nourished the body, but did little else.

'Then the Enumerations will help you,' said Ahriman. 'Rise into the low spheres and visualise the paths each card will take, the interactions as they strike one another, the ripples they cause in the system. Learn to read the geometric progression of potentiality as each permutation gives birth to a thousand more outcomes regardless of how similar the beginning parameters were. In the forgotten ages, some people knew this as chaos theory, others as fractal geometry.'

'I can't do it,' protested Lemuel. 'Your brain was crafted for that sort of thing, but mine wasn't.'

'It is not my enhanced cognition that allows me to see the cards fall. I am not a mathematical savant.'

'Then you do it,' challenged Lemuel.

'Very well,' said Ahriman, rebuilding the house of cards with calm dexterity. When the pyramid was complete, he turned to Lemuel. 'Name a card.'

Lemuel thought for a moment.

'The Chariot,' he said at last.

Ahriman nodded and closed his eyes, standing before the desk with his hands at his sides.

'Ready?' asked Lemuel.

'Yes.'

Lemuel banged the table and the cards fell to the floor. Ahriman's hand darted out like a striking snake and snatched a single gilt-edged card from the air. He turned it over to reveal a golden chariot drawn by two winged white horses. He placed the card face up on the desk.

'You see? It can be done.'

'Astartes reflexes,' said Lemuel.

Ahriman smiled and said, 'Is that what you think? Very well. Shall we try once more?'

Once again, Ahriman built the house of cards and asked Lemuel to name a card. Lemuel did so and Ahriman closed his eyes, standing before the precariously balanced cards. Instead of keeping his arms at his sides, he extended a hand with his thumb and forefinger outstretched, holding his fingertips close together, as though gripping an invisible card. His breathing deepened, and his eyes darted back and forth behind their lids.

'Do it,' said Ahriman.

Lemuel thumped the desk and the cards collapsed in a rain of images. Ahriman didn't move, and a single card fluttered through the air to slide precisely between his fingertips. Lemuel was not the least bit surprised when the Librarian flipped it over to reveal a divine figure bearing a fiery sword in his right hand and an eagle-topped globe in his left hand. Angels flew above the figure, blowing golden trumpets from which hung silk banners.

'Just as you wanted,' said Ahriman. 'Judgement.'

FOUR DAYS LATER, Lemuel was once again ensconced within Ahriman's library, though this time he had been promised remembrances instead of instruction. Almost a year after being denied the opportunity to descend to the surface of Ullanor, Lemuel had hoped for a firsthand account of Horus Lupercal's ascension to Warmaster. In this, he was to be disappointed.

When Lemuel asked about the Great Triumph, Ahriman had shrugged, as though it had been a trivial encounter, something not worthy of remembrance.

'It was a private affair,' said Ahriman.

Lemuel almost laughed before seeing that Ahriman was deadly serious.

'Why would you want to know of it anyway?'

'Seriously?'

'Yes.'

'Maybe because the Emperor himself was there,' said Lemuel, struggling to understand why Ahriman would think it strange he would want to know of such a singular event. 'Or perhaps because the Emperor has returned to Terra and the Great Crusade has a new commander. Horus Lupercal is the Warmaster. Such an event is a turning point in the affairs of mankind, surely you must see that?'

'I do,' nodded Ahriman, 'though I fear I would make a poor teller of the tale. I am sure others will recount it better than I in times to come.'

Ahriman sat behind his desk, sipping crisp, corn-coloured wine from an oversized pewter goblet. Lemuel sensed there was more to his reluctance to speak of Ullanor than any doubt as to his ability to give a good enough rendition.

There would be little in the way of remembrance; something was preying on Ahriman's mind, something that had happened upon the surface of Ullanor, but whatever it was, Lemuel would not hear it today.

To see an Astartes troubled by concerns beyond the battlefield was surprising, and he regarded Ahriman with new eyes. Even stripped out of his armour and clad in a crimson tunic and khaki combat fatigues, Ahriman was enormous. Encased in his battle-plate, his limbs were smooth and clean, machine-like, but now Lemuel could see the bulging musculature of his biceps and the undulant ridges of his pectorals. If anything, an Astartes without his armour was *more* frightening. His proportions were human, but also alien and gigantic.

Lemuel had come to know Ahriman well since leaving Ullanor; not well enough to yet count them as friends, but well enough to read his moods. Of his remembrancer friends, he had seen little, for Camille and Kallista spent the bulk of their time in the company of Ankhu Anen in the *Photep's* library, learning to develop their nascent abilities. As little as he had seen of his female friends, Lemuel had seen nothing at all of Mahavastu Kallimakus.

'Lemuel?' said Ahriman, snapping his thoughts back to the present.

'I'm sorry,' said Lemuel. 'I was thinking about a friend and hoping he was well.'

'Who?'

'Mahavastu Kallimakus, scribe to the primarch.'

'Why would he not be doing well?'

Lemuel shrugged, unsure how much he should say.

'He seemed out of sorts the last time I saw him,' he said, 'but then he's a very old man, prone to the aches and pains of age. You understand?'

'Not really,' admitted Ahriman. 'I am as fit now as I was two centuries ago.'

Lemuel chuckled and said, 'That should amaze me, but it's astonishing how quickly you become accustomed to the extraordinary, especially with the Thousand Sons.'

He lifted a modest, cut-crystal glass to his lips and drank, enjoying the rarity of a wine that didn't taste like it had been strained through a starship's urinary filtration system.

'How are you liking the wine?' asked Ahriman.

'It is a more refined taste than I am used to,' said Lemuel, 'flavoursome and forceful, yet with enough subtlety to surprise.'

'The grapes were grown in underground vineyards on Prospero,' explained Ahriman. 'It is a vintage of my own concoction, based on a gene-sample I took in Here-taunga bay on what was once the island of Diemenslandt.'

'I never took the Astartes for students of viniculture.'

'No? Why not?'

Lemuel cocked his head to one side, wondering if Ahriman was joking. Certainly the Chief Librarian of the Thousand Sons was a man of serious mien, but all too often he would puncture that with deadpan humour. From the hue of his aura, it seemed his question was honestly asked, and Lemuel floundered for an answer.

'Well, it's just that you are bred for war. I didn't think that left much room for less martial pursuits.'

'In other words you think we are only good for battle? Is that it? The Astartes are simply weapons, killing tools who cannot have interests beyond war?'

Lemuel saw a glint in Ahriman's eye and played along.

'You *are* very good at killing,' he said. 'Phoenix Crag taught me that.'

'You are right; we are very good at killing. I think that is why my Legion encourages its warriors to develop skills beyond the battlefield. After all, this crusade cannot last forever, and we will need to have a purpose beyond that when it is over. What will become of the warriors when there are no more wars?'

'They'll settle down and grow fine wine,' said Lemuel, finishing his glass and accepting another as Ahriman leaned over to pour. A shiver passed along his spine at the sheer absurdity of this moment. He chuckled and shook his head.

'What is funny?' asked Ahriman.

'Nothing really,' he said. 'I was just wondering how Lemuel Gaumon, a sometime academic, sometime dilettante of the esoteric came to share a glass of wine with a genetically engineered post-human? Two years ago, if someone had told me I'd be sitting here with you like this, I'd have thought they were mad.'

'The feeling is mutual,' Ahriman assured him.

'Then let us drink to new experiences,' said Lemuel, raising his glass.

They did, and they enjoyed the strangeness of the moment. When he judged sufficient time had passed, Lemuel said, 'You never answered my question.'

'Which question?'

'When you were training me with the trionfi cards,' said Lemuel. 'When I asked what kind of diviner you were, one with an innate connection to the aether or one who has to struggle for every morsel of truth? I get the feeling it's the former.'

'Once I was, yes,' said Ahriman, and Lemuel read pride in his aura, but also regret. 'I could pluck the future from the aether without effort, guiding my Fellowship along the most productive paths in war and study, but now I have to work hard for even a momentary glimpse into the patterns of the future.'

'What changed?'

Ahriman stood and circled the table, picking up the deck of cards and shuffling them expertly. He could have been a croupier or a cardsharp, thought Lemuel. The ease and dexterity with which Ahriman flicked the cards around his fingers was incredible, and he didn't seem to notice he was doing it.

'The tides of the Great Ocean are ever-changing, and its influence rises and fall. What was once a raging torrent can dwindle to a trickling brook in a fraction of a second. What was a gentle wave can rise to an all-consuming typhoon. Each practitioner's powers rise and fall with its moods, for it is a fickle mistress whose interest flits like a firefly in the dark.'

'You speak of it as though it were a living thing,' said Lemuel, seeing the wistful, faraway look in Ahriman's eyes. Ahriman smiled and replaced the cards on the desk.

'Perhaps I do,' he said. 'The ancient sailors of Terra often claimed they had two wives, their earthly mates and the ocean. Each was jealous of the other and it was said that one or the other would claim a seafarer's life. To live so close to the aether is to live with feet in two worlds. Both are dangerous, but a man can learn to read how they shift and dance in and out of sync with one another. The trick is to read those moments and crest the wave of power while it lasts.'

Lemuel leaned forward and tapped a finger on the gold-backed cards.

'I don't think that's a trick I've mastered,' he said.

'No, divination is not your forte,' agreed Ahriman, 'though you show some skill with aetheric reading. Perhaps I will schedule some time with Uthizzar of the Athanaens for you. He can develop this area of your psyche.'

'I keep hearing of these cults, but why such specialisation?' asked Lemuel. 'The sangomas I learned from were men and women who served the people of their townships in many different ways. They didn't confine themselves to one area of expertise. Why does your Legion break up its teachings into different cults?'

'The sangoma you speak of skimmed the tiniest fraction of learning from the Great Ocean, Lemuel. The lowliest Probationer of any Thousand Sons cult understands and practices more of the mysteries than even the most gifted sangoma.'

'I don't doubt that,' said Lemuel, taking another sip of wine. 'But, still, why so many?'

Ahriman smiled and said, 'Finish your drink, and I will tell you of Magnus's first journey into the desolation of Prospero.'

* * *

'PROSPERO IS A paradise,' began Ahriman, 'a wondrous planet of light and beauty. Its mountains are soaring fangs of brilliant white, its forests verdant beyond imagining and its oceans teem with life. It is a world returned to glory, but it was not always so. Long before the coming of Magnus, Prospero was all but abandoned.'

Ahriman lifted a box of cold iron from the top shelf of his bookcase and placed it on the desk before Lemuel. He opened the lid to reveal a grotesque skull of alien origin, its surface dark and glossy as though coated in lacquer. Elongated, with extended mandibles and two enormous eye-sockets behind them, it was insectoid and utterly repellent.

'What's that?' asked Lemuel, curling his lip in revulsion.

'This is a preserved exo-skull of a psychneuein, an alien predator native to Prospero.'

'And why are you showing it to me?'

'Because without these creatures, the cults of the Thousand Sons would not exist.'

'I don't understand.'

'I'll show you,' said Ahriman, lifting the skull from the box. He held it out to Lemuel and said, 'Don't worry, it is long dead and its residual aura has long since dissipated into the Great Ocean.'

'Still, no thanks. Those mandibles look like they could tear a man's head off.'

'They could, but that was not what made the psychneuein so dangerous. It was its reproductive cycle that was its most potent weapon. The female psychneuein is drawn to psychic emanations and has a rudimentary fusion of telepathic and telekinetic powers. When fertile, the female psychically projects a clutch of its eggs into the brain of a host being with an unprotected mind, vulnerable to the power of the aether.'

'That's disgusting,' said Lemuel, genuinely horrified.

'That is not the worst of it.'

'It's not?'

'Not by a long way,' said Ahriman, with amused relish. 'The eggs are small, no larger than a grain of sand, but by morning the following day, they will hatch and begin to feed on the host's brain. At first the victim feels nothing more than a mild headache, but by afternoon he will be in agony, raving and insane, as his brain is devoured from the inside out. By nightfall, he will be dead, his skull a writhing mass of plump maggots. In the space of a few hours, the grubs have picked the carcass clean and will seek a dark place to hide in which to pupate. By the following day, they will emerge as adults, ready to hunt and reproduce.'

Lemuel felt his guts roil, trying not to imagine the agony of being eaten alive by a host of parasites in his brain.

'What a horrible way to die,' he said, 'but I still don't understand how such vile creatures shaped Prospero and the Thousand Sons?'

'Patience, Lemuel,' cautioned Ahriman, sitting on the edge of the desk. 'I am getting to that. You know of Tizca, the City of Light, yes?'

'It is a place I am greatly looking forward to seeing,' said Lemuel.

'You will see it soon enough,' smiled Ahriman. 'Tizca is the last outpost of a civilisation wiped out thousands of years ago, a city where the survivors of a planet-wide cataclysm found refuge from the psychneuein. We suspect some freak upsurge in the Great Ocean triggered an explosion of uncontrolled psychic potential within the population, driving the psychneuein into a reproductive feeding frenzy. The civilisation of Prospero collapsed and the survivors fled to a city in the mountains.'

'Tizca,' said Lemuel, thrilled to be learning the lost history of Prospero.

'Yes,' confirmed Ahriman. 'For thousands of years, the people of Tizca endured, while all they had built in the millennia since leaving Terra fell to dust. The surface of Prospero is dotted with the remains of their dead culture. Empty cities are now overgrown with forests and vines, the palaces of their kings overrun with wild beasts.'

'How did they survive?'

'They salvaged enough knowledge and equipment from the destruction to construct techno-psychic arrays and sustainable energy sources, which then allowed them to build giant hydroponic gardens deep in the caverns of the ventral mountain ranges.'

'Where you grow the fruit for delightful wines,' said Lemuel, raising his glass in a toast, 'but that's not what I meant. How did they survive the psychneuein?'

Ahriman tapped his head and said, 'By developing the very powers that made them so vulnerable. The psychneuein were drawn to Tizca in their thousands, but the survivors were able to train their most gifted psykers to use their minds to erect invisible barriers of pure thought. They were primitive, bombastic powers compared to the subtle arts we employ today, but they kept the creatures at bay. And so, the practitioners of the mysteries remained locked in their limited understanding of the Great Ocean's power until the coming of Magnus.'

Lemuel leaned in and placed his wine glass on the edge of the desk. The origin myths of the primarchs were often shrouded in allegory and hyperbole, embroidered over time with all manner of fanciful details involving tests of strength, contests of arms or similarly outlandish feats.

To hear of a primarch's deeds on his home world from a warrior of his Legion would surely be the greatest achievement of any remembrancer, an authentic account as opposed to one embellished by people like the iterators. Lemuel's pulse rate rose in expectation, and he felt a chill gust at his shoulder, like the breath of an invisible passer-by. He frowned as he saw a shimmer of red in the cut crystal of his wine glass, the hint of a golden eye looking back at him from the liquid.

Lemuel glanced over his shoulder, but there was no one there.

Looking back at his glass, it was simply wine. He shook off the unease the image had conjured. Ahriman was looking at him with an amused expression on his face, as though expecting him to say something.

'You were saying,' said Lemuel, when Ahriman didn't continue, 'about Magnus?'

'I was,' said Ahriman, 'but it is not my story to tell.'

Confused, Lemuel sat back in his seat and asked, 'Then whose story *is* it to tell?'

'Mine,' said Magnus, appearing at Lemuel's shoulder, as if from thin air. 'I shall tell it.'

CHAPTER
SEVENTEEN

The Desolation of Prospero/The Fallen
Statue/Fresh Summons

IT SEEMED LIKE the grossest insult to be seated in the presence of so mighty a being, but no matter how Lemuel tried to rise, the muscles in his legs wouldn't obey him.

'My lord,' he finally managed.

The primarch wore a long, flowing robe of crimson edged with sable, secured at the waist by a wide leather belt with a jade scarab design at its centre. His curved blade was sheathed across his back, and his bright hair was pulled into a series of elaborate braids entwined like the roots of a giant tree.

Magnus filled the library with his presence, though he appeared to be no bigger than Ahriman. Lemuel blinked away a hazed outline of the primarch and stared into his single eye, its amber iris pinpricked with white magnesium. Where his other should have been was blank flesh, smooth as though it had never known an eye.

'Lemuel Gaumon,' said Magnus, and the syllables of his name flowed like honey from the primarch's mouth, like a word of power or some hidden language of the ancients.

'That's... that's me,' he stammered, knowing he sounded like a simpering idiot, but not caring. 'I mean, yes. Yes, my lord. It's an honour to meet you, I never expected to, I mean...'

His words trailed off as Magnus raised a hand.

'Ahriman was telling you of how I founded the cults of Prospero?'

Lemuel found his voice and said, 'He was. I would be honoured if you would take up where he left off.'

The request was audacious, but a newfound confidence filled him with sudden brio. He had the distinct impression that Magnus had not arrived here by accident, that this encounter was as stage-managed as any of Coraline Aseneca's supposedly improvised theatre performances.

'I shall tell you, for you are a rare man, Lemuel. You have vision to see what a great many people would run from in fear. You have promise, and I intend to see it fulfilled.'

'Thank you, my lord,' said Lemuel, though a tiny warning voice in his head wondered exactly what the primarch meant by that.

Magnus brushed past, touching Lemuel's shoulder, and the sheer joy of the contact swept any concerns away. Magnus rounded Ahriman's desk and lifted the gold-backed cards.

'A Visconti-Sforza deck,' said Magnus. 'The *Visconti di Modrone* set if I am not mistaken.'

'You have a good eye, my lord,' said Ahriman, and Lemuel suppressed a snigger, wondering if this was what passed for humour among the Thousand Sons.

Ahriman's words seemed sincere, and Magnus shuffled through the pack with even greater dexterity than had his Chief Librarian.

'This is the oldest set in existence,' said Magnus, spreading the cards on the desk.

'How can you tell?' asked Lemuel.

Magnus slipped a card from the deck and held up the six of denari. Each of the pips was a golden disc bearing either a fleur-de-lys or a robed figure carrying a long staff.

'The denari suit, which corresponds to what is now known as diamonds, bears the obverse and reverse of the golden florin struck by Magister Visconti sometime in the middle of the second millennium, though the coins he designed were only in circulation for a decade or so.'

Magnus put the card back in the deck and moved over to Ahriman's bookcase, scanning the contents briefly before turning back to face Lemuel. He smiled, his manner genial and comradely, as though he were sharing a joke instead of a priceless morsel of remembrance.

'When I came to Prospero they said it was as though a comet had borne me to the ground, for the impact I had on them was as great,' said Magnus with an amused smile. 'The Tizcan commune, which was the name the survivors of the psychneuein gave to their little enclave, was a place rooted in tradition, but they had some skill in wielding the power of the aether. Of course, they didn't know it by that name, and the powers they had, while enough to keep the psy-predators at bay, were little more than the enchantments of idiot children.'

'But you taught them how better to use their powers?'

'Not at first,' said Magnus, lifting a golden disk inscribed with cuneiform symbols from Ahriman's bookshelf. He looked at it for a moment before replacing it with an almost imperceptible shake of his head. As he turned away, Lemuel saw that it was a zodiacal timepiece.

'I was… young back then, and knew little of my true potential, though I had been taught by the greatest tutor of the age.'

'The Emperor?'

Magnus smiled.

'None other,' he said. 'I was schooled in the ways of the commune, and I quickly learned everything they had to teach me. In truth, I had outstripped the learning of their greatest scholars within a year of my arrival. Their teachings were too dogmatic, too linear and too limiting for my mind's potential. My intellect was superior in every way to those that taught me. With my teachings, I knew they could be so much more.'

Lemuel heard arrogance in Magnus's voice. The primarch's power was immense and beyond mortal understanding, but there was none of the humility he often heard when talking with Ahriman. Where Ahriman recognised his limits, Magnus clearly felt he had none.

'So how did you teach them?' asked Lemuel.

'I took a walk into the desolation of Prospero. True power comes only to those who have fully tested themselves against their greatest fears. Within the commune, I knew no fear, no hunger or want and had no drive to push my abilities to their full potential. I needed to be tested to the very limits of my powers to see if I even *had* limits. Out in the wilds, I knew I would either find the key to fully unlock my powers or die in the attempt.'

'A somewhat drastic solution, my lord.'

'Was it, Lemuel? Really? Is it not better to reach for the stars and fail than never to try?'

'Stars are giant flaming balls of gas,' said Lemuel with a smile. 'They tend to burn people who get too near.'

Ahriman chuckled. 'The remembrancer knows his Pseudo-Apollodorus.'

'That he does,' agreed Magnus with a satisfied smile. 'But I digress. A year after my coming to Prospero, I walked from the gates of Tizca and marched into the wilderness for nearly forty days. To this day, it is known as the desolation of Prospero, but such a title is a misnomer. You will find the landscape quite beautiful, Lemuel.'

Lemuel's heartrate spiked, remembering how Ahriman had told him he had seen a vision in which he had been standing on Prospero.

'I am sure I will, my lord,' he said.

Magnus poured a glass of wine and began his tale.

'I WALKED FOR hundreds of miles, travelling roads that passed through broken cities of iron skeletons of tall towers, empty palaces and grand amphitheatres. It was a civilisation of great worth, but it had fallen in a single day, not an uncommon fate among worlds during the madness of Old Night. I came at last to a city, a sprawling ruin at the foot of a cliff that seemed familiar, though I had never before set foot beyond the walls of Tizca. I spent a day and a night wandering its forsaken streets, the shadow-haunted buildings and empty homes that echoed with the last breaths of those who had dwelled within them. It touched me in a way I had not thought possible. These people had lived sure in the knowledge that they had nothing to fear, that they were masters of their destinies. The coming of Old Night changed all that. It had shown them how horribly vulnerable they were. In that moment, I vowed I would master the powers I had at my command, so that I would never fall prey, as they had fallen, to the vagaries of an ever-changing universe. I would face such threats and overcome them.'

Again, Lemuel felt the full force of the primarch's confidence, as if it was suffusing his skin and invigorating his entire body.

'I climbed a slender pathway up the cliff and came to a bend in the road, where a long-dead sculptor had erected a tall statue of a great bird carved from multi-coloured stone. It was a splendid creature with outstretched wings and the graceful neck of a swan. It perched precariously on the edge of the cliff. This statue had endured for thousands of years, rocking and swaying, but always keeping its balance perfectly. But no sooner had I beheld its grandeur than it toppled from its plinth and was dashed to pieces at the bottom of the cliff, far, far below. The sight of that falling statue filled me with an almost inconsolable sense of loss I could not explain. I abandoned my trek into the mountains and returned to the base of the cliff, where, needless to say, the statue lay smashed into many pieces.

'Where it had hit, the ground was covered with a carpet of shards, some small and some large, but shards and shards and more shards for as far as a man could walk in an hour. I spent the whole day just looking at the shards, measuring them and feeling the weight of them, and just pondering why the statue had chosen that moment to fall.'

Magnus paused, his eye misty and distant as he relived the memory.

'You say "chosen" as though the statue had been waiting for you,' said Lemuel. 'Isn't it possible that it was a coincidence?'

'Surely Ahriman has taught you that there are no such things as coincidences.'

'I mentioned it once or twice, yes,' said Ahriman dryly.

'I spent the night there and awoke the next morning full of enthusiasm. I spent many days on this carpet of broken stone shards, and eventually I noticed a very strange thing. There were three large stones on the ground, forming a triangle that was precisely equilateral. I was amazed. Looking further, I found four white stones arranged in a perfect square. Then I saw that by disregarding two of the white stones and thinking of a pair of grey stones a metre over, it was an exact rhombus! And, if I chose this stone, and that stone, and that one, and that one and that one I had a pentagon as large as the triangle. Here a small hexagon, and there a square partially inside the hexagon, a decagon, two triangles interlocked. And then a circle, and a smaller circle within the circle, and a triangle within that which had a red stone, a grey stone and a white stone.

'I spent many hours finding even more designs that became infinitely more complex as my powers of observation grew with practice. Then I began to log them in my grimoire; and as I counted designs and described them, the pages began to fill as the sun made countless passages across the sky. Days passed, but my passion for the designs I was seeing was all-consuming.'

'And that's how Amon found him,' said Ahriman, 'squatting in a pile of broken stones.'

'Amon?' asked Lemuel. 'The captain of the 9th Fellowship?'

'Yes, and my tutor on Prospero,' said Magnus.

Lemuel frowned at this apparent contradiction, but said nothing as Magnus continued.

'I had begun my second grimoire when Amon found me. Now, Amon is a quiet, private fellow, not easily given to company. Like many such solitary men, he is a poet and deeply interested in the hidden nature of things. When I saw him, I cried, "Amon, come quickly! I have discovered the most wondrous thing in the universe". He hurried over to me, anxious to see what it was.

'I showed him the carpet of stones, but Amon only laughed and said, "It is nothing but scattered shards of stone!" I took his hand and proceeded to show my old tutor the harvest of my many days study. When Amon saw the designs he turned to my grimoires and by the time he was finished with them, he too was overwhelmed.'

As much as Lemuel was having trouble following Magnus's logic, it was impossible not to be swept up by his enthusiasm. He saw that Ahriman was similarly carried along by the irresistible tide of the primarch's passion for his tale.

'Now Amon was much moved,' said Magnus, 'and he began to write poetry about each of the incredible designs. As he wrote and contemplated, I became sure that the designs must mean something. Such order and beauty was too monumental to be senseless. The designs were there, the workings of the universe laid bare.

'Together, Amon and I returned home, where he read his poetry, and I showed the masters of Tizca the workings in my grimoires. These were great men, and their love of beauty and nature was marvellous to behold. So amazed were they that they joined me on a pilgrimage back to the cliff where the statue had fallen. The shards were just as I had described them, and the masters of Tizca were overcome with emotion, filling their own grimoires with fantastical writing. Some wrote about triangles, others described the circles, while yet others concentrated all their attention on the glittering spectrum of coloured stones.'

Magnus directed all his attention on Lemuel, his amber eye flickering with internal fires.

'Do you know what they said to me?' asked Magnus.

'No,' breathed Lemuel, hardly daring to add his voice to the telling.

Magnus leaned down.

'They said, "How blind we have been". All who could see the designs knew that they had to have been put there by a Primordial Creator, for nothing but such a great force could create this immense beauty!'

Lemuel could picture the scene, the sheer immensity of the cliff, the broken carpet of multi-coloured shards and the awed gathering of students of the esoteric and the outlandish. He sensed their awe and felt the tide of history rising up to sweep away the old beliefs and leave a new way in its wake. Lemuel felt as though he were there, as though he inhabited the body of one of the venerable philosophers of Tizca, and found his mind opening to a host of new possibilities, like a blind man suddenly shown the sun.

'It was amazing,' he whispered.

'That it was, Lemuel. That it was,' said Magnus, pleased he truly appreciated the significance of what he was being told. 'It was a great moment in the history of Prospero, but as is the way of history, nothing of import is ever achieved without bloodshed.'

Lemuel felt his chest constrict with panic, feeling the horrible sensation of impending danger, as though he stood on the cusp of an abyss, waiting for a shove in the back.

'We had been lax in our mental discipline,' said Magnus, and a trace of sadness entered his voice. 'Such was our excitement at what I had found that we allowed our guard to drop.'

'What happened?' asked Lemuel, almost afraid of the answer.

'The psychneuein,' said Magnus. 'They were drawn to us in their thousands, blackening the sky with their numbers as they descended like a plague from ancient times.'

Lemuel drew in a breath, picturing the dark swathes of psy-predators as they swarmed from their darkened caves, organically shifting clouds of deadly clades, the relentless buzzing of thousands of crystalline wings the sound of inevitable doom.

'The males swarmed in, a hurricane of snapping mandibles and tearing claws, and fifty men died in the time it takes to draw breath. Behind the males came the females, engorged with clutch upon clutch of immaterial eggs. Their furious reproductive hunger was insatiable, and dozens of my friends fell to their knees in horror as they felt the psychneuein eggs take root in their brains. Their screams will stay with me forever, Lemuel. It is the sound of brilliant men who know that soon they will be raving madmen, their brains pulped masses of digestible tissue.'

A hushed silence filled the library, as the visceral terror of that notion took hold.

Magnus poured wine for them all before continuing.

'The beasts swirled around us, battering us with psychic thrusts, scrabbling at our mental barriers to seed our minds with their eggs, and only the strongest of us remained. Amon and eight of the masters of Tizca stood with me, and as the psychneuein attacked again, I knew this was what I had been seeking all along, a true test of my abilities. I would finally discover whether I had limits. I would see if I was the master of my powers or was to be found wanting.'

To look at Magnus as he told his story, Lemuel couldn't believe that such a warrior could ever be found wanting. Even telling the story gave his skin a faint luminosity, a heat that flowed through his veins. Magnus's amber eye had darkened to a fiery orange, the glittering sparks in its depths now swimming in his pupil.

'Then, as the psychneuein came at us again, something magnificent happened. I felt something move within me, I felt *changed*, as though an immense power that had lain within me, dormant and untapped, surged to life. As I contemplated the moment of my death, raging fires erupted from my hands. I hurled torrents of flame into the sky, as though I had always known I had such powers, and smote hundreds of psychneuein to ruin with every gesture.

'Memphia and Cythega, masters who had seen the patterns in the red stones, stood at my side, and walls of flame sprang up at their command. Ahtep and Luxan-htep plucked beasts from the air and dashed them on the rocks with the power of their minds, for they had found the spiral patterns of white stones. Hastar and Imhoden had seen the eight-angled crown of shards and willed the vital fluids within the psychneuein to boil within their exo-skeletons. Amon had been first among the hidden masters to see the patterns in the shards, and his mastery of them was second only to mine. Images of the future and imminent danger seared though his mind, and he cried words of warning to his fellows, telling them of dangers to come and of how they might avoid them.

'Phanek and Thothmes had seen the dance of squares, circles and triangles, the interaction of line and curve speaking to them of the hidden thoughts of all. They sensed the lust within the psychneuein to plant their psychic seed within our minds, the relent-less animal hunger that drove them to feed and propagate. They reached into the minds of the beasts and twisted their perceptions so that they became blind to us.'

'The cults of the Thousand Sons,' said Lemuel. 'That's where they came from.'

'Just so,' said Magnus. 'The subtle nuances of the Great Ocean were revealed to me that day, and when we returned to Tizca the members of my fellowship returned to their pyramid libraries to contemplate what they had learned. I watched over their deliberations and guided their studies, for I had seen the patterns of the broken statue first and knew better than any man how to wield the power of the aether. The nine masters devoted their every waking moment to what they had learned in the desolate wastelands, honing their unique abilities to become the first Magister Templi of the Prosperine cults.

'As word of their power spread throughout the adepts of Tizca, devotees flocked to study at their feet, hungry to learn the new ways to harness the power of the Great Ocean.'

'And what of you?' asked Lemuel. 'Why did you not become a cult leader?'

'Because I became the Magus,' said the primarch, 'Master of all the cults.'

'Magus? That's the highest rank isn't it?' asked Lemuel.

'No,' said Magnus, 'there is one rank above it, that of Ipsissimus, a being free from limitations, who lives in balance with the corporeal and incorporeal universe; for all intents and purposes, a perfect being.'

Lemuel heard Magnus's pride and knew there could be only one man in creation that could match such a description, one man who Magnus looked up to above all others.

'The Emperor, beloved by all,' said Lemuel.

Magnus smiled and nodded, folding his arms across his wide chest.

'Indeed, Lemuel,' he said, 'the Emperor. And it is with news of my father I come to the Library of Ahriman.'

Lemuel was instantly alert. Any scrap of information about the Emperor, the architect of humanity's fate, and the powerhouse behind the monumental undertaking of the Great Crusade, was eagerly seized upon by the remembrancers. To hear such news first-hand from one of the primarchs would be an honour indeed.

'Now that the last elements of the Legion have rendezvoused, we are summoned to my father's side once more.'

'Are we returning to Terra?' asked Ahriman. 'Is it time?'

Magnus hesitated, deliberately teasing the moment out.

'It is not for Terra that we set our course, but the Emperor promises the most serious of conclaves, the most momentous of gatherings, where the greatest questions of the age are to be debated.'

Lemuel gasped. Such news was grand indeed, but there was more to this singular piece of information than Magnus was letting on.

He smiled, buoyed up with sudden confidence.

'There's more isn't there, my lord?' he asked.

'He is perceptive, this one,' said Magnus with a nod to Ahriman. 'I think you are right, my friend; a stint with Uthizzar will hone his abilities nicely.'

Magnus turned to Lemuel once more and said, 'This conclave will be the crux of our Legion's existence, my friend. This will be our defining moment, where the Emperor at last acknowledges our worth.'

'You have seen this, my lord?' asked Ahriman.

'I have seen many things,' said Magnus. 'Great events are in motion, the wheel of history is on the turn and the Thousand Sons will be at the forefront of the new universal order.'

'Where will this gathering take place?' asked Ahriman.

'Far from here,' said Magnus, 'on a world named Nikaea.'

CHAPTER EIGHTEEN

Nikaea/Thrown to the Wolves/The Emperor's Right Hand

CATARACT CLOUDS OBSCURED the surface, a striated covering shot through with pyroclastic sparks and umber lightning. Nikaea was a new world, its geology unfinished and its final form not yet set. Tectonic movement and kilometres-deep pressure waves rippled below the crust, sending shockwaves through the mantle, and ripping some continents apart while slamming others together.

Two Stormbirds and a Stormhawk knifed through the clouds like swooping birds of prey, their crimson hulls painted with corrosive rain as they descended through the volatile atmosphere. Nikaea was a world in flux, its character in the throes of violent birth.

Space around the planet was a choppy soup of electromagnetic static, the approaches lousy with spatial debris caught in the whirling, inconstant gravity waves that rendered geomagnetic guidance systems inoperative.

Only by following a constant beacon of incandescent light that speared into the heavens from the world below could any craft hope to navigate the Nikaea system. To attempt to find Nikaea, let alone a fixed point on its surface without the aid of this signal would have been impossible for any but the luckiest pilots in the galaxy. It had taken an entire year for the 28th Expedition to travel from Hexium Minora to this remote corner of the galaxy.

Ahriman sat up front in *Scarab Prime*, the consoles before the pilots alive with flickering lights, vector diagrams and tri-dimensional contour maps of the jagged terrain. Pulsing cables connected the pilots to the avionics package, allowing them to fly purely on instruments, which was just as well, as the juddering canopy of the cockpit was smeared with ash and smoke.

Though the thought was faintly blasphemous, Ahriman hoped the Machine-God was watching over them. To lose control above such a hostile world was as sure a death sentence as could be envisaged.

Not that the pilots were actually guiding the Stormbird; that duty fell to Jeter Innovence, the Navigator strapped to the converted gravity harness where Ahriman normally performed his close-protection duties when flying into harm's way. Innovence had protested at being forced to leave his hermetic dome aboard the *Photep*, but had recanted his objections when told who he would be guiding and whose light he would be following.

Magnus the Red sat behind the Navigator, resplendent in a gloriously embroidered tunic of red and gold, shawled with a weave of golden mail hung with feathers and precious stones. In honour of the occasion, each of Magnus's forearms was sheathed in an eagle-stamped vambrace, and he wore an entwined lightning bolt girdle around his torso.

His hair was loose, glossy and mirror sheened, the colour of arterial blood.

No finer warrior scholar existed in the galaxy.

The slight form of Mahavastu Kallimakus sat beside Magnus, the heavy robes he wore unable to mask his gaunt frame. Kallimakus was venerable, as Lemuel had described, but Ahriman had not realised how much the primarch's control over him was costing the remembrancer. A heavy satchel of blank books rested against the fuselage, fresh pages for the scrivener to fill with Magnus's words and deeds.

Ahriman caught the primarch's eye, today an excited eclipse of pale blue and hazel flecks.

'We are close, Ahzek,' said Magnus, 'in every sense.'

'Yes, my lord. We land in less than ten minutes.'

'So long? I could have guided us in half the time!' cried Magnus, glaring at the recumbent form of the Navigator. His anger was false, and he laughed.

Magnus slapped a luminescent hand upon the Navigator's shoulder, causing him to flinch.

'Ah, don't mind me, Innovence,' said Magnus. 'I'm simply impatient to see my father once more. You are doing a grand job, my friend!'

Ahriman smiled. The melancholy that wreathed Magnus's soul after Ullanor had dispelled when word came of the conclave on Nikaea. The year spent traversing the immaterium from Hexium Minora had seen a frenzy of research and study aboard the *Photep* as Magnus handed out theoretical proofs, philosophical arguments and convoluted logic conundrums for his sons to solve in order to sharpen their minds. Nikaea promised to be the vindication of the Thousand Sons, and neither Magnus nor his Legion would be found wanting.

Ahriman turned back to the cockpit. According to the unwinding telemetry, they were practically on top of their destination, but the cloud cover was still impenetrable.

'Taking us down,' intoned the pilot. 'Beginning approach. Ground landing protocols exchanged and verified. Tether signal accepted and control relinquished.'

The pilots sat back as control of the aircraft was surrendered to Custodes ground controllers. The aircraft dipped its nose and went into a steep, looping descent. Ahriman had a brief, sinking sensation in his gut before his enhanced physiology compensated. The clouds streaked past the canopy. The glass slithered with moisture and streaks of grey, muddy ash.

Then they were below it, and the landscape of Nikaea was laid out before them.

It was black and geometric, a profusion of angular debris strewn upon the ground like the primordial shapes that lay at the heart of everything, and which had yet to be cloaked with the lie of individuality. Perfect spheres rose from the basalt ground, rippled with the liquid lines of their formation. Vast cubes sat side by side upon stepped volcanic plains, arranged in convoluted patterns that seemed a little too random to be random at all.

Magnus appeared at his side, like an excited Probationer about to take the *Liber Throa* and become a Neophyte. The primarch peered through the canopy and took in the geometric precision of the landscape.

'Incredible,' he whispered. 'The genesis of a world. The order of the universe described in mathematics, perfect shapes and geometry. How like my father to choose this place. He knew it would speak to me. It is the shards of my youth on a planetary scale.'

The Stormhawk dipped lower, banking its wings on its final approach, and a vast, conical landmass slid into view. It was a gigantic stratovolcano, steep-sided and rugged with hardened lava, tephra and blackened ash.

It pierced the clouds, and Ahriman knew with utter certainty that a great amphitheatre was carved within its heart. A column of purest light soared from the summit crater, invisible to mortal eyes, but a blazing spear piercing the heavens to those with aether-sight. A gathering thundercloud, shot through with golden lightning, filled the sky above the volcano.

Ahriman had felt the light's presence as soon as the ships of the 28th Expedition had translated into the Nikaea system, but to actually see it ahead of him was like waking from a coma into a brightly lit room.

'Throne, it's glorious,' said Magnus. 'That is true power, a mind that can reach across the galaxy and bind an empire together in the dream of Unity. It humbles me to know we serve so magnificent a master.'

Ahriman didn't answer. His mouth was dry and his heart thundered in his chest.

The light *was* magnificent. It was glorious and incredible in its potency and purity.

Yet all he felt was a mounting sense of dismay.

'I have seen this before,' he said.

'When?'

'On Aghoru,' breathed Ahriman, 'when I swam the Great Ocean hunting the threads of the future. When I met Ohthere Wyrdmake, I saw this: the volcano, the golden light.'

'And yet you said nothing? Why did you keep it to yourself?' asked Magnus.

'It made no sense,' said Ahriman, unable to keep the dread from his voice. 'The visions were fragmentary, disjointed. It was impossible to tell what it meant.'

'No matter,' said Magnus.

'No,' said Ahriman, 'I believe it matters. I believe it matters very much.'

* * *

LANDING LIGHTS WINKED in an ever-decreasing cruciform pattern as the Custodes' remote pilots reeled the Stormhawk in. The other two craft remained in their holding pattern, and would not descend until the first bird was clear. The Stormhawk slammed down in a hammer blow of burnt metal and gritty sulphurous backwash. As soon as it landed, a strip of white light extended onto the platform as a blast-shielded door lifted open.

Elongated shadows stretched from the detachment of warriors in armour of blood red and amethyst that marched from the side of the mountain. Massively wrought and precise, the honour guards of Astartes took up their position before the Stormhawk's assault ramp. Some carried gold-bladed rhomphaia while others drew enormous silver-bladed swords, which they reversed and set on the platform with their gauntlets resting on the pommels.

The Stormhawk's ramp lowered with a whine of pneumatics, and Magnus the Red descended to the surface. Followed by Ahriman and the shuffling form of Kallimakus, the primarch stepped from the ramp and took a deep breath of the hot, burnt air of Nikaea.

Kallimakus let out a soft gasp, and sweat gathered on Ahriman's forehead, though he said nothing. A detachment of nine Sekhmet warriors formed up behind Magnus, subtly matching themselves before the warriors on the platform.

These were no ordinary Astartes; these were the elite of two Legions. The sword-armed warriors were no less a force than the Sanguinary Host, the elite protectorate of the Lord of the Blood Angels. The Phoenix Guard of Lord Fulgrim stood with them, their long-bladed rhomphaia held ramrod-straight at their sides, perfectly poised and immaculately presented.

Their presence could mean only one thing.

Two giant figures emerged from the volcano, walking side by side like old friends. Ahriman's heartbeat spiked at the sight of them, the first a gloriously caparisoned warrior in armour of gold and purple, with flaring shoulder-guards and a billowing cape of scarlet and gold. His hair was brilliant white, bound at his temples by a band of silver, and his face was one of perfect symmetry, like divinely-proportioned Euclidian geometry.

The second figure wore armour of deepest crimson, the colour vital and urgent. Wings of dappled black and white rustled at his back, the feathers hung with fine loops of silver wire and mother of pearl. Hair of deepest black framed a face that was pale and classically shaped, like one of the thousands of marble likenesses that garrisoned the Imperial Palace of Terra. Yet this was no lifeless rendering of a long-dead luminary; this was a living, breathing angel made flesh, whose countenance was the most beauteous in existence.

'Lord Sanguinius,' said Ahriman in wonder.

'And Brother Fulgrim,' completed Magnus. 'Firmitas, utilitas, venustas.'

It seemed they heard him, for they smiled in genuine pleasure, though the words must surely have been lost in the feral growl of the Stormhawk's cooling engines.

The primarchs were illuminated in the reflected glow of the volcano, their smooth features open and welcoming. They wore the faces of eager siblings pleased to see their brother, though they had seen one another only recently at Ullanor.

Magnus stepped towards Fulgrim, and the master of the Emperor's Children opened his arms to receive his brother's embrace. They spoke words of greeting, but they were private, and Ahriman allowed himself to look away from the majesty of the Phoenician's countenance. Next, Magnus turned to Sanguinius, and the Primarch of the Blood Angels kissed his brother's cheeks, his greeting heartfelt but reserved. Only now did Ahriman notice the warriors accompanying each primarch. Sanguinius had two attendants, one a slender ascetic with a killer's eyes and another with such pale skin that the veins of his face were clearly visible beneath.

Ahriman took his place beside Magnus as he and Sanguinius parted. Magnus turned to him and said, 'Brother Sanguinius, allow me to introduce my Chief Librarian, Ahzek Ahriman.'

The Lord of the Angels turned his attention upon him, and Ahriman felt the full force of his appraisal. Like Russ before him, Sanguinius evaluated Ahriman swiftly, but where Russ sought out weakness to exploit, Sanguinius looked for strength to harness.

'I have heard much of you, Ahzek Ahriman,' said Sanguinius, his voice surprisingly gentle. For all its apparent softness, there was violent strength concealed within it, like a riptide beneath a placid seascape. 'You are thought highly of by many beyond your Legion.'

Ahriman smiled, pleased to hear such praise from the lips of a primarch.

'My lord,' he said. 'I serve the Emperor and my Legion to the best of my ability.'

'And what abilities they are,' said Sanguinius with a knowing smile. The primarch turned to introduce the warriors at his side. 'Magnus, this is Raldoron, Chapter Master of my protectors,' said Sanguinius, placing an elegantly sculpted hand on the shoulder of the warrior with the lethal eyes. Next he turned his attention to the warrior with the pale skin. 'And this is Captain Thoros, one of our most vaunted captains of battle.'

Both warriors gave deep bows, and Ahriman had a sudden flash within his mind, like a single, incongruous pict frame slipped within the passage of one moment to the next: A screaming, multi-limbed arachnid beast, all fangs and blade-limbs. So swift was it, Ahriman wasn't even sure he'd seen it, but it lingered like a harbinger when he looked at Thoros.

He shook off the image as Fulgrim turned to his warriors. Both were proud and haughty with an air of casual superiority that immediately made Ahriman wary. As flawlessly presented as their primarch, they were perfect in every way, but had none of the humility of Sanguinius's praetorians.

'Magnus, allow me to present my Lord Commanders, Eidolon and Vespasian.'

'A very real pleasure to meet you all,' said Magnus, bowing to his brother primarchs' warriors, honouring them as he honoured their masters.

'Well,' said Fulgrim, 'this promises to be a momentous day, brother, so shall we get on?'

'Of course,' said Magnus. 'I am eager to begin.'

'As are we all,' promised the Phoenician.

SANGUINIUS AND FULGRIM led them into the heart of the volcano, the tunnels within glassy and smooth, indicating they had been formed with industrial-scale meltas. They cut through the heart of the volcano, wide enough for the three primarchs to walk abreast, spiralling upwards through the solidified lava. The tunnels were lit with fiery luminescence, as though the molten heat of the magma at the volcano's heart was seeping up from below.

Ahriman removed his helmet to better appreciate the startling geology of the volcano, seeing shifting bands of crystalline layers through the translucent rock, like the sedimentary bands of an exposed rock face.

'This world may be young, but this volcano is old,' noted Ahriman, seeing the glances passing between Fulgrim's lord commanders as he spoke. He couldn't read their auras, and nor could he establish a link to his Tutelary. The glare of the Emperor's light was too powerful, overshadowing everything with its intensity.

Ahriman wondered if Magnus was similarly blinded by it.

He watched Magnus and his brothers as they spoke in low tones, relishing the sight of his primarch in the company of peers who harboured no ill-will towards him. Yet despite the bonhomie, their discourse was superficial. The more Ahriman studied the ebb and flow of their conversation and body language, the more he saw the supple flex of linguistic sparring.

The primarchs spoke of past campaigns, old glories and shared experiences, treading only on the comfortable ground of memory. Any hint that the subject of their meandering words might turn to matters of the future or the nature of the conclave were subtly deflected by Fulgrim, turned around and steered to safer ground.

He's hiding something, thought Ahriman, *something he doesn't want us to know about this gathering.*

Magnus must also be aware of it, but his primarch gave no sign that he was anything other than a willing actor in this unfolding drama. Ahriman looked at the Emperor's Children behind and before them, now seeing them as a prisoner escort instead of an honour guard

He wanted to warn Magnus, but nothing he might say could change their course. Whatever awaited them in the great amphitheatre he knew lay at the heart of this volcano, they had no choice but to face it. This was one destiny where the future was immutable and changeless.

The coiling passage wound ever upwards, and Ahriman knew they were close the summit.

The glow of the walls grew brighter, and Ahriman saw the extra light was coming from a vaulted antechamber of mirror-smooth basalt and glass. Servitors awaited their arrival with refreshments, and padded couches lined the walls.

'These will be your private chambers during recesses in the conclave,' said Sanguinius.

'They are quite sufficient,' replied Magnus.

Ahriman wanted to scream at the stilted formality of it all. Couldn't Magnus see that something was terribly wrong here? Sweat beaded on Ahriman's face and neck. He had the overwhelming urge to retreat to the waiting Stormhawk, fire up its engines and fly back to the *Photep*, never to return to Nikaea.

A pair of bronze doors led into the heart of the mountain, and the future pressed in from the other side.

'Is there anything else you require, friend Ahzek?' asked Lord Commander Eidolon.

Ahriman shook his head, the effort of keeping his expression neutral almost beyond him.

'No,' he managed, 'though I thank you for your concern.'

'Of course, brother,' said Eidolon, and Ahriman caught the inflexion on the last word.

Sanguinius turned and nodded to Raldoron and Thoros, who took up position on either side of their master and threw the bronze doors open.

It was all Ahriman could do not to scream a warning at Magnus. The Primarch of the Blood Angels marched through the great portal into the golden light with Fulgrim at his side. They beckoned Magnus to follow them.

Magnus turned to face Ahriman, and he saw the hurt of impending betrayal in his eye.

'I know, Ahzek. I know,' said Magnus wearily. 'I see now why we are here.'

Magnus turned and followed his brothers into the light.

AHRIMAN FOLLOWED MAGNUS through the doors, entering a grand amphitheatre hewn from the sharp-sided inner slopes of the volcano's crater. Thousands of figures filled its carved black benches, looking down into the amphitheatre. Most were robed adepts of high rank, though Ahriman saw groupings of Astartes scattered throughout the tiers. The stone floor of the amphitheatre was polished black marble, inlaid with a vast eagle of gold.

Sanguinius and Fulgrim led them to the centre of the arena, and Ahriman was struck by the appropriateness of the term, reminded of old Romanii legends that described how captured members of an underground sect had been thrown to the wolves and eaten alive for the perverse enjoyment of the crowd.

Though the world around them was raging in its birthing pangs, the air within the volcano was utterly still, the tempests beyond its tapered peak kept at bay by the hidden workings of the Mechanicum.

Ahriman's stride faltered as he saw the pyramid-stepped dais at the opposite side of the amphitheatre and the being that awaited them. This was the epicentre of the light and the beacon that had guided them through the maelstrom of spatial interference around Nikaea. So bright that he was almost obscured by his own brilliance, the Emperor of Mankind sat upon a carved throne of soaring eagle's wings and grasping claws coloured with blood red rubies. A golden sword lay across his lap, and he bore an eagle-topped orb in his left hand.

Flags of black silk and gold embroidery rippled above the Emperor, borne aloft by silver cherubs with glittering clarions that filled the air with a tuneless fanfare. At once, Ahriman was reminded of the Visconti-Sforza card that Lemuel had asked him catch.

'Judgement,' he whispered, wondering how he could have missed so obvious a portent.

Custodes warriors flanked their master and formed an armoured wall before the dais. Ahriman's doubts fled in the face of so wondrous an individual, for what could trouble a mind so blessed with this vision of perfection before it? He could not see the Emperor's face, merely impressions. A thunderous brow and stern, patrician features cast in a mould of dashed hope.

'Clarity, Ahzek,' said Magnus. 'Stand with me, and rise into the Enumerations. Retain your keenness of thought.'

Ahriman tore his gaze from the Emperor with effort and stepped alongside Magnus. He whispered the names of the first masters of Tizca over and over until he achieved the peace of the lowest sphere. Reaching that made advancing to the higher spheres easier, and Ahriman's thoughts returned to something approaching equilibrium with every step he took.

Freed from the clutter of emotion, he turned his attention to studying their surroundings as thoroughly as he might peruse any grimoire. He saw that the Emperor was not alone on the dais. The praetorian beside the Emperor was a warrior Ahriman had met once before on Terra, Constantin Valdor.

From the look of the curling script that snaked all around his armour, Valdor had prospered in the ranks of the Custodes, his proximity to the Emperor surely marking him as its most senior member.

A man in the plain dark robes of an administrator stood next to Valdor, an unassuming man rendered fragile and insignificant next to the giant Custodes warrior. This man too, Ahriman recognised, his long mane of white hair and all too human frailties marking him out as Malcador the Sigillite, the Emperor's trusted right hand and most valued counsellor.

To have earned a place in such rarefied company marked Malcador out as exceptional, even among a gathering of the most brilliant minds in the galaxy. He had not risen to such prominence by any virtue of eugenics, but by the simple brilliance of his mortal wisdom.

A red-robed fusion of machine parts and organics was surely Kelbor-Hal, the Fabricator General of Mars, but the others on the dais were unknown to him except by reputation: the green-robed Choirmaster of Astropaths, the Master of Navigators and the Lord Militant of the Imperial Army.

The lowest tier of the amphitheatre was punctuated by cantilevered boxes, like those in a playhouse reserved for kings. A short flight of steps led from each box to the floor of the amphitheatre. Figures were sitting in the boxes, but Ahriman couldn't focus on them or discern any traits of height, bulk or appearance. Instead of defining forms, he saw shadows and reflections, each box filled with bent creases of light. Though there were unmistakably people within each box, technological artifice concealed them from sight.

Falsehoods.

Whoever occupied the boxes retained their anonymity by virtue of chameleonic cloaks that shielded them from the casual sight of observers. But Ahriman was no casual observer, and not even the overwhelming light of the Emperor could completely obscure the titanic forces lurking beneath the falsehoods.

Ahriman turned his attention from the hidden viewers as Sanguinius and Fulgrim reached a raised plinth before the dais. Its only furniture was a simple wooden lectern such as a conductor of an orchestra might use to rest his sheet music upon. Magnus and Ahriman halted before the plinth, and the nine warriors of the Sekhmet stood sentinel with their masters

The Blood Angels and Emperor's Children dropped to their knees before the Emperor, and the Thousand Sons followed suit. Ahriman saw the dread of this moment in his dark eyes reflected in the polished black floor.

'All hail the supreme Master of Mankind,' said Sanguinius, his soft voice filling the amphitheatre with its quiet strength. 'I present before you, Magnus the Red, Primarch of the Thousand Sons and Lord of Prospero.'

'Rise, my sons,' said a voice that could only be the Emperor's. Ahriman had not seen him speak, but a reverent silence filled the amphitheatre, an utter absence of sound that seemed impossible with so many thousands gathered here.

Ahriman rose to his feet as Malcador the Sigillite descended the steps of the dais, bearing an eagle-topped sceptre that Ahriman recognised as belonging to the Emperor. It dwarfed the man, but Malcador appeared not to notice its bulk. Instead, he carried it as lightly as a walking cane. A pair of acolytes followed the Sigillite, one bearing rolled parchments, the other a smoking brazier in blackened iron tongs.

Malcador crossed the gleaming floor of the amphitheatre and stood before the three primarchs. The Sigillite's white hair pooled around his shoulders like snowfall and his skin was the texture of old parchment. He was just a man, yet had lived out the spans of many men. Some put this down to the finest and most subtle augmetics or a rigorous regime of juvenat treatment, but Ahriman knew of no means that could sustain a mortal life for so long.

Malcador had the wisdom of aeons in his dark, deep-set eyes, wisdom won over the passage of centuries spent at the side of the greatest practitioner of the arts in the galaxy. *That* was how Malcador endured, not through cheap tricks or the artifice of technological trinkets, but by the Emperor's design.

He held the staff up before Magnus, Fulgrim and Sanguinius, and Ahriman saw that his hands were thin, bony and frail. How easy it would be to break them.

'Fulgrim, Magnus, Sanguinius,' said Malcador with what Ahriman felt was woefully misplaced familiarity. 'I'd like you all to place your right hand upon the staff, if you please.'

All three primarchs did so, sinking to their knees so their heads were level with Malcador's. The venerable sage smiled before continuing.

'Do you all swear that you shall do honour to your father? In sight of those assembled here on Nikaea, will you solemnly swear that you will speak the truth as it is known to you? Will you do glory to your Legions and to your brothers by accepting the judgement this august body shall reach? Do you swear this upon the staff of the father who sired you, schooled you and watches over you in this hour of upheaval and change?'

Ahriman listened to the core of the Sigillite's words, seeing past the fine homilies and noble ideals to the truth beneath. This was no simple Oath of the Moment; this was an oath sworn by a defendant on trial for his life.

'Upon this staff I swear it,' intoned Fulgrim.

'By the blood in my veins I swear it,' said Sanguinius.

'I swear to uphold all that has been said upon this staff,' said Magnus.

'Let it be so recorded,' replied Malcador with a stiff formality that went against his normally affable demeanour. His acolytes stepped in towards the kneeling primarchs, the first unrolling a slender parchment with the words Malcador had said written upon them. He held it pressed flat to Magnus's vambrace while the second ladled a blob of hot wax from his brazier and poured it onto the parchment. This was then embossed with an iron stamp bearing the eagle and crossed lightning bolts seal of the Emperor. The servitors repeated this with Fulgrim and Sanguinius, and when they were done they retreated behind Malcador.

'There,' said the Sigillite. 'Now we can begin.'

HOODED ADEPTS LED the Thousand Sons to the box on the lower tiers of the amphitheatre above where they had entered. Magnus and his warriors took their places within the box as Fulgrim and Sanguinius were led to their seats. Excited conversation began once more.

Ahriman found himself drawn inexorably to the Emperor. High in the Enumerations, he was freed from the impact of emotion, and found he could see the Master of Mankind clearly, reading the reluctance etched into his regal features.

'He doesn't want this,' said Ahriman.

'No,' agreed Magnus. 'Others have clamoured for this, and the Emperor has no choice but to appease his supporters.'

'Clamoured for what?' asked Ahriman. 'Do you know what is going on?'

'Not entirely,' hedged Magnus. 'As soon as I heard Fulgrim's voice, I knew something was amiss, but the heart of it eludes me.'

As he spoke, Magnus tapped his thigh, making a series of apparently innocuous movements with his fingers, as though he were loosening stiff joints. Ahriman recognised them as the somatic gestures of the Symbol of Thothmes, the means by which a sanctum could be made secure from observation. It was also a symbol for silence in the presence of the enemy.

Beside the primarch, Mahavastu Kallimakus faithfully recorded their words, his eyes fixed ahead without really seeing what was going on. Only a man completely under the sway of another could be so unaffected by the grand company assembled beneath the stars.

'In any case,' said Magnus, 'I believe we are about to learn the nature of this gathering.'

Ahriman looked back to the floor of the amphitheatre, seeing Malcador standing at the plinth with a sheaf of notes spread on the lectern before him. He cleared his throat, the acoustics of the volcano's crater amplifying the sound until even those ensconced at the back of the amphitheatre could hear him clearly.

'My friends, we gather here on the birthing rock of Nikaea to speak on a subject that has vexed the Imperium since its inception. Many of you here today have come not knowing the substance of this conclave or the nature of this debate. Others know it all too well. For that I apologise.'

Malcador consulted his notes once more, squinting as though having trouble reading his own handwriting.

'And now to the heart of the matter,' said Malcador. 'This gathering will address the question of sorcery in the Imperium. Yes, gentlemen, we are here to resolve the Librarian Crisis.'

A gasp of astonishment rippled from the tiers of the amphitheatre, though Ahriman had guessed what the substance of Malcador's words would be as soon as he mounted the plinth.

'This is an issue that has divided us for many years, but here we will end that division. Some will maintain that sorcery is the greatest threat facing our dominion of the galaxy, while others will rail against what is said here, believing that fear and ignorance drives their accusers' hands.

'Let me assure you all that there is no greater crisis facing the Imperium, and the heroic undertaking upon which we are all embarked is too vital to risk with discord.'

Malcador drew himself up to his full height and said. 'That being said, who among you shall speak first?'

A gruff voice cut through the chatter from the tiers.

'I shall speak,' it said.

Undulant light in the box opposite the Thousand Sons rippled as a powerful figure threw off his false-hood. The warrior's beard was waxed, and he wore a snarling wolf's head across his shaved scalp. The skin of its forelegs was draped over his barrel chest and its pelt formed a ragged cloak.

Armoured in stormcloud grey and bearing his eagle-headed staff across one shoulder, Ohthere Wyrdmake, Rune Priest of the Space Wolves, stepped down into the amphitheatre.

CHAPTER NINETEEN

Witch Hunters/The Heart of a Primarch/
Magnus Speaks

THE LIBRARIAN CRISIS: like a guilty secret, it lurked behind the veneer of Unity, a dull ache that the body of the Imperium had tried to forget, like a frightened man ignoring a pain in his belly for fear of what might come to light under the glare of examination. Librarians had first been introduced to the Legions when Magnus, Sanguinius and Jaghatai Khan had proposed a regime of psychic training and development that went hand in hand with the already rigorous creation process of an Astartes warrior.

The Emperor had sanctioned these first experiments as a means of directing and controlling the power of emerging psykers within the Astartes, and Librarius departments were formed within the Thousand Sons, Blood Angels and White Scars to train them. The Librarians they had crafted had proven to be loyal warriors and potent weapons in the Legion's arsenal. Such was the success of these early experiments that Magnus pushed for his program to be expanded, allowing other Legions to benefit from his research.

With the success of the early experiments, many primarchs came to see the usefulness of Librarians, and allowed warrior-scholars from the Thousand Sons to form Librarius departments within their ranks. Not all the primarchs saw this as a good thing, and from the earliest days of its inception, the Librarian program was beset by controversy.

Psychic powers came with dark heritage, for the Great Crusade was rebuilding the lost empire of humanity from the wreckage left after Old Night, a cataclysm brought about, it was claimed, by the uncontrolled emergence of psykers all across the galaxy. As much as Magnus and his compatriots vouchsafed the integrity of the Librarians, they would always bear the stigma of those who had brought humanity to the edge of extinction.

Though there had been squabbles and division over the employment of Librarians, those divisions had been manageable and without real weight. The Thousand Sons heard the accusations levelled at them and stoically ignored them, content that they acted with the Emperor's blessing.

Like an untreated wound, those divisions had festered and spread, threatening to become a rift that would never be sealed. And so, with Horus Lupercal anointed the Warmaster and his retreat to Terra imminent, the Emperor chose this moment to heal that rift and bring his sons together as one.

History would recall this assembly as the Council of Nikaea.

Others would know it as the trial of Magnus the Red.

OHTHERE WYRDMAKE CROSSED the amphitheatre and stepped onto the plinth before the Emperor's dais. Ahriman willed Wyrdmake to see him, to feel the full weight of his treachery.

'I trusted him,' said Ahriman, bunching his fists. 'He was just using me to betray us. All along, it was a lie.'

His anger fled as another thought intruded.

'Oh Throne!' he exclaimed. 'The things I told him. Our ways and our powers. This is all my fault.'

'Calm yourself, Ahzek,' cautioned Magnus. 'Do nothing to prove him right. In any case, it was I who urged you to place your trust in Wyrdmake. If this travesty of a conclave is anyone's fault it is mine for not giving credence to the strength of my doubters.'

Ahriman forced himself back into the higher spheres, focusing on those that enhanced clarity and speed of thought. He kept away from those of empathy and strength.

Wyrdmake lifted his wolf-helmed head to face the glares of the Thousand Sons, his lined face pulled into a scowl of primal loathing. Such was its venom, Ahriman wondered how he could not have seen so brutal and violent a core to the Rune Priest. He had always known the Space Wolves were a butcher's blade of a Legion, powerful and unsubtle, but to see that so clearly defined on one man's face was still a shock.

'I will not waste time with fancy words,' said Wyrdmake. 'I am called Ohthere Wyrdmake of the Space Wolves, and I fought in the murder-make with the Thousand Sons on Shrike. I stood alongside its warriors on the baked salt flats of Aghoru, and I name them a coven of warlocks, every one of them a star-cunning sorcerer and conjurer of unclean magic. That is all I have to say, and I swear its truth upon my oath as a warrior of Leman Russ.'

Ahriman was astonished at the archaic wording of the accusation. Was this the forgotten ages, when men were ruled by superstition and fear of the dark? He cast around the amphitheatre, horrified at the sagely nodding heads and expressions of outrage directed their way.

Malcador stood at the edge of the dais and rapped his staff on its marble floor. All eyes turned upon him.

'You level a terrible accusation upon your brother Legion, Ohthere Wyrdmake,' said Malcador. 'Are there any who substantiate your claims?'

'Aye, Sigillite, there are,' replied Wyrdmake.

'Who stands with this accusation?' called Malcador.

'I do,' said Mortarion, emerging from beneath a false-hood and revealing his identity to the onlookers. As Ohthere Wyrdmake returned to his seat, Mortarion walked to the centre of the amphitheatre. Whether by coincidence or design, the Death Lord took exactly twenty-eight paces from the podium, and Ahriman again saw the recurrence of the number seven. Mortar-ion was clad exactly as he had been on Ullanor, as though he had been waiting for this moment since then.

Before Mortarion could speak, Magnus rose to his feet and slammed his hand down on the obsidian coping before him.

'Is this what passes for due process?' demanded Mag-nus. 'Am I to be tried by faceless observers who hide behind their falsehoods. If any man dares accuse me, let him speak to my face.'

Malcador rapped his staff once more and said, 'The Emperor has commanded it, Magnus. No man's testi-mony is to be corrupted by fear of whose eyes are upon him.'

'It is all too easy to hide behind cloaks of anonymity and cast your venom. Far harder to look the object of your wrath in the eye while you do it.'

'You will have your chance to speak, Magnus. No deci-sion will be made until all those who wish to speak have done so. I promise you,' said Malcador, adding. 'Your father promises you.'

Magnus shook his head as he returned to his seat, his anger still simmering.

Mortarion had not moved during Magnus's outburst, as though his brother primarch's outrage was an inconsequential thing, something to be endured for the brief annoyance it caused. Ahriman dearly wished he could summon Aaetpio, but sensed the ensuing conflagration would be akin to letting a Pyrae Zealator loose in a promethium-soaked warehouse.

Mortarion bowed curtly to the Emperor and began his oration.

'Brother Malcador claims that his issue has vexed the Imperium,' said Mortarion, his rustle-soft tones like the dry hiss of wind over aeons old sand dunes, 'but he is wrong to believe there is anything complex about the issue. I have seen the devastation that unchecked sorcery leaves in its wake, worlds burned to cinders, populations enslaved and monsters unleashed. Sorcery brought these worlds to ruin, sorcery wielded by men who peered too deeply into dark places they should have known to leave well alone.

'We all know of the horror of Old Night, but I ask you this simple question: what brought about that galactic holocaust? Psykers. Uncontrolled psykers. The threat of these people is horribly real, and you all know the danger they represent. Some of you may even have seen it first-hand. The psy-engines and occullum of Terra search out the latent witch-genes among humanity and the Black Ships of the Silent Sisterhood trawl the stars for these dangerous individuals. Did the Emperor, beloved by all, build these machines for no reason? No, they were built to protect us from these dangerous mutants, using their powers in service of their selfish ends.

'*That* is the difference. Where an astrotelepath or Navigator uses his powers for the good of others, allowing distant worlds to communicate or guiding the Expeditionary Fleets of the Imperium across the stars, the sorcerer uses his power for personal gain, for earthly power and dominance.

'Yes, the Imperium needs certain empowered individuals, but only those sanctioned and rigidly controlled. We know where power unchecked inevitably leads. You have all heard the stories of Old Night, but who among you has really seen what that means?'

Mortarion swung his manreaper, the deathly haft finally coming to rest upon his shoulder.

'The Death Guard have seen,' said Mortarion, and Ahriman wanted to laugh at his absurd theatrics. Though Mortarion played the role of the outraged righteous man, he was relishing his part in what he saw as the downfall of the Thousand Sons.

'On Kajor my Legion encountered a warrior race of humans that had fallen to barbarism. Extensive orbital surveys detected no trace of advanced technology, yet it took my Legion nearly six months to bring Kajor to submission. Why? They were savages, armed with little more than blades and crude flintlock carbines. How could such a feral race of savages hold the Death Guard at bay for so long?'

Mortarion paced as he spoke, the haft of the manreaper marking time to his steps with a solid *tunk* every step he took. 'They held us at bay because they had fell powers and unseen allies. Every night, creatures of witchery hunted in the shadows and killed for the joy of killing. Blood red hounds stalked the darkness of the forests with savage instinct, and juggernauts of thunder broke our lines with every charge.'

The Death Lord paused a moment to let that last fact sink in. That anything could sunder a Death Guard formation was nothing short of a miracle. Though his desert wheeze was faint, no word of his narration escaped the attention of those gathered in the amphitheatre.

'My warriors have fought xenos species of every stripe and defeated them, but these were not creatures of flesh and blood. These were summoned into life by Kajori warlocks. These magi conjured lightning from their flesh, set fires with their thoughts and cracked the very earth with their shouted oaths! No power comes without a price, and with every victory we won, we discovered what that truly meant. At the heart of every city we captured, my warriors found vast structures we came to know as Blood Fanes. Each one was a charnel house of bones and death. We destroyed every one, and with each one lost, the strength of our foes waned. In the end, we ground down every ragamuffin force they sent against us. Surrender was not in their blood and they died to a man, destroyed by a ruling caste of warlocks who could not bear to relinquish their power. I still think of Kajor and shudder.'

Mortarion finished his tale in front of the Thousand Sons, the last syllable leaving his lips as he looked up at Magnus.

'Now I do not accuse my brother of such barbarism, but no evil begins with such monstrous acts. If it did, no sane man would ever consider it. No, it begins slowly, a small step here, a small step there. By such acts is a man's heart turned black and rotten. A man may begin with noble intentions, believing that such small trespasses are minor things compared to the good he will do at the end of his course, but every act matters, from the smallest to the greatest.

'Tales of the Thousand Sons' victories are legion, but so too are the whispers of their sorceries. In the past I have led my warriors into battle alongside those of Magnus and am well aware of what his Legion can do, so I can vouch for the truth of what Ohthere Wyrdmake says. It is sorcery. I have seen it with my own eyes. Like the magi of Kajor, the cult warriors of Magnus conjure lightning and fire to smite their foes, while their brethren crush their enemies with invisible force. I do not lie when I say that I knew fear that day, the fear that I had broken one army of warlocks only to find myself with another at my side.'

'You all know I distrust the institution of Librarians within the ranks of the Astartes, fearing for what the Thousand Sons are trying to seed within our Legions. No Librarians sully the ranks of the Death Guard, and nor will they while I draw breath. I have held my tongue until now, confident that others wiser than I knew best, but I can keep silent no longer. When Brother Russ and Brother Lorgar spoke of the battles fought to subdue the Ark Reach Cluster, I found myself compelled to break my bonds of silence, though it tears my heart to name my own brother a warlock. I cannot stand by and watch his obsessions drive him and his Legion into the abyss of damnation. Know that I speak not out of hatred, but out of the love I have for Magnus. This is all I have to say.'

Mortarion turned and bowed once more to the Emperor before returning to the box he shared with other warriors of his Legion.

Ahriman turned to Magnus, as he heard the high, sharp crack of glass. The heat of Magnus's anger was radiating from his body. The primarch's fists were balled on the obsidian coping, and Ahriman saw the volcanic stone had softened and run like the wax of an invocation candle. Blobs of what had once been glassy rock dropped to the floor where they shattered as their customary atomic structure reasserted its reality.

'My lord?' hissed Ahriman, all thought of Enumerations forgotten as a hot rush of imparted fury passed between them with a flash of psychic osmosis. He reached out to Magnus, his fingertips lightly brushing his primarch's arm.

Magnus felt his touch and turned his gaze upon him. Ahriman recoiled from the depthless pit of his eye, the entire structure of it a wheeling lattice of unknown colours, as though every facet of emotion fought for dominance. Ahriman's heart lurched at the anger and need for vindication he saw there, a furious battle between raging instinct and higher intellect. He saw Magnus's desire to lash out at his attackers, the animal heart that cursed his brother for his limited understanding. Holding that back was the towering intellect that held court over his base emotions, a mind that had looked deep into the warp and seen it looking back at him.

In that moment of connection, Ahriman looked into the core of his primarch's incandescent form, the incredible fusion of genius and chained aether bound in the creation of his incredible mind and body. To see the white-hot furnace of so mighty a being's innermost construction was to stare into the heart of a newly-birthed star.

Ahriman cried out as he saw Magnus's life unfold in the space of what could have been an instant or could have been a span of aeons. He saw discourses between luminous minds in a cavern far beneath the earth, and a wondrous figure descending to Prospero atop a golden mountain range. All this and more poured into Ahriman without heed that his mind was vastly incapable of absorbing such enormous quantities of memory and knowledge.

He comprehended only a fraction of what he saw, but it was enough to press him back into his seat. Breath laboured in his chest and the awful rush of information pouring into him threatened to unseat his reason.

'Stop,' begged Ahriman as more knowledge than had been won by entire civilisations thundered into his mind, squeezing his genhanced faculties to the limits of their endurance. His vision greyed, and blood vessels haemorrhaged in his eyes. His hands trembled, and he felt the onset of a violent grand mal seizure, one that would almost certainly kill him.

Magnus closed his eye, and the raging torrent ceased.

Ahriman gasped as the flood abated, and a drawn out moan escaped his lips. Dread knowledge and buried secrets surged within him, each one a lethally volatile revelation.

He fell from the bench as his overloaded consciousness shut down in an attempt to rebuild the shattered architecture of his mind.

WHEN HE OPENED his eyes, he was lying on one of the padded couches in the vaulted antechamber beneath the amphitheatre. The pain had diminished, but his head felt as though it was encased in an ever-shrinking helmet of invisible steel. Light made his head hurt, and he raised a hand to shield his face. His mouth was dry and a bewildering series of images danced on the periphery of his vision, like a million memories crowding for attention.

'Enter the sixth Enumeration,' said a mellifluous voice that calmed and soothed him. 'It will help you restore your thoughts.'

'What happened?' he managed, trying to focus on the owner of the voice. He knew he recognised the speaker, but so many names and faces crowded his mind that he could not sort through them. 'I don't remember.'

'It's my fault, my son,' said the voice, and Ahriman was finally able to perceive the figure kneeling beside him. 'And I am truly sorry.'

'My lord Magnus?' he asked.

'In the flesh, my son,' said Magnus, helping him sit up.

Bright lights pounded behind his eyes and he groaned, feeling like his brain was trying to press its way out of his skull. The Sekhmet were assembled in the chamber, some drinking from silver goblets, others guarding the doors.

'You had quite a shock to the system,' said Magnus. 'I allowed my anger to get the better of me and let the walls enclosing my essence fall. No one mortal, not even an Astartes, should drink from that well. You'll have a monstrously sore head, but you will live.'

'I do not understand,' said Ahriman, pressing his palms to his temples.

'Knowledge is like strong liquor, my son,' said Magnus with a smile. 'To imbibe too much, too fast, will get you drunk.'

'I have never been drunk. I don't think it's possible for me.'

'It's not, not really,' said Magnus, handing him a goblet of cool water, 'at least not on alcohol. How much do you remember about what happened?'

'Not much,' admitted Ahriman, draining the goblet in a single swallow.

'That's probably for the best,' said Magnus, and Ahriman was not so far removed from his senses that he didn't catch the relief in his primarch's voice.

'I remember the Death Lord,' said Ahriman, 'chastising us and twisting facts to suit his accusations, but after that, nothing.'

A sudden thought occurred, and he asked, 'How long have I been unconscious?'

'Just over three hours, which was probably a blessing.'

'How so?'

'You were spared the tedious parade of close-minded bigots, superstitious fools and throwbacks naming us heretics, sorcerers, blood-mages and sacrificers of virgins. Wyrdmake and Mortarion have assembled quite a coven of witch hunters to condemn us.'

Ahriman rose to his feet, his legs unsteady beneath him as the room spun around him. His enhanced physiology fought to compensate, but it was a losing battle. He would have fallen but for Magnus's steadying hand. He forced the dizziness down and took a cleansing breath.

Ahriman shook his head. 'I feel like I have been stepped on by *Canis Vertex*.'

'You would,' said Magnus, 'but you'll want to recover your wits quickly, my son.'

'Why, what is happening?'

'Our accusers have said their piece,' said Magnus with relish, 'and now it's my turn.'

EXPECTANT SILENCE FILLED the amphitheatre as Magnus strode towards the plinth. He walked with his head held high and his feathered cloak trailing behind him, looking straight at the Emperor's dais. This was no walk of the accused, but the stride of the righteous man fighting against unjust accusers.

Ahriman had never been prouder to be one of his Thousand Sons.

Magnus bowed to the Emperor and Malcador then turned to give Fulgrim and Sanguinius bows of comradeship. In a move that spoke of grace in the face of adversity, he also gave Mortarion and Ohthere Wyrdmake courteous acknowledgements. Magnus was every inch the gentleman polymath who never forgot himself, even as his enemies united against him. He mounted the plinth and rested his hands on the wooden lectern.

He paused, sweeping his gaze around the assembled men and women, favouring them all with his attention.

'The fearful and unbelieving, the abominable and the murderers, the whoremongers and sorcerers, idolaters and all liars, shall have their part in the lake which burneth with fire and brimstone,' said Magnus, as though reading from a text. 'Those words are from a book written thousands of years ago in the forgotten ages, ironically from a passage named *Revelations*. This is what people thought in those barbaric times. It shows what savagery we came from, and how easy it is for our species to turn upon one another. These words of fear sent thousands to their death over the millennia, and for what? To salve the fears of ignorant men who had not the wit to embrace the power of new ideas.'

Magnus stepped from the plinth, circling the amphitheatre like a lecturing iterator. Where Mortarion had hectored the assembly with venom, Magnus spoke as though every member of the assembly, from the lowliest adept to the Emperor himself, were old friends gathered for a good-natured debate.

'If one of us were to walk among the people of those times, they would kill us for the technology we possess, thinking it witchcraft or unclean devilment. For example, before the writings of Aristarchus of Samos, men believed that Old Earth was flat, an unbroken plain where the oceans simply fell from the edges. Can you imagine anything more ridiculous? Now we take the sphericity of planets for granted. Much later, priestly scholars taught that Terra was the centre of the cosmos, and that the sun and planets revolved around it. The man who challenged this geocentric foolishness was tried for heresy, and forced to recant his beliefs. Now we know our place in the galaxy.'

Magnus paused before Mortarion, meeting the hostile glare of the Death Lord with one of quiet amusement.

'From the deepest desire often comes the deadliest hatred,' he said, 'and false words are not only evil in themselves, but they infect the hearts of all who hear them with evil. Imagine what we will know in a thousand years and think, really *think*, what we are doing here.'

Magnus turned from Mortarion and walked to the centre of the amphitheatre, lifting his hands out to his sides and slowly turning on the spot as he spoke.

'Imagine the Imperium of the future, a golden utopia of enlightenment and progress, where the scientist and the philosopher are equal partners with the warrior in crafting a bounteous future. Now imagine the people of that glorious age looking back through the mists of time to this moment. Think what they will know and what they would make of this travesty. They would weep to know how close the flame of enlightenment had come to being snuffed out. The art and science of questioning everything is the source of all knowledge, and to abandon that will doom us to slow decay, an Imperium of darkness and ignorance, where those who dare to pursue knowledge, whatever the cost to themselves, are regarded with suspicion. That is not the Imperium I believe in. That is not the Imperium I wish to be part of.

'Knowledge is the food of the soul, and no knowledge can be thought of as wrong, so long as each seeker after truth is master of what he learns. Nothing worth knowing can be taught, it must be learned with the blood and sweat of experience, and there are no greater scholars of that ilk than the Thousand Sons. Even as we fight in the forefront of the Emperor's Crusade we study the things others ignore, questing for knowledge in the places others fear to tread. There are no truths unknown, no secrets too hidden and no paths too labyrinthine for us to follow, for they lead us upwards to enlightenment.

'Hard-won knowledge is of no value unless it is put into practice. Knowing is not enough; we must apply. Willing is not enough; we must *do*!'

Magnus smiled, and Ahriman saw he had won over great swathes watching him.

'With that in mind, I beg your indulgence a little longer,' said Magnus, 'and a tale I will thee tell.'

'THERE IS AN ancient legend of Old Earth that speaks of three men of Aegina, who lived in a cave deep in the mountains,' said Magnus, with the warmth of a natural storyteller. Though he had heard this story before, Ahriman found himself captivated by Magnus's voice, the natural charisma that loaded every commanding word.

'These men lived shut off from the light of the world and they would have lived in permanent darkness but for a small fire that burned in a circle of stones at the heart of the cave. They ate lichen that grew on the walls and drank cold water from an underground stream. They lived, but what they had was not living.

'Day after day, they sat around the fire, staring into the flickering embers and dancing flames, believing that its light was all the light in the world. The shadows made shapes and patterns on the walls, and this delighted them greatly. In their own way they were happy, moving from day to day without ever wondering what lay beyond their flickering circle of light.'

Magnus paused in his recital, allowing the audience to imagine the scene and picture the dancing shadows on the cave walls.

'But one day a mighty storm blew over the mountains, but so deep were the men that only the merest breath of it reached their cave. The fire danced in the wind and the men laughed to see new patterns on the wall. The wind died and they went back to contemplating the fire, much as they had always done.

'But one of the men got up and walked away from the fire, which surprised the other men greatly, and they bade him return to sit with them. This lone man shook his head, for he alone had a thirst to learn more of the wind. He followed it as it retreated from the cave, climbing steep cliffs, crossing chasms and negotiating many perils before he finally saw a faint haze of light ahead of him.

'He climbed out of the cave, emerging onto the side of the mountain, and looked up at the blazing sun. Its light blinded him and he fell to his knees, overcome by its beauty and warmth. He feared he had burnt out his eyes, but in a little while his vision returned, and he hesitantly looked around him. He had come out of the cave high on the mountain's flank, and the world was spread out before him in all its glory: glittering green seas and endless fields of golden corn. He wept to see such things, distraught that he had wasted so many years in darkness, oblivious to the glory of the world around him, a world that had been there all along, but which his limited vision had denied him.'

The primarch stopped, looking up to the stars, and his rapt audience followed his gaze, as though picturing the blazing sun of his story.

'Can you imagine what it felt like?' asked Magnus, his voice wracked with emotion. 'To have spent your entire life staring at a small fire and thinking it was the only light in the world, only to be then confronted by the sun? The man knew he had to tell his friends of this miraculous discovery and he made the journey back to the cave where the other men sat, still staring into the fire and smiling vacuously at the shadows on the wall. The man who had seen the sun looked at the place he had called home and saw it for the prison it truly was. He told the others what he had seen, but they were not interested in far-fetched tales of a burning eye in the sky – all they wanted to do was live their lives as they had always lived them. They called him mad and laughed at him, continuing to stare at the fire, as it was the only reality they knew.'

Ahriman had first heard this story as a Philosophus in the Corvidae Temple when Magnus had mentored him prior to facing the Dominus Liminus. He heard the same note of bitterness in the primarch's voice that he had heard then, a precisely modulated pitch that conveyed the proper measure of anguish and frustration at the blindness of the men in the cave. How, Magnus's tone said, could anyone turn away from such light once they knew of its existence?

'The man could not understand his friends' reluctance to travel to the world above,' continued Magnus, 'but he resolved that he would not take their refusal to come with him as an end to the matter. He would *show* them the light, no matter what, and if they would not come to the light, then he would bring it to them.

'So the man climbed back to the world of light and began to dig. He dug until he had widened the cave mouth. He dug for a hundred years, and then a hundred more, until he had dug away the top of the mountain. Then he dug downwards, a great pit in the heart of the mountain, until he broke through into the cave where his fellows sat around the fire.'

Magnus fell silent, his words trailing off, though Ahriman knew it was a theatrical pause rather than any real moment of introspection. Knowing how the story ended, Ahriman was not surprised Magnus had stopped here. In the original version of the tale, the man's friends were so terrified by what they were shown that they killed the man and retreated deeper into the cave with their fire to live their lives in perpetual twilight.

The tale was an allegorical parable on the futility of sharing fundamental truths with those with too narrow perceptions of reality. By telling it selectively, Magnus had broken his covenant with the audience, but none of them would ever know. Instead, he continued his tale with fresh words woven from his imagination.

'The men were amazed at what he showed them, the light they had been missing for all their lives and the golden joy that could be theirs were they just brave enough to take his hand and follow him. One by one, they climbed from their dark cave and saw the truth of the world around them, all its wonders and all its beauty. They looked back at the dank, lightless cave they had called home and were horrified by how limited their understanding of the world had been. They heaped praise upon the man who had shown them the way to the light, and honoured him greatly, for the world and all its bounty was theirs to explore for ever-more.'

Magnus let his new ending wash over the amphithe-atre, and no member of the Theatrica Imperialis had given so commanding a performance. A rolling wave of applause erupted from the tiers, and Magnus smiled, the perfect blend of modestly and gratitude. Sanguinius and Fulgrim were on their feet, though Mortarion and the Death Guard remained as stoic as ever.

As pitch-perfect as Magnus's delivery had been, Ahriman saw that not all of the audience were won over, though it was clear the case against Magnus and the Thousand Sons was no longer as cut and dried as his accusers had hoped.

Magnus raised his hands to quell the applause, as though abashed to be so acclaimed.

'The man knew he had to show his friends the truth of the world around them,' he said, 'and just as it was his duty to save his friends from their dull, sightless existence, it is our duty to do the same for humanity. The Thousand Sons alone of all the Legions have seen the light beyond the gates of the empyrean. That light will free us from the shackles of our mundane percep-tions of reality and allow the human race to stand as masters of the galaxy. Just as the men around the fire needed to be shown the glorious future that lay within their grasp, so too does humanity. The knowledge the Thousand Sons are gathering will allow everyone to know what we know, to see as we see. Humanity needs to be led upwards with small steps, with their eyes gradually opened lest the light blind them. That is the ultimate goal of the Thousand Sons. Our future as a race is at stake. My friends, I urge you not to throw away this chance for enlightenment, for we are at a tipping point in the history of the Imperium. Think of the future and how this moment will be judged in the millennia to come.'

Magnus bowed to the cardinal points of the amphitheatre.

'Thank you for your attention,' he said. 'That is all I have to say.'

CHAPTER TWENTY

Heresy/The Librarians/Judgement

MAGNUS POURED HIMSELF some water, smiling as he paced the reception room beneath the amphitheatre. The Sekhmet stood to attention, each one sensing that this trial would soon be over. Ahriman's head still ached and the pressure on his thoughts was making him uneasy, as though it would prove too much for his skull to contain.

With the end of Magnus's performance, Malcador had called a recess to the proceedings. What had begun in betrayal and infamy had come to triumph, for few could fail to be moved by Magnus's great oration.

'I will admit to some trepidation when the day's events became clear to me,' said Magnus, handing a goblet of water to Ahriman. 'But I feel confident I have swayed the doubters to our side. Mortarion is too fixed in stone ever to change, but Sanguinius and Fulgrim stand with us. That will count for a great deal.'

'It will, but many others are concealed behind their falsehoods. The masses are behind us, but the judgement could still go against us. I do not understand why we are even here, it is insulting!' spat Ahriman, throwing down his goblet.

'You need to calm yourself, Ahzek,' said Magnus. 'There was no choice but to call this conclave. The fearful need reassurance that their voices are being heard. You saw that the Emperor did not want this. Believe me, I feel your anger, but you must keep it in check. It will not serve us here.'

'I know, but it galls me that our fate rests in the hands of such blinkered fools!'

'Be careful,' warned Magnus, moving to stand before him. 'You will mind your words. You are as dear to me as any son, but I will not stand to hear insults upon my father's wisdom. Give in to such impulses and you will only confirm everything they say about us.'

'I apologise, my lord,' said Ahriman, trying to will himself into the lower Enumerations, but the calm of the spheres eluded him. 'I mean no disrespect, but it is hard to imagine that others cannot see what we see, and almost impossible to remember what it was like not to know the things we know.'

'The curse of assumed knowledge is a challenge all enlightened individuals face,' said Magnus, softening his tone. 'We must remember that we once walked in their shoes and were blind to the truths of the universe. Even I knew nothing of the Great Ocean until my father revealed its glory to me.'

'No,' whispered Ahriman with sudden, instinctive clarity. 'You already knew of it. When the Emperor showed you its wonders and dangers you feigned not to know, but you had already peered into its depths and seen *them*.'

Magnus was at his side in an instant, towering over him with his flesh and eye a seething crimson. Ahriman felt the searing heat of Magnus's presence, realising that he had crossed a line without knowing it even existed. In that moment, he knew he understood very little about his primarch, and wished that every scrap of knowledge that had passed between them earlier could be washed away.

'Never say that again, ever,' said Magnus, his eye boring into him like a diamond drill.

Ahriman nodded, but behind Magnus's anger was something else, a wordless fear of buried secrets returning to the light. Ahriman couldn't see it, but he saw an image of the silver oakleaf cluster he wore on his shoulder-guard.

'Ohrmuzd? Throne, what did you do?' asked Ahriman, as a memory that did not belong to him threatened to surface in his mind. He saw a dreadful bargain, a pact sealed with something older and more monstrous than anything Ahriman could ever imagine.

'I did what I had to,' snapped Magnus, forestalling any further words. 'That is all you need to know. Trust me, Ahzek, what was done was done for the right reasons.'

Ahriman wanted to believe that, he *needed* to believe it, but there was no disguising the vanity and obsession that lay behind the secret bargain. He sought to pierce the shrouds and veils of self-justification and perceive the dark secret that lay beyond, but Magnus plucked the stolen memory from his mind.

'What was it?' demanded Ahriman. 'Tell me. What are you hiding from us?'

'Nothing you need know about,' said Magnus, flushed and on the verge of... On the verge of what? Anger? Guilt?

'You have no idea,' he continued. 'You can't know what it was like. The degradation of the gene-seed was too extreme and the corruption in the damaged helices was too complex and mutating too quickly to stabilise. It was... It was...'

'It was what?' asked Ahriman when Magnus didn't continue.

'The future,' whispered Magnus, his complexion ashen. 'I see it. It's here. It's...'

Magnus never finished his sentence.

Like the mightiest tree in the forest felled by a single blow, the Primarch of the Thousand Sons dropped to his knees.

As Magnus fell, Ahriman saw a storm of amber fire raging in his eye.

Light filled his vision, fireflies that burst briefly to life and then vanished.

Magnus opened his eyes to see sparks flying as stone chipped stone, and primitive smithing tools shaped a blade of napped flint. He saw the sword take shape, the workmanship little better than that of the pre-Neanderthal civilisations of Old Earth. Yet this was no human artifice, and this craftsmanship was sophisticated and undoubtedly alien. The proportions of the blade and grip were subtly wrong, the hands that fashioned them blue black and downy with a fine comb of russet hair.

Nor was this a normal blade, it was sentient. The word didn't fit, but it was the most appropriate one Magnus could find. It was forged by alien metallurgists in ways too inhuman to be understood, imbued with the power of the fates.

It was a nemesis weapon, crafted to slay without mercy.

Magnus recoiled from the blade, horrified that an intelligent race would dare craft such a dreadful tool of destruction. What reason could there be to bring such a vile thing into being?

Was this the future or the past? It was impossible to tell with any certainty. Here in the Great Ocean (for where else could he be?) time was a meaningless framework that gave mortal lives a veneer of meaning. This was a realm of immortals, for nothing could ever really live or die here.

Energy was eternal, and as one form ended, another rose in a never-ending cycle of change.

No sooner had he considered the question of past and future than the image splintered into a million shards, spinning in the darkness like a microscopically magnified view of an exploding diamond.

Magnus had ventured deeper into the Great Ocean than anyone other than the Emperor, and he had no fear of his surroundings, only an insatiable desire to know the truth of what he was seeing. Spiteful laughter, like that of a hidden observer, wove around him with the ethereal echoes of a long-departed jester. From its resonances, a chamber resolved out of the darkness, a fire-blackened place of reeking evil and blood.

Arterial spray looped over the walls, and patterns of acrid quicklime on the floor stung his nostrils. Figures moved in the darkness, ghostly and too faint to make out. Magnus reached out to a figure garbed in armour the colour of quarried stone, but the vision faded before he could see more than the tattoos covering the warrior's scalp.

His odyssey continued, and Magnus allowed himself to be borne upon the rolling tides of the Great Ocean. Briefly, he wondered what had become of his corporeal body, for he knew he had not deliberately loosed his body of light from his flesh. That this had come upon him without warning was unusual, but fear would only make any phantom hazards more tangible.

He saw worlds on fire, worlds wracked with endless battles and entire systems ablaze with the plague of war. This was a vision of things that could never be, for these worlds were battlegrounds of Astartes, slaughterhouses where brother warriors who had marched from Terra to the edges of known space tore at each other with blades and fists. As distasteful as such visions were, Magnus did not let them affect him. The Great Ocean was a place where anything was possible and its capricious tides ever sought to unseat a traveller's equilibrium.

The abominable stench of the charnel house rose in an overpowering wave, a potent cocktail of rotting organic matter and escaping corpse gasses. Magnus felt his gaze drawn to a forsaken world, a world once verdant and fecund, but which had fallen to disease and corruption. He saw it had not gone without a fight, its landscape bearing the scars of the war waged to subdue it. The battle had been fought on the microscopic level, the armies of bacteria and virus numbering in their trillions.

Every living thing on this world was now a factory for disease, where aggressive microbes bent their mindless wills towards reproduction and spreading their infection further.

The planet's ending had never been in doubt, but it could no more surrender to its fate than the corruption could stop its destructive assault. It had become a world of stagnation, its marshes and forests turgid oceans of filth and oozing pestilence.

Magnus saw a rearing mass of metal in the heart of a swamp, the rusted hulk of a starship that rose like an iron cliff or an ocean-going vessel sinking to its doom. Putrescent things made their homes in its rusted superstructure, and something monstrous made its lair in its dead heart. Magnus had no clue what that might be, but saw the glitter sheen of metal and knew that the nemesis blade of the alien craftsman had found its way here.

The thought filled Magnus with panic as he heard the roar of gunfire and saw a host of marching warriors in the livery of the Luna Wolves fighting towards the crashed starship. He shouted and screamed at them, seeing his brother at the forefront of his warriors. Horus Lupercal was oblivious to him, for this was not reality, merely a fleeting glimpse of a future that might never come to pass.

The chronology of events fractured, like individual frames of a picter stitched together at random: a friend cast aside and now a bitter foe; a throne room or a command bridge; a beloved son cut down by a traitor's sword, and the steeldust shimmer of a blade that would strike the blow to change the universe; a beloved father cut down by a rebellious son.

He saw a towering temple, a giant octagonal building with eight fire-topped towers surrounding the dome at its centre. Multitudes gathered before this house of false gods, and warriors in the ceramite plates of Astartes gathered before a mighty bronze gateway. A wide pool glistened like oil and two warriors argued at its side as the crescent reflection of the new moon wavered in the water.

Booming laughter broke the scene apart, and Magnus saw Horus Lupercal once more, a titanic figure of awesome potency. Yet this was not his brother, this was a monster, a primal force of destruction that sought to put the great works of his father to the flame. With every sweep of Horus's clawed hand worlds died, consumed in the flames of war that spread across the face of the galaxy like a rapacious infection. An insane conductor weaving a symphony of destruction, Horus systematically reduced the Imperium to cinders, turning brother upon brother as they bled in the carnage.

Magnus peered into the thing that wore Horus's face, but saw nothing of his brother's nobility or regal bearing, only hatred, spite and regret. The thing's gaze met the twin orbs of Magnus with malicious glee, and Magnus saw that Horus's eyes were amber pits of fire.

'How does it feel, brother?' asked Horus. 'To look upon the world as you once did?'

'As it always does, Horus,' replied Magnus. 'Here I am as I will myself to be.'

'Ah, vanity,' said Horus, 'the simplest temptation to set.'

'What are you?' demanded Magnus. 'You are not my brother.'

'Not yet, but soon,' answered the monster with a maddening grin. 'The new moon waits on Khenty-irty to begin his transformation into Mekhenty-er-irty.'

'More riddles?' said Magnus. 'You are nothing more than a void predator, a collection of base impulses and desire given form. And I have heard that name before.'

'But you don't know what it means.'

'I will,' said Magnus. 'No knowledge is hidden from me.'

'Is that what you think?'

'Yes. My brother would never unleash this madness.'

'Then you don't know him, for it is happening right now. The pawns of the Primordial Annihilator are already in motion, setting the traps of pride, vanity and anger to ensnare the egos of the knights required to topple the king.'

'You lie.'

'Do I?' laughed Horus. 'Why would I attempt to deceive you, brother? You are Magnus of the Thousand Sons. There are no truths unknown to you, no knowledge hidden from you. Isn't that what you said? You can see the truth of this, I know you can. Horus Lupercal will betray you all. He will set the Imperium ablaze in his quest for power. Nothing will survive; all will become a nuclear cauldron of Chaos, from the supermassive heart of the galaxy to the guttering stars in its halo.'

'Where will this miraculous transformation take place?' asked Magnus, fighting to keep the growing horror from his voice.

'On a little moon,' giggled the monster, 'in the Davin system.'

'Even if I believe you, why tell me?'

'Because it has already begun, because I enjoy your torment, and because it is too late to stop this,' said Horus.

'We'll see about that,' promised Magnus.

HE OPENED HIS eye, and the Horus monster was gone.

Ahriman and the Sekhmet surrounded him, their faces filled with dread.

'My lord?' cried Ahriman. 'What happened?'

His hand flashed to his face, where the sacrifice he had made so long ago had once sat. The skin was smooth and unblemished with no lingering trace of the completeness his body of light enjoyed in the Great Ocean.

Magnus shrugged off the Sekhmets' help and climbed to his feet. He could already feel the sands of time moving across the face of the galaxy, and had a brief flash of a chiming bronze timepiece with a cracked glass face and mother of pearl hands.

'We need to go,' he said, reacquainting himself with his surroundings by focusing on the trails of spilled water.

'Go?' asked Ahriman. 'Go where?'

'We must return to Prospero. There is much to do and precious little time.'

'My lord, we cannot,' said Ahriman.

'Cannot?' thundered Magnus. 'Not a word you should use in reference to me, Ahzek. I am Magnus the Red. Nothing is beyond my powers.'

Ahriman shook his head and said, 'That is not what I mean, my lord. We are summoned back to the amphitheatre. We are called to judgement.'

THE STARS HAD moved on, though sulphurous clouds obscured many of them. Ahriman had the powerful sense of their shame, as though they wished to turn their faces from events below. Ever since Magnus had fallen, Ahriman had sought to recover the memory that lurked just on the edge of his consciousness.

Try as he might, it would not come, and though he knew trying to force it would only cause it to recede, his need to know was greater than his capacity for reasoned thought. Whatever Magnus had done involved his twin brother, but the truth was locked in the deepest well of buried memory.

A sombre mood had fallen upon the thousands gathered within the crater of the volcano, in stark contrast to the ebullience that had filled it as Magnus had spoken.

'Why do I feel like I have already been condemned?' asked Magnus, looking over at the dais at the opposite end of the amphitheatre, where Malcador conversed with the Emperor.

'Maybe we have,' answered Ahriman, seeing Mortarion's look of triumphant vindication. Sanguinius had ashen tears painted on his cheeks, and Fulgrim could not look at them, his sculpted features tormented with guilt.

'I care not anymore,' hissed Magnus. 'Let us be done with this and begone.'

The atmosphere hung on a knife edge, like a bubble stretched to the point where its surface tension could no longer maintain its integrity. Not a single voice could be heard, only the rustle of hessian robes and bated breath.

That silence was broken when Malcador stood and moved to the front of the Emperor's dais, rapping his staff three times upon the marble.

'Friends, this council is almost at an end,' he began. 'We have heard learned discourse from both sides of the divide, but the time has come to pronounce judgement and restore our harmony. With great solemnity has this matter been weighed, for it is an issue that could tear us asunder if we are not united. I ask now, would any here gathered add their voices to what we have already heard? Speak now or forever keep your counsel.'

Ahriman scanned the crowd, hoping either Sanguinius or Fulgrim or some as yet unrevealed ally might emerge from beneath a falsehood to stand with them. No one moved, and he had all but given up hope of salvation when he saw a power-armoured individual bearing a long, skull-topped staff rise from his seat in the high tiers.

'I, Targutai Yesugei, of the Borjigin Qongqotan clan would speak,' said the warrior, his voice gruff and heavily accented with the distinctive final obstruent devoicing and vowel shortening of a native Chogorian.

Targutai Yesugei's armour was winter white and trimmed with crimson, the shoulder-guard bearing the golden lightning bolt of the White Scars. His staff marked him out as a one of the Khan's Librarians. His scalp was shaven, save for a long scalp lock worn like a topknot, and a crystalline hood rose from the shoulders of his armour, framing a tanned, weather-beaten face crisscrossed with ritual scars.

At a nod from Malcador, Yesugei made his way to the floor of the amphitheatre, walking with the calm dignity of the noble savage.

Nor was he alone.

From scattered positions all around the amphitheatre, robed Astartes Librarians made their way to join the White Scar warrior, and Ahriman's heart leapt as he saw the heraldry of the Dark Angels, the Night Lords, Ultramarines and Salamanders.

The twelve Librarians congregated before the Emperor's dais, and Ahriman instantly knew that none of these warriors had ever met, just as he knew that their choosing to speak at this moment had not been planned.

'Twelve of them standing before their king,' said Magnus with a soft smile. 'How apt. As all the ancient gods were attended by twelve knights, so too are we.'

The Librarians knelt before the Emperor, their heads bowed, and Ahriman studied the symbols stitched on their surplices.

'Elikas, Zharost, Promus, Umojen,' said Ahriman, 'these men are the chief Librarians of their Legions.'

'And they side with us,' said Magnus in wonder.

Targutai Yesugei rose to his feet, and the Emperor gave a brief nod that spoke volumes.

The warrior of the White Scars mounted the plinth, and Ahriman was impressed by the solemnity he saw in Yesugei's eyes, a profound wisdom won through centuries of study and hard-fought battles.

'I am White Scar, Stormseer of Jaghatai Khan,' he said, 'and I speak with truth as my guide. This I swear on honour of my clan, may my brothers cut out my heart if I lie. I listen to words said by honourable men, but I not see as they see. They look with eyes blind to world around them. They understand with minds not willing to see truth of this galaxy.

'The warrior chosen by Stormseers is not evil, and nor is power he wields. He is weapon, like Land Raider and bolt gun. What fool casts aside weapon before battle? Like all weapons, it is dangerous without much training, and all here know danger of rogue psyker; Lord Mortarion tell us of it. But what is more danger, a trained warrior who understand his powers or a warrior with power who knows nothing of its use? Like all things, power must be yoked to its true purpose before it can be unleashed. The psyker must be moulded by men of great skill as a sword is crafted by forger of steel. He must be taught way of the Stormseer and must prove his worth many times before he may bear the skull staff of the warrior-seer.'

Yesugei lifted his staff and aimed it towards the green-robed Choirmaster of Astropaths and black-suited Master of Navigators, sweeping it across the width of the dais. The gesture was subtle, for it also included the Emperor.

'To damn psykers as one evil is to forget how Imperium depend on them. Without mind-singers each world is adrift and alone, without star-seekers there is no travel between them. Men who speak against

Primarch Magnus speak with the blurred vision of ancients. They do not see consequences of what they seek. What they ask for will doom us all. My truth, I pledge on this oath-sworn staff. If any doubt me, I stand ready to cross blades with them.'

Targutai Yesugei bowed once more and stepped from the podium, returning to the ranks of his brother Librarians. Ahriman looked over at Magnus. Like him, his primarch was moved by Yesugei's words, captivated by their simple honesty and by the recognition of the hypocrisy inherent in the accusations levelled against the Thousand Sons.

'Surely the council cannot find against us now,' said Ahriman.

'We will see,' replied Magnus as the Emperor rose from his throne.

THUS FAR, THE Emperor of Mankind had viewed the conclave's proceedings from afar, an observer who hears all and deliberates without giving any clue to his thoughts. Now he moved to the edge of the dais, his armour shimmering in the light as the stars shone brightly once again. Ahriman tried to shift his consciousness into the Enumerations to keep his perceptions clear, but the power of the Emperor was too great and too magnificent to ever truly allow clarity of thought.

Every soul in the amphitheatre stared in wonder at this paragon of all that was good in humanity, the apotheosis of mankind's dreams and hopes. His every word was seized upon and written in a thousand places, like the words once transcribed as the faithful recitation of a god from the forgotten ages. The scrivener harness of Mahavastu Kallimakus clattered to life in anticipation.

Thoughts of Kallimakus were forgotten as a warm sensation of approbation washed over him. Ahriman recognised this feeling for what it was, the influencing of another person by instilling a measure of your psyche into their aura. Ahriman could perform a similar feat, though on a handful of people at most. To reach out to so many thousands at once spoke of power beyond measure.

The Emperor's sword was drawn, and his gaze locked with that of Magnus, as though they engaged in silent communion unheard by any others. Ahriman tore his gaze from the Emperor and saw that Magnus was pinned to his seat, his body rigid and his skin pale. His eye was tightly closed, and Ahriman saw an almost imperceptible tremor in his flesh, as though powerful currents of electricity were tearing through him.

'If I am guilty of anything, it is the pursuit of knowledge,' hissed Magnus through clenched teeth. 'I am its master, I swear it.'

Ahriman could hear no more, for Magnus suddenly drew a gasping breath, like a drowning man upon finding the surface of an ocean.

'Hear now the words of my ruling,' said the Emperor, and the amphitheatre filled with the sound of scratching quills. 'I am not blind to the needs of the Imperium, but nor am I blind to the realities of the hearts of men. I hear men speak of knowledge and power as though they are abstract concepts to be employed as simply as a sword or gun. They are not. Power is a living force, and the danger with power is obsession. A man who attains a measure of power will find it comes to dominate his life until all he can think of is the acquisition of more. Nearly all men can stand adversity, but few can stand the ultimate test of character, that of wielding power without succumbing to its darker temptations.'

As much as the Emperor was addressing the entire amphitheatre, Ahriman had the powerful sense that his words were intended solely for Magnus.

'Peering into the darkness to gain knowledge of the warp is fraught with peril, for it is an inconstant place of shifting reality, capricious lies and untruths. The seeker after truth must have a care he is not deceived, for false knowledge is far more dangerous than ignorance. All men wish to possess knowledge, but few are willing to pay the price. Always men will seek to take the short cut, the quick route to power, and it is a man's own mind, not his enemy or foe, that will lure him to evil ways. True knowledge is gained only after the acquisition of wisdom. Without wisdom, a powerful person does not become more powerful, he becomes reckless. His power will turn on him and eventually destroy all he has built.

'I have walked paths no man can know and faced the unnameable creatures of the warp. I understand all too well the secrets and dangers that lurk in its hidden darkness. Such things are not for lesser minds to know; no matter how powerful or knowledgeable they believe themselves to be. The secrets I have shared serve as warnings, not enticements to explore further. Only death and damnation await those who pry too deeply into secrets not meant for mortals.'

Ahriman blanched at the Emperor's words, feeling their awful finality. The promise of extinction was woven into every word.

'I see now I have allowed my sons to delve too profoundly into matters I should never have permitted them to know even existed. Let it be known that no one shall suffer censure, for this conclave is to serve Unity, not discord. But no more shall the threat of sorcery be allowed to taint the warriors of the Astartes. Henceforth, it is my will that no Legion will maintain a Librarius department. All its warriors and instructors must be returned to the battle companies and never again employ any psychic powers.'

Gasps of astonishment spread through the amphitheatre, and Ahriman felt his skin chill at the absolute nature of the Emperor's pronouncement. After everything that had been said, he couldn't believe the judgement had gone against them.

The Emperor wasn't finished, and thunder rolled in his voice.

'Woe betide he who ignores my warning or breaks faith with me. He shall be my enemy, and I will visit such destruction upon him and all his followers that, until the end of all things, he shall rue the day he turned from my light.'

BOOK THREE

PROSPERO'S
LAMENT

CHAPTER
TWENTY-ONE

Something of my Own/Paradise/
Treachery Revealed

LEMUEL FOUND MAHAVASTU Kallimakus on the edge of the great walls of Tizca. The old man was asleep in a padded chair with a sketchpad open across his lap. Lemuel kept his footsteps light, not wishing to wake his friend if he didn't need to. The five months on Prospero had been good for Mahavastu, the fresh sea air and temperate climate restoring his ravaged physique and putting fresh meat on his bones.

Prospero had been good for them all. Lemuel had shed much of his extra weight and now carried himself with a confidence born of knowing that he was looking better than he had in decades. Whether that was down to the agreeable lifestyle on Prospero or his growing skills in aetheric manipulation, he couldn't say.

Lemuel cast his eyes out over the view, alternating with glances down at the charcoal lines on Mahavastu's sketchpad. The view was one of rugged splendour, high mountains, sweeping forests and a deep blue sky of incredible width. In the far distance, a jagged series of spires indicated the ruins of one of Prospero's lost cities of the ancients. Mahavastu's rendition of the view was less than impressive.

'I told you I was no artist,' said Mahavastu, without opening his eyes.

'Oh, I don't know,' said Lemuel. 'It has some rustic charm to it.'

'Would you hang it on your wall?'

'A Kallimakus original?' asked Lemuel, taking a seat. 'Of course. I'd be mad not to.'

Mahavastu chuckled dryly.

'You always were a terrible liar, Lemuel,' he said.

'It's what makes me such a good friend. I'll always tell the truth, because you'll always know if I don't.'

'A good friend *and* a great remembrancer,' said Mahavastu, taking Lemuel's hand. The old man's fingers were like twigs and without strength. 'Stay awhile if you have the time.'

'I'm meeting Kallista and Camille for lunch later, but I always have time for you, old friend. So, leaving aside your obvious talent, what's brought the artistic urge out in you?'

Mahavastu looked down at the sketchpad and smiled ruefully. He flipped it closed, and Lemuel saw a look of aching sadness on the old man's face.

'I wanted something for myself,' he said, with a furtive glance over his shoulder. 'Something I knew *I* had done. Do you understand?'

'I think so,' said Lemuel guardedly, remembering the panicked words they had exchanged on Aghoru before the Thousand Sons' dreadful battle with the Syrbotae giants in the Mountain.

'I remember leaving Prospero with the restored Legion so long ago,' said Mahavastu. 'It was a glorious day, Lemuel. You would have wept to see it. Thousands upon thousands of warriors marching through the marbled processionals with rose petals falling from an empty sky and the cheers of the populace ringing in our ears. Magnus honoured me with a place in the triumphal march, and I have never felt such pride as I did that day. I could not believe that I, Mahavastu Kallimakus, was to chronicle the annals of Magnus the Red. There could be no greater honour.'

'I wish I could have seen it, but I doubt I was even born then.'

'Most likely not,' agreed Mahavastu, with tears in his eyes. 'A Legion on the verge of destruction had been reunited with its lost primarch. He had saved them from the abyss. I treasure that memory, but the time since then feels like another has lived my life. I remember fragments, but none of it feels real. I have filled a library's worth of books, but they are not my words. I cannot even read them.'

'That's what I came to tell you, my friend,' said Lemuel. 'I think I may be able to help you with that. Remember I said I had a partial copy of the *Liber Loagaeth* in my library back on Terra, but how I'd never been able to source the *Claves Angelicae*, its twin book with the letter tables?'

'Yes, I remember.'

'I have found a copy.'

'You have? Where?'

'In the library of the Corvidae,' said Lemuel. 'Ever since we returned to Prospero, Ahriman has stepped up my training. He's had me practically chained to a desk under the tutelage of Ankhu Anen, who is a scholar quite beyond anything I've ever experienced. I have to admit, I didn't care for him when I first met him, but he's been of immense help in my studies. I asked him about the book and he had a library servitor fetch it as though it was nothing at all.'

'Then you intend to translate what I have been writing?'

'In time, yes,' said Lemuel. 'It's a difficult language to crack, even with the letter keys. There are whole word groups that don't look like real language at all. I'm going to see if Camille can use her psychometry to help me with it.'

Mahavastu sighed and said, 'I wish you wouldn't.'

Lemuel was taken aback.

'You don't want to know what you've been writing all this time?' he asked.

'I think I am afraid to know.'

'Afraid of what?'

'I am a scribe, Lemuel. I am an *exceptional* scribe, and I do not make mistakes. You of all people know that. So why appoint me as a scribe only to prevent me from knowing what it is I write. I believe the words I have written are not meant for mortal eyes to see.'

Lemuel took a deep breath, shocked at the fear he heard in Mahavastu's voice.

'I am an old man, Lemuel, and I am tired of living like this. I want to leave the crusade and return to my homeland. I want to see Uttarpatha before I die.'

'The records of the crusade will be poorer for your absence, my friend.'

'Come with me, Lemuel,' urged Mahavastu, keeping his voice low. 'There is a curse upon this world, you must know that.'

'A curse? What are you talking about?'

'This world was destroyed once before through the arrogance of its people, and all human history tells us that men do not learn from their mistakes, even those as advanced as the Thousand Sons.'

'The people back then didn't understand their abilities,' said Lemuel. 'The Thousand Sons have mastered their powers.'

'Do not be so sure, Lemuel,' warned Mahavastu. 'If they had truly mastered their powers, why would the Emperor forbid them to wield them? Why would he have ordered them back to Prospero except to more fully dismantle their Librarius?'

'I don't know,' said Lemuel, 'but how galling must it be to be told that all the great things they've done and all the knowledge they've accumulated is worthless and forbidden?'

'That is exactly what I mean,' said Mahavastu. 'They have been forbidden to pursue their esoteric leanings, yet they do so regardless. Your continued instruction is in defiance of the Emperor's edicts! Had you thought of that?'

A hot flush settled in Lemuel's belly at the thought of defying the word of the Emperor. He *hadn't* thought of it like that at all, for he saw no harm in the skills he was acquiring. The long journey back to the Thousand Sons home world had been a time of rest for the remembrancers, but upon arrival on Prospero their training had been, if anything, more intensive than ever.

'This Legion is doomed,' said Mahavastu, taking Lemuel's hand once more and surprising him with its strength. 'If they continue down this path, it will not be long until their defiance comes to light, and when that day comes...'

'What?'

'Be anywhere in the galaxy, but do not be on Prospero,' said Mahavastu.

THE MEETING WITH Mahavastu had unsettled Lemuel, and his thoughts were troubled as he made his way through the city towards his rendezvous with Camille and Kallista. Tall buildings of white and gold lined wide boulevards of pollarded trees. Luscious green fronds hung low over the streetscape, heavy with fruits of yellow and red.

As usual, the sun was warm, and balmy ocean-scented winds sighed through streets busy with people. The inhabitants of Tizca were tall and uniformly attractive. They had welcomed the return of the Thousand Sons elements of the 28th Expedition, and the remembrancers that came with them. Lemuel had found much to like on Prospero, not least its people.

Tizca was a wondrous city of glorious architecture, open spaces, lively theatres and beautiful parklands. The White Mountains and Acropolis Magna provided a stunning backdrop to the city, and the great pyramids and silver towers of the Thousand Sons cults towered over everything. In any other city, such dominating architecture would have been oppressive, but such was the harmony with which the pyramids were constructed that they seemed as natural a part of the landscape as the mountains themselves.. Even the pyramid of the Pyrae, with its titanic guardian and burning finial blended with the city's aesthetic.

The months he had spent on Prospero had given Lemuel a good grounding in the city's geography, and such was the intuitive design of its layout that it was possible to navigate its many streets after only a short time.

Currently, he was heading east towards the Street of A Thousand Lions and Voisanne's. Tucked away in one of Occullum Square's radial streets, Lemuel had discovered Voisanne's on one of his morning walks, a modest bakery-cum-restaurant that did the most incredible confectionaries. Though he had kept off most of the weight he had lost since Aghoru, he still liked to treat himself to something sweet when he felt in need of comfort.

Today was one of those days.

Mahavastu had picked a scab Lemuel hadn't even realised was there. Like everyone within the Imperium, he had learned of the Edicts of Nikaea and the ramifications they would have. Though these edicts had come directly from the Emperor, dissenting voices already wondered how many of the Astartes Legions would actually obey the ruling.

That was a problem for someone else to deal with, and Lemuel hadn't been surprised when Ahriman continued his training on the voyage back to Prospero.

Lemuel had simply taken the fact that the Thousand Sons were continuing their education of the remembrancers to mean that they were utterly certain of their abilities. Now he wondered if that were true. *Were* they meddling with powers that ought to be abhorred?

Lemuel had heard the story of Prospero's fall, but he hadn't really given any thought as to *why* it had fallen. Ahriman spoke of Old Night as an unavoidable catastrophe, but was that really true? Might those millennia of horror been avoided had humanity left well alone the powers that he used with such familiar ease?

He looked towards the water-locked Pyramid of Photep, the glittering spire immense and shimmering with heat haze reflecting from its mirrored skin. Primarch Magnus dwelt within this mighty structure, its gold and silver embellishments shining as though afire in the noonday sun.

Lemuel entered a street lined with statues of rearing silver lions. Each was subtly different in pose and size from the others, as though a vast pack had been gilded then brought to Tizca and placed upon tall plinths of polished marble. He touched the leftmost lion for good luck, smiling at the notion that one particular lion could be luckier than another.

Two particularly regal beasts framed the entrance to a small area of parkland, and Lemuel paused to watch a group of Tizcan citizens practicing tàijíquán under the watchful eye of a warrior of the Thousand Sons. He found calm in the slow, precise movements, letting the soothing repetitions and graceful unity ease his troubled mind.

Lemuel took in deep breaths as the class breathed, finding his hands moving in unconscious imitation. He smiled and his grim mood vanished. Lemuel moved on down the street and emerged into a vast square, though such a term was misleading for the open space was perfectly circular.

Numerous streets, eighty-one to be precise, radiated from Occullum Square, and the centre was taken up by a tall column in the Doric fashion with a flaming urn at its summit. A great relief carved on its square plinth depicted a personification of Prospero grieving for her lost civilisation, while an armoured figure with one eye lifted her up. Some said the tower was all that remained of a device once used by the ancients of Prospero to communicate with Terra in the days before Old Night, but no one had been able to make it work again.

It was market day, and the square was packed with stalls, traders and good-natured bartering as the people of Tizca haggled for silks, produce and handmade ornaments. It reminded Lemuel of home, and he had a sudden pang of nostalgia for the heaving, bustling, sweating markets of the Sangha commercia-subsid.

He threaded the crowds, politely declining offers of food and drink while stopping to purchase two crystal vials of scented oil. Lemuel headed south, taking Gordian Avenue until it cut east into a narrow street overhung with trellis and hanging fruit.

Voisanne's was at the end of the street, and he saw Camille and Kallista waiting for him. He smiled and waved at them. They waved back, and he bent to plant chaste kisses on both womens' cheeks.

'You're late,' said Camille.

'My apologies, ladies,' said Lemuel. 'I was purchasing gifts for you from the market, and it took longer than usual to haggle the merchant down from his ruinous prices.'

'Gifts?' asked Kallista, brightly. 'Then you're forgiven. What do you have for us?'

Lemuel placed a crystal vial before each woman and said, 'Fragrant Boronia oil. I have no doubt your quarters are equipped with oil burners, so two droplets in water will fill your rooms with sweet floral undertones and a light, fruity scent that will refresh you and revitalise your creative energy. At least that's what the merchant assured me would happen.'

'Thank you, Lemuel,' said Camille, unstoppering the vial and sniffing its contents. 'Chaiya will love it. She loves our rooms to smell pretty.'

'Very nice,' added Kallista.

'It's nothing, ladies,' said Lemuel, 'just a trifle to apologise for my lateness.'

'I thought you were late *because* you bought us these?' said Camille.

'Actually it was Mahavastu that made me late,' said Lemuel with enforced levity. 'You know how the old man likes to tell an endless, rambling story.'

Camille looked askance, but Kallista nodded, and Lemuel was about to turn and ask for a menu when a waitress arrived bearing a tray of food. She placed a bowl of fruit before Kallista, a crème-filled pastry in front of Camille and frosted confections of spun sugar, sweet pastry and fruit for Lemuel.

The waitress went back inside, and Camille took a bite of her pastry.

She sighed with pleasure.

'Wonderful,' she said, 'but I don't think I'll ever get used to them knowing what I'm going to order before I even ask for it.'

'I know,' said Lemuel. 'I'd be worried if it wasn't for the fact they bring what I absolutely want every time.'

'True,' agreed Camille. 'I'll let them off then. So, how was he?'

'Who?'

'Mahavastu, you said you saw him earlier.'

'Oh, he's, well, he's fine, if a little homesick, I think. He was talking about wanting to go home, to Terra, I mean.'

'Why?' asked Kallista. 'Why would anyone want to leave Prospero? It's paradise.'

'He's getting old, I suppose. He wants to go home before it's too late.'

'I'll miss the old man,' said Camille. 'He has interesting tales.'

'Yes,' agreed Lemuel, uncomfortable with keeping the conversation on Kallimakus, as though it revived an old itch. 'Still, how are you two fine ladies getting on?'

'Good,' said Camille, taking another bite of her pastry. 'I've catalogued most of the ruins around Tizca, and Khalophis is taking me further out into the Desolation soon. He's taking me to one of the older cities. One of the first to be lost when Prospero fell, so he says.'

'Should be fascinating, my dear,' said Lemuel, 'but please be careful.'

'Yes, father,' smiled Camille.

'I'm serious,' said Lemuel. 'You don't know what might be out there.'

'Okay, okay, I will.'

'Good. And you, my dear Kallista? What progress have you made recently? Is Ankhu Anen still working you hard in the Athenaeum?'

Kallista nodded enthusiastically. She had blossomed since coming to Tizca, and even in a city of handsome people, Kallista Eris still stood out. Rumour had it she was being courted by a rakishly handsome captain of the Prospero Spireguard. Not that Lemuel was short of offers of companionship, but he had his own reasons for maintaining his solitary lifestyle.

Since Nikaea, the frequency of Kallista's nocturnal seizures had steadily lessened to the point they dared hope they had ceased altogether. She still carried her bottle of sakau, but had not needed it for months.

'Yes, Lemuel, he is. The Athenaeum is filled with texts said to pre-date Old Night, but they're written in ancient Prosperine, which no one speaks anymore. I can help with the translation by linking back to the minds of the writers. It's slow work, but it's shedding a lot of light on what society was like before it collapsed. You should pay us a visit, I'm sure you'd find it fascinating to see how the planet's developed since then.'

'I'll do that, my dear,' promised Lemuel. 'Ahriman has me very busy, but I'm sure he wouldn't mind me calling on you.'

'I'd like that,' said Kallista, finishing her fruit and taking a sip of water.

They chatted of inconsequential things for the rest of the afternoon, enjoying the warm sunshine and conversing as friends do. Some wine was brought, a crystal-white blend that Lemuel laughed to see was the vintage developed by Ahriman. As Lemuel poured the last of their second bottle, Camille brought the subject around to their hosts.

'So, how much longer do you think we have before the Thousand Sons redeploy?' she asked.

It was a question lightly asked, but Lemuel saw the undercurrent of anxiety behind it. Normally, he did not use his ability to read auras around his friends, understanding their need for privacy, but there was no mistaking Camille's desire to stay on Prospero.

'I don't know,' said Lemuel honestly. 'Ahriman hasn't said anything, but with the other Legions earning glory in battle, I know they're eager for a tasking order. The Emperor's Children on Laeran, the Luna Wolves on One Forty Twenty, the Ultramarines at Mescalor; it's been over two years since Ark Reach and yet the Thousand Sons are idle while their brothers make war.'

'Do you think it has anything to do with Nikaea?' asked Kallista.

'I think it must,' said Lemuel. 'From what I hear, the Crimson King couldn't leave Nikaea fast enough. According to Ahriman, the primarch has had all his warriors buried in their cult's libraries since they got back.'

'I heard that too,' said Kallista with a conspiratorial smile. 'I even overheard Ankhu Anen talking to Amon about it.'

'Did you hear what they were looking for?'

'I think so, but I didn't really understand what they said. It sounded like they were looking for ways to project a body of light farther than ever, whatever that means.'

'What do you suppose that's in aid of?' asked Camille.

'I have no idea,' said Lemuel.

HORROR. SHOCK. DISBELIEF. Anger.

All these emotions surged through Ahriman's body as he listened to his primarch's words. Together with the other eight captains of the *Pesedjet*, he stood upon the labyrinth spiral of Magnus's inner sanctum within the Pyramid of Photep. Slatted shafts of late afternoon sunlight cut the gloom, yet he could feel only oppressive darkness pressing in on him. He couldn't bring himself to believe what he had just heard. Had anyone other than Magnus said these treacherous words, he would have killed them.

From his position on the spiral, he could see each of his fellow captains. Phosis T'kar's brow was knotted in fury, his fists bunched in rage. Beside him, Phael Toron ground his teeth, and black mosaic chips wobbled in their mortar beds as their anger manifested around them.

Hathor Maat affected an air of calm, but his anguish was clear to see in the radiant aether light pulsing behind his features. Khalophis and Auramagma glowed with the power of their shock, sparks of flame bursting to life at their fingertips.

Uthizzar looked dreadful, his ashen face crumpled by the weight of unimaginable treachery yet to come as he felt the primarch's sense of betrayed grief as his own.

Ahriman had known something unthinkable was coming. He had felt it for months, knowing that Magnus was keeping a monstrous secret from his captains while he worked feverishly and alone in his private library and the vaults beneath Tizca. Amon and Ankhu Anen had shared Ahriman's knowledge that something was wrong, but even their combined power was unable to pierce the veils of the future to see what so concerned their primarch.

'This cannot be,' said Hathor Maat, for once articulating the feelings of his brothers with perfect understanding. 'You must be wrong.'

No captain of the Thousand Sons would normally dream of uttering such a thing to Magnus, yet this was a matter of such outrageous impossibility that the words had been on the verge of spilling from Ahriman's lips.

'He is not,' said Uthizzar, unashamed tears spilling down his face. 'It will come to pass.'

'But Horus,' said Phosis T'kar. 'He couldn't... He won't. How could he?'

Phosis T'kar could barely say the words. To voice them would give them solidity and make them real.

'How can you be sure?' asked Khalophis.

'I saw it,' said Magnus, 'beneath the amphitheatre of Nikaea. I saw the face of the monster, and though I wish it were not so, I saw the truth of its words. Since our return from Nikaea, I have travelled the Great Ocean and followed the paths of the future and the past. A billion threads of destiny from long ago have woven this one crucial filament upon which the fate of the galaxy hangs. Either we save Horus or we will be dragged into a war more terrible than any of us can imagine. I travelled the distant lands of the past, pushing the limits of my power to unlock the truth, and this has been coming for a very long time.'

Magnus opened his great grimoire and traced his finger down the latest pages filled with his writings.

'An ancient prophecy of the Aegyptos speaks of a time in the far future when all is war and the god of the sky, Heru, is initially set to protect his people from chaos,' he read. 'Much of that prophecy has been lost, but Heru turns on another god named Sutekh, a dazzling golden god, for dominion over all. In this form Heru was known as Kemwer, which means the Great Black One in the old tongue.'

'What do ancient legends have to do with Horus Lupercal?' demanded Phosis T'kar.

'Heru is but one of the names of an even older god, whose name can be translated as Horus,' said Magnus. 'The clues have been there all along, if only we had the wit to see them. Alas for so much has been lost. Even as we expand our knowledge, we forget so much.'

'Does the prophecy say any more?' asked Uthizzar.

Magnus nodded.

'It tells that neither side will be victorious, but says that many of Horus's brother gods sided with him in the struggle,' he said. 'If Horus wins, he will become known as Heru-Ur, which means Horus the Great.

Should Sutekh lose, his land will become barren and desolate for all time.

'The early tales of the god Horus say that during a new moon, he would be blinded and was named Mekhenty-er-irty, which translates as He who has no Eyes. This was a very dangerous time, for until the moon rose again, Horus was a tremendously dangerous figure, oft-times attacking those who loved him after mistaking them for hated foes.'

'Why would Horus Lupercal do such a thing?' asked Amon. 'What possible reason could there be?'

'An insult to his pride?' suggested Auramagma. 'Ambition? Jealousy?'

'No,' said Ahriman, recognising emotions that would cause Auramagma to strike a brother. 'Such things drive mortals to war, not primarchs. Something else is at the root of this.'

'Then what?' demanded Hathor Maat. 'What madness could possibly make Horus Lupercal turn traitor?'

There. It had been said out loud, and only now did Ahriman dare look at Magnus. The primarch was dressed like a mortuary priest, and his shoulders were slumped in the manner of a man awaiting the executioner's axe. Clad in a simple robe of crimson, and cloaked in a white shroud, Magnus waited for his sons to work through their emotions to a place of rationality.

Ahriman wished Magnus had not told them of his vision, for there was solace in ignorance. For the first time in his life, Ahriman wished to *un-know* something.

Horus Lupercal was going to betray them all.

Even thinking the words seemed like a betrayal of the Warmaster's honour and nobility.

'Well?' demanded Hathor Maat. 'What could it be?'

'Something will take root in his soul,' said Ahriman, feeling the words come without conscious thought, as though he knew the answers, but didn't have the right words to articulate them. 'Something primordial and yet corrupt.'

'What does that even mean?' snapped Phosis T'kar. 'You think a simple void-predator can violate the flesh of a primarch? Ludicrous!'

'Not violate, but I... I don't know,' said Ahriman, looking directly at Magnus. 'I don't know, but on some level it is true. I am right, am I not?'

'You are, my son,' agreed Magnus sadly. 'There is much I do not yet understand of what is happening to my brother, but time is running out to stop it. The Luna Wolves will soon be making war on a moon of Davin, and the fates are conspiring to fell Horus with a weapon of dreadful sentience. In his weakened and blinded state, the enemies of all life will make their move to ensnare his warrior heart. Without our intervention, they will succeed and split the galaxy asunder.'

'We have to warn the Emperor,' said Hathor Maat. 'He has to know of this!'

'What would you have me tell him?' roared Magnus. 'That his best and brightest son will betray him? Without proof, he would never believe it. He would send his war dogs to bring us to heel for employing the very means that have allowed us to know of this betrayal! No, there is only one option open to us. We must save Horus ourselves. Only if we fail do we take word to the Emperor.'

'What can we do to stop this?' asked Uthizzar. 'Ask and we obey.'

'The works I have had you researching since Nikaea hold the key to Horus Lupercal's salvation,' said Magnus. 'With your help, I will project myself across the warp and shield my brother from his enemies.'

'My lord,' protested Amon. 'That evocation will require power of undreamed magnitude. I am not even certain such a thing can be done. Nothing we have found is conclusive in how effective such a ritual could be.'

'It *must* be done, Amon. Begin assembling the thralls,' ordered Magnus. 'Bind their power to mine and they will fuel my ascent.'

'Many will not survive such a ritual,' said Ahriman, horrified at the casual disregard in which Magnus held their lives. 'To burn out so many thralls will cost us greatly.'

'How much greater the cost if we do nothing, Ahzek?' said Magnus. 'I have made my decision. Assemble the coven in the Reflecting Caves in three days.'

THE BILL ARRIVED without them asking for it, and Lemuel signed the credit slip. He had a pleasant buzz from the wine and saw that Kallista and Camille were just as mellow. The food had been exquisite and the service attentive. Once again Voisanne's had lived up to its reputation, and the afternoon had passed in a wonderfully convivial manner.

'Thank you, Lemuel,' said Kallista. 'Very kind of you.'

'Not at all. Two such lovely ladies should never have to pay a bill.'

'Sounds good to me,' said Camille with a nod.

They pushed their chairs back and stood as the staff cleared their plates and glasses.

'So where are you off to now?' asked Camille.

'I think a stroll around the market before I head back to my quarters,' said Lemuel. 'I have some passages of Rosenkreutz's *Fama Fraternitatis* to read before my instructions with Ahriman tomorrow, and after two bottles of wine, it may take a few readings to sink in.'

'What kind of book is it?' asked Kallista.

'Its about a monk who told of supernatural beings that move unknown among us, and have done since the earliest days of civilisation, healing the sick and studying the laws of nature for the betterment of mankind.'

'Riveting stuff,' said Camille, gathering her belongings.

'It is actually,' said Lemuel, warming to the subject. 'It appeals to the very best in human nature. After all, what could be nobler than the idea of helping one's fellow man without thought for reward or material gain? Wouldn't you agree, Kallista? Kallista?'

Kallista Eris stood beside the table, her fingers clutching the back of her chair, her knuckles white with the effort. Her skin was flushed and tendons pulled taut in her neck. Her eyes rolled back and a trickle of bloody saliva ran from the corner of her mouth.

'No,' she hissed.

'Oh, Throne, Kalli!' cried Camille, reaching for her. 'Lemuel, catch her!'

Lemuel reacted too slowly to catch Kallista as her legs gave way. She loosed a screeching wail of agony and spun around, crashing down onto their table, sending empty glasses and bottles flying. The table overturned and she landed in the debris, thrashing like a lunatic. The crystal bottle of oil shattered along with the glasses, and the sharp scent of berries and melon filled the air.

Camille was by her side in an instant.

'Lemuel! Get her sakau, it's in her bag!' she cried.

Lemuel dropped to his knees, all traces of intoxication purged from his system as adrenaline pumped into his body. Kallista's bag lay beneath the overturned table, and he scrambled over to it, emptying its contents onto the cobbled ground.

A notebook, pencils, a portable vox-recorder and assorted items a gentleman wasn't supposed to see fell out.

'Hurry!'

'Where is it?' he cried. 'I don't see it!'

'It's a green glass bottle. Cloudy, like spoiled milk.'

'It's not here!'

'It must be. Look harder.'

A crowd of concerned onlookers had gathered, but thankfully kept their distance. Kallista howled, the sound shot through with such agony that it seemed unthinkable a human throat could produce it. Amid the detritus of her bag and the broken glass from their table, Lemuel saw the bottle Camille had described and lunged for it. He scrambled over to Camille, who was desperately trying to hold Kallista down. The pretty remembrancer was stronger than she looked, and even with the help of a man in the red-trimmed robes of a physician she was able to throw them off.

'Here, I've got it!' he shouted, holding the bottle out.

Kallista sat bolt upright and stared directly at Lemuel. Petechial haemorrhaging filled her eyes with blood, and thick streamers of it poured from her nose and mouth. It wasn't Camille looking at him; it was a monster with snarling fangs and predator's eyes. It was older than time, stalking the angles between worlds with immeasurable patience and cunning.

'Too late for that,' she said, slapping the bottle from Lemuel's hand. It broke on the cobbles, the viscous liquid mingling with the spilled dregs of wine.

'The wolves will betray you and his war dogs will gnaw the flesh from your bones!' cried Kallista, and Lemuel lurched back as she lunged towards him, clawing at his eyes. She landed on him, her legs clamped around his waist and her hands locked around his throat.

He couldn't breathe, but before she could crush his windpipe, she screeched and her back arched with a terrible crack. The killing light went out of her, and she flopped back, her hands scrabbling for her notebook.

Lemuel saw the awful pleading in her eyes.

'Get her some paper!' yelled Camille.

CHAPTER
TWENTY-TWO

The Thousand Sons/Into the Desolation

THREE DAYS AFTER Kallista's attack, Ahriman finally spoke of the origins of the Thousand Sons. Lemuel wasn't in the mood for remembrances, having spent a couple of sleepless nights with Camille at Kallista's bedside. She lay in a medicae unit in the Pyramid of Apothecaries, hooked up to a plethora of machines, the purpose of which Lemuel didn't know. Some appeared to be specialised devices of the Corvidae, but Ankhu Anen refused to say what they were doing for her.

The attack had leeched the strength and vitality from her, as though she shrank within herself before their eyes. Every time Lemuel tried to rest, he saw her blood-red eyes, and sleep eluded him. Seeing Kallista like that had terrified him more than he liked to admit.

Malika had suffered seizures like Kallista's in the months before she…

No, don't think like that.

No sooner had Lemuel thrust the pen and notebook into Kallista's hands than she had filled page after page with nonsensical doggerel.

Ankhu Anen was examining it even now, hoping to divine some truth from it, and Lemuel hoped he would find something. At least it would make Kallista's pain meaningful.

'Do you wish to hear this?' asked Ahriman, and Lemuel focussed on his words.

They sat in one of the high terraced balconies of the Corvidae temple, an arboretum with an angled glass roof overlooking the city far below, though the temperature was precisely modulated to mimic the sensation of being outdoors. The terrace was positioned at the southern corner, allowing Lemuel to see the pyramid of the Pyrae cult and the Titan battle-engine guarding its entrance. He'd heard it was a prize of battle, taken by Khalophis on the field of Coriovallum, and that it had once belonged to the Legio Astorum. It seemed in somewhat bad taste to have an Imperial war machine taken as a trophy, but from what he knew of Khalophis, that seemed about right.

'Sorry, I was just thinking of Kallista,' said Lemuel.

'I know, but she is in good hands,' promised Ahriman. 'If anyone can decipher Mistress Eris's writings, it will be Ankhu Anen. And our medicae facilities are second to none, for we practise ancient as well as modern branches of medicine.'

'I know, but I can't help but worry, you understand?'

'I do,' replied Ahriman. 'More than you might think.'

'Of course,' nodded Lemuel. 'It must be hard to lose comrades in battle.'

'It is, but that is not what I meant. I was referring to those who die not in battle.'

'Oh? I was led to believe the Astartes were more or less immortal?'

'Barring battlefield injury, we may well be. It is too soon to tell.'

'Then how could you possibly know how I feel?'

'Because I too have lost someone I loved,' said Ahriman.

The surprise of such words coming from an Astartes shook Lemuel from his bitter reverie, and he narrowed his eyes. Ahriman was once again unconsciously touching the silver oakleaf cluster on his shoulder-guard.

'What is that?' asked Lemuel.

'It was a talisman,' said Ahriman with a rueful smile. 'A charm, if you will. My mother gave one each to my twin brother and I when we were selected as student aspirants to the Thousand Sons.'

'You have a twin?'

'I *had* a twin,' corrected Ahriman.

'What happened to him?'

'He died, a long time ago.'

'I'm sorry to hear that,' said Lemuel, finding the notion that Astartes warriors had lives before their transformation into super-engineered post-humans something he hadn't considered. Such were the enormous divergences from the human norm that it was easier to assume the Astartes sprang full-grown from some secret laboratory. It put a human face on an inhuman creation to know that Ahriman had once had a brother, a relationship that most mortals took for granted.

'What was his name?'

'He was called Ohrmuzd, which means "sacrifice" in the ancient tongue of the Avesta.'

'Why are you telling me this?'

'Because it will be useful,' said Ahriman. 'For both of us, I think. The doom of Ohrmuzd is also the story of how the Thousand Sons came to be. Do you wish to hear of it?'

'I do,' said Lemuel.

'FROM THE VERY beginning, we were a troubled Legion,' said Ahriman. 'The primarch tells me our gene-stock was harvested at an inauspicious time, a time of great cosmic upheaval. The warp storms that had all but isolated Terra in the lightless age of strife were resurgent once more and the effects were felt all across the world: madness, suicide and senseless violence. The last of the pan-continental despots had been toppled and the world was only just lifting its head from the ashes of that global conflict. It seemed like these were the last, dying paroxysms of the wars, which was true to an extent, but there was more to it than that.'

'You were there?' asked Lemuel. 'To see all that?'

'No, but I was a quick learner. I was one of the lucky ones, conceived and born among the wealthy tribes of the Achaemenid Empire. Our kings had allied with Earth's new master more than a century before, and we were spared the horrors of atomic war or the invasion of the Thunder-armoured warriors.'

'The proto-Astartes.'

Ahriman nodded, saying, 'Brutal and unsubtle creations, but sufficient for the job of conquest. They were ordinary men, the fiercest warriors of the Emperor, within whose bodies he had implanted full-grown biological hardware and mechanical augmentations to boost their strength, endurance and speed. They were monstrous things, and most were eventually driven insane by the demands their enhanced physiques made upon them.'

Lemuel noticed the inflexion Ahriman put on the word *enhanced*, reading his thinly-veiled criticism of the Emperor's first creations.

'With the end of the wars, the Emperor tightened his grip on Terra and turned his gaze to the heavens, knowing that he had achieved only the first step on the road to Unity. He knew the Thunder Warriors would never be able to join him on his quest to unite the disparate threads of humanity and bind them together once again. He would need another army, an army as superior to the Thunder Warriors as they were superior to mortal men. But first he would need generals, mighty soldiers who could lead them in battle.'

'You're talking about the primarchs, aren't you?'

'I am, yes. The Emperor created the primarchs using lost science and technology he had uncovered in his long wars. With the aid of rogue geneticists from the Martian Hegemony, he crafted beings of such luminosity that their like could never be conjured again. They were the pinnacles of genetic evolution, but they were lost to the Emperor before they could reach maturity. You have heard the legends, surely?'

'I have, but I assumed they were just that, legends.'

'No,' said Ahriman, shaking his head. 'They are truths enhanced by myths to allow men to better immortalise their deeds. It is far easier to march into the fires of war following a warrior whose origins are legendary than one who has no such glorious pedigree.'

'I suppose so,' agreed Lemuel. 'I hadn't thought of it like that.'

'Few do,' said Ahriman with a smile. 'But I was talking about me.'

'Sorry, go on.'

'My people's biological heritage was uncontaminated by many of the inherited flaws and viral defects so common to the other tribes of Earth, so the Emperor walked among us with his army of scientists, testing each and every family grouping for the requisite genetic markers. In my brother and I, he found what he was looking for and, with my parent's blessing, took Ohrmuzd and I to a secret place deep within the high mountains at the crown of the world. Before we left, our mother gave each of us one of these talismans, said to represent the strength of Dhul-Qarnayn, the greatest ruler of the Achaemenid. She bade us keep them close, telling us that the power of the ancient king would keep us safe.'

Ahriman pulled a leather cord from around his neck, revealing a silver pendant the size of a coin upon which was embossed the image of an oak leaf. It was the twin of the one set in Ahriman's shoulder-guard.

'Foolish superstition of course. How could a king who has been dust for tens of thousands of years protect the living? Though it went against the new creed of reason, we kept our talismans close throughout our training.'

'What sort of training?'

'Tests of strength, speed and mental agility. From an early age, the people of my culture were taught to value truth over all things, and Ohrmuzd and I were the sons of royalty, so we had long since learned to hunt and kill and debate. We excelled in all aspects of our training, and our biological advancement was a source of great pleasure to the scientists who attended us and monitored our progress. There were many of us training beneath the mountains, but gradually we were channelled into different groups, and Ohrmuzd and I were overjoyed at being kept together while many other siblings were split up.

'We grew rapidly and trained harder than any have trained before or since. Our prowess was unmatched and we marched into battle to quell the last pockets of resistance and rebellion on Terra to test our battle skills. Armoured in the latest battle-plate and equipped with the most destructive weapons, none could match us, and we were named the Thousand Sons.

'When the time came to leave Terra, it was a great moment. Not even the triumph at Ullanor can compare with the moment of grief as an entire world wept to see the architect of Unification depart. The alliance of Terra and Mars was complete, and the Mechanicum had outdone itself, building fleets of ships to allow the Emperor to take to the stars and complete his Great Crusade of Unity. The skies over Terra were thick with starships, hundreds of thousands of them organised into more than seven thousand fleets, reserve groups and secondary, follow-on forces. It was an armada designed to conquer the galaxy and that was exactly what we set out to do.'

Ahriman paused in his tale to look out over Tizca far below, his eyes lifting to the black mirror of the ocean. Lemuel saw a faraway look in his eyes, and had the powerful sense that Ahriman was telling this tale as much for his own benefit as for Lemuel's.

'The early years of the Crusade were a joy to us, a time of war and conquest as we swept through the solar system and reclaimed it once more. Beyond the boundaries of Terra, hostile xenos species had taken root, and we culled them without mercy, blackening their worlds and leaving nothing in our wake but ashes.'

'That doesn't sound like the Great Crusade,' pointed out Lemuel. 'I thought it was all about enlightenment and the advance of reason. That sounds like conquest for the sake of it.'

'You have to understand that we were fighting for the survival of the species then. Terra was surrounded on all sides by predatory races, and to survive we fought fire with fire. It was a glorious time, where the Astartes learned of the sheer, unstoppable fury we could bring to bear. War forges a man's character, and that is no less true of a Legion. Whether it was the echoes of our gene-sires in our blood, I do not know, but each of the Legions began to take shape beyond simply a name. The Ultramarines gained a reputation for order and discipline, fighters who learned from each engagement and applied that knowledge to the next. The World Eaters, well, you can imagine how they learned to fight.'

'And the Thousand Sons?'

'Ah... There we come to the first cracks in our great adventure,' said Ahriman.

'Cracks?'

'Our character manifested itself five years into the crusade. Our warriors began to display abilities far beyond anything we had expected. I could see things before they happened, and Ohrmuzd could craft lightning from the air. Others amongst our Legion could perform similar feats. At first we were jubilant, thinking this to be latent power encoded into our genes by the Emperor, but soon our joy turned to horror as first one warrior, then more began to change.'

'Like Hastar on Shrike,' said Lemuel.

'The flesh change, yes,' said Ahriman, rising and moving to the edge of the arboretum. Ahriman gripped the railing, staring off into the far distance. Lemuel joined him, fighting off mild vertigo as he looked down.

'The first warrior died on Bezant, his flesh turned inside out and his powers beyond his control. Something took his flesh, ripped him apart and made him a vessel for a xenos beast from the Great Ocean. We thought this was just a fluke occurrence, but it was not; it was an epidemic.'

'It was really that bad?'

'It was worse than you can imagine,' said Ahriman, and Lemuel believed him. 'It was not long before others noticed it. Many of the Legions had been reunited with their sires, and some of them found the notion of our powers to be hateful. Mortarion was the worst, but Corax and Dorn were not much better. They feared what we could do, and spread their lies to anyone who would listen that we were witches practising unclean sorcery. Little did any of them realise they were condemning the very powers that allowed them to travel between the stars or spread their malicious rumour-mongering.'

Lemuel saw the anger in Ahriman's face, the bitterness of memory causing the plants nearby to wither and blacken. He felt a nauseous twist in his gut and swallowed a mouthful of bile as Ahriman continued.

'With every passing year, more and more of our warriors would succumb to the flesh change, though we grew ever more adept at spotting the signs and taking steps to contain them. Perversely, the more warriors suffered the change, the stronger our powers became. We learned how to keep the worst of the flesh change at bay, but more and more of us were falling prey to it and the voices of our persecutors were growing ever more strident. There was even talk of disbanding us and expunging us from Imperial history.'

Lemuel shook his head.

'That's the thing about history,' he said. 'It has a habit of remembering the things you'd like to forget. No one can erase that much, there will always be some record.'

'Don't be so sure, Lemuel,' said Ahriman. 'The Emperor's wrath is a terrible thing.'

Lemuel heard the sorrow in Ahriman's voice and wanted to ask more, but the tale was not yet done.

'Ohrmuzd and I were at the forefront of the Thousand Sons, its greatest warriors and most powerful practitioners of the arts. We thought we were immune to the flesh change, that our power was too great for it to touch us. How arrogant we were! Ohrmuzd fell prey to its effects first, and I was forced to secure him as he fought against his rebelling flesh.'

Ahriman turned to Lemuel, and Lemuel quailed before the intensity of his gaze.

'Imagine your body turning on you, every molecule refusing to hold to its genetically-encoded purpose, with only your strength of will preventing your flesh from uncontrollably mutating, all the while knowing that eventually you must weaken and it will take you.'

'I can't,' said Lemuel. 'It's beyond me.'

'I did what I could for Ohrmuzd, but soon after his succumbing, I too was afflicted. I did not go into stasis with the rest of our fallen brothers, doomed to wait out the entirety of the Great Crusade until a cure could be found, for I was able to stave off the change, though it was a battle I knew I was destined to lose.'

Ahriman smiled, and the twisting pain in Lemuel's guts subsided.

'Then, a miracle happened,' he said. 'We reached Prospero and the Emperor found Magnus.'

'What was it like?' asked Lemuel. 'To be reunited with your lost sire?'

'Magnus was our salvation,' said Ahriman, with no small amount of pride. 'We descended to the planet's surface at the Emperor's side, though I remember little of the first meeting of father and son, for my body was wracked with pain as I fought to hold myself together. It was a dark time for our Legion, and yet a joyous one. It was clear to us that we could not go on as we were, for the flesh change was taking too many of us, and there was nothing we could do to stop it. Even as we despaired, we rejoiced, for we were finally reunited with the genetic father of our Legion.'

Lemuel smiled to hear the fond recollection in Ahriman's voice. The Captain of the 1st Fellowship looked over to the Pyramid of Photep, and an unreadable expression crossed his face, like a man afraid to face a guilty memory he has buried deep.

'Within a day of the Emperor leaving Prospero, more and more of the Legion fell prey to the change. Though I had resisted it longer than any other had before, I too succumbed and my body began to rebel. My powers raged uncontrolled, but all I remember of that day is the horror of knowing that soon I would be little better than some of the monstrous things we had slain in our expansion from Terra. Soon, I would need to be put down like a beast.

'Then I remember a soothing voice in my head, soft and silky, like I imagined a father's would be when comforting a sick child. Darkness stole over me, and when I awoke, my physique was unblemished and without a mark. The flesh change had almost destroyed us, yet we were whole and in control of our bodies once more. The Legion had been saved, but I felt no joy that day, for a piece of me had died.'

'Your twin brother,' said Lemuel.

'Yes. I was whole, but Ohrmuzd had died. His body was too ravaged by the flesh change, and nothing could be done to save him,' said Ahriman. 'I took his silver oakleaf and incorporated it into my armour. His memory deserved no less.'

'Again, you have my condolences,' said Lemuel.

'None of us could recall anything of how this miracle came to pass, but we were alive, though barely a thousand of us were left.'

'The Legion name,' said Lemuel.

'Literally,' agreed Ahriman. 'Now we truly were the Thousand Sons.'

Lemuel frowned and said, 'Wait, that doesn't make sense. You were known as the Thousand Sons before you reached Prospero, yes?'

'Yes.'

'Why?'

'Why what?'

'Why that name in particular? The Legion's name only makes sense *after* Magnus saved you on Prospero,' said Lemuel. 'Yet you were known as the Thousand Sons before then. So is it just a stupendous coincidence that there happened only to be a thousand survivors?'

'Now you are thinking like a Practicus,' said Ahriman with a smile. 'I keep telling you that there is no such thing as coincidence.'

'So what are you telling me? That the Emperor saw what was happening to you and knew that Magnus would save a thousand of you?'

'Perhaps. The Emperor has seen a great many things,' said Ahriman, though Lemuel sensed evasion in his words. 'Yes, Magnus saved us, but he never said how he did it.'

'Does it matter?' asked Lemuel. 'He saved you. Isn't that enough?'

Ahriman turned his gaze to the heavens. 'That remains to be seen, but I think it *will* matter. I think it will matter a great deal.'

As MUCH AS she was worried about Kallista, Camille was relishing her day of exploration too much to worry about her stricken friend. She had rolled out of bed, kissed Chaiya goodbye, and made her way to the rendezvous with Khalophis without so much as a second thought for Kallista Eris. She felt guilty about that, but not so guilty she was going to miss out on the chance of exploring the Desolation of Prospero.

Khalophis's disc-speeder brought them to the ruined city in less than an hour, which had disappointed Camille until he told her how far and fast they had travelled. Tizca was far behind them, and she wondered why everyone still called the lands beyond Tizca the 'Desolation', as nothing could be further from the truth. The landscape was as lush as anything she could ever imagine. Vast forests and wide open plains spread to the horizons, and crystal clear rivers spilled in foaming waterfalls from the mountains.

Khalophis had steered the speeder with delicate skill, which she found surprising. She expected him to fly brusquely and without finesse. The sense of speed as they flew through this bountiful land had been exhilarating, and the thrill of being allowed to explore the far cities of Prospero was as close to perfect as she could imagine.

Camille looked up at the high stacks of blackened iron and stone towering above her Their structures were wrapped in greenery and swayed gently in the chill winds funnelled down from the end of the valley. Hundreds of skeletal frames arranged in what looked like grid patterns dotted the valley mouth, and the ground underfoot was like faded rockcrete, cracked and split by patient weeds.

Broken piles of stone clustered the bases of the structures, like cladding or flooring pushed from the structures they had once enclosed by the relentless forces of nature.

Over the course of the morning and early afternoon, they had discovered some that still had elements of their internal structure intact, but these were few and far between.

Khalophis followed her, his boltgun slung casually over his shoulder as he watched her capturing pict images of the structures. She already had a library's worth of images, but the things she had touched so far had yielded little of interest.

'Have you found anything yet?' asked Khalopis. 'These ruins bore me.'

'Nothing yet,' said Camille.

'We should go. This valley has seen some psychneuein activity of late.'

Lemuel had mentioned psychneuein once. They sounded vile, but with a warrior like Khalophis to protect her, she wasn't unduly worried.

'We can't go yet,' she said, ducking into the shadows of a largely intact structure that echoed with shadows and decay. 'So far, everything I've touched has been machine-formed and without memory. They're no use to me. This one's in pretty good condition, so it might house something of value.'

The interior of the building stank of neglect and damp, its shadows refuges for the wild animals that called the Desolation of Prospero home. Light broke in through holes in the walls and speared down from above. Dust hung in the air, drifting motes of light in the splintered breeze.

Camille drew in a deep breath, tasting the age of the structure in the musty fragrances. There was history here, stories she could unlock if she could only find something that had once belonged to a living, breathing person.

'This way,' she said, heading towards a sagging steel stairway that led to the next level.

'That doesn't look safe,' said Khalophis, eyeing the rusted handrails.

'I'm touched by your concern,' said Camille, 'but it's lasted a thousand years like this. I expect it'll last another afternoon, don't you?'

'I don't know, I'm not an engineer.'

She tried to figure out if he was joking, but gave up when his expression didn't change.

'Okay then,' she said, turning away. 'I've climbed my share of rickety stairs, and this one looks fine.'

She turned and made her way upstairs, hoping that the forces of comedic timing weren't about to deposit her in a heap of broken stairs and embarrassment. Fortunately, they held, though they creaked and groaned alarmingly as Khalophis put his weight on them.

The upper level was as desolate as the lower, the grey floor covered in dust, droppings and debris from the levels above. Most of the higher floors had collapsed, leaving the building as little more than a hollow chimney, with occasional nubs of floor slabs and structural spars jutting into thin air. Birds fluttered above, and she caught the faint rustle of wings from high up nests.

'What do you hope to find here?' asked Khalophis. 'Everything's decayed. If there was something to be learned here, don't you think we would have found it by now?'

Camille flashed him a confident smile.

'You can't look the way I can,' she said.

Khalophis grunted, 'None of you remembrancers have done anything worth a damn since you joined us. It was a waste of time bringing you here. I haven't seen anything special yet.'

She ignored him and moved through the remains of the building, stopping every now and then to examine the debris for anything that might prove useful. Assorted pieces of what might once have been personal effects lay in some of the piles, but they were as lifeless as the ruins themselves.

Something moved above her, a creak of stone and a soft, animal growl. Camille looked up, seeing a flitting shadow, a startled bird whose nest she'd unwittingly approached too closely. She peered into the corner of the building, seeing a collection of wooden spars and what looked like sheet metal arranged too neatly to be random.

'Do you have any lights in that armour of yours?' asked Camille. 'Or a torch?'

'I can do better than that,' said Khalophis with relish.

He extended his hand, and a flaring ball of light appeared in the air before him. It burned brighter than a welder's torch, and shone stark light throughout the derelict structure.

'Very impressive,' said Camille, squinting against the brightness.

'This is nothing. It's almost insulting to use my powers for something so trifling.'

'Fair enough, but it's a little bright. Can you dim it down a little?'

Khalophis nodded and the light's intensity dimmed to a level where Camille could see. High-contrast lighting threw deep black shadows and revealed the decay of the structure in all its glory. For all that the ruined building had little in the way of memory, Camille felt a momentary pang of sadness for the civilisation that had passed away thousands of years before her birth.

People had lived and died here, spending the span of their years dreaming of better days, and working to provide for themselves and their families. They were now dust, and to be so forgotten struck a real chord in Camille. She moved around the barricades – there could be no other purpose for such an assembly of items – and saw a host of cobwebbed skeletons, the bones held together by what looked like some kind of hardened resin.

'They didn't realise how easily it could all be taken away,' she said.

'What?'

'The people who lived here,' said Camille, kneeling beside the nearest body. Though she was no expert in the study of bones, its size suggested it was a man's. 'I'll bet none of them woke up and thought, "this is the day our world ends, so I'd better make it count".'

She looked up at Khalophis and said, 'Nothing is permanent, no matter how much we might think it is. I suppose that's what I'm learning here.'

'Some things will endure,' said Khalophis with the certainty of a zealot. 'The Imperium.'

'I expect you're right,' said Camille, not wishing to get into a discussion on the Imperium's future with him.

She peeled off one of her gloves and gingerly touched the skeleton, half-expecting it to crumble to dust at her touch. It was a miracle none had succumbed to the ravages of time already, but the hardened resin appeared to be the cause of their preservation.

She heard a rustle of frightened birds from high above, but shut out the noise as she ran her hand over the hardened clavicles to the dead man's skull, noticing that the cranial lid was detached. It hung from one side of the skull, like a hinged door that had been pushed open from the inside.

She closed her eyes, letting the familiar warmth flow from her hand and into the relic of past times. The power moved within her, and she felt the urgency of the man whose skull she touched pulling her down into his life, sensing the swell of his emotions as they reached out to her.

Too late, Camille saw they were of pain and madness. She tried to withdraw her hand, but the red rush of agony was too swift for her, and searing pain stabbed into her brain like a hot lance. Blood streamed from her mouth as she bit her tongue. Camille screamed as the man's last, anguished moment ripped through her. Horrible images of feasting white maggots, ruptured flesh and dying loved ones burned their way into her consciousness.

She shook as though seized by a high-energy current, her teeth grinding and her sinews cracking as her mouth tore open in a soundless scream.

Then it was over. She felt rough hands pull her away, and the moment of connection with the dead man was broken. Bruised afterimages remained imprinted on her vision, and she gasped with the horror of his last moments. She had touched the dead before, and had always been able to insulate herself from their endings, but this had been too dreadful and too intense to ignore. She tasted metal and spat a mouthful of blood.

'I told you we should not have lingered,' snarled Khalophis.

'What?' was all she could manage, seeing Khalophis towering over her. One heavy gauntlet gripped her shoulder. The other was wreathed in flickering orange flame.

'Psychneuein,' hissed Khalophis, dragging her towards the stairs.

Then she heard it, a droning buzz like a hive of vespidae, and the excited flutter of what sounded like an explosion of wings as a flock of predatory birds took flight.

CHAPTER TWENTY-THREE

Pyrae Unleashed/If you're Dead/
The Reflecting Cave

'RUN!' SHOUTED KHALOPHIS, as the frantic buzzing noise grew louder. Camille looked up to see an organically shifting swarm of winged clades launching themselves from hidden lairs in the darkness of the ruined structure.

Terror flooded her limbs with paralysing stillness.

The chittering clatter of insect limbs rattled from the steel structure as scores of psychneuein boiled down the length of the building, frantic with alien hunger. Camille saw hundreds of them, vile insect-like monsters with grasping limbs and feeding proboscis. The droning buzz of hundreds of wings and the chitinous *clacking* of snapping mandibles grew steadily in volume.

Something moved behind her, and she turned to see one of the hideous, beetle-like creatures. It had a glossy, segmented body and six spindly limbs that oozed a repellent resin. Its wings moved too fast to see, like oil spilled on water, and it stank of spoiled meat.

Razored mandibles jutted from its swollen head, its surface grotesquely textured like a human brain studded with multi-faceted eyes that threw back her horrified reflection.

The creature launched itself forward, but erupted in flames before it reached her. The charred corpse struck her in the chest and disintegrated into hot ashes. She screamed, and frantically brushed the smoking remains from her lap as Khalophis swept her up into the crook of his arm as easily as a man might pick up a small child.

'I told you to run,' he snapped. 'You mortals never listen.'

Khalophis set off towards the stairs, but a host of psychneuein crawled up from below.

'Damn things,' said the Astartes, flicking his free hand towards them. A wall of red flame erupted from the ground, consuming the creatures in seconds. No sooner had he despatched the psychneuein than more landed on the overhanging girders and piles of rubble. Camille counted at least a dozen.

As though a single intelligence controlled the beasts, they took flight at the same instant. They swooped towards them, the screech of their wings like a war cry.

'You think it's that easy?' roared Khalophis, filling the air around them with balls of phosphorent flame, spinning them around like whipping poi. The psychneuein hovered at bay, hissing and spitting as the fiery spheres wove a flaming lattice around their prey. More of the creatures appeared with every passing second.

Khalophis set her down and said, 'Stay behind me. Do what I say when I say it and you will live. Understood?'

Camille nodded, too terrified to speak.

The Astartes warrior hurled a torrent of fire from his hands towards the largest group of psychneuein, and they screeched in rage as they erupted in flames. A chop of his left hand sent a spear of fire into a psychneuein that dared swoop down at him from above. His right hand shot out, and an invisible blaze of heat rippled outwards. A dozen beasts spontaneously exploded as the molecules of their bodies were superheated to explosive temperatures.

The air was blisteringly hot, and Camille felt her skin burning in the fire shield around them. Secondary fires were filling the air with sooty, carbonised smoke. Her eyes stung with the heat, each breath laboured and painful.

'I can't breathe!' she gasped.

Khalophis glanced down at her. 'Deal with it.'

More of the psychneuein came at Khalophis, but none could breach his protective barriers of heat. Camille pulled her body into a tight ball on the floor, covering her mouth with her hand. She tried to keep her breaths shallow, but terror was working against her and she felt her vision greying.

'Please,' she gasped with the last of the oxygen in her lungs.

Khalophis bent down and hauled her to her feet.

'Stand here,' he said. 'Stay within the heat haze and you will be able to breathe.'

Camille could barely hold herself upright, but she felt the heat vanish, as though the door to a meat locker had just opened in front of her. She sucked in greedy mouthfuls of cold air, seeing a ripple in the filmy atmosphere surrounding her. Beyond the haze, fires and smoke raged unchecked as Khalophis's power consumed anything flammable within reach. None of it touched her, as though she were enclosed in a hermetically-sealed bubble.

Khalophis fought with the fury of a gladiator as the psychneuein assailed him from every side. There seemed to be no end to their numbers as they hurled themselves at the warrior with furious abandon.

'Burn, you freaks!' shouted Khalophis, killing with jets of flame, daggers of fire and waves of superheated air. Even in her terror, Camille heard the strain in his voice. The power of the Pyrae was phenomenal, but so too was the cost.

With every display of psychic mastery, the fury of the attacking monsters doubled.

She tried to recall what Lemuel had told her of the psychneuein, but could remember little other than the fact that they reproduced by stinging you and laying their eggs in your body. One fact leapt to the front of her consciousness, and despite the heat, a sudden chill travelled the length of her spine.

'It's your powers!' she yelled. 'They're being drawn to us because of your powers! It's driving them wild. You have to stop using them!'

Khalophis sliced half a dozen psychneuein from the air with a shimmering fire sword that sprang from his fist. In that brief lull, he turned to her, his face dripping in sweat, his eyes sunken and exhausted.

'The fire is all that's keeping us alive!' he cried, sweeping the blade around as three more came at him.

'It's what will get us killed if you don't stop using it!'

A hissing psychneuein landed on the broken remains of a fallen wall, its thorax bulging and dripping. A long stinger whipped at its rear and she screamed as it leapt at Khalophis.

'Behind you!' she yelled.

Khalophis dropped to one knee and immolated the monster with a glance. A clutch of monsters took its place, their stingers erect and wickedly barbed. Never mind the eggs, being stung would kill her before they could use her body as an incubator.

Khalophis snarled and the fire sword vanished. He swung his bolter around, racking the slide and firing a three round burst into the group of psychneuein.

'Back towards the stairs!' shouted Khalophis, firing as he went. 'If we can reach the speeder, we'll be safe.'

Camille nodded, trying to keep behind the warrior as her insulating cocoon vanished.

The entire floor was ablaze, pools of molten steel and dissolving carcasses littering the ground. Again the smoke tarred her lungs, and she coughed as her body fought for oxygen. A psychneuein slammed into Khalophis, its body ablaze from the fires, and the giant warrior stumbled. He batted it away, but the momentary lapse of concentration caused his barrage of bolter fire to falter.

Three psychneuein darted in, their stingers plunging into Khalophis's armour. Two stingers broke on impact, but the third stabbed into his waist through the coiled cabling beneath his breastplate. He grunted and crushed the beast with his fist. His bolter roared and psychneuein burst like target dummies.

Khalophis expertly switched magazines on his bolter and loosed another burst of shots as more of the beasts flew in. The fire had taken hold of the entire building, and Camille felt the floor shift underfoot as beams melted in the intolerable heat. The buzz of wings was almost obscured by the crackle of flames and creaking structural elements.

'The stairs!' she cried.

The way down was ablaze, the sagging ironwork red hot and melting. No way down there.

Khalophis saw it at the same time and shook his head, as though disgusted at her fragility.

'Hold on,' he said as he slung his bolter and tossed her over his shoulder.

The psychneuein boiled towards them, but Khalophis was already on the move. He ran through the flames, head down like a living battering ram. Psychneuein smashed against him, some breaking open on his armour, others stabbing him with their long stingers. Camille cried out in pain as a barb protruding from his shoulder-guard tore into her side. She looked up in time to see that Khalophis was running towards a sheet of dancing flame. She cried out as he leapt into it.

Searing heat surrounded her, but the blazing wall parted like a stage curtain as Khalophis loosed one last burst of his powers.

Then they were falling. Camille closed her eyes as the ground rushed up towards her. Khalophis braced his legs as he dropped, slamming down on the move and carrying on as though his leap through the flames was nothing at all. Camille felt a rib break with the impact of slamming against his armour, but gritted her teeth against the pain. Khalophis kept running, smashing through the low doorway that led back to the outside world in an explosion of stone and plaster dust. He fired his bolter one-handed over his shoulder. Alien screeches told Camille that every one of them was a killing shot. Whatever else she thought of Khalophis, he was a superlative warrior.

Camille drew gloriously fresh air into her lungs and, almost immediately, her vision cleared and her breathing eased.

The psychneuein swarmed from the ruined building. Smoke poured from its shattered windows and leaping flames licked up its length. Its structure bowed and shuddered as load-bearing elements melted. Spalling brickwork and stone tumbled from its upper levels.

Khalophis unceremoniously dumped her from his shoulder, and she bit back a scream as the splintered ends of her broken rib ground together.

'Get in,' ordered Khalophis, and she looked behind her to see the welcome form of the disc-speeder. He threw his bolter into the vehicle and climbed into the pilot's seat.

Camille dragged herself upright using the speeder's exhausts and painfully opened the crew compartment hatch as its engines spooled up with a rising whine.

The swarming psychneuein were almost on top of them, the buzz of their frantic wings deafening. Less than twenty yards separated them from the vanguard of the monsters.

'Hurry, for Throne's sake, hurry!' she shouted, pulling herself inside.

'Are you in?' Khalophis demanded.

'I'm in,' she said, pressing herself into one of the bucket seats and hauling the restraint harness around her body. The whine of the engines changed pitch, and the speeder leapt forward, the phenomenal acceleration slamming her head against the fuselage. She kept her eyes shut for long seconds, hardly daring to breathe as the long seconds ticked by.

The engine noise deepened, and Khalophis's voice crackled over the intercom.

'We're clear,' he said. 'Are you all right back there?'

She wanted to snap at him, but that was the pain talking.

Instead she spat a mouthful of blood and nodded.

'Yeah, I guess,' she said. 'I think I broke a rib, my lungs feel like I've swallowed a gallon of burning tar and thanks to your lead foot I've got a splitting headache, but I'll live.'

'Good enough,' said Khalophis. 'Alive is all I need.'

'I'm touched by your concern,' she said, before adding, 'but thanks for saving my life.'

Khalophis didn't acknowledge her, and they spent the journey back to Tizca in pained silence.

* * *

A SOFT HUMMING filled the medicae bay. Kallista reclined in bed, eyes closed, her chest rising and falling with rhythmic breaths. Her skin was grey, its surface dull and lustreless. Her hair had been shaved, and Lemuel wished he could do more for her than simply sit by her bedside and hold her hand.

He and Camille had taken alternating shifts to sit by her bedside, but Lemuel had been here for nearly forty-eight hours and was beginning to feel like lead weights were attached to his eyelids. A bank of walnut-panelled machines with numerous gold-rimmed dials and pict-slate readouts chirruped beside Kallista's bed. Lengths of copper wiring coiled from jack plugs in their sides to points across her skull, and crackling globes buzzed softly along their top edges.

Kallista's eyes fluttered open and she smiled weakly at the sight of him.

'Hello, Lemuel,' she said, her voice like footsteps on dead leaves.

'Hello, my dear,' he replied. 'You're looking well.'

Kallista tried to laugh, but she winced in pain.

'Sorry,' said Lemuel. 'I shouldn't make you laugh, your muscles are all strained.'

'Where am I?'

'In the neuro-wing of the Pyramid of Apothecaries,' said Lemuel. 'After what happened to you, it seemed the most sensible place to bring you.'

'What did happen to me? Did I have another attack?'

'I'm afraid so. We tried to get your sakau, but you were too far gone,' said Lemuel, deciding to keep silent about what Kallista had said to him in her delirium.

Kallista lifted her arm to her forehead, trailing a collection of clear tubes and monitoring cables from a canula piercing the back of her hand. She touched her head and frowned, gently feeling the stubble and brass contacts on her scalp.

'Yes, sorry about your hair,' said Lemuel. 'They had to shave it to attach those contacts.'

'Why? What are they for?'

'Ankhu Anen brought the devices from the Corvidae temple. He was a bit cagey when I asked what they were, but eventually he said that they monitor aetheric activity in your brain and quell any intrusions. So far, they seem to be working.'

Kallista nodded and surveyed her surroundings.

'How long have I been here?'

Lemuel rubbed his hands over his chin. 'My beard says three days.'

She smiled and pushed herself further up the bed. Lemuel poured some water, and she gratefully drank the entire glass.

'Thank you, Lemuel. You are a good friend.'

'I do my best, dearheart,' he said, before adding. 'Do you remember anything about what you saw? I only ask because Ankhu Anen seemed to think it might be important.'

Kallista bit her bottom lip, and he saw an echo of the fearful look he'd seen at Voisanne's.

'Some of it,' she said. 'I saw Tizca, but not like we know it. There was no sunshine and the only light was from the fires.'

'Fires?'

'Yes, the city was burning,' said Kallista. 'It was being destroyed.'

'By whom?'

'I don't know, but I saw the shadow of a stalking beast in the thunderclouds, and I could hear howling from somewhere far away,' said Kallista, tears gathering in her eyes and spilling down her cheeks. 'Everything was burning and glass was falling like rain. All the shards were like broken mirrors and every one of them had the image of a single staring eye looking back at me.'

'That's quite a vision,' said Lemuel, taking her hand and stroking her upper arm.

'It was horrible, and it's not the first time I've had one like it. I didn't recognise Tizca the first time I saw it but, now that I'm here, I'm sure it was the same one.'

A sudden thought occurred and she said, 'Lemuel, did I write anything this time?'

He nodded.

'Yes,' he said, 'but it didn't make any sense. Ankhu Anen is trying to decipher it now.'

Kallista closed her eyes and wiped away her tears. She took a shuddering breath, and then smiled as someone opened the door behind him. Lemuel turned and saw a tall, broad-shouldered man in the uniform of a captain in the Prospero Spireguard. He was ludicrously handsome, with dark features and as chiselled a jaw as any heroic image of Hektor or Akilles.

Lemuel disliked him almost immediately on principle.

The man's crimson uniform jacket was immaculately pressed, decorated with brass buttons, gold frogging and numerous polished medals. He carried a silver helmet in the crook of his arm, and a long curved sabre was belted at his hip next to a gleaming laspistol.

'Sokhem,' said Kallista with a grateful smile.

The soldier gave Lemuel a quick nod of acknowledgement. He held out his hand and said, 'Captain Sokhem Vithara, sir. 15th Prosperine Assault Infantry.'

Lemuel took the proffered hand and winced at the strength of Vithara's grip.

'Lemuel Gaumon, remembrancer, 28th Expedition.'

'A pleasure,' said Vithara. 'Kalli's told me of you friendship, and I thank you for that, sir.'

Lemuel felt his dislike melt away in the face of Vithara's winning smile and natural charm. He forced himself to smile, knowing he was no longer needed.

'Nice to meet you too, Captain Vithara,' he said, rising and scooping up his coat. 'I'll leave you two alone now.'

He gently lifted Kallista's hand and planted a kiss and said, 'I'll come and see you later, my dear.'

She gripped his shoulder and pulled him close, whispering urgently in his ear.

'I want to leave Prospero,' she said. 'I can't stay here. None of us can.'

'What? No, my dear, you're in no state to go anywhere.'

'You don't understand, Lemuel. This world is doomed, I've seen its death throes.'

'You don't know for sure what you saw,' said Lemuel, pulling himself upright.

'Yes I do,' she said. 'I know all too well what it was.'

'I can't leave,' said Lemuel. 'There's so much I've yet to learn from the Thousand Sons.'

'You can't learn if you're dead,' said Kallista.

Lemuel left Kallista and Captain Vithara together and made his way from the neuro-wing. Though he had no desire for Kallista beyond friendship, he had to admit to a pang of jealousy at the sight of her handsome suitor.

He smiled at the thought, recognising how foolish it was.

'You are a hopeless romantic, Lemuel Gaumon,' he said. 'It will be the death of you.'

As he made his way to the exit, a door slid open ahead of him, and his good mood evaporated in an instant as he saw an Astartes warrior who looked like he'd just returned from a war zone. His armour was scorched black in places, and numerous barbs jutted from his shoulder-guards and thighs. He recognised Khalophis, but it wasn't his appearance that halted Lemuel in his tracks.

He carried Camille in his arms, and she looked dreadful.

Blood matted her hair and clothes. Her skin was a painful red, and she held a hand pressed to the side of her chest, stifling pained gasps with every step Khalophis took.

'Camille!' cried Lemuel, running over to her. 'What in the world happened?'

'Lem,' she wept. 'We were attacked.'

'What?' asked Lemuel, looking up at the hulking form of Khalophis. 'By whom?'

'Get out of my way, mortal,' said Khalophis, moving past Lemuel.

He turned and jogged to match the warrior's pace.

'Tell me what happened,' he said.

'She was exploring the ancient ruins, even after I told her it was dangerous, and we disturbed a nest of psych-neuein.'

Lemuel's blood chilled at the mention of Prospero's indigenous psy-predators.

'Throne, no!' he said, standing directly in front of Khalophis. The Astartes glared down at him, and Lemuel thought he was going to walk straight through him.

'Camille, listen to me,' said Lemuel, lifting her eyelids. Her pupils were dilated and almost entirely black. He didn't know if that was good or bad. 'How are you feeling?'

'Like I've been run over by a Land Raider,' she snapped. 'Any more stupid questions?'

'How is your head?' he asked, speaking slowly and clearly. 'Do you have a headache?'

'Of course I do. Thanks to Khalophis, I think I breathed in a lifetime's worth of smoke.'

'No, I mean... Do you feel any different?' asked Lemuel, struggling for the right words. 'Is your head painful in a way that feels, I don't know, strange?'

'I'm not sure,' she said, catching the edge of his panic. 'Why? What's wrong with me?'

Lemuel ignored her question and spoke directly to Khalophis, 'Get Camille to a bay right now, and send for Lord Ahriman. Hurry! We don't have much time!'

THE REFLECTING CAVE was filled with light, myriad pin-pricks of soul-light that flickered form precisely shaped crystals held by the thousand Thralls standing at the intersection points of the cavern's energy lines. Located almost a full mile beneath the city of Tizca, the crystal cave was enormous, fully three kilometres across at its widest point, and its stalactite-hung roof chimed with the sound of soft bells.

Fireflies danced within the walls, throwing back the lights carried by the Thralls and illuminating the figures and apparatus at the centre of the enormous cave.

An elongated bronze device, like a gigantic telescope, descended from the central point of the roof. Its surface was graven with unknown symbols and studded with vanes of silver, while a polished green crystal fully three metres across terminated the base of the bronze mechanism.

Magnus the Red stood directly below the device, looking up through the crystal into the night sky directly above the centre of Occullum Square. He was naked but for a loincloth, his flesh bare to the elements and gleaming with oil.

Ahriman watched as Amon massaged a mixture of sandalwood, jasmine and benzoin oil into Magnus's flesh. Uthizzar scraped the excess oil from the primarch's body with a bone-bladed knife as Auramagma held a smoking censer that filled the air with the fragrance of cinquefoil. Phael Toron stood next to Ahriman, his body language stiff and awkward.

Phael Toron's 7th Fellowship had spent the majority of the Great Crusade on Prospero, missing much of the great learning undertaken by the Legion since Magnus had led them from their adoptive home world. His warriors had quickly accepted the new teachings, but it was going to take time for them to fully adjust.

'Is this all necessary?' asked Toron, indicating the strange paraphernalia arranged beneath the bronze mechanism. A rectangular white slab like an altar was hung with a heavy chain of magnetised iron. At each of the cardinal points around the slab were four concave mirrors that focussed the light from the crystals carried by the Thralls. Five concentric circles enclosed the altar, and within the circuits of the four outermost circles were unknown words that left a bad taste in Ahriman's mouth when he had tried to read them.

'The primarch tells us so,' said Ahriman. 'He has looked long and hard into the necessary rituals to hurl his body of light halfway across the galaxy.'

'This smacks of unclean spirit worship to me,' said Toron.

'It is not,' Ahriman reassured him. 'We have learned much since leaving Prospero, Toron, but there are things you have yet to fully understand. This is absolutely necessary if we are to save Horus.'

'But why here, hidden from sight in a cave?'

'Look to your history,' said Ahriman. 'The first mystical rites were conducted in caves. We are the initiates of Magnus, and when we are finished, we will emerge into the light of the stars, reborn and renewed in our purpose. Do you understand?'

Toron gave a curt bow, cowed by the aetheric flare in Ahriman's aura. 'Of course, Lord Ahriman. This is all very new to me.'

'Of course, forgive my choler,' said Ahriman. 'Come, it is time.'

They stepped forward, and their Thrall attendants moved in to drape white chasubles over their armour, tying them at the waist with narrow gold chains.

Ahriman received a crown of vervain leaves threaded with a silver cord, and Toron was handed a glittering athame with a silver blade and obsidian handle.

Together, they walked to Magnus as Uthizzar stepped away and retrieved an iron lantern from his Thrall. Amon cleaned his hands of oil with a silk cloth, and robed Magnus in white before lifting a charcoal brazier that smoked with the aroma of alder and laurel wood.

'Your flesh is anointed, my lord,' said Amon. 'You are untainted.'

Magnus nodded and turned to Ahriman.

'The Crimson King requests his crown,' he said.

Ahriman approached Magnus, feeling the heat of his master's skin and the meditative power churning within him. Magnus lowered his head, and Ahriman placed the crown of vervain leaves upon his brow, letting the silver cord settle around his ears.

'Thank you, my son,' said Magnus, his eye glittering with violet fire and hazel flecks.

'My lord,' said Ahriman with a bow. He retreated from Magnus, and turned to receive a heavy book bound in faded leather and stitched with gold. An iron pendant, worked in the form of a snarling wolf's head against a crescent moon, lay along the valley at the meeting point of its pages.

This was the Book of Magnus, its contents the distilled wisdom of all that Mahavastu Kallimakus had written in his long years of unthinking service to the Thousand Sons. To look upon it was an honour, but to hold it and be expected to read from its pages was the culmination of a lifelong dream for Ahriman.

Yet, for all that he had rebuked Phael Toron, Ahriman couldn't help but wonder if the man's unease was justified. The ritual Magnus had them performing was uncannily similar to many they had destroyed during the glory days of the Great Crusade.

'Are we of one mind?' asked Magnus. 'We can go no further without complete accord. The harmony of our assembly is all, for it bears that most precious cargo: the human soul.'

'We are in accord,' said the captains with one voice.

'Our work starts in the darkness, but comes into the light,' continued Magnus. 'My form must be reduced to the chaos of its component parts, and the whole will be greater than the sum of its parts. This great work we are upon is our most determined effort to lay claim to mastery of our fate. By such works we show that we are not content to simply be pawns in the Great Game, but will play upon our own account. Man the dabbler becomes man the decider. Too few have the courage to take arms against an uncaring galaxy, but we are the Thousand Sons; there is nothing we dare not do!'

Magnus nodded to Auramagma, who turned to the white slab as the thousand Thralls began chanting in monotonous, meaningless syllables. The light from the Thralls' crystals pulsed, as though with the heartbeat of the cave itself.

Auramagma turned right as he reached the slab, circling around it with the brazier forming a ring of aromatic smoke. Ahriman followed him, reciting angelic words from the Book of Magnus, the power of them a fulsome texture on his lips.

Phael Toron came after him, bearing the athame upon his outstretched palms, and following him came Uthizzar with the unlit lantern. Lastly came Amon, who bore the heated brazier in his armoured gauntlets. The five sons of Magnus processed around the white slab nine times before halting as Magnus took his place in the centre.

The Primarch of the Thousand Sons lay down upon the altar, his white robes spilling over its edges. Ahriman kept reading from the Book of Magnus as Uthizzar lit the lantern with a taper from Amon's brazier. Aura-magma held the censer aloft as Phael Toron stepped towards the recumbent form of Magnus.

Ahriman saw a ripple of light converging from all around them as streamers of aether drifted down from the crystals carried by the thousand Thralls. Within moments, the entire floor of the cave was awash with smoky light, the combined essence of the Thralls seeking an outlet for their energy. The light gathered in the mirrors, focusing its magnified illumination upon Magnus's body, imparting a ghostly aura to his still form.

'It is time,' said Magnus, 'Ahzek, give me the Moon Wolf.'

Ahriman nodded and lifted the iron pendant from the book. The moon glittered silver in the cavern's light, and the fangs of the wolf shone like icicles. He lowered the pendant into Magnus's flattened palm, looping the chain over his outstretched fingers.

'This was given to me by Horus Lupercal on Bakheng,' said Magnus. 'It was part of his armour, but a lucky shot broke it from his pauldron. He gave it to me as a keepsake of that war, and joked that it would guide me in times of darkness. He was egotistical even then.'

'Now we'll see if he was right,' said Ahriman.

'Yes we will,' said Magnus, closing his eye and making a fist around the pendant. His breathing slowed, becoming shallower as he concentrated on the love he bore for his brother. Within moments, a swelling bloodstain appeared on Magnus's shoulder and he groaned in pain.

'What in the name of the Great Ocean is that?' cried Phael Toron.

'A sympathetic wound,' said Amon. 'A repercussion, a stigmata, call it what you will. We have little time; the Warmaster has already been wounded.'

'Toron,' hissed Ahriman, 'you know your role. Fulfil your duty to your primarch.'

The athame twitched on Phael Toron's palms, lifting up and twisting in the air until it hung directly over the primarch's heart. The silver cord within the vervain crown unwound of its own accord and slithered over the edge of the altar to bind itself to the magnetised chain.

'I will travel the Great Ocean for nine days,' said Magnus through gritted teeth, and Ahriman was astonished. To travel for so long was unheard of. 'No matter what occurs, do not break my connection to the aether.'

The five warriors surrounding Magnus shared a look of concern, but said nothing.

'You must not falter,' said Magnus. 'Continue, or all this will be for nothing.'

Ahriman lowered his gaze and continued to read, not understanding the words or how he knew their pronunciation, but speaking them aloud just the same. His voice grew in volume, moving in counterpoint to the chanting of the Thralls.

'Now, Toron!' cried Magnus, and the athame plunged down, stabbing into the primarch's chest. A red bloom of glittering, iridescent blood spilled from the wound. Instantaneously, the swirling light found its outlet, and searing white beams erupted from the mirrors and surged into the hilt of the athame.

Magnus arched his back with a terrible roar. His eye snapped open, its substance without pupil or iris, but awash with all manner of incredible colours.

'Horus, my brother!' cried Magnus, his voice laden with the echoes of the thousand souls fuelling his ascent. 'I am coming to you!'

And a terrifying, angelic form shot up from Magnus's body in a blazing column of light.

CHAPTER
TWENTY-FOUR

She was my World/Whatever the Cost/The Price

LEMUEL WAS FRANTIC with worry. He couldn't find Ahriman, and Camille was running out of time. A week that had started out so well had turned to one of the worst in the space of a couple of days. Two of his dearest friends were gravely ill, and a third was suffering at the hands of a master who used him without care for his wellbeing.

Events were spiralling out of control, all his grand ideas for what he had hoped to learn from the Thousand Sons as insubstantial as mist. He had learned a great deal, but what use was power when those you loved could slip away from you without warning?

He had shed too many tears for lost loved ones. He wasn't going to shed any more.

Camille lay in a bed not dissimilar to Kallista's, though without the variety of equipment hooked up to her cranium. Cuts and grazes had been dressed, and her lungs had been flushed of carbon, ash and trace elements of metal oxides. The wound in her side had been

413

treated and dressed, and she had been declared physically fit and prescribed strong pain balms and three days of bed rest.

After what Ahriman had told him, Lemuel worried that Camille didn't have three days.

He had begged Khalophis to find Ahriman, only to be told that Ahriman was 'with the primarch' and could not be disturbed. Though Lemuel's body clock was turned upside down, he guessed it was early morning. Looking at a chrono above the nurse's station he saw that ten hours had passed since Khalophis had brought Camille in.

Still, Ahriman had not come or even acknowledged Lemuel's calls for aid.

When he returned to Camille's room, Lemuel found an attractive ebony-skinned woman sitting by her bed, holding her hand and mopping her brow with a cloth. The elegant sweep of the woman's bone structure told Lemuel she was a native of Prospero.

'Chaiya?' he asked.

The woman nodded and favoured him with a nervous smile. 'You must be Lemuel.'

'I am,' he said, rounding the bed and taking Chaiya's hand. 'Can we talk outside?'

Chaiya glanced over at Camille. 'If there is something you wish to say concerning Camille's health, I think you should tell her first, don't you?'

'Under normal circumstances, I'd agree with you,' said Lemuel, 'but two of my best friends have been admitted to this facility, and my usual good manners are in short supply. So please indulge me.'

'It's all right, Lemuel,' said Camille. 'You know me, if there's news to be told, I'd rather hear it first-hand. Say what you have to say.'

Lemuel swallowed. Having to voice his suspicions to Camille's lover was bad enough; admitting them to her face was almost too much to bear.

'The psychneuein I told you about, it turns out they lay their eggs in a rather unorthodox manner.'

Camille smiled, the muscles on her face relaxing.

'It's okay,' she said, 'none of them stung me. Khalophis kept me safe. If anything, you should be checking him out to see if he's going to become a mother.'

Lemuel sat on the edge of the bed and shook his head. 'That's not how they reproduce, Camille. As I said, it's rather unorthodox…'

He explained what Ahriman had told him of the reproductive cycle of the psychneuein, trying to emphasise that it wasn't even certain that she was in any danger. Chaiya's expression told him he wasn't doing a very good job.

'You think that's what this headache is?' she asked.

'It might be,' he said. 'I don't know. I hope not.'

'You *hope* not? What kind of lame answer is that?' snapped Camille. 'Get me a damn brain scan or something! If I've got some alien's eggs in my head, I bloody well want to know about it.'

Lemuel nodded and said, 'Of course. I'll see what I can do.'

'No,' said Chaiya. 'I'll do it. I have friends in the Thousand Sons. It will be better if I ask.'

'Yes, yes,' nodded Lemuel. 'That sounds wise. Very well, I'll… I'll wait here shall I?'

Chaiya leaned over and gave Camille a kiss.

'I'll be back as soon as I can,' she said before heading out of the room. Left alone with Camille, Lemuel took a seat and smiled weakly, crossing his hands in his lap.

'I'll never make a physician, will I?'

'With that bedside manner? Not anytime soon, no.'

'How's your head anyway?'

'Still sore.'

'Oh.'

'I did get a bumpy ride in Khalophis's speeder. I banged my head pretty good on the seat.'

'I'm sure that's it then,' said Lemuel.

'Liar.'

'All right,' he snapped. 'So what do you want me to say? That I think alien eggs are going to hatch in your head and eat your brain while you're still alive? I'm sorry, I can't say that.'

She watched him silently.

'Yeah, definitely need to work on that bedside manner,' she said.

Her forced humour broke the dam within him, and he buried his head in his hands and wept. Tears flowed freely and his chest heaved with sobs.

Camille sat up.

'Hey, I'm sorry, Lemuel, but I'm the one in bed here,' she said gently.

'I'm sorry,' he managed eventually. 'You and Kallista, it's too much. I can't lose you both, I just can't.'

'And you're not damn well going to,' said Camille. 'We'll figure this out. If there's going to be any tinkering done with my head, there's probably no better planet to be on, is there?'

Lemuel wiped his wet eyes with a sleeve and smiled.

'I suppose not. You're being very brave, you know that?'

'I *am* on some pretty strong meds, so I wouldn't give me too much of the credit.'

'You're braver than you think,' said Lemuel. 'That counts for a lot. Believe me, I know.'

'Yeah, me and Kalli are going to be fine, you wait and see,' she said.

'Yes,' said Lemuel bitterly. 'That's all I ever do.'

Camille reached out and took his hand, letting her eyes drift closed.

'No,' she said. 'That's not true is it? You did all you could to save her.'

Lemuel pulled his hand free.

'Don't. Please.'

'It's all right,' said Camille. 'Tell me about Malika.'

HE BEGAN HESITANTLY, for it had been many years since he had spoken of Malika. The words were too tangled in grief to come easily, but he haltingly told Camille of the brightest, most beautiful woman in the world.

Her name was Malika, and they had met at a fund-raising dinner held by the Lord of the Sangha district to procure monies that would allow him to purchase a quarry's worth of Proconnesus marble from the Anatolian peninsula to donate to the Imperial Masonic Guild. The current Guildmaster, Vadok Singh, had promised a prominent location for the statues that would be crafted from the blocks, perhaps even the Emperor's Investiary, and rumour had it the commission had been awarded to no less a sculptor than Ostian Delafour.

Such things took money, and the wealthiest citizens of the district had been summoned to show their devotion financially. Lemuel was a rich man, and had built a sizeable estate, thanks to a combination of business acumen and the ability to read people's auras to know when he was being played false. He owned property throughout Mobayi, and was well-liked, having turned much of his wealth to philanthropic works.

Malika was the daughter of the Lord of the Sangha district, and they had fallen in love that night beneath the stars and over a bottle of palm wine. They were married the following year, in a ceremony that cost more than many of the families living on Lemuel's lands made in a year. Lemuel had never been happier, and as he spoke of the first seven years of marriage, his face lit up with golden memories.

The first signs of Malika's diminishing health came with severe migraines, unexplainable blackouts and short-term memory loss. Physicians proscribed pain balms and rest, but nothing helped alleviate her symptoms. The diagnoses of the finest medical practitioners from all across the Nordafrik districts were sought, and eventually it came to light that Malika had developed a highly aggressive astrocytoma, a malignant brain tumour that he was told was incredibly difficult to treat.

Surgery alone could not control the tumour, as its cells had extended their cancer throughout her brain. Radiation therapy followed numerous surgical procedures alongside aggressive chemotherapy in an attempt to control any further tumour growth, but the physicians told Lemuel that the heterogeneous nature of her ailment was making it difficult to treat. As one cell type was destroyed, they said, others lurked in the wings to take over the job of destroying Malika's brain.

Lemuel watched his wife fade away and there was nothing he could do about it. Such helplessness was anathema to him, and he turned to ever more esoteric methods in his attempts to save her, despite the futility of their likely effect. No treatment was too ridiculous, for Lemuel was willing to try anything to save his beloved wife.

Any chance was better than none.

Lemuel employed homeopathic and naturopathic experts to administer holistic courses of herbal treatments, while Ayurvedic practitioners placed equal emphasis on the wellbeing of her mind and spirit. Qi gong, acupuncture, controlled breathing, hypnosis and orthomolecular therapies were all tried, but none of them had any effect whatsoever.

Lemuel refused to give up. His researches had led him to the farthest corners of knowledge, and he uncovered many texts that spoke of forces beyond human understanding. In these books he recognised his own abilities and read of others that could heal the sick, raise the dead and call forth powers that were unearthly and abhorred.

That didn't matter. He would do whatever it took to save his wife.

She begged him to stop, but he would not listen. She had made peace with her mortality, but Lemuel could not. He wept as he told Camille of how she had watched from their roof veranda as he left on an expedition to the mountains of the Himalazia in search of hidden masters said to have achieved mastery over body and mind.

If anyone could help, it would be them.

Laden with all his wealth, he and his followers travelled far into the mountains and almost died in the frozen winds that scoured these highest peaks. It proved to be a wasted journey; the builders of the Emperor's palace had long since displaced any hidden masters that might once have lived in these mountains.

By the time he returned to Mobayi, Malika was dead.

'SHE WAS THE world to me,' said Lemuel as he finished his tale.

'I'm so sorry,' said Camille. 'I never knew. I mean, I saw something of her when I touched you on Aghoru, but I didn't know. Why did you never tell us about Malika?'

Lemuel shrugged.

'I don't like telling people that she died,' he said. 'The more people I tell, the more it sinks in that she's really gone. It makes it more real and more unchangeable, somehow.'

'You think you can change that she died?'

'For a while I thought I could,' said Lemuel. 'Some of the books I read spoke of bringing the dead back to life, but they were maddeningly vague. Nothing worked, but when the opportunity came to be selected for the

Remembrancer Order, I jumped at the chance to petition the Thousand Sons.'

'Why the Thousand Sons?'

'I'd heard the rumours,' said Lemuel. 'Hadn't you?'

'I don't listen to rumours,' said Camille, smiling. 'I just start them.'

Lemuel chuckled.

'Touché, my dear,' he said. 'I spent a long time listening to rumours in my search for a cure for Malika, and I'd heard a great deal spoken about the sorcery of the Thousand Sons. I heard whispers of how a great many of them had been horribly afflicted with dreadful mutations, and of how Magnus had saved his Legion. I thought that if I could learn from them, I might learn how to bring Malika back.'

'Oh, Lemuel,' said Camille, taking his hand and kissing it. 'Trust me, there's no bringing anyone back. I know; I've touched the dead and I've listened to their lives. I've felt their love and their pain. But, through all of that, I've felt the joy they took in life when they were alive, the people they knew and loved. In the end, that's the best anyone can hope for, isn't it?'

'I suppose so,' agreed Lemuel, 'but I tried so hard.'

'She knew that. Through everything, she knew you loved her and were trying to save her.'

'Could I give you something of hers?' asked Lemuel. 'Maybe you could read it?'

'Of course, whatever I can do, Chaiya. You know that,' said Camille, her voice drowsy.

Lemuel frowned. 'Did you just call me Chaiya?'

'Sure... why? That's your... name...' said Camille. 'Isn't it... my love?'

Lemuel's stomach lurched as Camille's hand fell from his and her eyes widened. She gasped for air, and the entire left side of her face seemed to slip, as though invisible hands were moulding her flesh into a lopsided grimace.

'Oh, no! Camille! Camille!'

Her hands bunched into fists as they wrung the sheets on the bed, and her body stiffened with the force of the seizure. Her eyes stared with manic fury, and blood-flecked saliva drooled from the corner of her mouth. Camille's face was a mask of wordless pleading, her entire body wracked with pain.

Lemuel turned towards the door.

'Help! Throne of Terra, help me please!' he yelled.

'Can you see them?' asked Phosis T'kar.

'Yes,' replied Hathor Maat. 'Seeing them isn't the problem. It's doing something about it that's the problem.'

'Please,' begged Lemuel. 'Whatever you can do.'

Camille's room had become a hive of activity since he'd called for help. Chaiya had returned, not with medical staff or any form of imaging equipment, but with two captains of the Thousand Sons. She had introduced them as Phosis T'kar of the 2nd Fellowship and Hathor Maat of the 3rd.

Evidently she *did* have friends in high places.

While Phosis T'kar held Camille motionless with the power of his mind, the absurdly pretty Hathor Maat placed his hands on either side of her skull. His eyes were closed, but from the motion of his pupils, it was clear he visualised with other senses.

'There are six of them, buried deep and growing fast,' he said. 'Ugly white things. They're not yet larval, but it won't be long before they pupate.'

'Can you save her?' asked Chaiya, her voice as brittle as cracked crystal.

'What do you think we're trying to do?' snapped Phosis T'kar.

'They're cunning little bastards,' hissed Hathor Maat, twisting his head and moving his hands around

Camille's skull. 'Organic tendrils, like anchors, are burrowing into the meat of the brain, tethering themselves to the nerve fibres. I need to burn them out slowly.'

'Burn them out?' asked Lemuel, horrified at the idea.

'Of course,' said Maat. 'How else did you think I was going to do it? Now be quiet.'

Lemuel held onto Chaiya's hand, and she to his. Though they had not met before today, they were united in their love for Camille. From the straining muscles in her neck and arms, Lemuel could tell that Camille's body was trying to thrash out its agony on the bed, but Phosis T'kar kept her immobile without apparent effort.

'I see you,' said Hathor Maat, curling his finger as though hooking a fish. Lemuel smelled a sickly aroma of something burning.

'You're hurting her!' he cried.

'I told you to be quiet,' barked Hathor Maat. 'The tiniest fraction of a misstep and I may end up burning out the mechanism that allows her to breathe or pumps blood from her heart. I have its body and am slowly boiling it alive.'

He laughed with relish.

'Oh, you don't like that do you?' he said. 'Trying to dig your hooks in deeper, eh? Well, let's see about that.'

Hathor Maat dug his fingers downwards, spreading the tips wide and smiling as the smell of burning meat grew stronger. He worked within Camille's skull for over an hour before nodding to himself. .

'One. Two. Three. And four... Got them,' he said.

'You got them all?' asked Lemuel.

'Don't be foolish, that was just the tendrils of the first egg. They're tenacious and aren't going without a fight. It's loose now, but we need to get it out fast before it reattaches. Phosis T'kar?'

'Got it,' said the Captain of the 2nd Fellowship.

Phosis T'kar placed his hand beside Camille's ear and twisted his extended fingers as though attempting to pick the most complex of locks. His fingers were incredibly dextrous, and Lemuel held his breath as Phosis T'kar gradually drew his fingers back towards his palm.

'Inkosazana preserve us!' cried Lemuel as something wet and wriggling emerged from Camille's ear. It looked like a spined slug, and its slimy body writhed as it was drawn forth by Phosis T'kar's incredibly precise power.

The slug-like creature plopped down into a gleaming kidney bowl, leaving a sticky trail of blood and slime behind it. Just looking at it made Lemuel feel sick.

'Would you like to do the honours?' asked Phosis T'kar handing Lemuel the kidney bowl with a grin.

'Oh, absolutely,' replied Lemuel. He tipped the bowl and dropped the pre-larval psychneuein to the tiled floor of the medicae bay.

He stamped on it and ground it to a gooey paste with his heel.

'One down, five to go,' said Hathor Maat, his skin streaked in sweat. 'Just as well I love a challenge.'

BEYOND THE PYRAMID of Apothecaries, a light rain fell over Tizca. Rain was uncommon over the city and its inhabitants came out onto the streets to feel it on their skin. Children played in the rain, and the streets echoed with squeals of delight as they splashed in puddles and stood beneath spouting gutters.

It continued for days, drowning the city every morning.

No one knew where it came from, for the techno-psychic arrays built into the mountains were normally an entirely reliable means of predicting and controlling the planet's climate.

Some rain was, of course, necessary to keep the ecosystem in balance, but this was beyond anything the inhabitants of Tizca had ever experienced. The buildings glistened with rainwater and the streets flowed with gurgling rivers.

Questions were asked of the Thousand Sons, but no answer was forthcoming as to the cause of the unseasonable rains. Fully half the Legion's captains were *in absentia*, and those who remained had no answer.

On the sixth day, an impromptu parade was held through Occullum Square where the crowd threw off its clothes and cavorted naked in the rain. Tizca had no standing force of enforcers, so elements of the Prospero Spireguard were deployed to return the deliriously naked dancers to their abodes. The seventh day saw several members of the parade fall ill with a deadly form of viral pneumonia, and the following morning riots broke out in front of the Pyramid of Apothecaries as frightened people demanded a vaccine. Sixty-three people died before the Spireguard restored order, and a sullen mood fell upon the city.

On the ninth day, the rains finally ceased, and the sun broke through the dark clouds that hung like disapproving judges over the heart of the city. A luminous beam of light shone down on Tizca, bathing it in golden radiance and striking the flaming urn atop the great column at the centre of Occullum Square.

Mahavastu Kallimakus wrote that it was like the light of heaven returning to Prospero.

DEEP WITHIN THE Reflecting Caves, that light retuned to its source.

Magnus opened his eye, and the athame withdrew from his flesh, its blade crumbling to dust as soon as it came into contact with the air. Ahriman let out a relieved sigh as Magnus sat up, swinging his legs over the side of the white slab and blinking furiously in the darkness.

Only the dim glow that swam in the walls illuminated the chamber. Of the thousand Thralls, only eighteen remained alive, though their bodies were gaunt and drained, the glow from their crystals faint and almost extinguished.

'My lord,' said Amon, coming forward with a goblet of water. 'It is good to see you.'

Magnus nodded, and Ahriman saw how pale his skin had become. His long red hair was matted with sweat, and Ahriman thought he could see the writhing veins and pulsing organs beneath the primarch's skin. That was a lie, for Ahriman had seen into the heart of Magnus, and there was nothing so mundane as liver, lungs or kidney within that immortal frame.

Phael Toron, Uthizzar and Auramagma crowded in, their joy at seeing Magnus returned beyond measure. Only Ahriman held back, his emotions mixed at what they had done. For nine long days they had stood vigil over their beloved primarch, neither eating nor sleeping nor partaking of food or water. No words had passed between them, and no communication had been attempted with their brothers on the surface.

'Was it worth it?' asked Ahriman. 'Did you succeed?

Magnus fixed him with his single eye, a dull orb of watery blue, and shook his head slowly.

'No, Ahzek, I think that I did not,' said Magnus. 'Just as I attempted to save my brother from the abyss, others were ready to push him in.'

'Others?' snarled Auramagma. 'Who?'

'A wretch named Erebus who serves my erstwhile brother, Lorgar. It seems the powers that seek to ensnare Horus Lupercal have already claimed some pieces on this board. The Word Bearers are already in thrall to Chaos.'

'Lorgar's Legion have betrayed us also?' asked Phael Toron. 'This treachery runs deeper than we could ever have imagined.'

'Chaos?' said Ahriman. 'You use the term as if it were a name.'

'It is, my son,' said Magnus. 'It is the Primordial Annihilator that has hidden in the blackest depths of the Great Ocean since the dawn of time, but which now moves with infinite patience to the surface. It is the enemy against which all must unite or the human race will be destroyed. The coming war is its means of achieving the end of all things.'

'Primordial Annihilator? I have never heard of such a thing,' said Ahriman.

'Nor had I until I faced Horus and Erebus,' said Magnus, and Ahriman was shocked to see the barest flicker in his primarch's aura.

Magnus was lying to them. He *had* known of this Primordial Annihilator.

'So what do we do now?' asked Uthizzar. 'Surely now we must warn the Emperor?'

Magnus hesitated before nodding slowly.

'Yes, we must,' he said. 'If my father is forewarned, he can take arms against Horus before it is too late.'

'Why will he believe us?' asked Ahriman. 'We have no proof.'

'I have the proof now,' sighed Magnus wearily. 'Now return to your cult temples and await my summons. Amon, attend upon me; the rest of you may leave.'

The Captains of Fellowship turned and made their way towards the crystal steps that led out of the cave.

'Ahriman,' said Magnus, 'bend all the power of the Corvidae to unravelling the strands of the future. We *must* know more of what is to come. Do you understand me?'

'I do, my lord,' replied Ahriman.

'Do whatever it takes,' said Magnus. 'Whatever the cost may be.'

* * *

LEMUEL AWOKE TO find Ahriman standing over him. His mentor had a stern look in his eye, and Lemuel immediately felt the tension in the room. He stifled a yawn, realising he'd fallen asleep next to Kallista's bed once again. Her eyes were closed, though it was hard to tell whether it was in sleep or unconsciousness. Camille sat across from him, her breathing still that of a sleeper.

Camille had recovered well from her ordeal with the psychneuein eggs, quickly returning to her normal, vivacious self.

'My lord?' he said. 'What is it?'

Amon and Ankhu Anen stood behind Ahriman, making the room feel suddenly small.

'You should leave, both of you,' Ahriman told him.

'Leave? Why?'

'Because you will find what has to happen here unpleasant.'

'I don't understand,' he said, rising from his chair and moving protectively towards Kallista. Camille woke and looked up, startled, as she saw Astartes filling the room.

'Lem?' she asked, immediately picking up on the tension. 'What's going on?'

'I don't know yet,' he said.

'I do not expect you to understand,' said Ahriman with real regret in his voice. 'But events are in motion that require us to know of the future. Our normal methods of gathering such information are denied to us, so we must seek other avenues.'

'What are you going to do? I won't let you hurt her.'

'I am sorry, Lemuel,' said Ahriman. 'We have no choice. This *has* to happen. Believe me, I wish it did not.'

Amon moved towards the bank of walnut-panelled machines and turned all the dials to the their middle positions. The light began to fade from the crackling, buzzing globes and the needles on the brass readouts nosed their way down.

'What is he doing?' Camille wanted to know. 'Lord Ahriman, please?'

Ahriman said nothing, his face betraying his unease.

'You wanted to know what this machine was for?' said Ankhu Anen, taking Lemuel's arm. The giant Astartes easily pulled him away from Kallista's side and handed him off to Ahriman. 'It is an aetheric blocker. It isolates the subject's mind from the Great Ocean. We used such devices to subdue our brothers when the flesh change came upon them. It was the only way to stop it. Your friend's mind is locked open to its roaring tides, and, but for these devices, aetheric energy would be pouring into her.'

'Can you... shut her mind to it?' asked Camille, standing protectively beside her friend.

The Astartes said nothing, and Lemuel read the truth in their auras.

'They can,' he said, 'but they won't.'

'She should be dead already,' hissed Ankhu Anen, dragging Camille out of the way. 'She has a unique link to future currents, and we must make use of all the tools available to us.'

'Tools? Is that all we've been to you?' asked Lemuel, struggling uselessly in Ahriman's grip. 'All this time, were you just using us?'

'It was not like that,' said Ahriman, casting a poisonous glance at Ankhu Anen.

'Yes it was,' said Lemuel. 'I see that now. You think you're so clever, but you're blinded by your belief in the superiority of your knowledge. You can't even contemplate that someone else might know better than you.'

'Because no one else *does*,' snapped Ahriman. 'We do know better than anyone else.'

'Maybe you do, but maybe you don't. What if there's something you're missing? What if there's some little piece of the puzzle you don't know about?'

'Be silent,' ordered Ankhu Anen. 'We are the architects of fate, not you.'

'So what happens when you turn those machines off?' asked Camille, taking Lemuel's hand as they realised the futility of resisting the Astartes physically.

'We will listen to what she has to say and we will learn of the future.'

'No, I won't let you,' said Lemuel.

'No?' sneered Ankhu Anen. 'Who are you to bark orders at us, little man? You think because Ahriman has taught you a few parlour tricks that you are one of us? You are mortals, your abilities and intellect are beneath our notice.'

'Ahriman, please!' begged Lemuel. 'Don't do this!'

'I'm sorry, Lemuel, but they are right. Kallista is dying anyway. At least this way her death will mean something.'

'That's a lie!' shouted Lemuel. 'If you do this, you'll be killing her. You might as well put a bullet in her brain and be honest about it.'

Amon removed some of the contact points on Kallista's skull and consulted the readouts on the aetheric blocker. He nodded to Ankhu Anen and said, 'It is done. I have kept some of the blocks in place, but her mind is open to the aether now. Just a fraction, but it should be enough to generate divinatory activity.'

Kallista's eyes fluttered open and she drew in a panicked breath as awareness was forced back to the surface of her consciousness. Her lips moved and breaths of hoarse air gusted from somewhere deep inside her. The temperature in the room fell sharply.

'A million shards of glass, a million times a million. All broken, all shattered glass. The eye in the glass. It sees and it knows, but it does nothing...'

Her eyes drifted shut and her breathing deepened. No more words were forthcoming, and Ankhu Anen leaned over her, prising the lids of her eyes open.

'Increase the flow of aetheric energy,' he ordered. 'We can get more out of her.'

'Please,' begged Camille. 'Don't do this.'

'Ahriman, she's an innocent, she doesn't deserve this,' cried Lemuel.

The Thousand Sons ignored them, and Amon again adjusted the dials on the machine. The needles dipped even farther, and Kallista's body jerked on the bed, her legs kicking the covers from her feet. Lemuel didn't want to watch, but couldn't tear his eyes from the dreadful sight.

She screamed, and the words poured from her in a flood as the temperature continued to plummet.

'It's too late... the Wolf is at the door and it hungers for blood. Oh, Throne... no, the blood! The Ravens, I see them too. The lost sons and a Raven of blood. They cry out for salvation and knowledge, but it is denied! A brother betrayed, a brother murdered. The worst mistake for the noblest reason! It cannot happen, but it must!'

Sweat poured from Kallista's face. Her eyes bulged in their sockets and every muscle and sinew of her body stretched to breaking point. The effort of speaking was too much, and she fell back, her frame wracked with agonising convulsions.

Lemuel felt Ahriman's grip slacken, and he looked up to see regret written across his face. He extended his aura, projecting his disgust and sadness at Kallista's treatment by the Thousand Sons into Ahriman's. The effect was subtle, but Ahriman looked down at him with an expression that was part admiration and part remorse.

'That will not work on me,' said Ahriman. 'You have learned much, but you don't have the strength to influence me with the little power you have.'

'Then you're just going to let this happen?'

'I have no choice,' said Ahriman. 'The primarch has demanded it be so.'

'Lem, they're going to kill her,' pleaded Camille.

Ahriman turned to face her saying, 'She is already dead, Mistress Shivani.'

He nodded to Amon. 'Allow the aether free reign within her. We must know everything.'

Magnus's equerry turned back to the machine and turned all the dials to zero. The needles fell slack and the lights winking on its surface extinguished. The glass readouts on the machine cracked with frost and the globes misted over. Lemuel felt cold like the chill at the end of the world.

The effect on Kallista was instantaneous. Her back arched and her eyes snapped open. Blazing light streamed out, like the furnace breath of an incinerator. It illuminated the room with a sickly blue-green light, throwing shadows of things that didn't exist across every wall. The ghostly howls of a million monsters ripped from her throat, and Lemuel smelled the awful stench of roasted human flesh.

Smoke poured from Kallista's body, and even the Astartes were horrified at what was happening to her. The flesh bubbled and smoked on her bones, peeling away in blackened flakes as though the target of an invisible flamethrower. Her body hissed and spat as it was reduced to jellied runnels of boiling fat and meat.

Yet through it all, she still screamed.

Long after her heart and lungs and brain were blackened husks, she kept screaming. The sound cut through Lemuel like a hot knife, twisting in his guts with treacherous force. He dropped to his knees as a screeching whine, like a host of fingernails dragged down a slateboard, bit into his head. Camille was screaming, her grip on his hand as powerful as a clamping vice.

Then, with a terrible ripping, tearing sound, it was over.

Lemuel blinked away bright sunbursts, feeling his stomach lurch at the stench of burned meat that hung like a miasma in the air. He pulled himself to his feet, dreading what he would see as much as he *needed* to see what had become of Kallista Eris.

Nothing remained of the beautiful remembrancer save a blackened outline seared onto the sheets, and smoking pools of rendered flesh that drooled from the bed in long, rubbery ropes.

'What did you do?' he whispered, tears streaming down his face. 'Oh, Kallista, you poor, poor girl.'

'We did what we needed to,' hissed Ankhu Anen. 'I make no apologies.'

'No,' said Lemuel, turning to help Camille to her feet. 'You didn't need to do this. This was murder, plain and simple.'

Camille wept with him, burying her head in his shoulder and clawing at his back with heaving sobs of grief.

Ahriman reached out to him.

'I am truly sorry, my friend,' he said.

Lemuel shrugged off his hand, moving past Ahriman towards the door with his arms wrapped tightly around Camille.

'Don't touch me,' he said. 'We are no longer friends. I don't know if we ever were.'

CHAPTER TWENTY-FIVE

The Warning/You were Right/Too Close to the Sun

Magnus sat in the centre of the Reflecting Cave, allowing the resonant harmonies of the silent crystals to fill him with calm. His meditations had lasted two nights and he had finally achieved the calm he needed to make his journey. He was not alone, for nine hundred Thralls stood in their appointed positions around the chamber, each holding a glimmering crystal into which they had bound their lifeforce.

No more Thralls could be spared, for all those that had taken part in the last ritual had since perished. Nine hundred was fewer than Magnus would have liked, but nine hundred would have to do. What other choice was there?

The spell he had crafted required sacrifice. Its power was beyond anything he had ever conjured, even within the secrecy of his Sanctum or in the days when he had struggled to cure his Legion of their terrible mutations.

The Thralls' lives were forfeit, but it was a sacrifice each made willingly. Their brothers had died in vain as

Magnus had tried to save Horus. They would die to allow Magnus to take warning of that treachery to the Emperor, and none begrudged their lord and master the light of their lives.

Magnus opened his eye as Ahriman approached.

'Is everything prepared?' he asked.

Ahriman was robed in white, and he bore the Book of Magnus before him like an offering. Magnus read his favoured son's concern, but he alone of all his warriors could be entrusted with this spell, for only Ahriman had the clarity of thinking and detached command of the Enumerations necessary to intone the incantation with the required precision.

'It is, my lord,' said Ahriman, 'but again I ask you, is this the only way?'

'Why do you doubt me, my son?' asked Magnus.

'It is not that I doubt you,' said Ahriman hurriedly, 'but I have studied this evocation and its power is unlike anything we have ever attempted. The consequences–'

'The consequences will be mine alone to bear,' interrupted Magnus. 'Now do as I ask.'

'My lord, I will always obey, but the spell to break into the alien lattice-way calls for bargains to be struck with the most terrible creatures of the Great Ocean, beings whose names translate as… daemons.'

'There is little beyond your knowledge, Ahriman, but there are yet things you cannot know. You of all men should know that "daemon" is a meaningless word conjured by fools who knew not what they beheld. Long ago, I encountered powers in the Great Ocean I thought to be sunken, conceptual landmasses, but over time I came to know them as vast intelligences, beings of such enormous power that they dwarf even the brightest stars of our own world. Such beings can be bargained with.'

'What could such powerful beings possibly want?' asked Ahriman. 'And can you ever really be sure that you have the best of such a bargain?'

'*I* can,' Magnus assured him. 'I have bargained with them before. This will be no different. If we could have saved the gateway into the lattice on Aghoru, this spell would be unnecessary. I could simply have stepped into it and emerged on Terra.'

'Assuming a gateway exists on Terra,' cautioned Ahriman.

'Of course a gateway exists on Terra. Why else would my father have retreated there to pursue his researches?'

Ahriman nodded, though Magnus saw he was far from convinced.

'There can be no other way, my son,' said Magnus. 'We talked about this before.'

'I remember, but it frightens me that we must wield powers forbidden to us to warn the Emperor. Why should he trust any warning sent by such means?'

'You would have me trust the vagaries of Astrotelepathy? You know how fickle such interpretations can be. I dare not trust a matter of such dreadful importance to mere mortals. Only I have the power to project my being into this alien labyrinth and navigate my way to Terra with news of Horus's treachery. For my father to believe me I must speak to him directly. He must bear witness to the acuity of my visions, and he must know what I know with the totality of my truth. Heard third-, fourth- or fifth hand through a succession of intermediaries will only dilute any warning until it is too late to do anything. *That* is why it must be this way.'

'Then it must be done,' said Ahriman.

'Yes, it must,' agreed Magnus, rising from the floor of the chamber and walking with Ahriman to the point beneath the bronze mechanism that lay below

Occullum Square. Magnus looked up through the green gem at its base, as though looking to Terra itself.

'It *will* be dangerous,' admitted Magnus, 'but if there is anyone who can do it…'

'It is you,' finished Ahriman.

Magnus smiled and said, 'Watch over me, my son?'

'Always,' said Ahriman.

MAGNUS FELT THE world fall away from him, shedding his corporeal body as a serpent sheds its skin and rises renewed. Ancients watching such creatures believed they knew the secrets of immortality and named their houses of healing in their honour. To this day, the symbol of the Apothecary, the caduceus, bore serpents entwined in a double helix.

Chains of flesh were shrugged off, and Magnus distilled his molten core into a seething arrow aimed from Prospero to distant Terra. With a thought, he shot up through the Occullum and into the heavens. His body of light was a beautiful thing, existence as it was meant to be experienced, not the mundane solidity endured by mortals.

Magnus shook off his revelries, for the energy of the spell was propelling him ever onwards. He felt Ahriman's words, the words of ancient sorcerers of Terra, wrapping his incandescent body in purpose, the life energies of the Thralls empowering him with their vitality.

This was a dangerous spell, and no other being would dare wield it.

The blackness of space dissolved, and the raging torrents of the Great Ocean surrounded him. Magnus laughed with the pleasure of it, rejoicing in the familiar energies and currents that welcomed him like a long lost friend.

He was a bright star amid a constellation of supernovas, each a flickering ember next to his beatific glory.

Here in the Great Ocean, he could be whatever he wanted to be; nothing was forbidden and anything was possible.

Worlds flashed past him as he hurtled through the swelling tides of colour, light and dimensions without name. The roiling chaos of the aether was a playground for titanic forces, where entire universes could be created and destroyed with a random thought. How many trillions of potential lives were birthed and snuffed out just by thinking such things?

Predators avoided him as he sped towards his destination like the most incredible comet ever set loose in the stars. They recognised him and were fearful of his brilliance in a realm where the light of creation blazed in every breath. Stagnation was anathema to Magnus. All life needed to progress through a series of evolved stages to prosper, and change was part of the natural cycle of all living things, from the smallest single-celled organism to the radiant creature encased within the crude matter of humanity.

The nobility of his cause threw off sparks of potency that created phantom worlds and concepts in his wake. Entire philosophies and bodies of thought would be born in the minds of those lucky enough to have his leavings descend upon their dreaming minds.

His course altered, a roving thought steering him around a monstrously dark shadow, the heaving bulk of something enormous shifting in the depths of the Great Ocean. Magnus felt a glimmer of familiarity in the stirred-up memories, but suppressed it with a shudder that sent a torrent of nightmares into the dreams of the tribal warriors of a feral world soon to encounter the 392nd Expeditionary Fleet.

There were no landmarks in the Great Ocean, its topography ever-mutable, yet this landscape of streaming colour and light was familiar by its very changeability. He had flown this shoal before, and he recoiled from it, concentrating on keeping his course true.

A shudder passed along his bright essence, and Magnus felt the first clutch of his Thralls die. Their soul lights winked out and a measure of his incredible, ferocious speed bled away.

'Hold on, my sons,' he whispered, 'just a little longer.'

What he sought was close, he could feel it: the same subtle vibration in the fabric of the Great Ocean that had drawn him to Aghoru. It was faint, like a distant heartbeat hidden within a rousing drum chorus.

Its creators had selfishly sought to keep it for themselves, little realising their time as masters of the galaxy was over. Even with their empire in decline, they kept their secret jealously close to their hearts.

Magnus sensed one of their hidden pathways nearby and opened his inner eye, seeing the glittering fabric of the Great Ocean in all its revealed glory. The hidden capillaries of the alien network were visible as radiant lines of molten gold, and Magnus angled his course towards the nearest.

Distance was a similarly meaningless concept here, and with a thought he spiralled around the golden passageway. He focussed his energy and unleashed it at the lattice in a blaze of silver lightning. Scores of his Thralls died in an instant, but the shimmer-sheen of the golden passage remained unbroken. Magnus hurled his fists against the impervious walls, snuffing out his Thralls by the dozen with every blow, but it was useless.

It had all been for nothing. He couldn't get in.

Magnus felt his glorious ascent slowing, and howled his frustration to the furthest corners of the Great Ocean.

Then he felt it, the familiar sense of something titanic moving in the swells around him, a continent adrift in the ocean with ancient sentience buried in its aetheric heart. Infinite spectra of light danced before him, more magnificent than the most radiant Mechanicum Borealis. Even to one as mighty as Magnus, the flaring eruption of light and power was incredible.

Its communication was sibilant, like sand pouring through the neck of an hourglass. It had breadth and depth, yet no beginning and no end, as though it had always existed around him and always would.

It spoke, not with words, but with power. It surrounded him, offering itself freely and without ulterior motive. The Great Ocean was truly a place of contradictions, its roiling, infinite nature allowing for the presence of all things, good and bad. Just as some entities within its depths were malicious and predatory, others were benevolent and altruistic.

Contrary to what most people believed, there *was* uncorrupted power here that could be wielded by those with the knowledge and skill to do so. Such gifted individuals were few and far between, but through the work of adepts like Magnus, it might yet be possible to lift humanity to a golden age of exploration and the acquisition of knowledge.

Magnus drank deep of the offered power and tore his way into the golden lattice. He felt its shrieking wail of unmaking as a scream of pain. Without a second thought, he flew into the shimmering passageway, following a route he knew would lead to Terra.

FAR BENEATH THE birthrock of the race that currently bestrode the galaxy as its would-be masters, a pulsing chamber throbbed with activity. Hundreds of metres high and many hundreds more wide, it hummed with machinery and reeked of blistering ozone. Once it had served as the Imperial Dungeon, but that purpose had long been subverted to another.

Great machines of incredible potency and complexity were spread throughout the chamber, vast stockpiles and uniquely fabricated items that would defy the understanding of even the most gifted adept of the Mechanicum.

It had the feel of a laboratory belonging to the most brilliant scientist the world had ever seen. It had the look of great things, of potential yet untapped, and of dreams on the verge of being dragged into reality. Mighty golden doors, like the entrance to the most magnificent fortress, filled one end of the chamber. Great carvings were worked into the mechanised doors: entwined siblings, dreadful sagittary, a rearing lion, the scales of justice and many more.

Thousands of tech-adepts, servitors and logi moved through the chamber's myriad passageways, like blood cells through a living organism in service to its heart, where a great golden throne reared ten metres above the floor. Bulky and machine-like, a forest of snaking cables bound it to the vast portal sealed shut at the opposite end of the chamber.

Only one being knew what lay beyond those doors, a being of towering intellect whose powers of imagination and invention were second to none. He sat upon the mighty throne, encased in golden armour, bringing all his intellect to bear in overseeing the next stage of his wondrous creation.

He was the Emperor, and though many in this chamber had known him for the spans of many lives, none knew him as anything else. No other title, no possible name, could ever do justice to such a luminous individual. Surrounded by his most senior praetorians and attended by his most trusted cabal, the Emperor sat and waited.

When the trouble began, it began swiftly.

The golden portal shone with its own inner light, as though some incredible heat from the other side was burning through the metal. Vast gunboxes fixed around the perimeter of the cave swung up, their barrels spooling up to fire. Lightning flashed from machine to machine as delicate, irreplaceable circuits overloaded and exploded. Adepts ran from the site of the breach, knowing little of what lay beyond, yet knowing enough to flee.

Crackling bolts of energy poured from the molten gates, flensing those too close to the marrow. Intricate symbols carved into the rock of the cavern exploded with shrieking detonations. Every source of illumination in the chamber blew out in a shower of sparks, and centuries of the most incredible work imaginable was undone in an instant.

No sooner had the first alarm sounded than the Emperor's Custodes were at arms, but nothing in their training could have prepared them for what came next.

A form pressed its way through the portal: massive, red and aflame with the burning force of its journey. It emerged into the chamber, wreathed in eldritch fire that bled away to reveal a robed being composed of many-angled light and the substance of stars. Its radiance was blinding and none could look upon its many eyes without feeling the insignificance of their own mortality.

None had ever seen such a dreadful apparition, the true heart of a being so mighty that it could only beat while encased in super-engineered flesh.

The Emperor alone recognised this rapturous angel, and his heart broke to see it.

'Magnus,' he said.

'Father,' replied Magnus.

Their minds met, and in that moment of frozen connection the galaxy changed forever.

OCCULLUM SQUARE WAS busy, though Lemuel saw an undercurrent of nameless fear in the auras of the traders and buyers. They haggled with more than usual bitterness, and the sparring back and forth was done with tired eyes and heavy hearts. Perhaps it was a mass hangover from the riots two weeks ago. No one had adequately explained why such violence had broken out on the streets of a city that had not known unrest in hundreds of years.

He sat with Camille on a wrought iron bench between Gordian Avenue and Daedalus Street, watching the crowds go about their business, pretending nothing was out of place, as though they were not living on a world ruled by warriors who regarded them as nothing more than playthings.

In the fortnight since Kallista's death, he and Camille had spent a great deal of time together, mourning their lost friend and coming to terms with their current situation. It had involved many stories, many tears and a great deal of soul-searching, but they had eventually reached the same conclusion.

'She thought this world was a paradise,' said Camille, watching the forced laughter of a couple strolling arm in arm beneath the shadow of the Occullum.

'We all did,' said Lemuel. 'I didn't want a tasking order to come for the Thousand Sons. I wanted to stay and learn from Ahriman. Look where that got us.'

'Kalli's death wasn't your fault,' said Camille, taking his hand. 'Don't ever think that.'

'I don't,' he said. 'I blame Ahriman. He may not have pulled the switches or pressed the buttons, but he knew what they were doing was wrong and he let it happen anyway.'

They watched the crowds for a moment longer, before Camille asked, 'Do you think he'll come?'

Lemuel nodded.

'He'll come. He wants this as much as we do.'

Camille looked away and Lemuel read the hesitation in her aura.

'We do both want this, don't we?' he asked.

'Yes,' said Camille, a little too quickly.

'Come on,' he said. 'We have to be honest with one another now.'

'I know, and you're right, it's time, but I–'

'You don't want to leave without Chaiya,' finished Lemuel.

'No, I don't. Does that sound stupid?'

'Not at all. I understand completely, but is what you have worth dying for?'

'I don't know yet,' said Camille, wiping the heels of her palms against her eyes. 'I think it might have been, but this is her home and she won't want to leave.'

'I won't force you to come, but you saw what I saw.'

'I know,' she said, through moist eyes. 'It'll break my heart, but I've made my mind up.'

'Good girl,' said Lemuel, hating that it had taken him this long to understand the truth.

Camille nodded towards Daedalus Street and said, 'Looks like your friend's here,' as a servitor-borne palanquin emerged and turned towards them. The servitors were bulk-muscled things, broad shouldered and wearing silver helmets and crimson tabards. The crowds parted for the palanquin, and it stopped before Lemuel and Camille.

The velvet curtain parted and Mahavastu Kallimakus emerged. A set of bronze steps extended from the base of the palanquin and he climbed down to join them.

'A grand conveyance,' said Lemuel, impressed despite himself.

'A waste of time that only serves to draw attention to my irrelevance,' snapped Mahavastu, sitting next to Camille on the bench. 'Sobek insisted I travel in it to save my old bones.'

The venerable scribe patted Camille's hand, his skin gnarled like old oak.

'I was sorry to hear of Mistress Eris's death,' he said. 'She was a quite lovely girl. A real tragedy.'

'No it's not,' said Lemuel. 'It would have been a tragedy if she died thanks to a weakness of her own making, but she was murdered, plain and simple.'

'I see,' said Mahavastu. 'What do I not know?'

'The Thousand Sons burned her out,' said Camille. 'They used her, and she died so that they could glimpse echoes of the future. Fat lot of good it did them. All she did was talk in riddles before it killed her.'

'Ah, I was told she had another of her unfortunate attacks at Voisanne's?'

'She did, but that was only the beginning,' said Lemuel, standing and pacing back and forth before the bench. 'They killed her, Mahavastu. It's that simple. Look, what do you want me to say? You were right, there is a curse upon the Thousand Sons. If what Kallista said means half of what we think it means, this world is doomed and it's time we were gone.'

'You wish to leave Prospero?' asked Mahavastu.

'Damn right I do.'

Mahavastu nodded. 'And you feel the same, Mistress Shivani?'

'Yeah,' she said. 'When Ankhu Anen moved me away from Kallista, I felt something of his memories, a fragment of something that passed between him and the other captains. I didn't get more than a flash, but whatever they know has them terrified. Something very bad is happening, and it's time we put some distance between us and the Thousand Sons.'

'Have you given any thought as to how we might do this, Lemuel?' asked Mahavastu.

'I have,' he said. 'There's a mass-conveyer in orbit right now, the *Cypria Selene*. It's completing an engine refit and is resupplying in preparation for despatch to

Thranx. She's scheduled to depart in a week, and we need to be on that ship.'

'And how do you propose we manage that?' asked Mahavastu. 'Its crew will be monitored, and we have no legitimate reason to be on the *Cypria Selene*.'

Lemuel smiled for the first time in weeks.

'Don't worry,' he said, 'I've learned a thing or two that should help with that.'

THE BOOKS WERE scattered like autumn leaves across the floor of his chambers, their pages torn and crumpled. The orreries were shattered and the astrological charts torn from the walls. The globe of Prospero was broken, its ochre continents lying in broken shards amid the cracked cerulean fragments of its oceans.

A torrent of destruction had swept through Magnus's chambers, but no thoughtless vandal or natural disaster had wreaked such havoc. The architect of this destruction squatted amid the ruin of his possessions with his head buried in his hands.

Magnus's white robe was stained and unkempt, his flesh worn with weeks of neglect, his body wracked by inconsolable grief. The shelves behind him were shattered, the timber splintered and broken to matchwood. Almost nothing remained in once piece. The mirrors were cracked and reduced to shattered diamonds of reflective glass.

Magnus lifted his head, out of breath from his rampage.

The exertion was nothing; it was the scope of what he had destroyed that took away his breath, the sheer, mind-numbing horror of what had been lost and could never be retrieved.

Only one thing had escaped his destructive rampage, a heavy lectern of cold iron upon which was chained the Book of Magnus, the grimoire of all his achievements, culled from the unexpurgated texts penned by Mahavastu Kallimakus.

Achievements.

The word stuck in his throat. All his achievements were lies in the dust.

It had all been for nothing. Everything was unravelling around him faster than he could weave it back together.

Magnus rose to his full height, his body diminished from its former glory, as though a fundamental part of him had been left on Terra after his confrontation with his father. The moment of connection they had shared had been sublime and horrendous. He had seen himself as others saw him, a monstrous, fiery angel of blood bringing doom down upon those mortals unlucky enough to fall beneath his gaze.

Only his father had recognised him, for he had wrought the life into him and knew his own handiwork. Magnus had experienced that awful self-knowledge in an instant, feeling it sear his heart and crush his soul in one dreadful moment of union.

He had tried to deliver his warning, showing his father what he had seen and what he knew. It hadn't mattered. Nothing he could have said would have outweighed or undone the colossal mistake he had made in coming to Terra. The treachery of Horus was swept away, an afterthought in the wake of the destruction Magnus had unwittingly unleashed. Wards that had kept the palace safe for a hundred years were obliterated in an instant, and the psychic shockwave killed thousands and drove hundreds more to madness and suicide.

But that wasn't the worst of it, not by a long way.

It was the knowledge that he had been wrong.

Everything he had been so sure of knowing better than anyone else was a lie.

He thought he had known better than his father how to wield the power of the Great Ocean. He believed he was its master, but in the ruins of his father's great work, he had seen the truth. The Golden Throne was the key. Unearthed from forgotten ruins sunken deep beneath the driest desert, it was the lodestone that would have unlocked the secrets of the alien lattice. Now it was in ruins, its impossibly complex dimensional inhibitors and warp buffers fused beyond salvage.

The control it maintained on the shimmering gateway at his back was ended, and the artfully designed mechanism keeping the two worlds apart was fatally fractured. In the instant of connection, Magnus saw the folly of his actions and wept to see so perfect a concept undone.

Unspoken understanding flowed between Magnus and the Emperor. Everything Magnus had done was laid bare, and everything the Emperor planned flowed into him. He saw himself atop the Golden Throne, using his fearsome powers to guide humanity to its destiny as rulers of the galaxy. He was to be his father's chosen instrument of ultimate victory. It broke him to know that his unthinking hubris had shattered that dream.

Without will, the spell that had sent him to Terra was nothing, and Magnus had felt the pull of flesh dragging his spirit back through the gateway. He did not fight it, but let his essence fly through the golden lattice to the tear he had so carelessly torn in its fabric. Vast shoals of void predators were already massing, swirling armies of formless monsters, fanged beasts and awesomely powerful entities that lived only for destruction.

Would the Emperor be able to hold them back?

Magnus didn't know, and the thought of so much blood on his hands shamed him.

He'd flown back through the timeless depths of the Great Ocean and awoken within the Reflecting Caves in the midst of a vast hall of the dead. The Thralls were no more, each and every one reduced to a withered, lifeless husk by the power of his spell.

Only Ahriman remained, and even he looked drained.

With tears in his eyes, Magnus retreated from the scene of his crime and all but fled to the Pyramid of Photep, ignoring Ahriman's shouted questions. Alone, amid the lies of his centuries of study, the red mist had fallen over his sight. He'd mocked Angron for his rages, but at the thoroughness of his destruction, he understood a measure of the satisfaction such violence could bring.

Magnus stood and walked from the ruin of his study, ashamed at his loss of control and needing to clear his head. The glass doors that led to his balcony were smashed, the glass lying in accusing shards that crunched as he stepped through the wreckage.

He leaned on the balcony railing, supporting his weight on his elbows and letting the cool wind ruffle his hair and caress his skin. Far below him, Tizca carried on as though nothing had happened, its people oblivious to the doom he had unleashed upon them all. They didn't know it yet, but a terrible retribution would soon fall upon them.

What form that retribution would take he did not know, but he recalled the Emperor's words at Nikaea, and feared the worst. People moved through Occullum Square and along the Street of a Thousand Lions, congregating in the many parks and Fountain Houses that dotted the western areas of the city where the bulk of its citizens dwelt.

The port was to the north, a walled area of the city built on the gentle slopes that led down to the curved bay. Golden beaches spread further along the coast before sweeping beyond sight into the Desolation. Hard against the flanks of the eastern mountains stood the Acropolis Magna, a raised spur of rock that had once been a fortress, but had long since fallen into ruin. A great statue of Magnus stood upon its highest point to mark the place where he had first set foot on the surface of Prospero.

How he wished he could take back those first steps!

Dozens of theatres clustered around the base of the Acropolis Magna, their tiers cut into the lower slopes of the rock, home to actors who strutted like martinets on each marbled proscenium. Five perfectly circular Tholus stood in areas of rolling parkland, open-air structures built according the principles of the Golden Mean. In the forgotten ages they had once housed temples, but were now used as sports arenas and training grounds.

Numerous barracks of the Spireguard dotted the city's plan, and Magnus felt a twinge of regret for these men and women most of all. They were all going to die for the crime of being born on Prospero.

The cult's pyramids dominated the skyline, looming from the gilded city like cut glass arrowheads. Sunlight reflected on them, dancing like fire in the polarised crystal. He'd seen the vision once before and had thought it allegorical. Now he knew better.

'All this will be ashes,' he said sadly.

'It does not have to be,' said a voice behind him.

Magnus turned, and harsh words died on his lips as he saw it was not an intruder that had spoken.

He had.

Or at least a version of him had.

The mirror hanging beside the doorway was broken, yet dozens of splinters still clung to the copper frame. In each of them, Magnus saw a shimmering reflection of his eye, one mocking, one angry, one capricious, another aloof. The eyes stared with sly amusement, each a different colour and each now regarding him with the same quizzical look.

'A mirror? Even now you appeal to my vanity,' said Magnus, dreading what this signified.

'I told you it was the easiest trap to set,' said the reflections, their voices slippery and entwined. 'Now you know the truth of it.'

'Was this always what you wanted?' asked Magnus. 'To see me destroyed?'

'Destroyed? Never!' cried the reflections, as though outraged by the suggestion. 'You were always to be our first choice, Magnus. Did you know that?'

'First choice for what?'

'To bring about the eternal chaos of destruction and rebirth, the endless succession of making and unmaking that has cycled throughout time and will continue for all eternity. Yes, you were always first, and Horus is a poor second. The Eternal Powers saw great potential in you, but even as we coveted your soul, you grew too strong and caused us to look elsewhere.'

The reflections smiled with paternal affection, 'But I always knew you would be ours one day. While suspicious eyes were turned upon you and your Legion, we wove our corruptions elsewhere. For that you have my thanks, as the Blinded One has lit the first fire of the conflagration, though none yet see it for what it is.'

'What *are* you?' asked Magnus, stepping through the doorway to re-enter the wreckage of his chambers. Hoarfrost gathered on the splintered glass and his breath misted before him.

'You know what I am,' said his reflections. 'Or at least you *should*.'

One splintered eye shifted, swirling until it became a fiery snake with multi-coloured eyes and wings of bright feathers: the beast he had killed beneath the Mountain of Aghoru. It changed again, morphing through a succession of shimmering forms, until Magnus saw the shifting, impossibly massive form of the shadow in the Great Ocean.

'I once named myself Choronzon to you, the Dweller in the Abyss and the Daemon of Dispersion, but those are meaningless labels that mortals hang upon me, obsolete the moment they are uttered. I have existed since the beginning of time and will exist beyond the span of this universe. Names are irrelevant to me, for I am every name and none. In the inadequate language of your youngling species, you should call me a god.'

'You were the one that helped me save my Legion,' said Magnus with a sinking heart.

'Save? No. I only postponed their doom,' said the shadow. 'That boon is now ended.'

'No!' cried Magnus. 'Please, never that!'

'There is a price to pay for the time I gave your sons. You knew this when you accepted the gift of my power. Now it is time to make good on your bargain.'

'I made no bargain,' said Magnus, 'not with the likes of you.'

'Oh, but you did,' laughed the eyes. 'When, in your despair, you cried out for succour in the depths of the warp, when you begged for the means to save your sons – you flew too close to the sun, Magnus. You offered up your soul to save theirs, and that debt is now due.'

'Then take me,' declared Magnus. 'Leave my Legion and allow them to serve the Emperor. They are blameless.'

'They have drunk from the same chalice as you,' said the eyes. 'And why would you wish them to serve a man who betrayed you? A man who showed you unlimited power and then told you not to use it? What manner of father opens the door to a world of wonder and then orders you not to step through? This *man* who planned to use your flesh to save his own from destruction?'

The images in the glass changed once more, and Magnus saw the Golden Throne, its mechanisms wreathed in crackling arcs of lighting. A howling, withered cadaver sat upon the throne, its once-mighty flesh blackened and metastasised.

'This is to be your destiny,' said the mirror, 'bound forever to the Emperor's soul-engine, suffering unendurable agony to serve his selfish desires. Look upon this and know the truth.'

Magnus tried to look away, but the horror of the vision was impossible to ignore.

'Why should I believe anything you say?' he cried.

'You already know the truth of your doom; I have no need to embellish. Look into the warp and hunt for your nemesis. He and his savage dogs of war are already on their way. Trust yourself if you do not trust me.'

Magnus closed his eye and cast his senses into the seething currents of the Great Ocean. Its substance was agitated, and roaring tides billowed with tempestuous force. All was chaos, but for a slender corridor of stillness, through which Magnus felt the passage of many souls.

He closed upon their lifeforce and saw the form his doom would take.

Magnus's eye snapped open and anger boiled over. His hand erupted in searing white fire, the most prosaic and primal of the arts, and his chambers were filled with billowing flames, burning everything within to cinders. Wood and paper vaporised in the white heat of Magnus's rage, and what little his despair had not destroyed, his rage consumed.

A column of blazing fire erupted from the summit of his pyramid, and a rain of molten glass shards fell from the summit. All eyes in Tizca turned towards the Pyramid of Photep, the plume of fire dwarfing that of the Pyrae.

Only the Book of Magnus remained inviolate, its pages impervious to the killing fire.

Nothing was left of the mirror, its fused shards bubbling in a molten pool at his feet.

'You can destroy them,' said the fading reflections in the liquid glass. 'Say the word and I will tear their vessels asunder, scattering them beyond all knowledge and hope of salvation.'

'No,' said Magnus, dropping to his knees with his head in his hands. 'Never.'

MAGNUS HAD NO knowledge of how much time had passed when he heard the crash of his door breaking open. He looked up to see Uthizzar enter his chambers, his youthful features shocked at the devastation he saw within. A squad of Scarab Occult came with him, their visors marred by a single vertical slash that obscured the right eye lenses of their helmets.

Magnus had heard that the tradition had become commonplace after the Council of Nikaea, but to see such a visible sign of his sons' devotion was a poisoned barb in his heart.

'Uthizzar,' said Magnus through his tears, 'get out of here!'

'My lord?' cried Uthizzar, moving towards Magnus.

Magnus raised a warding hand, his grief threatening to overwhelm him as he thought of all he had seen and all that the monstrous god of the warp had shown him.

Uthizzar staggered as the full force of Magnus's thoughts struck him like a blow. Magnus veiled his mind from the young telepath, but it was too late. Uthizzar knew it all.

'No!' cried Uthizzar, crushed by the gut-wrenching hurt of betrayal. 'It cannot be! You… Is it true? Tell me it is not true. What you did… What is coming…'

Magnus felt his heart harden, and cursed himself for such an unforgivable lapse of will.

'It is true, my son. All of it.'

He could see Uthizzar's eyes begging him to say he was joking, or that this was some hideous test. As much as Magnus wanted to save his sons from the sins of their father, he knew he couldn't. He had lied to himself and his warriors for too long, and this last chance for truth and redemption could not be squandered.

No matter what it entailed.

'We have to warn the Legion,' hissed Uthizzar, spinning on his heel and barking orders to the Scarab Occult. 'Mobilise the Spireguard and stand the fleet to battle orders. Disperse the Arming Proclamation to the civilian militias and issue a general evacuation order for non-combatants to the Reflecting Caves!'

Magnus shook his head, and a wall of unbreakable force sprang up before Uthizzar and his warriors, trapping them within his scorched and smoking chambers.

'I am sorry, Uthizzar, I really am,' said Magnus, 'but I can't let you do that.'

Uthizzar started to turn towards him, but before his son could look him in the eye, Magnus ended his life.

CHAPTER
TWENTY-SIX

A Good Student/My Fate is My Own/Dispersal

THE TANG OF salty air was strong. A stiff breeze blew in from the sea, and Lemuel felt a pang of nostalgia as he thought back to the sweeping coastlines of Nordafrik. The waters around his home had long since retreated, but the exposed seabeds shared the memory of their days at the bottom of the ocean with the air.

He shook off the memory. He needed all his powers of concentration.

The port area of Tizca was heaving with bodies: sweating stevedores, teamsters, servitors and load-lifters. The *Cypria Selene* was scheduled to break orbit in four hours, and the last-minute preparations for her departure were in full swing. Trucks, supply tankers, baggage lifters and water bladders carefully negotiated the busy port, and the noise of horns and shouting drivers rivalled the roar of engines.

The hot reek of burning metal saturated the day as shuttles and lifters screamed into the sky to deliver the last crewmembers and passengers to their berths. Few remained on Prospero, and a palpable sense of excitement suffused the port.

Lemuel's nerves were stretched bow-taut. Red-jacketed soldiers of the Prospero Spireguard circulated throughout the port, and officious docket-supervisors checked and rechecked passes and permits.

Beside him, Camille walked with her hands clasped demurely before her. She wore a long dress of emerald green, cut low and embroidered with black lace around the hems, sleeves and collar. She had balked at wearing the noblewoman's dress before Lemuel had pointed out that a patrician gentleman's consort would need to be seen in such a garment.

At this moment, that patrician gentleman was reclining in his palanquin, its ostentatious appearance enhanced by silk brocade and velvet cushions stolen from their living quarters. Bedecked in an exquisitely tailored suit, Mahavastu Kallimakus was failing miserably to look like an arrogant nobleman of Terra by looking down his nose as he tapped an ebony cane on the pillars of his conveyance.

Only Lemuel was spared the indignity of disguise, wearing his beige remembrancer's robes to masquerade as Mahavastu's personal scribe and eunuch escort to Camille. That last element of his disguise had raised a smile as they planned how best to reach a shuttle bound for the *Cypria Selene*. At least it had raised a smile with everyone except Lemuel.

Behind them came a team of bearers, nine servitors carrying a collection of steamer trunks filled with the mass of papers, sketchbooks and grimoires written by Mahavastu in the years he had spent as Magnus's puppet. Lemuel had urged Mahavastu to leave them, but the old man was adamant. The past needed to be preserved. History was history and it was not for them to judge what should be remembered and what should be forgotten.

'I won't be a burner of books,' said Mahavastu, and the discussion was ended.

They had entered the port area without incident, for centuries of peace and an increasingly compliant galaxy had made the people of Prospero complacent.

'So how are we going to do this?' asked Camille. It was the first thing she had said this morning, for there had been a furious row the previous night as she had told Chaiya of her decision to leave.

'Trust me,' said Lemuel. 'I know what I'm doing.'

'You keep saying that, but you never say what you're going to do.'

'I won't know until the time comes.'

'Well that's reassuring.'

Lemuel didn't reply, understanding the root of Camille's harsh words. They moved through the crowds, avoiding the main thoroughfares of wide-wheeled trucks as they ferried soldiers and crew to the loading berths. Tall-sided hangars, storage silos and fuel towers made up the bulk of the port facilities, and they threaded a path between them as they wound towards the silver platforms built on the edge of the shoreline.

A dozen craft growled in their berths, the last to join the orbiting mass-conveyer. This would be their last chance to get off Prospero.

Lemuel led them towards the launch bays as two more craft climbed into the sky on shrieking columns of jetfire. Camille walked alongside Mahavastu's palanquin, trying and failing to look decorous as the bulked-out servitors bore him without complaint. They made for an unusual spectacle, but one Lemuel hoped looked about right for passengers who had every right to be taking flight on the newly refitted *Cypria Selene*.

'This isn't going to work,' said Camille.

'It's going to work,' insisted Lemuel. 'It has to work.'

'No it won't. We'll be stopped and we'll be stuck on Prospero.'

'With that attitude we definitely will be,' snapped Lemuel, his patience wearing thin.

'Lemuel. Camille,' said Mahavastu from the palanquin. 'I understand we are all under a lot of pressure here, but if it wouldn't be too much trouble, would both of you please shut the shitting hell up!'

Both Lemuel and Camille were brought up short, shocked at the old man's language.

Lemuel looked up at Mahavastu, who seemed, if anything, more offended than them.

'I apologise for my profanity,' said Mahavastu, 'but it seemed like the only way to restore calm. Sniping at each other is only going to end things badly for us all.'

Lemuel took a deep breath.

'You're right,' he said. 'I apologise, my dear.'

'I'm sorry, Lemuel,' said Camille.

Lemuel nodded and led the way downhill again. At last they reached the entrance to the shuttlecraft launch platforms. This time there was a security checkpoint, as not even the citizens of Prospero left such dangerous places unsecured. Spireguard manned the entrance to the shuttle areas, and blue-robed officials checked the identity of everyone going through to the launch platforms.

'Now we get to see if all that training was worth it,' said Camille.

Lemuel nodded. 'Let's hope I was a good student.'

They approached the checkpoint, and Lemuel handed over a sheaf of papers taken from one of Kallista's notebooks to a bored-looking clerk. The words written there made no sense, but it would be easier if the mark couldn't understand them.

The clerk frowned, and Lemuel took that as his cue.

'Lord Asoka Bindusara and Lady Kumaradevi Chandra to take ship to the *Cypria Selene*,' said Lemuel, projecting a confidence he didn't feel into the man's aura. 'I am their humble servant and scrivener. Be so good as to indicate which of the waiting shuttles is the most regally appointed.'

Lemuel leaned in and whispered conspiratorially, 'My master has grown accustomed to the luxuries of Prospero. It wouldn't be pleasant for anyone were we to be assigned a craft that wasn't a damn palace, if you take my meaning.'

The clerk was still frowning at the words on the page. It wouldn't take long for him to see past Lemuel's bluff and understand he was looking at gibberish. Lemuel felt the man's bureaucratic mind processing the letters before him and increased his manipulation of his aura. Siphoning off the sanguine and the bile, he crafted the impression that the documents were travel passes and berthing dockets for three passengers and their luggage.

The clerk gave up with Lemuel's papers and consulted a data-slate of his own instead.

'I don't see your names,' he said with officious satisfaction.

'Please, check again,' said Lemuel, edging closer as a trio of shuttles blasted off from the shoreline. He sensed Camille and Mahavastu's panic behind him and increased his mental barrage. Even as he did so, he could feel that it wasn't working.

Lemuel heard a gasp of surprise from behind him, and a soothing blanket of acceptance settled over him. From the glassy look that came into the clerk's eyes, Lemuel saw it was affecting him too. Someone moved beside him and a woman's voice said, 'There has been a last minute addition to the passenger manifest, these are my guests aboard ship.'

Lemuel smiled as Chaiya rested her hand on the clerk's arm, feeling her influence spreading through him. It seemed every native of Prospero enjoyed a measure of psychic power, and he wondered how he hadn't noticed it before.

'Yes,' said the clerk, sounding unsure, but unable to say why. 'I see that now.'

He nodded as Chaiya's certainty increased, and he waved to the soldiers on either side of the gateway. The clerk stamped a lading billet for their steamer trunks and handed Lemuel four berthing disks, each with a stamped eye at its centre. Lemuel tried not to look as relieved as he felt.

'My lord thanks you,' he said as they swept through the gate.

No sooner were they hidden from sight of the clerk and his soldiers, than Camille threw herself into Chaiya's arms and kissed her. They embraced until Mahavastu coughed discreetly.

'You came!' said Camille, tears smudging the make-up around her eyes.

'Of course I came,' said Chaiya. 'You think I'd let you leave without me?'

'But last night–'

Chaiya shook her head. 'Last night you blindsided me with all your doomsaying talk. And the idea that you were leaving scared me. I don't want to leave Prospero, but if you think there's something bad coming, that's good enough for me. You've never been wrong before now. About anything. I love you and won't be parted from you.'

Camille wiped her eyes with the sleeve of her dress, ruining the fabric, but not caring.

'There is something bad coming, I know it,' she said.

'I believe you,' said Chaiya with a nervous laugh. 'If you're wrong we can always come back.'

Lemuel nodded towards the shuttle the clerk had assigned them.

'We'd better get moving,' he said. 'Ours is one of the last to leave.'

Their ragtag group followed the directions of blue-coated ground crew towards the berth of a sleek lighter of gleaming silver. Its wide wings enfolded them in shadow as they passed beneath them, and its flat-bottomed cargo bay was slung beneath the berthing frame they had to climb to reach the crew ramp.

Lemuel allowed himself a small smile of success.

Camille and Chaiya laughed and giggled as they walked hand in hand towards the lighter.

Even Mahavastu wore a smile.

The smiles fell from all their faces as an urgent voice called out, 'Stop. On the crew ramp, stay where you are.'

Lemuel's heart turned to a lump of ice as he turned to see who had hailed them.

A captain in the Prospero Spireguard was leading a detachment of soldiers towards them.

'This looks bad,' he said.

'You HAVE NOTHING to fear from me, Amon,' said Magnus. 'You have been my most faithful servant since I first came to Prospero. I could never harm you.'

'With respect, my lord, I am sure young Uthizzar thought the same,' said Amon, picking his way gingerly through the wreckage of Magnus's chambers. His grey hair was kept cropped close to his skull and his skin had the texture of aged vellum. He knelt beside Uthizzar's body and placed his hand upon the cracked and seared breastplate.

The bodies of the Scarab Occult lay around Uthizzar, their bodies twisted in unnatural ways and their flesh blackened as though consumed in the same fire that had destroyed Magnus's library.

'Tell me what happened,' said Amon.

Magnus lowered his head, unwilling to meet his oldest friend's gaze. The Captain of the 9th made no accusations – he didn't need to. No accusation could carry greater guilt than Magnus placed upon himself. Almost a week had passed since he had killed Uthizzar, a week in which he had almost given in to his self-destructive urges and turned his powers upon himself.

Fearing the worst, others had tried to enter his chambers, but Magnus had kept them all at bay until now. Magnus looked down at the grotesquely crumpled body of Baleq Uthizzar and sighed with regret and loss.

'It was an unforgivable lapse and should never have happened,' he said, 'but he knew too much and I could not let him leave.'

'Knew too much about what?'

'Come here,' said Magnus. 'Let me show you.'

Amon rose and followed Magnus onto the balcony overlooking the white city of Tizca. Magnus read the wariness in Amon's aura, and didn't blame him. He would be a fool not be wary. In all the long years since they had first spoken, as tutor and pupil, Magnus had never thought of Amon as a fool.

Magnus looked towards the noonday sky.

'Fly the Great Ocean with me,' he said.

Amon nodded and closed his eyes, and Magnus let his body of light float free of his flesh. The concerns of the mortal world lessened, but could not be wholly ignored. Tizca transformed from a place of cool marble to a glittering jewel of light, the tens of thousands of shimmering soul-lights who called the city home like tiny lanterns.

'How fragile they are,' said Magnus, though there was no one yet to hear him.

The warm glow of Amon's subtle body appeared next to him, and they flew into a sky of brilliant blue. The world around them deepened from blue to black, the stars pinwheeling around them like darts of phosphor.

The blackness of space transformed into the swirling, multi-coloured chaos of the Great Ocean, and both travellers felt the welcome rush of pleasure as its currents flowed around their ethereal forms.

Magnus led the way, streaking through the swirling abyss towards a destination only he was capable of finding. Amon followed him, his dutiful friend and beloved son. At length, they came to the region of stillness he had seen a week ago.

He felt Amon's horror as he beheld the vast fleet of ships, the slab-sided warships, the sleek strike cruisers and the monstrous monuments to destruction that were the Battle Barges. Hundreds of vessels drew ever closer to Prospero, ships of many flags and many allegiances, united with one shared purpose: annihilation.

Leading them was a feral blade of a ship, unsheathed to deliver the deathblow to its hated foe. Grey and fanged, it prowled the stars with carved eyes at its bladed prow piercing the depths of the Great Ocean with uncanny precision.

'Is that what I think it is?' asked Amon.

'It is,' confirmed Magnus.

They flew closer to the brutal vessel, the protective shields that kept void-predators at bay no match for travellers of such power. They passed through its layered voids, diving down through metre upon metre of adamantium hull plates, integrity fields and honeycombed bulkheads until they reached the heart of the ship.

The masters of this fleet gathered to plan the destruction of all that Magnus held dear, and the two sons of Prospero listened to their deliberations. Magnus was prepared for what he would hear, but Amon was not, and the flaring wash of his aetheric field sent a pulse of choleric energy through the ship's crew.

'Why?' begged Amon.

'Because I was wrong.'

'About what?'

'Everything,' said Magnus. 'All the things you taught me, I arrogantly assumed I already knew. You warned me of the gods of the warp and I laughed at you, calling you a superstitious old fool. Well I know better now, for I beheld such a being and thought I had the better of it, but I was wrong. I have done terrible things, Amon, but you must believe that I did them for the right reasons.'

Amon drifted down towards the master of this vessel and the steely-eyed killer in golden armour who stood next to him on a raised command dais. A group of identically armoured warriors stood at the base of the dais occupied by their leaders.

'The Council of Nikaea?' demanded Amon. 'Were they right to name us warlocks?'

'I fear they may have been, though only now do I understand that.'

'And for that we are to suffer?'

Magnus nodded and flew up through the ironwork of the starship, exploding outwards into the seething cauldron of the Great Ocean. Amon flew at his side, and they hurtled back to Prospero, exhaling pent-up breaths as they opened their eyes and looked down on the reassuringly familiar vista of Tizca.

'And the Legion knows nothing of this?' asked Amon.

'Nothing,' said Magnus. 'I have drawn a veil around Prospero. None see out, not even the Corvidae. Now the Thousand Sons must learn what it means to be blind.'

'So our punishment draws ever closer,' said Amon. 'What happens when it gets here?'

'You are kind, old friend,' said Magnus. 'It is *my* punishment.'

'Their axes will fall on the rest of us as well,' pointed out Amon. 'I ask again; what will we do when they get here?'

'Nothing,' said Magnus. 'There is nothing *to* do.'

'There is always something to do. We can destroy them before they even reach us,' hissed Amon, gripping Magnus's arm.

Magnus shook his head saying, 'This is not about whether we can defend ourselves against this threat. Of course we can. It is about whether we *should*.'

'Why should we not?' countered Amon. 'We are the Thousand Sons and nothing is beyond us. No path is unknown to us and no destiny is hidden from us. Instruct the Corvidae to pierce the veils of the future. The Pavoni and Raptora can enhance our warriors' prowess while the Pyrae burn our enemies and the Athanaeans read the minds of their commanders. When they come they will find us ready to fight.'

Magnus despaired, hearing only the urge to strike the first blow in Amon's voice.

'Have you not heard what I have said?' he pleaded. 'I do not strike because it is what the powers that have manipulated me since I came here want me to do. They want me to take arms against our doom, knowing that if I do it will only confirm everything those who hate and fear us have always believed.'

Amon looked out over the city, and his eyes took on a faraway look, tears of loss streaming down his cheeks.

'Before you came to Prospero, I had a recurring nightmare,' he said. 'I dreamt that everything I held dear was swept away and destroyed. It plagued me for years, but on the day you arrived from the heavens like a comet, the dream stopped. I never had it again. I convinced myself it was nothing more than an ancestral memory of Old Night, but it wasn't, I know that now. I foresaw this. The destruction of everything I hold dear is coming to pass'

Amon closed his eyes and he gripped the balcony with white-knuckled fury.

'I may not be able to stop it,' he said, 'but I am going to fight to protect my home, and if you ever held my friendship in any esteem, you would do the same.'

Magnus rounded on Amon.

'Despite everything I have done, my fate is my own,' Magnus said. 'I am a loyal son of the Emperor, and I would never betray him, for I have already broken his heart and his greatest creation. I will accept my fate and though history may judge us traitors, *we will know the truth*. We will know we were loyal unto the end because we accepted our fate.'

* * *

THE CAPTAIN OF the Spireguard stopped before him, and Lemuel reached out to soothe his aura. His terror made it difficult, but before he could reach out with any calming influence, he saw that the officer's aura was not expecting trouble, but wracked with grief.

Lemuel looked more closely, recognising the breadth of the man's shoulders, the immaculate pressing of the uniform and the gold frogging looped around his shoulders.

The captain removed his helmet, and Lemuel dared hope this enterprise wasn't doomed.

'Captain Vithara?' he said.

'Indeed, Master Gaumon,' said Captain Sokhem Vithara of the 15th Prosperine Assault Infantry. 'I hoped I would see you before you left.'

'Before we left?' asked Lemuel, confused as to why they weren't being frogmarched in manacles away from the lighter. The cargo bay doors were closing and they would be airborne in a matter of moments.

'Yes, I almost missed you because your names weren't on any of the manifests.'

'No,' agreed Lemuel with a guilty smile, 'they wouldn't be.'

'Still, I'm glad I caught you.'

'You are?' asked Camille. 'Why? What do you want?'

The young man struggled to find the right words, and in the end he gave up and just spoke in a confused torrent.

'I don't know for sure what happened to Kallista, but I know she does not want to remain here,' he said, and Lemuel struggled to hold his composure in the face of the young man's obvious grief. 'She wants you to take her away from here.'

Lemuel exchanged a worried look with Camille.

'That could be difficult,' he said.

'I know, I'm not making any sense,' said Vithara, 'but she said that she wanted to leave Prospero with her friends.'

'And she told you this?' asked Camille, enunciating each word carefully so there could be no misunderstanding. '*After* she died?'

Vithara's face was a mask of indecision and incomprehension.

'I believe so,' he said. 'I dreamed of Kallista last night, you see. She was sitting beside me in Fiorento Park and we watched the sunshine on the lake. We didn't say anything, we just held each other. When the reveille bell woke me this morning, I found a note beside my bed telling me to be at the landing platforms at this exact time. I don't remember writing the note, even though it was in my handwriting, but it was obviously Kallista's words. She wanted me to be here, and she wanted me to give you this.'

Vithara accepted a pale blue ceramic jar from one of his soldiers and held it out to Lemuel. Simply crafted, it was an urn in which one might keep a beloved family member's ashes.

Lemuel took the jar and smiled and said, 'You know, I believe you are absolutely right. Kallista did come to you last night, and since I am her friend, I will honour her wishes.'

'Then you think she really came to me last night?'

'I do,' said Lemuel, his own grief eased by the notion. 'I really do.'

Vithara saluted Lemuel and said, 'Thank you, Master Gaumon. I'll miss Kalli, but if this is what she wants then who am I to deny her?'

'You are a very noble man,' said Camille, stepping forward and planting a soft kiss on his cheek. 'I see why Kalli liked you.'

He smiled and nodded towards the crew compartment of the lighter, where an exasperated deck hand waited to close the hatch.

'You'd better go,' said Vithara. 'You don't want to miss the *Cypria Selene's* launch. After all, time and tide wait for no man.'

'Indeed they do not,' said Lemuel, shaking Vithara's hand. The servitors loaded the steamer trunks into the lighter as Mahavastu climbed down from his palanquin. Camille guided the venerable scribe onto the lighter as Vithara led his men from the landing platform.

Lemuel followed his friends onboard. As the hatch slid shut behind him, he had what he knew would be his last sight of Prospero.

He was wrong about that.

THE CYPRIA SELENE weighed anchor on schedule and eased clear of her berth with smooth grace. Silver jibs jutted into space from the central hub of the orbital docks, the space around it thick with manoeuvring warships. Thousand Sons battle-barges slipped their moorings and set sail for the outer reaches of the star system, and squadrons of strike cruisers flocked around them as they departed Prospero.

To coordinate so large a ballet of ships was no small feat. The *Photep* led an armada of ships with the power to level planets to the furthest edges of the star system, while the *Ankhtowë*, *Scion of Prospero* and the *Kymmeru* assumed equally-angled vectors, leading fleets to the corners of the Thousand Sons' domain.

The order to disperse the fleet had come with the highest alert prefixes, and the four battle groups made best speed for their destinations. None of the captains knew the nature of the alert, but all had been given strict instructions not to unlock their orders until reaching their assigned coordinates.

That such orders left Prospero dangerously undefended was clear to every shipmaster, but none dared disobey a direct command from the primarch himself. Whatever the purpose of this dispersal was not for them to question. Their only duty was to obey.

Military traffic took precedence over civilian vessels, and it took six hours for the *Cypria Selene* to work its way up the queue of ships awaiting a transit corridor. Eventually, the vessel's Master Steersman was able to pilot his way towards clear space and open up the plasma drives to take his vessel towards the coreward jump point.

From there, warp-willing, it would be a three-week journey to the Thranx system.

THE ANGLE OF launch had been good, and instead of taking four days to reach the coreward jump point, *Cypria Selene* achieved the necessary safe distance from the Prosperine star to safely activate its warp drives in three. The vessel's Navigator confirmed the warp-currents in the realm beyond were as calm as he had known them, and the Master of Cartography ran a final positional check before passing his jump calculations to the Navigator's module.

In the ship's observation dome, Lemuel and Mahavastu chatted about where they next planned to visit, while Camille and Chaiya held hands as they listened to the toneless jump countdown through speakers set into the wood-panelled walls.

Set high on the rear quarter of the *Cypria Selene*, the dome provided a commanding view over the vast superstructure of the mass-conveyer. Its hull stretched away from them for sixty kilometres, ending in a blunt wedge of a snout. For a vessel intended to carry vast quantities of war materiel, troops and bulk items of warfare and compliance, it was handsomely appointed.

The four of them had settled into ship-board life with ease, and the cabins they had been assigned by the misdirected clerk were clearly intended for highborn passengers.

'Give or take, you should be on Terra inside two months,' Lemuel told Mahavastu. 'You'll be back in Uttarpatha, cataloguing old records recovered from beneath the ruins. I hear they've finished collating the datacores of NeoAleksandrya, but there's bound to be more. They'd be mad not to want your help.'

'Perhaps,' agreed Mahavastu, leaning heavily on an ebony cane with a golden pommel inset with a jade eye. 'Though I fear I may be too old for such excitement.'

'Nonsense,' said Lemuel. 'There's life in you yet.'

'You are kind, Lemuel,' said Mahavastu, 'but I think perhaps I will instead concentrate on my memoirs. What I can recall of them.'

'I would be happy to read them.'

'Happier than I shall be to write them, I feel.'

Lemuel didn't reply, but simply smiled as Camille and Chaiya joined them at the edge of the observation dome. Perhaps sixty people had come to watch the ship translate into the warp, either curious to see how so enormous a vessel could travel between the stars or eagerly fearful to look into the mysterious realm of the warp.

If only they knew, thought Lemuel. *They would put out their eyes rather than look into a place of such dreadful power.*

'Almost away,' said Camille.

'Yes,' said Lemuel, nodding towards the glass dome as the countdown reached one minute. 'Part of me is almost sad.'

Aerial-like vanes extended along the entire length of the vast ship, causing the view to shimmer as void barriers powered up in preparation for the jump.

'Won't be long now,' said Camille, taking Lemuel's hand.

'And then this will all be over,' said Lemuel.

The count had reached thirty-three seconds when the alarms sounded.

The automated voice was cut off by a burst of shrieking static. A series of emergency lights flooded the interior of the dome with a red glow.

'What's happening?' cried Mahavastu.

Lemuel had no answer for him, but was spared from admitting his ignorance by an explosion of shimmering, ghostly light off the *Cypria Selene's* starboard bow. As though a yellowed fang had torn a terrible wound in the fabric of reality, a blooming froth of light spilled out and illuminated space around the mass-conveyer. It tore wider and wider, blistering streamers of unlight weeping from the wound like blood on a shroud.

Vast forms moved in the swirling vortex, shaped like gutting knives.

The first was a lean, feral-looking warship; its flanks slate-grey and brutally punctured with gun batteries and torpedo launchers. Its prow was shaped like a ploughshare, but this was no peaceable vessel, it was a ship of war.

Its angles were harsh, its lines sleek. It was a hunter of the stars and a killer of ships.

As it cleared the flaring tear in reality, scores of other fighting vessels jostled for position behind it, golden craft, black craft and a host of predatory vessels in identical livery to the fleet's leader.

Lemuel had seen this ship before, in the heavens above Shrike in the Ark Reach Cluster.

'Is that...?' gasped Lemuel.

'Unfortunately, yes,' said Mahavastu. 'I rather think it is.'

'You know that ship?' asked Camille. 'What is it?'

'It is the *Hrafnkel*,' said Mahavastu, 'the flagship of Leman Russ.'

CHAPTER
TWENTY-SEVEN

**Thunder from Fenris/So Much Will Be Lost/
Canis Vertex**

THE FIRST BOMBS from the Space Wolf fleet struck Prospero just before dawn. The orbital defence platforms had been caught completely unawares. One minute their augurs had been silent, the next a vast fleet of ships had appeared, a buckshot spread of torpedoes already arcing towards the orbital batteries and missile defences. Most were knocked out before they were able to launch a single weapon or power up a single gun. The lucky few that managed a snap shot were bracketed and obliterated moments later.

With no response from the ground, the armada moved into high anchor above Prospero and assumed a geostationary assault pattern. Thousands of weapons were trained on the planet below: energy weapons, mass-drivers and bombardment cannons. The ships drifted sedately, like grand liners in a regatta among the stars. The *Hrafnkel* opened the assault, its massive weapon systems blinking as etched lines of icy light stabbed down.

Moments later, the rest of the fleet opened fire.

* * *

THOUGH MAGNUS HAD kept his Legion blind to the approach of the Emperor's vengeance, the Raptora cult maintained a constant kine-barrier over the city of Tizca. Not even Magnus the Red could undo that protection without someone noticing.

The first warning anyone had of the imminent attack was a hot wind that seemed to come straight from the sky, pressing down on the city like the pressure before a storm. It tasted of metal and burnt oil. Static leapt from the pyramids' tops, sparking from silver tower to silver tower as if between the equipment in the laboratory of an insane Magos.

The sour grey of pre-dawn erupted in light as the lowered clouds were lit with inner radiance. This was swiftly followed by the tremendous crash of atmospheric discharge, like thunder without the lightning. Multiple sonic booms from hypersonic projectiles shattered the graveyard silence, and those citizens of Tizca who still slept were shaken from their beds by the echoes as percussive blasts rolled through the city.

Like a stabbing finger of raw light, the first energy lance struck Prospero a kilometre north-east of Tizca. It impacted in the wide ocean bay of the port and flashed a five-hundred metre column of seawater to superheated steam. A series of follow-on blasts seared into existence within seconds, marching vertical striations of incandescent brightness that sent up towering geysers of saltwater.

Banks of scalding fog rolled in from the ocean, boiling the flesh from the bones of early-morning dockworkers. Projectiles streaked through the lower atmosphere on trails of fire as shockwave fists pummelled the sea and sent foaming breakers crashing to shore.

Whole swathes of mountains simply vanished in towering mushroom clouds, magma bombs levelling entire peaks and filling the valleys with rubble. The earth shook with man-made thunder, the relentless pounding of the planet's surface like pile-driving hammers repeatedly slamming down. In orbit, more and more warships added the weight of their fire to the bombardment, hurling building-sized ordnance towards the planet below. The total saturation of the target area ensured that the city was completely engulfed, enough to level a continent's worth of metropolises.

Yet Tizca endured. The kine-shields of the Raptora were the strongest defences any city in the Imperium could boast. Harder than the thickest adamantium and more unyielding than layer upon layer of voids, the invisible umbrella of protection soaked up the violence of the bombardment, though at fearsome cost to the warriors who maintained it.

The entire populace of Tizca was awake now, moving onto the streets of their beloved city and looking up in confusion and wonder. There was little fear, for the destruction had not yet breached their protected environment. They watched, open-mouthed, as blinding energy weapons burned searing traceries in the sky above, while smudges of black smoke and fire painted the clouds as steel-jacketed shells flattened on the shield. Hastily-mustered Spireguard regiments poured onto the city streets and tried to usher people indoors, but the incredible spectacle was too entrancing to be ignored.

Magnus the Red watched as the lightstorm blistered and burst over his city. The sky was stained a bloody orange as airbursting incendiary rounds burned the clouds away, and a tear fell from his eye as he watched the land around Tizca die. The forests were burning to ash and the wild grasslands blazed with secondary fires, reducing the unspoilt countryside to a wasteland in a matter of minutes.

The Desolation of Prospero was complete.

'Now I know how you felt, father,' he whispered, sensing aetheric energy build in his fists, aching to be released. Magnus fought for calm, reciting the secret names of the Enumerations known only to him. This was his fate; this was what he had accepted as his punishment. He could not cast off his noble intent to pay for his mistakes.

No matter how much he ached to.

He watched the thunder batter itself uselessly against the shields of the Raptora.

'I am here,' he whispered to the heavens. 'Do what you will.'

THE APEX CHAMBER at the summit of the Corvidae pyramid was wreathed in smoke, aromatic fumes oozing from the stone, sweet and tinged with camphire and cedar. Veils hanging from the angled walls twisted in the warm winds billowing from outside, and Ahriman fought to hold onto the high Enumerations as the constant thunder tried to unseat him.

He sat before the Icon of the Corvidae, a wide crystal boulder shaped like a flat oval with a chunk of black spinel at its centre like the dilated pupil of an eye. The boulder had been hewn from the Reflecting Caves by the First Magister Templi of the Corvidae, and had been used as a focus for prognostication by the cult's devotees since its earliest days. It floated above a reflecting pool, its waters shimmer-dark and still despite the pounding of the earth.

Ahriman blinked as he caught a phantom image of a new moon in its depths.

Always capricious in its revelations, the Icon had been silent for weeks, with not even the most gifted of the Corvidae able to divine so much as a hint of the future. Ankhu Anen and Ahriman had both attempted to see beyond Prospero, but their visions had revealed nothing. Their subtle bodies had been unable to enter the Great Ocean at all, as though something was actively preventing them from venturing beyond Prospero's horizons.

Then the bombardment had fallen in a rain of thunder and steel.

Within moments of the first bombs landing, the warriors of the Corvidae mustered for war in the lower reaches of the Pyramid. Prospero was dying around them, though Tizca remained untouched. That wouldn't last long. The unseen attackers would soon realise they would need to come down and dig the Thousand Sons out the hard way.

Who were these mysterious enemies? Who would be insane enough to attack an Astartes Legion on its home planet? More importantly, how had they been able to bring such enormous firepower to bear without anyone being aware of it?

Ahriman needed answers before he issued a deployment order, and thus he attuned his mind to the crystal and went straight to the source of all knowledge on Prospero: Magnus the Red.

No one had seen the primarch for weeks, but the great column of fire from his pyramid had been visible all across the city. The mood of its people was fearful. Now Ahriman knew why.

'My lord, your sons require your guidance,' he said, drawing energy from Aaetpio to focus all his energy on the crystal eye. In the past few weeks, Aaetpio had been his constant companion, his Tutelary no longer needing his summons to attend upon him. Fluttering overhead with shimmering wings, Ahriman used his enhanced power to reach out with his mind towards the crystal within the Pyramid of Photep.

He felt the resonance of the crystals in the Apex Chambers of the other cult temples, the urgent cries for information from all the captains save Uthizzar. A faint glow shimmered in the depths of the crystal and the gemstone at its heart swam with motion, as though it were no longer solid, but liquid.

'My sons,' said Magnus, his voice echoing in Ahriman's mind. Its quality was sharp and edged as it sang from the crystal. 'This is our Legion's darkest hour, but also our moment of triumph.'

Ahriman felt the sudden joy of his brothers. Until this moment, he hadn't realised how much he had missed hearing his father's voice. He forced himself to concentrate on the matter at hand.

'My lord, what is happening?' he asked. 'Who is attacking us?'

'Leman Russ and his Wolves,' said Magnus matter-of-factly, as though such an occurrence was wholly expected, 'together with elements of the Custodes and the Silent Sisterhood.'

Ahriman was astonished, and his grip on the Enumerations would have slipped but for Aaetpio. Even so, it took a supreme effort of will to hold onto his clinical detachment.

'Why? What have we done to earn such violence?'

'Not you,' said Magnus. 'I have brought this upon us. This is my doom.'

'We need to deploy before they launch assault boats,' stated Phosis T'kar. 'The kine shield cannot be maintained any longer. I have lost too many warriors holding it this long.'

'Then lower it, my son,' said Magnus, 'for the Wolves are already on their way.'

'Then those treacherous bastards will learn what it means to attack the Thousand Sons,' snarled Khalophis. 'I will show them how the Pyrae make war.'

'Give us an order, my lord,' begged Hathor Maat. 'Please!'

The eye in the heart of the crystal dimmed, as though retreating into its depths. Ahriman saw the hesitation, and a memory threatened to swim to the surface of his mind, a fragment of his moment of connection to the primarch on Nikaea.

Khalophis had called the Space Wolves treacherous, but Ahriman knew the master of the Pyrae had it wrong. In this war, it wasn't the Space Wolves who would be thought of as traitors, it was the Thousand Sons.

'Leman Russ hates us, but even he would never dare attack us without orders,' said Ahriman, thinking aloud. 'This order must come from a higher source. It comes from the Emperor – it is the only explanation. My lord, what are you not telling us?'

'Always you were the perceptive one, Ahzek,' said Magnus, and the eye swam into sharp focus once more, its hue filled with resignation. 'I hid the truth from everyone, even myself, for so long that I was almost convinced it was simply a bad dream of another's life.'

Ahriman sensed the confusion of his brother Astartes, each of whom urgently wanted to take the field of battle. If the Space Wolves were coming, every second was precious. He wanted nothing more than to march out with his warriors, but what Magnus was telling him was too vital to be ignored.

'What did you do?' he demanded, all deference gone from his tone. 'When you saved us, what did you do? The pact you made with the powers of the Great Ocean, this is the price of it, is it not?'

'Yes, Ahzek,' said Magnus. 'To save my sons, I made a devil's bargain, and like the great doctor before me, I thought I had the best of it. All this time, I have been a blind fool, a puppet jerked on the strings of an intelligence greater than mine.'

A psychic shockwave sent a sharp fracture knifing through the crystal, and a jagged red line appeared in the centre of the eye.

'I was desperate. I had exhausted every other alternative to save you all,' hissed Magnus, his voice sending brittle cracks throughout the crystal. 'From the moment I turned my other eye inwards, I knew they were there: The Eternal Powers of the Great Ocean, beings older than time with power beyond imagining. Only they had the means to save you all from hideous mutation and death, so yes, I supped from their poisoned chalice. You were restored to me and I was content. What father would not do everything in his power to save his sons?'

'And for that we must suffer?' asked Hathor Maat. 'For that we are to be destroyed?'

'They think we are traitors,' said Ahriman, with the dawning horror of comprehension. 'All those who spoke against us at Nikaea will be vindicated if we fight back. Our inability to see the future... We thought it was because the Great Ocean's currents had turned from us, but it was you, wasn't it? You kept us from seeing the future. You dispersed the fleet. You *want* this. Is this why Uthizzar is absent? Did he learn what you planned for us?'

'Watch your tongue, Ahzek!' bellowed Khalophis. 'The primarch would never allow that.'

'He is right, Khalophis,' said Magnus, and the simple truth of his words broke their hearts. 'Uthizzar came to me, and in my weakness he read the truth of it. I could not allow him to warn you or our sacrifice would be for nothing. For the good of all, we must be destroyed.'

The scale of such a gross betrayal shocked them all to silence until Phosis T'kar responded in the only way he knew how.

'No one is being destroyed,' roared Phosis T'kar. 'If Russ's dogs want a fight, we'll give them one.'

'No! You must not,' said Magnus. 'The gathering darkness needs us to turn on our brothers. It wants two loyal Legions torn apart and broken on the anvil of blind hate before the coming war. We cannot allow that to happen, for the Emperor will have need of his loyal Wolves before the end. We must accept our fate and let our devastation run its course.'

Ahriman's anger cut through his state of detachment in the spheres and his fists clenched.

'All this time, you knew there would be a reckoning,' he said. 'We are the Red Sorcerers of Prospero, damned in the eyes of our fellows, and this is to be how our story ends, in betrayal and bloodshed.'

'It is the only way, Ahzek,' said Magnus. 'I am sorry.'

'No,' said Ahriman. 'It is not the only way. You may find it nobler to suffer your fate, but I will take arms against it.'

Ahriman focussed his will upon the crystals of his fellow Magister Templi.

'The Corvidae will fight the invaders,' he promised. 'My brothers, are you with me?'

'The Raptora are with you,' said Phosis T'kar.

'The Pavoni will fight,' said Hathor Maat.

'As will the Pyrae,' hissed Khalophis. 'Oh, the Pyrae will most definitely fight.'

THE LAND AROUND Tizca was in flames, a ruined wasteland from which nothing would ever rise again. The city's high marble walls, glorious museums, libraries, silver towers and great pyramids remained intact, the protection of the Raptora holding firm in the face of one of the most sustained and powerful bombardments ever unleashed in the history of the Imperium.

The mountains burned, the skyline forever changed by the world-shattering detonations.

Hot on the heels of the bombardment, the invaders came in their thousands. At first, the people of Tizca thought them to be particles of ash-blown grit, so numerous and so small were they. But as they closed, it became apparent that wave after wave of drop-ships, assault boats and gunships were inbound. Behind them came bulkier cargo transports bearing armoured vehicles and artillery pieces.

The kine-shields of the Raptora could not protect Tizca from the attack, but their cover was no longer needed. The bombardment from orbit had ceased, and packs of roaring Stormbirds led the charge, skimming low over the water towards the Tizca's port. Hundreds of craft flew over the churning seas, leaving foaming breakers in their wake. The idea that any enemy could reach the surface of Prospero to launch an assault had been discounted, and as a consequence, there were no anti-aircraft batteries to meet the oncoming craft.

The route into Tizca was wide open.

The first craft, an enormous, blade-like Stormbird with steel-grey sides and the image of twin wolves painted on its blunt, pugnacious prow smashed into the port. It blasted its way into the berths with a salvo of missiles and a sawing blast of cannon fire. Landing skids deployed at the last second, and the craft came down hard in the wreckage.

No sooner had it set down than the assault ramps dropped and a savage giant leapt down. His armour was hung with wolf pelts and his helmet bore two enormous fangs jutting from the lower portion of the faceplate.

Leman Russ set foot on Prospero, the first invader ever to do so. He roared to the skies, and the devastation wrought by his fleet above was pleasing to him. Two enormous wolves howled at his sides, and a score of his most powerful warriors fought their way into the port.

Dozens more craft smashed into the docking berths and explosions mushroomed skyward from damaged silos and ruptured fuel lines. Hundreds of warriors took the field of battle, a howling tide of warriors surging through the burning port towards the city proper.

Hundreds of smaller Thunderhawks roared in from the sea towards the undulating length of coastline between the port and the rearing escarpment of the Acropolis Magna in the east. Atop this glistening cliff of blond sandstone, the bronze statue of Magnus watched over his city with a stern, paternal gaze.

The eastern quarter of Tizca had been the original extent of the city before Magnus had designed the rest of its layout. Its street plan was chaotic and winding, and was a popular promenade for Tizca's more bohemian citizens. Old Tizca, as it was known, was built on a gentle slope that meandered down to the sea, its narrow, winding streets awash with Fountain Houses, intimate markets, chic eateries and theatres.

Dozens of Thunderhawks touched down on its wide, seafront esplanade, smashing through the marble sea-wall and unleashing hundreds of howling warriors with bright axes and wolf-skulled battle helms. Coordinated gunfire took down a number of invaders, the citizen militias of Tizca mobilising with military swiftness, but their weapons were nowhere near powerful enough to fell enough of their enemies.

As Russ's warriors loped through the burning wreck-age of the coastal districts, heavy landers crushed seafront structures and disgorged thundering tanks in the grey livery of the Space Wolves. Enormous Preda-tors, Land Raiders and Vindicators rumbled through the lower town, levelling buildings with their enormous cannons and mowing down anyone foolish enough to expose themselves.

Squadrons of Whirlwind rocket tanks rumbled from their transports and hunkered down in the ruins, turn-ing their boxy missile pods towards the Acropolis Magna. The pods vanished in fire and smoke, as rocket after rocket streaked skywards in rapid succession. A dozen or more impacted on the tip of the rock, obliterating the statue of Magnus in a storm of molten detonations. This symbolic act complete, the missile pods swivelled and yet more salvoes arced upwards to land with devastating results in the centre of Tizca. Raging thermals spread the fire from building to building, and the City of Light burned.

As the troop carriers and heavy landers touched down, sleek speeders screamed overhead, unleashing endless torrents of missiles into the city. Their fire was indiscriminate, the gunners instructed to fire at will. Hundreds of civilians died in the opening minutes of the aerial assault, and scores more were gunned down as hunting speeders strafed the streets with cannon fire.

The Skyguard Air Command launched every squadron of their two-man skimmers from their hangars to the south. These disc-like aircraft were armed with heat lances and missile pods, and the sky above the city became a frantic mess of gunfire, streaking missiles, explosions and dogfights as the two forces duelled for supremacy.

As the Space Wolves drew first blood, Prospero's military responded.

The citizen militias of Tizca rose in defence of their city, gathering what arms they could and taking up firing positions on rooftops and at windows. No one was fool enough to think they would be anything more than irritants to the Space Wolves, but to let the invaders simply walk into Tizca without a fight was as abhorrent as it was unthinkable.

The Spireguard, already on high alert after the commencement of the bombardment, moved out en masse under the guidance of the Corvidae. Magnus had blinded his Legion to the approach of the Space Wolves, but the immediate paths of the future were clear to those with eyes to see them.

Elements of the 15th Prosperine Assault Infantry, under Captain Sokhem Vithara, occupied the upper slopes of Old Tizca, anchoring their defence between the fire-wreathed pyramid of the Pyrae cult, the Skelmis Tholus a kilometre west and the Corvidae pyramid. Vithara set up his command post in the vestibule of the Kretis gallery, the oldest repository of artwork and sculpture on Prospero.

In the south-west of the city, the Prospero Assault Pioneers rallied what little was left of their soldiers after avalanches caused by the orbital shelling swallowed three of their barracks. The northern Palatine Guard deployed on the edges of the burning port, occupying the high parapets of overlooking libraries and galleries of the Nephra-te district. Their commander, Katon Aphea, was the heir apparent to one of Prospero's oldest families, a young and gifted officer with great potential. He anchored his defence on the Caphiera Tholus and positioned his troops with a tactical acumen that would have been lauded at any Imperial Army scholam.

Leman Russ and his Wolves overran Aphea's position in less than two minutes.

Tizca burned as dawn's light crept over the horizon, but for all that the Space Wolves had struck an overwhelmingly bloody blow, they had yet to face the city's true defenders.

The Thousand Sons deployed, and suddenly the fight took on a very different character.

AHRIMAN RAN THROUGH the streets on the edge of Old Tizca, his armour's autosenses easily penetrating the thick clouds of smoke pouring from the blazing buildings. The Scarab Occult marched with him, their hearts hungry for vengeance. Ahead, the Aquarion Fountain House burned, its graceful, columned structure and artfully carved fountains crumbling in the awful heat.

Heavy fighting engulfed the streets beyond the nearby Skelmis Tholus, with the 15th Prosperine Assault Infantry in contact with the invaders. The narrow streets formed natural choke points, and the Spireguard commander was using the terrain to his advantage.

Flames billowed further downslope, devouring structures set alight by the Space Wolves and threatening to spread further uphill. Warriors of the Pyrae were containing the blazes, hurling the fires back down the hill to block entire avenues and streets with seething walls of flame. The sky overhead was smeared with missile contrails and explosions, and a building behind Ahriman collapsed as an aircraft slammed into its roof, sending up plumes of smoke and fire. Blazing rafters and roof tiles spilled onto the street.

The air was hot and acrid, the smell of a city in its death throes.

Explosions and the constant bark of gunfire echoed from walls that had known only laughter and song. Drifting clouds of ash and burning parchment fluttered past, and Ahriman plucked a scrap of paper from the air.

'What is it?' asked Sobek.

'*Evidence of the Unseen*,' said Ahriman, reading the words on the smouldering parchment. '"The sea rises and the light falters. The moment we break faith with one another, the sea engulfs us and the light goes out. On that day, the sun will go down for the last time".'

Ahriman dropped the paper, watching it float off in the billowing thermals. The words were too apt to be coincidence, and he feared for what they represented. He watched the confetti of ashen books, scrolls and treatises dance like burning snowflakes above him.

'So much will be lost, but I will restore it,' he vowed. 'All of it, no matter how long it takes.'

Ahriman took a deep breath, the scale of such an undertaking not lost on him. His senses were stretched to the limits of perception, his mind alive with the flickering light of possible futures. He drew deeply on Aaetpio's well of power to enhance his awareness. His skin felt as though his Tutelary's fire was burning him. He had felt something like this once before, but forced that memory from his mind as he sensed the presence of inimical souls nearby.

'Scarab Occult!' shouted Ahriman, aiming his heqa staff towards one of the narrow streets leading down into the Old Town. 'Stand to.'

Flames and smoke belched from the street as a host of shadowy warriors smashed through the burning rubble and into the wider thoroughfare. Dust coated their armour and black, carbonised streaks marred the gleaming plate, but there was no mistaking the winter's grey of the Space Wolves.

The enemy Astartes had seen them, unsheathing bolters and viciously-toothed swords hung with wolf-tails.

The moment stretched for Ahriman. His perceptions raced down the length of his bolter, following the path his shot would take. In his fleeting vision he saw it smash through the visor of one of the Space Wolves, blowing out the back of his helm in an explosion of blood and brain matter. The precognitive flash froze him for the briefest second with the enormity of what it represented.

Astartes were at war with one another, and the sheer horror of that fact cost Ahriman a fraction of a second.

It was all the Space Wolves needed.

Though the Thousand Sons had been forewarned, still the Space Wolves fired first.

A hail of bolter fire slammed into Ahriman and the Scarab Occult. One warrior went down, his chest-plate broken open and his vital organs pulped by a mass-reactive shell. Two others dropped, but returned fire. The spell on Ahriman was broken, and his choler came to the fore as his bolter bucked in his hand and a Space Wolf was pitched backwards, his helmet a smoking ruin.

Another was lifted from his feet by Sobek, his Practicus using his kine powers to pound the wolf-cloaked warrior to destruction against the marble walls of the Fountain House. Three other Space Wolves jerked and spasmed as the Pavoni amongst his warriors vaporised the super-oxygenated blood in their veins. Flames licked from their eye-lenses, and they fell to the ground as their armour fused around them. The Tutelaries of the Scarab Occult spun around the Space Wolves, amplifying their masters' powers with gleeful spite.

The last three Space Wolves were blazing columns of fire, the plates of their armour black and molten, like onyx statues frozen in a moment of unimaginable agony.

Ahriman took a moment to contemplate what they had done. Aaetpio flickered above his head and he felt its urge to flow into him. Crackling arcs of crimson lightning flickered at his fingers and he suppressed them with a burst of impatience.

'Restrain yourself!' he snapped, not liking his Tutelary's eagerness one bit.

Sobek approached him, wringing his hands, asking, 'What did you say?'

'Nothing,' said Ahriman. 'It doesn't matter.'

'They caught us unawares, but we'll hurl them back to Terra,' said Sobek, and Ahriman saw the light of his Practicus's Tutelary echoed in the fiery gleam pulsing behind his visor.

'We have killed warriors of a brother Legion,' said Ahriman, wanting Sobek to appreciate the gravity of the moment. 'There is no going back from this.'

'Why should there be? We did not start this war.'

'That doesn't matter. We are at war and once you are at war, you fight until the bitter end. Either we defeat the Space Wolves or Prospero will be the Thousand Sons' tomb. Either way we lose.'

'What do you mean?'

'If we survive this attack, what then? We cannot remain on Prospero. Others will come and finish what Russ has begun. If we lose, well, that speaks for itself.'

Sobek hefted his heqa staff, its length rippling with fire.

'Then we had best not lose,' he said.

KHALOPHIS RECLINED UPON the crystal throne at the heart of the Pyrae temple. His armour reflected the flames billowing at the edge of the chamber. To anyone other than a cultist of the Pyrae, the chamber would have been unbearable, the air too hot to breathe, the fire too hot to endure.

Fire sprites and elemental aspects of the aether spun and danced in the air, leaving incandescent wakes behind their insubstantial bodies. Sioda hung over him like a fiery guardian angel, the Tutelary's form having swollen to enormous proportions since the treacherous bombardment had begun.

Armoured Neophytes surrounded him, arranged in the sacred six-pointed hexalpha pattern representing the volatile union of fire and water. They carried soulcrystals hewn from the Reflecting Caves, and flickering embers of life force burned within them.

'Are you sure of this, my lord?' asked Pharis, his Zelator's voice betraying his unease.

Khalophis grinned and flexed his fingers upon the carved armrests of the throne. Darting fire swam in its depths, and he felt the enormous rage of the wounded consciousness beyond the temple walls awaiting the chance to strike back at his enemies.

'I have never been more sure of anything, Pharis,' said Khalophis. 'Begin.'

Pharis backed away from his master, and nodded to the Neophytes. They bowed their heads and Khalophis gasped as their energies surged into him. The throne blazed with light, and he fought to direct the raging power that threatened to consume him.

'I am the Magister Templi of the Pyrae,' he hissed between clenched teeth. 'The Inferno is my servant, for I am the Lord of Hellfire and I will teach you to burn.'

Sioda swept down and enveloped his body. Khalophis felt his consciousness torn from his flesh to fill another body, one of iron and steel, of crystal and rage. No longer were his muscles fashioned from meat and tendons, but from enormous pistons and fibre-bundle hydraulics newly lined with psychically resonant crystals. The bolter was no longer his weapon, but vast guns capable of obliterating entire armies and fists that could tear down buildings.

Khalophis surveyed the battlefield with the eyes of a god, a towering avatar of battle roused to fight once more. His limbs felt stiff and new, his senses taking a moment to adjust to their enormous dimensions and ponderous weight. He flexed his new body. The metallic grinding of long dormant gears and the shriek of rekindled pneumatics cut through the clamour of battle.

Sioda's fire flowed along the incredibly complex mechanisms of his body, filling them with new life. He took a thunderous step forward and let loose an atavistic roar, his voice that of a braying war horn.

Like a mighty dragon woken from centuries of slumber, *Canis Vertex* marched into battle one more.

CHAPTER
TWENTY-EIGHT

The Line is Holding/They Will Turn On You
Too/Understand the Foe

THE JETBIKES WERE golden, with curved prows shaped in the form of eagles' beaks, their flanks carved to resemble swept-back wings. Phosis T'kar counted seven of them, swooping in low on an attack run towards his position at the end of the Raptora plaza. The warriors riding them were also golden, their red helmet plumes streaming behind them like pennants. Rapid-firing cannons blazed from underslung gun pods, ripping up the flagstone road leading from the Mylas agora.

Geysers of rock burst from every impact, but Phosis T'kar wasn't worried. He braced his weight on his right leg and snatched his hands through the air, as though sweeping a curtain open. Four of the jetbikes were plucked from the air as if they had reached the end of an unbreakable tether. Phosis T'kar slammed them against the high walls of the Timoran Library, shattering the statues of its first custodians.

The last three exploded as Hathor Maat sent a cataclysmic electrical surge through their engines. The burning wrecks smashed into the ground and tumbled end over end towards the Thousand Sons position, skidding to a halt less than a metre from Phosis T'kar.

'Custodes,' he grunted. 'They're not so tough.'

The northern reaches of Tizca were aflame. The port was a mass of reeking pillars of smoke, the stink of promethium mingling with the acrid reek of burning tar, rubber and metal. Thick clouds hung low over the city and ash fell like black rain. Men and women in their hundreds streamed past his position, heading towards the Pyramid of Photep laden with books and arms full of scrolls. The streets were littered with fallen tomes and fragments of statuary. Carved heroes of the Raptora had once looked down on the plaza, but shelling from enemy artillery had toppled all save a handful. Expressionless faces and outstretched hands lay strewn across the flagstones.

Mixed among the civilians were bloodied remnants of the Palatine Guard, shell-shocked men drenched in blood who staggered from the port in shock. These terrified survivors were all that remained of the soldiers tasked with containing the initial enemy landings.

'I've had word from the Athanaeans,' said Hathor Maat, jogging over from his position to Phosis T'kar's left.

'What is it?'

'The Wolf King is coming,' said Hathor Maat gleefully. 'They say he was first to land at the port and is fighting his way towards us.'

'Fighting?' said Phosis T'kar. 'I don't think there's much fighting going on. The Wolves are cutting through the Spireguard with ease.'

'You didn't really expect them to hold, did you?' said Hathor Maat. 'They're only mortals, and this is an Astartes fight.'

'Not just Astartes,' said Phosis T'kar, gesturing towards the wrecked jetbikes. 'Custodes want our heads on spikes too.'

'They all die just the same,' said Hathor Maat.

'Any word other than the location of the Wolf King?'

'Ahriman's got the northern perimeter sealed. He's holding the upper slopes of Old Tizca from the Acropolis to the eastern flank of Corvidae pyramid.'

'Leaving us with the western front from the Pavoni pyramid to the port.'

'Looks that way,' agreed Hathor Maat. 'The Athanaeans are taking up position in Occullum Square, they're going to feed us intel on the enemy plans as they get it. What's left of the Spireguard is taking up position with the Legion, but we can't count on them.'

'What about Khalophis?'

'No word yet.'

Explosions burst nearby as streaking missiles corkscrewed out of the sky and detonated overhead. Razored shrapnel scythed downwards, tearing a dozen civilians to bloody rags.

'Here they come!' shouted Hathor Maat, running back to his position.

A trio of boxy shapes moved through the smoke, the roar of their engines like the cry of living beasts. Trailing clouds of plaster-dust and fire, three enormous Land Raiders in the livery of the Space Wolves burst into the plaza. Behind them came the warriors of Leman Russ, hundreds of armoured fighters advancing in a howling tide of blades and bolts.

Among the warriors of Fenris were warriors in gold and red. They carried long spears with ebony hafts and shimmering blades. Phosis T'kar grinned at the thought of matching his strength against such warriors.

Packs of slavering wolves bounded across the plaza, their bared fangs flecked with scraps of uniform and flesh. The Thousand Sons opened fire, and the plaza erupted in a storm of gunfire. The din of shooting was eclipsed by the howls of the wolves. Phosis T'kar snapped his fingers and broke the alpha male of the pack in two. Bolter fire smacked armour plates and spun Space Wolves around, but the warriors of Russ were masters of charging from cover to cover and few were falling.

Heavy lasbolts flickered overhead, fizzing spears of impossibly bright energy. Explosions burst all along the Thousand Sons' lines as thudding bangs of bolter fire pummelled their positions. Pounding concussions ripped across the plaza, but the kine shields of the Raptora were proof against such attacks.

He concentrated on the lead Land Raider, reaching out and closing his fist. He wrenched his hand back, and the left sponson tore free of the vehicle in a blazing plume of white light. The heavy tank skidded around and slammed into the vehicle next to it, crushing the warriors advancing between them.

Phosis T'kar grinned.

'You didn't realise what you were getting into here, did you?' he said.

Another angry retort died in his mouth as sudden, cramping pain knotted in his belly, like someone had taken a fistful of his intestines and wrenched them upwards. He tasted bile and felt a sickly lather of sweat prickle on his skin.

Another vehicle exploded, its hull a writhing spider-web of coruscating lightning. The last vehicle erupted in flames as Auramagma's warriors hurled fireballs at its frontal glacis. It kept coming, shooting as it crushed priceless tomes and beautiful sculpture to shards beneath its treads. Auramagma himself stood atop a fallen master of the Raptora and wove sheets of white fire like a conductor before his orchestra.

'Too arrogant, that one,' said Phosis T'kar, recognising Auramagma's flaw while ignoring his own. A missile streaked out and slammed into the Land Raider's topside, skidding off its armour and exploding further behind it.

Phosis T'kar battered a handful of Space Wolves back with a flick of his wrist, hurling them beneath the tracks of the blazing Land Raider. Their armour broke open with satisfyingly wet cracks. No sooner had the vehicle crushed his victims than fire spewed from its insides. Its escape hatches slammed open as the blazing crew fought to escape the furnace of their vehicle. Auramagma let them burn.

Lightning danced through the Space Wolves, exploding their bodies within the armoured casing of their battle-plate. Hissing sheets of fire turned the ground molten, while the kine shields soaked up the weight of return fire. Phosis T'kar laughed to see his Legion unleashed, with no constraints to its full potential and no faint-hearts complaining because they could kill the enemies of the Imperium better than anyone else.

A sudden cold shiver made him start, the whisper of a ghostly touch at the back of his mind. He had felt it once before, but before he could recall where, a wolf leapt at him through the flames. Its fur was ablaze, and he reached up to flick it away with a gesture.

Nothing happened.

The wolf slammed into him and barrelled him to the ground. Its jaws snapped down, the fangs gouging deep furrows in his visor. Yellowed talons tore into his side, and he grunted as he felt them pierce his flesh. The wolf bit him in a frenzy, and Phosis T'kar fought to keep it from his throat.

His eyes met those of the beast, and he saw into its heart, the alien core of the being beneath the mask of the wolf. His eyes widened in recognition, but it was too late to do anything except fight.

The beast's jaw fastened on his neck, but before it could bite down Phosis T'kar slammed his fist into the wolf's belly. He pistoned his arm through its ribcage, crushing through ribs and vital organs to shatter its spine. The light went out of its eyes, and Phosis T'kar threw its body away in disgust. He climbed to his feet, looking at his hands in horror. He willed power to flow through them, but he felt nothing, no connection to the Great Ocean nor any hint of its fire.

A slender shape in form-fitting golden armour danced into view, a long-bladed sword lancing for his belly. He batted the blade away with his heqa staff and took stock of his attacker. It was a woman, but no ordinary woman. The lower portion of her face was obscured by a silver muzzle-mask and her dark eyes were tattooed with tears.

Now Phosis T'kar knew why his powers had failed. He heard screams of pain as the kine shields failed and more of the Silent Sisterhood made their presence felt. She came at him with a lancing thrust of her sword. He blocked it with his staff once more, sliding the hook down to the hilt of her blade and twisting.

She read the move and drew her blade back, spinning around and going low with a slender dagger aimed at his groin. Phosis T'kar stepped in to meet her and her dagger shattered on the plates of his thigh. He brought his knee up into her face and crushed the mask hiding her jaw. Blood and teeth flew from the impact, but the woman rolled out of reach.

All along the edge of the plaza, hundreds of armoured warriors came together in a battering clash of plate. No longer was this a battle to be fought with one side having the advantage; this was now a brutal, sweating, throat-tearing fight at close quarters.

Phosis T'kar unsheathed his combat blade and dropped into a fighting crouch before the armoured woman. He held his staff out before him with his knife high at his shoulder.

'Very well, null-maiden,' he snarled. 'I'll just kill you the old-fashioned way!'

Though his body lay recumbent on a crystal throne of golden fire, Khalophis marched through the ruins of Tizca with the strides of a mighty giant. Structures were children's building blocks, the fires flickering embers. People were specks to be crushed beneath his thunderous steps.

He marched past the Kretis gallery towards the Skelmis Tholus with the wide expanse of ocean at his right shoulder. The streets of Old Tizca were too narrow for a titanic battle engine such as *Canis Vertex*, and ancient buildings exploded as he smashed through them like some destructive colossus from ancient legends.

Gunfire lashed up, but none of it could harm him. He felt the heat of Sioda gather in his right arm, and unleashed a torrent of fire that bathed six streets in billowing clouds of sticky flames. He couldn't hear the screams, but he saw his howling victims falling to their knees and begging for salvation.

The guns of *Canis Vertex* were functional, but with his Tutelary's connection to the Great Ocean, his pyrokinetic abilities were boosted a hundredfold and he had no need of them. The mighty fists of the Titan were wreathed in flames, and with every gesture, tank-sized fireballs slammed into the enemy. Khalophis laughed as he spat tongues of flame from both arms, burning the invaders back to their ships.

The attacking forces had cut a deep wound into Tizca, but Khalophis saw how far the invaders had extended themselves in their urgent need to break the defenders in two. *Canis Vertex* could cut them off from their reserves, and the Thousand Sons' lines would drive them back to the ocean.

The Athanaeans dispersed word of the enemy movements, and the Corvidae met and countered any surprise attacks planned on a whim. The battle was by no means won by either force, but from his god's-eye view Khalophis could see the battle was turning in favour of the Thousand Sons.

'You bit off more than even you could chew,' roared Khalophis, the words coming out in the real world as a deafening blurt of eardrum-busting static from the engine's war horn.

Gunships and speeders slashed forwards, guns blazing and missiles arcing towards his armoured hide. Without voids, he would have been vulnerable, but a shield of flame turned shells to molten droplets of lead and detonated missiles before they could impact. He felt his Tutelary's savage joy, its power jostling for control, and he clamped down his authority.

It shrieked in jealous spite and Khalophis spasmed with a soul-deep sensation of nausea.

Canis Vertex halted its rampage and explosions erupted across its armoured chest as its aetheric armour vanished. Scenting blood, the Jetbikes, speeders and gunships closed in to deliver the deathblow.

'Get back,' he hissed. 'This is mine!'

Sioda screeched and angrily returned to the body of *Canis Vertex*.

A billowing flare of heat erupted from the Titan, and a dozen aircraft were swatted from the sky by the intense burst, their engines fused and pilots seared to charred bones.

Khalophis spat onto the floor of the Pyrae temple, the blood hissing as it boiled in the intense heat. His armour was smoking, and dark light built behind his eyes as he wept tears of fire that cut blackened scars down his cheeks.

* * *

THE LIBRARY OF the Corvidae, normally a place of quiet sanctuary and solitude was now a site of frantic activity. Ankhu Anen directed the labours of hundreds of scribes and servitors as they emptied the shelves and datacores of the library. The vast chamber contained hundreds of thousands of texts, too many ever to be evacuated in so short a time, but Ahriman's orders had been explicit.

Everything that could be saved was to be transferred to the Pyramid of Photep.

The light of fires filtered through the crystal walls, and danced over the steel and glass shelves of the library. Massively overladen bulk servitors carried panniers of books, and terrified scribes swept even more onto protesting load lifters.

He had tried to impose some kind of order on the evacuation of the library, but soon found that impossible. The panic of being so close to the fighting was a plague spreading through his minions, and his carefully ordered plans had fallen apart within moments.

'Ensure the Pnakotic manuscripts are kept separate from the Prophecies!' he shouted, seeing a tearful scribe bundling books from different eras together in a servitor's overflowing pannier. Scrolls and torn pages fluttered to the terrazzo floor. Dust fell from the high ceilings as something exploded nearby, and the library echoed with terrified screams.

Bodies flowed past him, their arms filled with heavy books and rolled-up maps and parchments. The Corvidae had collected so much in their researches into the future, so much that had yet to be studied and properly interpreted. How much knowledge of things to come would be lost in this senseless attack?

A wave of dizziness swamped him and he reached out to steady himself. His hand closed on the cold steel of a shelf and he glanced over at the book nearest his fingers. It was a tattered, worn, leather copy of *Liber*

Draconi, incongruously sitting next to the *Book of Atum* and twine-bound pages of the *Völuspá*.

He snatched his hand away as though burned.

'The dragon of fate,' he whispered.

Since his earliest days in the ranks of the Thousand Sons, Ankhu Anen had been haunted by dreams of a hissing dragon born of ice and fire. Its breath was the death of stars and its eyes the light of creation. Long had he sought the meaning of his dream, but the symbolism of dragons was manifold.

To some, the dragon represented intellectually superior man overcoming the untamed natural world, or creatures of primal chaos that could only be destroyed through disciplined marshalling of mental and physical prowess. To others, it was a symbol of wisdom, adopted by primitive emperors to enhance their perceived power. To Ankhu Anen it was a symbol of impending doom.

He backed away from the bookshelf, and looked up as a sudden premonition of danger flashed into his mind. A flaming mass was hurtling towards the temple, its form blurred and indistinct through the crystal panes.

Ankhu Anen turned and ran back towards the entrance of the library as a tremendous blast rocked the temple. Glass panes and adamantium columns shattered as a blazing, golden-skinned Thunderhawk gunship smashed into the temple. The wreck spun as its remaining wing caught one of the enormous structural members and it slammed into the ceiling before dropping to the floor of the library with a thunderous explosion.

Razor-sharp fragments and blazing sheets of jet fuel sprayed out from the wreckage, and the dry pages contained within the library eagerly caught light. Ankhu Anen was hurled through the air by the force of the blast, slamming into a high shelf and crashing through it to land on an overturned load lifter and its spilled cargo of books. The shelf buckled and crashed down on top of him in a rain of twisted metal and glass.

Ankhu Anen tried to extricate himself from the remains of the shelving unit, but fell back as searing pain flared in his leg and chest. Taking a deep breath, he took stock of his wounds. His leg was pinned beneath a fallen column, and a jutting spar of steel protruded from his chest. The fall had torn the wound gapingly wide, and blood pumped from his ruptured heart. Not even his secondary organ would be able to keep up with so rapid a loss.

Flaming liquid spread through the library, clawing at groaning shelves and seeking out fresh paper to sate its rapacious appetite. Dead and dying scribes surrounded Ankhu Anen, their bodies shredded by flying debris or burned beyond recognition. He looked up to see a shimmering rain of glass falling from the enormous, smoking hole the crashed gunship had torn. It was like a waterfall of crystal, and as he stared at the mesmerising sight, he saw a golden eye reflected in the shards as they fell in slow motion. The eyes watched him sadly, and Ankhu Anen had the powerful sense that they could easily save his life, yet chose not to.

'Why?' he begged, but the eyes had no answer for him.

A faint scratching of metal sounded at his ear, and he twisted to call for help, but his words trailed off as he saw a black raven watching him with its head cocked to one side. Its wings were glossy and black, though he could see psyber-implants worked with great subtlety into its skull. The bird regarded him quizzically, and he smiled at the sight of his cult's symbol.

'What are you?' he asked. 'A vision of the future? A symbol of salvation?'

'Neither, I think,' said a coarse voice at his shoulder, and Ankhu Anen twisted to see a warrior in armour the colour of a winter's morn. It shimmered as though sheened with a layer of frost, and Ankhu Anen saw nothing but hatred in the Space Wolf's body language. The raven took flight with a sharp caw and landed upon the warrior's shoulder-guard.

The warrior carried a long staff topped with a golden eagle, and a host of warriors flooded into the Corvidae library behind him. They were golden and grey, and they carried long-necked weapons with blue flames at their hissing nozzles.

'Who are you?' cried Ankhu Anen, trying to summon the aether to strike down this impertinent invader. No power was coming, and he felt the ache of powerlessness as a jagged pain in his heart.

'I am called Ohthere Wyrdmake, Rune Priest to Amlodhi Skarssen Skarssensson of the 5th Company of Space Wolves,' said the warrior, removing his helmet to reveal a bearded warrior of great age with pale eyes and a braided beard. A leather skullcap covered the top of his head, and Ankhu Anen saw a willowy female in skin-tight armour of bronze and gold behind him. Her eyes were dead and unforgiving, and he recoiled from the emptiness he saw within them.

'Wyrdmake? The dragon of fate,' hissed Ankhu Anen, his eyes widening in understanding. 'It's you... It's always been you.'

The Rune Priest smiled, though there was no amusement, only triumphant vindication.

'Dragon of fate? I suppose I am,' he said.

Ankhu Anen tried to reach his heqa staff, but it was lost in the devastation of the crash. He tried to pull his leg free.

'Do not struggle,' said Wyrdmake. 'It will make your death easier.'

'Why are you doing this?' begged Ankhu Anen. 'This is a dreadful mistake, you must see that! Think of all that will be lost if you do this terrible thing.'

'We are obeying the Emperor's will,' said Wyrdmake, 'as you should have done.'

'The Thousand Sons *are* loyal,' gasped Ankhu Anen, and a froth of bubbling blood spilled from his mouth. 'We always were.'

Wyrdmake knelt beside Ankhu Anen and pressed an icy gauntlet to his face.

'Do you have a valediction? Any last words before you die?'

Ankhu Anen nodded, as the future opened up before him. Through gurgling, bloody coughs he hissed his final prophecy.

'I can see the aether inside you, Rune Priest,' he hissed with the last of his strength. 'You are just like me, and one day those you serve will turn on you too.'

'I almost pity your delusion,' said Wyrdmake, shaking his head, 'almost.'

Wyrdmake stood to his full height and waved more of the warriors with flame-weapons forward. Ankhu Anen heard the whoosh of streaming jets of fire destroying a hundred lifetimes worth of knowledge, and tears gathered in the corners of his eyes.

'You will tell me one thing before you die,' said Wyrdmake. 'You will tell me where I can find the star-cunning one called Ahzek Ahriman.'

PHOSIS T'KAR HAD the advantage of weight and strength, but the null-maiden was lightning quick and her blade whipped like a silver snake. They duelled in the ruins of the plaza amid of a sprawling mêlée of armoured bodies. Blackened hulks of wrecked tanks littered the plaza, and glass fell in a glittering crystal rain from smoking holes punched in the Raptora pyramid.

Statues fell from its golden ledges to shatter on the stone below, and the constant thud of artillery impacts further east set a rhythmic tone for the battle. Fire bathed the combatants in a ruddy orange light, and Phosis T'kar felt a liberating sense of his own strength even as his aetheric powers were denied him.

He spun his staff in lazy circles as the Sister of Silence stared at him with her dead eyes.

'There is nothing to you, is there?' he said. 'I pity most mortals who cannot see what I see, but you? You live in dead space with silence as your only companion. It will be a mercy to end your life.'

The woman did not reply and launched a rapier-quick thrust to his throat. Phosis T'kar swayed aside and swept his arm out as she came in for a reverse stroke. Her blade whipped around his forearm, cutting a grove around his gauntlet, and he lunged towards her with his staff outstretched.

She bent back beneath his strike, sweeping her legs out and hammering her heel into his knee. His armour cracked and pain shot up his thigh. Phosis T'kar stepped back, favouring his good leg, and grinned.

'You're quick, I'll give you that,' he said.

She didn't answer and dodged his next attack with similar grace. A flurry of shots sent up geysers of rock-dust beside them and he flinched back from the heavy impacts.

'Time to end this,' he said.

The woman came at him again, and this time he made no move to stop her. Her sword plunged into his chestplate, slicing through the compound ceramite and armaplas, but before it could penetrate the ossified bone-shield over his ribs, he stamped forward and rammed his combat knife up into the woman's arm.

The blade sliced between her radius and ulna, and she screamed in agony.

'Not so silent now, eh?' he snarled, dragging her towards him. She fought against his strength, but her struggles only intensified her pain. Phosis T'kar slammed his helm into her face, and the Sister of Silence's head caved in.

He wrenched his combat knife clear as he felt his power surge back into his limbs with a frisson of painful pleasure. Utipa flared into existence above him, and he welcomed his Tutelary's presence, feeling its return boost his power. Phosis T'kar sheathed his bloody blade and unslung his bolter, ramming a fresh magazine home and racking the slide. He snapped the silver blade protruding from his chest, and turned from the body before him, jogging back to the fighting and firing his bolter at targets of opportunity as he went.

The raging combat swirled like a seething tide, with neither force quite able to gain the upper hand. The Space Wolves fought with furious abandon, utterly directed and focussed, but without the clarity of vision to appreciate the whole picture. The Thousand Sons fought with clinical detachment, every warrior having achieved the lower Enumerations to better focus their skills. As Astartes, they were trained to excel in the brutality of close combat, but Magnus had taught them there was always another, cleverer way to win.

'Understand the foe,' Magnus had said, 'and you will know how to beat him.'

It was a lesson the Space Wolves and Custodes had taken to heart, for how else would they have thought to bring the null-maidens of the silent sisterhood with them? Knowing that gave Phosis T'kar all he needed to turn this battle around.

He ran through the thick of the fighting, casting his mind out into the swirling mass of heaving emotions. The red mist of anger and hatred hung over the struggling fighters, but three patches of deadness were like islands of silence amid the oceans of carnage.

'Got you,' he hissed.

He saw Hathor Maat fighting back to back with Auramagma, and shot his way through the crush of bodies to reach his fellow captains. A warrior in grey armour slashed at him with a saw-bladed axe, but Phosis T'kar wrenched it from his grip with a thought, and drove the screaming teeth into the warrior's face without breaking stride.

His pace slowed as he came within range of another null-maiden. He stopped and climbed onto an empty plinth that had once supported the statue of Magister Ahkenatos, pulling his bolter tight into his shoulder, and scanning for the dead zones within the battle through Utipa's eyes.

His Tutelary swooped over the battlefield, and Phosis T'kar felt a sudden burst of pain in his chest. He looked down. The wound was still bleeding, which was odd. Then he saw the iridescent shimmer to his blood and sensed its ambition. He knew what it meant, but angrily clamped down on the sudden fear that accompanied such recognition.

Taking a deep breath, he focussed on what he was seeing through Utipa's eyes.

He saw the first of the null-maidens, and shifted his aim towards her. She fought in the midst of a knot of Space Wolves and Custodes against Hathor Maat's warriors. The bolter slammed back against his shoulder, and the woman collapsed, the back of her neck and shoulder torn off by the blast of the shell.

Following Utipa's guidance, he found the second null-maiden and put a bolt round through her chest. The third he killed with a snap-shot as she fled to the cover of one of the wrecked Land Raiders.

Immediately, the Thousand Sons went on the offensive. Lightning flashed from Hathor Maat's hands, and

Auramagma threw out blazing streams of liquid fire. Kine shields flared to life and the Space Wolves were hurled back from the edges of the pyramid.

Phosis T'kar roared and leapt from the plinth.

Bolts of pure force slammed into his enemies, scattering them before him like a charging cavalryman. As much as he had felt a strange sense of freedom when stripped of his power, it was a moment of fleeting enjoyment compared to this.

Hathor Maat and Auramagma appeared at his side, and he read their joy at this sudden turn in their fortunes. Auramagma was as feral as the Space Wolves, while Hathor Maat was pathetically relieved to have his powers back.

The Thousand Sons formed on their captains, a fighting wedge of lightning-wreathed killers, plunging into the body of the Space Wolf army like a lance. The Space Wolves and Custodes fell back before them, helpless without any means of combating the lethal powers of the Thousand Sons.

A terrible howl of fury echoed around the plaza, and every pane of glass within the Raptora pyramid exploded into diamond fragments. They fell in a crystal rain that reflected the fire and smoke of battle in every shard.

Phosis T'kar dropped to one knee, his autosenses screaming with the overload of sound.

'What in the name of the Great Ocean...?' he managed before he remembered where he had heard that howl before.

'Shrike,' said Hathor Maat, recalling the same thing.

The Space Wolves parted, and Phosis T'kar saw the enormous majesty of the Wolf King and a coterie of gold-armoured giants striding through the battle lines towards them.

CHAPTER
TWENTY-NINE

I Must Not/Power Without Control/Syrbotae Down

OLD TIZCA WAS no more. The peaceful warren of anti-quated streets he had so enjoyed exploring as a youth on Prospero was now ashes and burning rubble. War-riors picked careful paths through the smouldering ruins, firing from the hip or fighting with axes and swords. The coastline was invisible, obscured by fog-banks of artillery fire. Spurts of yellow fire followed by dull metallic coughs snatched at the clouds, and another portion of his beloved city would vanish in a rippling series of fiery detonations.

Magnus watched the death of Tizca from the highest balcony of his pyramid, the one structure that had so far escaped the destruction. Nothing reflective remained in his chambers, nowhere for the insidious voice of his temptation to wheedle and cajole him into making yet another error of judgement.

He gripped the edge of the balcony and wept bitter tears for his lost world and his dying sons. What had once been a wondrous beacon of illumination for all who cared to look upon it was now a maelstrom of battle.

The northern spur of the city was a raging inferno, its palaces ablaze and its parklands ashen wastelands. Further south, the port was a giant black stain on the horizon, its structures demolished in the wake of his brother's attack.

He sensed Leman Russ in the western reaches of the city, fighting at the Raptora pyramid. Constantin Valdor was at his side and the warrior named Amon. With his inner eye, Magnus felt the courage and elation of the Thousand Sons who fought alongside Phosis T'kar, Hathor Maat and Auramagma. It grieved him to know that most of these men would soon be dead, for the Wolf King left only desolation in his wake.

In the east, Ahriman and his warriors were holding the invaders at bay. Not even the savagery of the Wolves or the power of the Custodes could break through Ahriman's defences, his warriors using their predictive powers to counter every assault.

Few Sisters of Silence fought in the east, for the majority were at the side of Leman Russ and Valdor. The attackers had not brought enough of the null-maidens to take Tizca, assuming the assault would be little more than a mopping up operation. They thought the bombardment from orbit would be enough, and that alone angered him.

Though the majority of the Spireguard had been swept away in the opening moments of the battle, the Thousand Sons had rallied magnificently and prevented the battle becoming a rout. A thin line of warriors in crimson armour linked the six pyramids of Tizca, forming a circular perimeter with Occullum Square at its centre. The Pyramid of Photep was the southernmost of the pyramids, the glittering water surrounding it awash with sodden pages of ancient wisdom lost forever in the name of fear.

Crackling currents of aether surged through his body, begging to be released and let loose among the foe. Magnus fought to hold it in check. The fire of the Great Ocean battered him, like the most desirable addiction calling to him across the veil between worlds.

Magnus wanted nothing more than to descend to the streets of Tizca and turn back the invaders, to show them the true extent of his powers. His fingers sparked at the thought. He clenched his fists and turned his thoughts inwards.

He heard the voices of his sons crying out to him, begging him to take the field of battle, but he ignored them, forcing their voices from his head.

It was the hardest thing he had ever done.

One plea threatened to cut through his resolve, the voice of his dearest son.

Help us, it said.

'I cannot, Ahzek,' he said between clenched teeth. 'I *must* not.'

SMOKE FILLED THE streets around the outer precincts of the port, choking the light and oxygen from the day. Booming explosions marched through the city like the tread of drunken gods, and the bark of gunfire mingled with screams in a pitch perfect rendition of a hellish choir. Phael Toron ducked back behind a fallen statue to reload his bolter as a stuttering blast of fire tore through the walls of the Fountain House. A hundred warriors of his Fellowship held this portion of the perimeter, with a further two hundred on either side of him. Three times the enemy forces had tried to break through from the port, and three times the guns and blades of the 7th had hurled them back.

Phael Toron's warriors knew this part of Tizca like no other, and the divinatory commands from the Corvidae allowed them to coordinate their defences with perfect cohesion. Coupled with the information gathered by the Athanaeans, the defences were always perfectly aligned to meet every attack.

Corpses littered the streets; both enemy and friend, for the defences had not been held without cost. Blood splashed the pristine marble of the walls and rivers of vital fluid flowed in the cracks in the streets. Phael Toron had exhausted twelve magazines, and only a regular supply of ammunition from Spireguard squads had kept their guns firing.

A cramping pain clenched in his gut and he grunted as an unidentifiable sickness sent spasms through his limbs. He shook off the sensation, forcing down the bilious phlegm building in his throat and shaking out the sudden blurring of his vision. He blinked away bright spots before his eyes as a series of fiery blasts ripped through their lines.

'Watch the right!' he shouted, seeing three of his warriors torn apart in a blitzing stream of cannon-fire. The distinctive thumping noise told Phael Toron it was too heavy for an infantry gun. Crimson-armoured warriors dashed through the rubble towards the gap, bearing heavy weapons. He risked a glance over the fallen statue of a golden lion.

The district between the port and the Timoran Library was unrecognisable, its colonnaded processionals and arched follies now a tumbledown wasteland of blazing ruins and jumbled stone. The salty tang of sea air was laden with chemical pollutants from the blazing port, the enormous volume of gunfire and the pyres of burning books.

Space Wolves and golden warriors moved cautiously through the smouldering remains of what had once been a gallery of pre-Old Night sculpture, their forms unknown and of obviously alien manufacture. They were now crushed fragments beneath the invaders' boots, and Phael Toron felt the aether simmering beneath his skin as Dtoaa amplified his choler. He took a deep breath, reining in his emotions. The Enumerations weren't helping, and he could feel his Tutelary's raging desire to hurt the attackers threatening to overwhelm his tactical sense.

'That would make me little better than them,' he hissed, forcing its red rage down.

Another spray of bullets tore a line through the golden lion, chewing up the soft metal as though it were as porous as sandstone. Phael Toron rolled away from the disintegrating lion and scrambled over to the cover of a fallen arc of stonework. He recognised it as part of the gallery's domed roof, and looked over his shoulder to see a plume of grey smoke coiling from the building's interior. Streaking contrails of speeders flashed overhead amid a series of stuttering, strobing detonations.

Portions of the gallery crashed down to the east, burying at least thirty of his warriors beneath tonnes of rubble and sending up a billowing cloud of dust. No sooner had the walls of the gallery fallen than an ululating howl erupted from the invaders.

'Push them back!' he shouted, swinging around the fallen portion of the dome and opening fire, pumping shot after shot into the mass of charging Space Wolves. His warriors followed suit, filling their designated fire sectors with lethally accurate bolter fire. Some of the enemy warriors went down, but not enough. Phael Toron estimated at least six hundred Space Wolves were pushing hard from the port.

They were feral barbarians, with none of the grace and poise an Astartes should possess. Their armour was hung with fetishes, skulls and furs, like some primitive tribe of savages that deserved no less a fate than extinction.

Many charged into battle without helms, either casting them aside in their bloodlust or too stupid to care about protecting their most vital organ. Phael Toron made them pay for that by picking his targets, blasting skulls from shoulders with every shot.

Gunfire streaked back and forth, fizzing lines of fire that filled the air with explosive shells. He ducked back behind the ruins of the dome, hearing the hard thud of bolt rounds against its copper-sheathed surface.

A warrior in red scrambled into cover with him, and he nodded curtly at his Philosophus, Tulekh. The man was a fine adept and had mastered his powers more quickly than any of the 7th Fellowship. Even Phael Toron had struggled to master the breadth and power of abilities brought back to Prospero by Magnus and the Legion. Where the other Fellowships employed their mystical abilities, the 7th fought this battle with conventional means.

'We can't hold them like this,' said Tulekh. 'We need to use our powers!'

'Not yet,' said Phael Toron. 'They are weapons of last resort.'

'This *is* the last resort!' urged Tulekh. 'What else is there?'

Phael Toron knew the man was right, but still he hesitated. His men were nowhere near as experienced at wielding the Great Ocean's powers as the other Fellowships, and he feared to unleash them in so violent a cauldron. But as Tulekh said... what else was there?

'Very well,' he said at last. 'Pass the word that everyone is to use whatever means they need to push these bastards back into the sea.'

Tulekh nodded and Phael Toron read his ferocious anticipation as the order was given.

He looked around the fallen dome and drew in a breath as he saw a monstrous shape thumping through the rubble behind the Space Wolves, a grey giant of thick ceramite plates and whirring, clanking mechanics. The dreadnought was dust-covered and fire-blackened, its hull dented with impacts and its back banner in flames.

One arm was a bloodied, electrically-sheathed fist, the other a whirring, rotating launcher that spun up to replenish its ammo from a giant missile hopper at its shoulder.

'Move!' shouted Phael Toron as a series of warheads spat from the launcher and streaked towards them.

The missiles slammed into the ruins of the dome, and a tremendous explosion hurled him through the air. The blast tore his bolter from his grip and he slammed down into a crater sloshing with blood. He rolled and reached for a weapon, but there was nothing within reach.

Shredded corpses of Thousand Sons were strewn around the crater, their bodies catastrophically mangled by gunfire and explosions. Once again, the nauseous cramps seized him, and he bent double as he felt Dtoaa's power flow into him, unbidden and unstoppable.

All around Phael Toron, the rubble rose up into the air and the blood boiled at his feet. The power of the Great Ocean flowed through him, but deep in the cellular core of him, a dreadful flaw was already unmaking him.

THE THOUSAND SONS were dying. Scores died in the opening minutes of the Wolf King's attack, his fury unstoppable and his power immeasurable. Clad in the finest battle-plate and armed with a frostblade that clove warriors in two with single strokes, his fury was that of a pack hunter who knows his brothers are with him. His huscarls were grimly efficient butchers of men,

their Terminator armour proof against all but the luckiest shots and blades.

Though Phosis T'kar could see no more of the hateful
Sisters of Silence, he knew they were there, for his powers were weakening, bleeding from his hands like ink
from a splintered quill. The Custodes slew with powerful strokes of their Guardian Spears, hewing armour
and flesh with efficient strokes that hit with precisely
the force required to do the job of killing.

Phosis T'kar felt his Tutelary's impotent rage as its
power was leeched away. He drew ever more deeply on
his own reserves of power, feeding them with the very
essence of his soul, turning his emotions outwards as he
and his men fought for their very survival.

Enemy warriors surrounded them, warriors who
moments before had been on the brink of defeat. The
lance of the Thousand Sons had plunged into the body
of the Wolves and cut deep towards the heart, but Russ
had deflected the fatal stroke. Worse, it had been turned
back against them. The Space Wolves clawed at them,
the Custodes cut them down and the slavering wolves
bit and snapped at the edges of the battle.

'We have to pull back!' shouted Hathor Maat over the
thunderous din of gunfire and clashing blades. 'We are
over-extended.'

Phosis T'kar knew he was right, but could focus on
nothing save the monstrously powerful form of Leman
Russ as he slaughtered the Thousand Sons without a
care for the priceless repositories of knowledge and
experience that he was snuffing out with every blow.

'Do it,' he snarled. 'Re-form the perimeter.'

Hathor Maat read the fury in his voice and asked,
'What are you going to do?'

'I can end this,' he said. 'Now do it!'

Hathor Maat needed no second telling, and the order
was passed through the ranks of the Thousand Sons. In

disciplined groups, the warriors of the 2nd, 3rd and 8th
Fellowships collapsed their lines and fell back. Sensing
they had regained the initiative, the Space Wolves
surged forwards as they scented victory.

'You think we'd make it that easy for you?' hissed
Phosis T'kar. He whipped his heqa staff around and
surged into the heaving mêlée with a roar of hatred to
equal any lupine howl. A blast of blue fire hissed from
his staff, spearing into the chest of the warrior before
him and setting him alight. He gave an animal bray of
pain, and fell back as Phosis T'kar and his coven pushed
into the mass of enemy warriors.

A fiery bloom of light erupted beside him, and he saw
that Auramagma and his warriors were with him. Phosis T'kar knew he should be angry with the captain of
the 8th for disobeying his order, but instead felt only
hateful vindication. Jets of white-hot fire streamed from
Auramagma's hands, melting ceramite plates as though
they were softened wax. Burning wolves howled their
agony to the sky, and dying warriors had the air sucked
from their lungs by the superheated blasts that consumed them.

Phosis T'kar's bolt pistol boomed and blew off the
head of a Custodes warrior who'd lost his helmet. His
staff swept fiery arcs as it split armour like eggshells. He
killed with brutal skill, feeling a blazing heat surge
within his body. His eyes filled with light and his limbs
burned with fire.

Ahead, he could see the Wolf King and his golden
allies. His vision narrowed until all he could see was the
path his staff would take as it shattered armour and
burned his foes with fire. He killed warriors by the
dozen, feeling the sensation in every cell of his flesh.

His arm swept up and down like a piston, smashing
though armour and shattering bone with a strength he
had never known. His body seethed with power, but his

every iota of attention was fixed on his prey. The enemy fell back from him in horror, unable to match his power. He hurled warriors aside like straw, battering them into the ground with waves of thought until they were little more than smears of gore on the marble. The power flowing through him was incredible.

Phosis T'kar looked over as Auramagma faced the Wolf King with fire wreathing his limbs in searing light. His fellow captain loosed a flood of aether at the primarch. Phosis T'kar roared in triumph as the flames engulfed Leman Russ, and Auramagma's fire met the chill armour of Leman Russ in an explosion of light like the birth of a star. Russ barely blinked, but the effect on Auramagma was as incredible as it as horrific.

The enormous power of Auramagma turned from the Wolf King's armour as light is reflected from a mirror, and his screams were hideous to behold as the aether's spite burned its creator. Auramagma howled in such agony that all who heard his screams were moved to pity as the aether devoured his very essence. A blazing pyre of agony, Auramagma fled through the crush of bodies, and the Space Wolves parted before him, none willing to go near so damned a soul.

At last Phosis T'kar hammered his way through to the golden warriors surrounding Russ and laughed as he saw their terror of him. Their leader turned to face him, and Phosis T'kar relished the look of disgusted hatred he saw. Dark hair spilled from beneath his red-plumed helm, and Phosis T'kar saw he had the eyes of a killer.

'Valdor,' hissed Phosis T'kar, the word slithering and wet.

Constantin Valdor held his long-bladed polearm extended before him. 'What are you?' he bellowed, and Phosis T'kar laughed at the foolishness of such a question.

'I am your death!' he boomed, but the words were mangled and distorted by the twisted shape of his mouth. Phosis T'kar loomed over the chief Custodes, and only now did he feel the changes wrought upon his body.

His flesh was a riot of form and function, its every organ and limb reshaped by a madness of transformation. Flesh and armour ran together in a hideous meld of organic and inorganic material, and the bubbling meat of his body seethed with unbridled ambition. How could he not have noticed so profound a change? The answer came to him as soon as the question formed in his mind.

His flesh was no longer his to call his own. Utipa's presence filled him, its hateful relish and patient malice unlocking the rampant potential locked in his genetic makeup. A wild and untamed transformative power that had lain dormant and contained within him was now given a free rein, unleashing nearly two centuries of change in as many minutes.

In Valdor's eyes, Phosis T'kar saw what he and the Legion had become, and knew then that this fate had always been theirs. Valdor came at him with his Guardian Spear aimed at his heart, and Phosis T'kar finally understood why his primarch had chosen not to fight.

'Monster!' cried Valdor, driving the spear into his mutant flesh.

'I know,' said Phosis T'kar sadly, dropping his weapons and closing his eyes.

The golden blade clove his heart, and death was a welcome release.

PHAEL TORON ROSE out of the crater in blaze of lightning. Hissing blood streamed from his armour and whipping arcs of power blazed at his fingertips. His armour shone with inner luminescence as though it contained the fiery heart of a plasma reactor. With eyes saturated with aetheric energy, Phael Toron saw the hellish battlescape before him in all its visceral horror.

The host of Leman Russ and the Custodes had all but won the field of battle. Like a sword thrust at the unprotected vitals of a reeling foe, the Space Wolves had cut deep into Tizca. The perimeter of the Thousand Sons was holding, but that it would soon break was beyond question. No force in the galaxy could resist so furious an attack, so lethal a drive and a foe so utterly without mercy: no force but the Thousand Sons with the power of the Great Ocean at their command.

Phael Toron saw the ruin of his Fellowship, the broken bodies and the shattered skulls taken as trophies by howling Space Wolves. He took in the vista with a glance and his rage spilled out in a torrent of force. Those enemy warriors closest to him were hurled back, the armour peeled from their bodies and their flesh torn from their bones. The furred abominations that ran with Russ's warriors exploded in bright smears, their inner light snuffed out in an instant with alien cries of rage.

Phael Toron floated over the battlefield, his arms extended from his side as he swatted enemy warriors from his path with his thoughts. He laughed at the ease with which he commanded such powers, delirious with the sensations flooding him. How he had feared these powers and dreaded the difficulty in commanding them, but this was no more difficult than breathing!

His warriors followed behind him, the fire that flowed from his hands pouring into them and filling them with light. The power was wild, but Phael Toron didn't care, letting the chaotic energies flow from the Great Ocean with him as its willing conduit.

A blizzard of explosive shells streamed from the cannons of three dreadnoughts, wolf-clad machines adorned like totemistic idols. Phael Toron unmade the first, disassembling it into its component parts with a gesture. He felt the anguish of the desolate scrap of flesh at its heart as it died, and took pleasure in its terror. In a fit of dark amusement, he turned the remaining two upon one another, letting their guns rip each other apart until nothing remained save torn fragments of smoking metal.

All around him, the warriors of the 7th Fellowship burned with the same fire that poured into him. As he grew in power and confidence, so too did his warriors, their transformation an echo of his own.

A pair of Predator battle tanks opened fire on him. He lifted the vehicles from the ground and hurled them out to sea, laughing at the horrified faces of the Space Wolves. They fell back, gathering in frightened packs as they cowered in ruins of their own making.

Phael Toron's body shook with the force of the power passing through him, and he fought to control it, remembering the catechisms and higher Enumerations that Magnus and Ahriman had taught him. Power was only useful when it was controlled, they had told him, and Phael Toron understood the truth of that as he felt his grip on its leash slipping. Dtoaa, once his Tutelary, now his devourer, swooped down and filled him with more power than even the greatest master of the aether could contain.

'No!' he cried, feeling the savage glee of Dtoaa as their roles were suddenly reversed.

Agonising pain tore through him, and Phael Toron screamed as his limbs ruptured with the force of the energies pouring into him. His body could not contain such titanic forces and no mental discipline could prevent what has happening to his flesh from taking place.

Phael Toron threw back his head and gave one last scream of horrified understanding before his body exploded with the violence of a newborn star.

* * *

A KILOMETRE TO the east, Khalophis marched *Canis Vertex* towards the smoking, fire-blackened ruin of the Corvidae pyramid. Thick columns of smoke poured from the giant building as its priceless and irreplaceable tomes burned.

Tiny figures in gold and grey fled from his titanic strides. Missiles and hard rounds melted on his fire shield. He was invulnerable and invincible. How could he go back to making war like everyone else after such an experience? To control maniples of robots through the psychically-resonant crystals was sublime, but to command a god of the battlefield was the greatest joy of all.

What his weapons did not burn, his enormous, splay-clawed feet crushed, and he left a trail of devastation more thorough than any the Space Wolves might have made. Khalophis did not care. Buildings could be rebuilt, cities renewed, but the chance to bestride the world as a colossus of metal might never come again.

From his throne in the Pyrae pyramid, he felt the aetheric fire burning his skin, but knew he had to maintain his control over the Titan. Lives and the future of Prospero depended upon it. Utipa's fire ran like molten gold through the limbs of *Canis Vertex*, though he felt its desperate urge to command, to wreak harm like he could only dream. Khalophis jealously held onto his control, even as he felt Utipa's power increase with every life taken and structure obliterated.

He forced himself to concentrate on the battle, sweeping his gaze over the city to see where his immense firepower and strength would be best employed.

The port was the key. Heavy transports bearing yet more soldiers from orbit swooped low over the sea to debark warriors by the hundred with every passing minute. Further out, Tizca's northern perimeter was still holding. Ahriman and the Corvidae stood shoulder to

shoulder with the Athanaeans and Spireguard, fighting
with rare courage to hold the seaborne invaders at bay.

Ahriman could do without his help for the time
being.

To destroy the port would deny the invaders the
beachhead they needed to complete the destruction of
the Thousand Sons. Khalophis steered his mighty
charge towards the port, fists spitting flame and death
with every stride.

Khalophis did not perceive the environment around
Canis Vertex as its long-dead Princeps once had. He felt
the ebb and flow of battle more keenly than any
Moderati. Aetheric energy washed from the battle at the
Raptora pyramid and he smiled to know such power.

No sooner had he attuned his senses to the battles
raging below him than he felt the sudden surge of
energy on the far side of the Corvidae Pyramid. He felt
Phael Toron's presence, but his eyes snapped open as he
felt the incredible power building in the Captain of the
7th.

Too late, he halted *Canis Vertex's* forward momentum.

'Throne, no,' he hissed as a howling column of searing white fire, fully a thousand metres in diameter,
erupted skyward in a blaze of hellish light. The clouds
vanished in an instant as a second sun shone throughout Tizca.

Canis Vertex reeled from the blast, and Khalophis felt
the enormous, surging swell of aetheric energy pour
through the gaping rent torn in the fabric of the world.
It blew out his flame shield in an instant, stripping the
Titan back to its bare metal and beyond. The crystals
bonded with its complex locomotive mechanisms shattered, and Utipa screamed in triumph as it wrested
control from him.

Its triumph was short lived as the Titan's molten
skeleton buckled in the intolerable heat.

Its limbs folded beneath its enormous bulk, and the battle engine crashed down on the Corvidae pyramid, completing the destruction Ohthere Wyrdmake had begun.

Khalophis fought to sever his connection to the doomed war engine, but Utipa would not release its grip, and aetheric feedback lashed back upon him. He drew on all his power as Magister Templi of the Pyrae to hold back the fire, but no power in the galaxy could withstand so monstrous a force.

Khalophis had a moment to savour the irony of his death before the fire consumed him utterly, and the entire pyramid of the Pyrae exploded in a searing fireball of glass and steel.

CHAPTER THIRTY

The Last Retreat/The Truth is my Weapon/
Wolf-Sign

AHRIMAN SHOOK HIS head, wondering why he was lying flat on his back amid a growing cloud of dust and rubble. He didn't remember falling or being struck, but rolled onto his side as a surging pain and cramp seized his limbs. He grunted in pain, knowing all too well what that pain signified.

He rolled to his feet and looked to the west in time to see a seething column of bitter fire piercing the heavens. A surge tide flowed from the Great Ocean into the world, and the cramping pain in his muscles told him how powerful he could be if he would only unleash those powers. Shimmering light built behind his eyes and raw aether dripped from his fingertips, liquefying the ground where it touched into a soup of impossible form.

Every single warrior, friend and foe, had been struck down by that terrible explosion, the shockwaves spreading through the city like an earthquake. What buildings were left standing after the punishing barrages were brought down and cast to ruin by its force.

The light diminished as whatever vessel had torn the veil between worlds open was destroyed. Ahriman saw a blazing humanoid form lurching drunkenly on the horizon, like a burning wicker man set alight by highland savages to please their heathen gods of the harvest.

A flickering image appeared in his mind, a taunting vision of a future he could not change, and he closed his eyes as the towering battle engine that had fallen on Coriovallum died for a second time. Ahriman had seen where it would fall, but had no desire to watch the destruction of the Corvidae pyramid.

He heard the earth-shattering sound of screaming steel and breaking glass, the sound of all that might yet be known reduced to ashes and lost hope. The monstrous battle engine crashed to earth, sending another powerful tremor through the city as the Pyrae temple exploded in a simultaneous fireball.

Ahriman stared in open-mouthed horror at this trifecta of destruction. This was the death knell for his Legion. The perimeter was no more. The entire north-west sector was gone, and the enemy would pour through in unstoppable numbers as soon as they realised the boon they had just been handed.

The lull created by the destruction balanced on a knife edge, and the Thousand Sons were the first to recover their wits. As the Space Wolves picked themselves up, the Scarab Occult struck with a dreadful torrent of lethal powers. Blazing cones of lightning seared the enemy, gleeful arcs of crackling power leaping from warrior to warrior. Hissing fire swept through the streets, devouring all it touched, melting stone and ceramite and flesh in the inferno of its incredible heat.

At first, Ahriman dared to hope that the surging aetheric energy might yet be their salvation, but his hopes were dashed seconds later. A warrior ten metres to his left screamed in abject horror as his body erupted in a mass of hideous growths. His armour buckled and cracked as his mutant flesh spilled out with horrid fecundity. Another warrior followed, seconds later, his body borne aloft on a seething geyser of blue flame that consumed him in the time it took to draw breath.

Yet more hideous changes were being wrought upon the Thousand Sons, vile appendages erupting from splitting armour plates, squamous limbs and rugose growths pushing like jelly from gorgets and through bullet wounds with grotesquely wet sounds.

Warriors screamed and fell to their knees as decades of suppressed flesh change ripped its way to the surface. Dozens were falling prey to its malign influence with every second, and the cries of horror were not confined to the Space Wolves. The Spireguard fell back from their erstwhile allies, as the degenerate *things* the Thousand Sons were becoming turned on them with mindless hunger to feed their rampant growth.

'Everyone back!' shouted Ahriman, knowing that this position was lost.

Those Thousand Sons who resisted the flesh change took up the cry, and even a cursory glance told Ahriman they were the oldest and most experienced warriors of the Legion. He was glad to see that Sobek was amongst them. With the remnants of the Spireguard, he and his Practicus led the survivors back through the ruined edges of Old Tizca, moving swiftly along shell-cratered streets and avenues filled with fire and rubble.

Ahriman checked his weapon loadout, seeing he had a mere five magazines remaining to him. His heqa staff was still a potent weapon, its length crackling with invisible lines of force. He willed it to powerlessness, for he dared not wield it with so much wild energy filling the air. He would have need of his staff before the end of the fight, but he forced all thought of its use from his mind until he needed it most.

No sooner had he quelled his powers than he sensed a ghostly presence probing the aether around him, a questing tendril that spoke of another mind seeking his. Ahriman felt the primitive cunning of a hunter, the patience and animal circling that spoke of long years spent on the frozen tundra with nothing to warm the flesh but fur torn from the still warm corpse of native prey-beasts.

It took no great skill to recognise the presence, for he had swum the Great Ocean with this seeker. Ohthere Wyrdmake was hunting him, and Ahriman allowed his aetheric presence to bleed into the air, psychic spoor to draw the Rune Priest to him.

'Come find me, Wyrdmake,' he whispered. 'I welcome it.'

Ahriman led his tattered remnants through the ruins of his beloved city, picking up scattered warbands of shell-shocked Thousand Sons warriors from the west and east as they converged on Occullum Square. He counted several hundred close by, and only hoped there were others deeper in the city, for they would need more if they were to hold the Space Wolves and Custodes at bay.

Occullum Square was just ahead, and as Ahriman saw the toppled, bullet-ridden statues of a number of lions, he suddenly recognised where his line of retreat had led: the Street of a Thousand Lions. He almost laughed as he saw that the leftmost lion in the street had escaped destruction, its golden hide as polished and pristine as if it had only recently left the sculptor's workshop. He paused in his flight from Old Tizca and reached up to touch the rearing beast.

'Maybe you really are lucky,' he said, feeling foolish but not caring. 'I could use some of it if you have any to spare.'

'Superstition doesn't suit you,' said a voice behind him, and Ahriman smiled with genuine relief as he saw the limping form of Hathor Maat in the midst of the retreating warriors. Ahriman ran over to meet him, and they embraced like devoted brothers.

'What happened?' asked Ahriman, turning from the rearing lion.

'The Wolf King,' replied Hathor Maat, and Ahriman needed no further clarification.

'Phosis T'kar?' he asked as they set off south once more.

Hathor Maat looked away, and Ahriman saw the dreadful waxiness to his skin, an unhealthy pallor that was as alien and abhorrent to a biomancer as any gross mutation. To see the normally absurdly handsome Hathor Maat so broken was almost as unsettling as anything Ahriman had seen in the course of this nightmarish battle.

'The flesh change took him,' said Hathor Maat, the terror of what he had seen haunting his eyes. 'Valdor of the Custodes killed him, but I think Phosis T'kar let him. Better death than to live as a monster. Auramagma is gone too.'

Ahriman had no special regard for Auramagma beyond his status as a fellow captain, but he grieved the loss of Phosis T'kar. If he lived through this horror, he would grieve his friend in the proper manner, and once again he realised that only death allowed him to recognise a fellow warrior as a true friend.

He forced his grief for Phosis T'kar down, keeping to the lower Enumerations to close himself off from the loss. He wondered how the loss had affected Hathor Maat. Coagulated blood coated the left side of Maat's skull, but that was the least of his concerns. His skin shimmered with an internal light that rippled with the urge to change, and Ahriman hoped the vain warrior would resist the temptation to use his powers to stop it.

'Where are we going?' gasped Hathor Maat as they ran.

'The second line of defence,' said Ahriman.

'What second line of defence?'

'An east to west line between the pyramids of the Athanaeans and the Pavoni, with the Great Library at its centre and the Pyramid of Photep at its back.'

'That's a long line,' pointed out Hathor Maat.

'I know, but it is shorter than the last one. If we can hold it long enough to allow the bulk of Tizca's citizens to reach whatever safety the Pyramid of Photep can provide, then we'll have achieved something worthwhile.'

'It's not much.'

'It is all we can do,' said Ahriman, running south while casting hurried glances over his shoulder as he heard the first signs of pursuit. The horrific spawn many of his warriors had become would delay the Space Wolves, but Russ's butchers would carve their way through them soon enough. Ahriman swallowed his anger, knowing it would do no good, for it had too many targets. He had anger enough to last a thousand lifetimes.

Anger at the unthinking violence Russ and the Custodes had unleashed against them.

Anger at the death of so many brave warriors who deserved better.

Anger at how easily he had allowed himself to turn away from asking questions that needed to be asked.

But most of all, anger at Magnus for leaving them to face their doom alone.

AHRIMAN LED HIS warriors across Occullum Square, past the great urn-topped column at its centre, which, like the lion, had miraculously avoided destruction in the shelling. The square was a mass of people fleeing the wrath of the Space Wolves and Custodes, for the blades and bullets of the enemy were uncaring which of the city's inhabitants they cut down. Panicked people poured into the square from all its radiant streets, heading towards its southernmost exit, a wide avenue incongruously named the Palace of Wisdom.

A shattered arch lay in ruins around its entrance, and toppled columns lay strewn next to shattered statues of long-dead scholars of the Athanaeum. The gold-skinned form of Prospero's Great Library was barely visible through the smoke pouring from its shattered sides, and beyond it, the gleaming crystal form of Magnus's great pyramid reared over all.

More survivors of the aetheric burst and the Titan's fall poured into Occullum Square, and Ahriman estimated at least three thousand warriors of his Legion. Compared to the strength that had been fighting at the start of the battle it was pitifully few, but it was more than he had expected. How many, he wondered, had fallen to the enemy, and how many to the flesh change running rampant through their ranks?

He pushed the question aside. It was irrelevant, and he had more important matters to deal with. He ran towards the Palace of Wisdom, leaping a marble representation of the mad Scholar Alhazred with Sobek and Hathor Maat to either side of him. The Palace of Wisdom was paved with black marble slabs, each one engraved with an uplifting, cautionary or instructional quote from some of the Great Library's most prominent contributors. Dust, rubble and panicked citizens of Tizca obscured many of the slabs, but sensing a cosmic order to those that remained, Ahriman kept his eyes fixed on the ground as he ran.

The first slab bore the words: *without wisdom, power will destroy the one who wields it.*

Knowing there was no such thing as coincidence, Ahriman focussed his attention on each slab as he ran across it.

Seekers desire power but not wisdom. Power without wisdom is dangerous. Better to have wisdom first.

Those who have knowledge do not predict. Those who predict do not have knowledge.

If you abuse power, you will be burned and then you will learn. If you live.

And lastly, Ahriman smiled with grim amusement as he saw a slab that read, *Only the fool wishes to go into battle to beat someone for the satisfaction of beating someone.*

The significance of these words was not lost on him and he wondered why he had been chosen to see them. There was little he could do to affect the destiny of the Thousand Sons.

Only one being on Prospero could do that.

THE THOUSAND SONS formed up on the edges of the once-verdant park of the Great Library. Hathor Maat and Sobek formed the Scarab Occult and ragged warbands in a line of armoured bodies across the park, their guns pointed to the north. A mist of burnt sap and greenery clogged the air, and the smoke from the ashen forest hung low to the ground, like a noxious fog swirling around their ankles. The Great Library was in ruins behind them, its structure now barely recognisable as a pyramid. Its glassy sides were bathed in golden light from the fires raging throughout its many galleries. Its tip had caved in, and smoke poured from its collapsed summit like billowing spurts of lava from a steep-sided volcano.

Ahriman started as a memory overlaid his vision of the Great Library.

'What?' asked Hathor Maat, seeing his look of consternation.

'It wasn't Nikaea at all,' said Ahriman. 'I did not see the volcano at all. It was this… I saw this.'

'What are you talking about?'

'On Aghoru,' said Ahriman with mounting horror, 'I foresaw this, but I did not recognise it. I could have warned Magnus. I could have stopped this.'

Hathor Maat dragged him around.

'If you saw this, it was going to happen no matter what. There's nothing you could have done,' he said

'No,' said Ahriman, shaking his head. 'It doesn't work that way. The currents of the future are all echoes of *possible* futures. I could have–'

'Could have is irrelevant,' snapped Hathor Maat. 'You didn't see this. Neither did Amon, Ankhu Anen or Magnus or anyone else in the Corvidae. So stop worrying about what you didn't see, and pay more attention to what's right in front of you!'

The sheer incongruity of Hathor Maat giving him advice broke the spell of immobility that held him. Ahriman nodded and turned from the Great Library, concentrating his attention on their defensive line. It was easier to defend than the last one, but still too long for the number of warriors they had left.

The parkland was filled with ruined pavilions, low walls and decorative follies. On any normal day, its paths and arbours would be filled with citizens and scholars reading words of wisdom beneath the balmy sun. Ahriman had spent many a day beneath its green and pleasant boughs, ensconced in many a quaint and curious volume of forgotten lore. Now he looked on its walls, fallen trees, broken plinths and shaded hollows as defensive positions.

'We'll hold one attack, maybe two,' he said, reading the contours and angles of the devastated park. 'Then we must fall back to the Pyramid of Photep.'

'I think that might be optimistic,' said Hathor Maat, as Leman Russ led six thousand Astartes and Custodes towards their position like the closing jaws of a hungry wolf. It was a sight calculated to break the defenders' will, but Ahriman recalled a quote from a leader of Old Earth and lifted his voice so every Thousand Sons' warrior could hear him.

'The patriot volunteer, fighting for his country and his rights, makes the most reliable soldier on Earth,' he cried, pulling his bolter in tight to his shoulder. He aimed along the top of the gun and smiled without humour as he saw Ohthere Wyrdmake slotted neatly between the open sights of his bolter. The Rune Priest was way out of range to take the shot, but Ahriman had no intention of ending their enmity with something so banal as a bolter shell.

He handed his weapon to Sobek and turned to Hathor Maat.

'Remember on Aghoru when I told you we allowed our powers to define us, and that we needed to learn to fight as Astartes again?'

'Of course,' said Hathor Maat, confused as to Ahriman's meaning. 'What of it?'

'This is that moment,' said Ahriman, removing his helmet and dropping it to the blackened grass. 'Fight these dogs and show them that of all the mistakes they have ever made, underestimating us will be their most heinous. Fight them hard, but no one must use their powers or it will be their undoing.'

'What are you talking about? What are you going to do?'

Ahriman sat cross-legged on the blackened grass and gripped his heqa staff, its gold plated length and blue copper bands crackling with awakened power.

'Ignoring my own orders,' he said, and closed his eyes.

AHRIMAN LIFTED HIS body of light from his corporeal form with a breath. The raging currents of the Great Ocean lapped close to the surface of the world, making the transition as easy as it had ever been. The force of the tides battering his subtle flesh was enormous, driven to fury by the heightened emotions at work within the cauldron of combat in the material universe.

The flesh change sought to claim him, but he forced it down, knowing this was probably the last time he would fly the Great Ocean. He rose higher, seeing the blazing, serpentine curve of Tizca's outline and the red haze that lay over its once-proud architecture.

'Such hatred,' he whispered. 'Did we ever deserve so much?'

He flew from the park of the Great Library, fighting to hold his course in the face of battering currents and dangerous breakers. He felt the raw wound where the aether had broken through in the north-west, hearing the echo of a soul in torment as it was torn apart by the rapacious void-predators who gathered around the pulsing wound in the hope that it would open once more.

The line of enemy warriors shone with brilliant vividness: golden and red, vibrant and so sure of their purpose. They could not see how they might be wrong. Ahriman saw a mysterious cloud of deception lying over them and pitied them their ignorance.

'If you knew how you had been betrayed, you would join forces with us and end this.'

Darkened shrouds hung over the advancing warriors and tanks, areas of dead space where Sisters of Silence guarded the host's captains. Ahriman avoided them, knowing he would be hurled back to his body should he venture within such a hateful darkness. His foeman would never set foot within such darkness, for he was as hypocritical as the rest of them.

Ahriman smiled as he saw Ohthere Wyrdmake, so proud, so arrogant and so filled with anger that it was a wonder he could function as a human being. As much as he told himself he did this for his Legion's survival, Ahriman was forced to admit he was going to enjoy this mission of revelation.

He reached down with ghostly hands and wrenched Wyrdmake's body of light from his flesh, tearing up with such violent suddenness that the Rune Priest's armoured limbs went as rigid as a fresh-carved statue. His comrades and acolytes rushed to his aid, but Wyrdmake was beyond their help now.

Ahriman released his nemesis as his shimmering form took shape, coalescing into a bright replica of the man below. His aura blazed with shock and anger, but that quickly turned to sly hatred as he saw who floated before him.

'Warlock,' spat Wyrdmake.

'Is that all you have for me, old friend?' asked Ahriman, folding his arms. 'Insults?'

'I have sought you this day,' said Wyrdmake.

'I know, I felt your clumsy pursuit. A Neophyte of Prospero could have sensed you. How did you acquire my psychic trace?'

'Your brother in the library gave you up,' said Wyrdmake triumphantly.

Ahriman laughed.

'Is that what you think happened?' he asked. 'If Ankhu Anen did so, it was because he *wanted* you to find me. He knew I would kill you if you did.'

'I think not,' said Wyrdmake, a golden staff appearing in his hands.

Ahriman shook his head and the staff exploded into shards of fading light.

'In this place, in this realm, do you really think we will fight like that?'

Wyrdmake hurled himself towards Ahriman, his hands outstretched like claws and his face transforming into that of a snarling wolf with its jaws poised to tear out his throat. Ahriman surged to meet him and they came together in a blazing explosion of power.

Wyrdmake clawed at him, but Ahriman moved like quicksilver, evading every strike and rising higher and higher into the Great Ocean. Spinning like intertwined spirals of genetic code, they streaked through the aether, Wyrdmake attacking in a frenzy of claws and snapping bites, Ahriman deflecting every strike with graceful precision.

'You are the same as me,' he said, evading yet another raging attack.

Wyrdmake broke away from Ahriman's blazing form and shook his head, the wolf-form retreating within his shimmering flesh.

'I am nothing like you,' he snarled. 'My power comes from the natural cycle of birth and death of Fenris. I am a Son of the Storm. I am nothing like you.'

'And yet you are not on Fenris,' said Ahriman. 'We call it by different names, but the power you use to call the storm and split the earth is the same power I use to scry the future and shape the destiny of my Legion.'

'Is this all *you* have for *me*?' snapped Wyrdmake. 'Lies? I can believe nothing you say.'

'Lies?' said Ahriman. 'Look at what you are doing to my world. I have no need of lies. The truth is my weapon.'

No sooner had the words left him than he shot forwards, his essence enveloping Wyrdmake's. He stabbed a spear of brightness into the Rune Priest, but this was no assault on Wyrdmake's body of light. It was a spear of truth.

'You cannot understand the truth without understanding the omnipresent character of the *untruth* you are bound to. Enlightenment is fruitless until you free yourself from the lie. The power of truth will merge with you when you become free from all forms of deception. This is my gift to you, Ohthere Wyrdmake!'

Ahriman poured everything into the Rune Priest: the corruption of Horus and the betrayal of everything the Emperor had sought to create, the monstrous scale of the imminent war and the horror that lay at the end of it. Win or lose, a time of ultimate darkness was coming, and as Ahriman opened Wyrdmake to all that he had seen, he too learned all that had driven the Space Wolves and the Custodes to make such furious war upon the Thousand Sons.

He saw the honeyed words of Horus and the sinister urgings of Constantin Valdor, each spoken with very different purposes, but designed to sway Leman Russ towards a destination of total destruction.

The scale of this betrayal shocked him to the root of all that he was. Ahriman had come to terms with Horus

Lupercal's betrayal, for it had its origins in the snares and delusions woven by beings to whom the passage of vigintillions of aeons were but the blink of an eye. This? This was all too human treachery. These were lies, told for noble reasons, but which had brought about the unintended consequences of Prospero's destruction.

Anger overtook Ahriman, and he hurled himself at Wyrdmake once more, tearing into his subtle body with unthinking anger. Wyrdmake fought back, but his struggles were feeble, his mind aflame with the horrors Ahriman had shown him.

They fell through the Great Ocean, the weight of their emotions dragging them back to their bodies. Shoals of void-predators came with them, terrible abominations of nightmares undreamed, abortions of monstrous appetite and fiends of insatiable hunger. Ahriman felt their presence, and shaped them further with the most hideous imaginings he could conjure, phage beasts of fang and claw, nameless forms and vampiric bloodlust.

At last they returned to the hate-bathed city of Tizca, its ghostly image like looking through a thick fog or a grimy window. Ahriman saw the fighting raging through the blasted park, the clash of Space Wolves and Thousand Sons as both forces tore at one another for all the wrong reasons. Sobek, Hathor Maat and the Scarab Occult stood sentinel over his body as the fighting pushed the Thousand Sons' line inexorably back.

Leman Russ was a blazing column of light as he killed warriors by the score, and Ahriman knew that nothing could stop this feral god from tearing the Thousand Sons apart. His two wolves, representations of light and dark, smashed warriors from their feet and ripped them to pieces, their savagery the equal of their master. Ahriman dragged his gaze from the Wolf King and his bestial companions, and held the slumped Wyrdmake before him.

The Rune Priest was a broken shadow of his former haughty self. His subtle body haemorrhaged life energy and his aura flickered with the damage Ahriman's truth had wrought upon his mind.

All his certainty was undone and his soul was bare, raw and undefended.

'This is for Ankhu Anen,' said Ahriman, and he threw Wyrdmake to the void-predators. They closed on his helpless form with hungry savagery, snapping and tearing with warp-sharpened claws and vorpal fangs. It was over in seconds, the glowing morsels of the Rune Priest's soul devoured and lost forever.

Ahriman watched with no small amount of satisfaction as Ohthere Wyrdmake's armoured form collapsed, the body of flesh unable to survive the death of the soul. Part of him recoiled from so dark a deed, but the heart of him rejoiced to see his enemy so wholly destroyed.

Ahriman opened his eyes and took a deep breath, feeling the many repercussions that coloured his flesh like angry bruises. The sounds of battle were deafening, and the howling of wolves echoed throughout what was left of Tizca. In an instant, he saw that the battle for Tizca was as good as over. Prospero was lost.

His grip on his heqa staff was rigid, and he saw its gold and blue banding fade until its entire length was utterly black. The symbolism was unmistakable.

'So be it,' he said.

AHRIMAN FOUGHT BACK to back with Hathor Maat, holding their line together in the face of the savagery of the Space Wolves and the Emperor's praetorians. Chainblades rose and fell, their jagged, icy teeth red with Astartes blood, and bolters fired hard rounds that impacted and penetrated their targets without time to arm.

Their line had not held against the unbridled savagery of Leman Russ, and this final stand was being made in the shadow of the Pyramid of Photep. Shards of crystalline glass floated on the oil-scummed waters surrounding

Magnus the Red's lair. The surviving populace of Tizca, who had escaped the initial wrath of the invaders, sheltered within, the last of a great lineage of scholars who had not only endured Old Night, but thrived in its wake.

Armoured vehicles crushed statues and fallen tree trunks, their guns trained on the vast pyramid behind the battle. The struggling warriors were too enmeshed for any of the gunners to draw a clear shot, and so they contented themselves with demolishing the sanctum of their enemies' primarch. The Pyramid of Photep shimmered in the fading light, its gleaming surface and silver towers bathed in the hellish light of its own destruction. Explosions bloomed upon the mighty crux ansata engraved on its front, and glass rained from its ruptured flanks.

Ahriman knew the end was upon them, for fewer than fifteen hundred of the Legion remained alive. Such a force could conquer planets and quell entire rebellions with ease, but against more than three times their number and facing no less a warrior than a primarch, this was a battle that could only end one way.

To fight was to doom both Legions in the coming war, but Ahriman could no more let these barbarians despoil his world without a struggle than he could undo the past. The Wolf King had built pyres of irreplaceable knowledge and smashed priceless artefacts unique in all the galaxy with the careless stoke of his frostblade.

Such ignorance and thoughtless destruction could not go unanswered.

'I said you were being optimistic,' said Hathor Maat, punching his heqa staff through the neck of a helmetless Space Wolf. Blood squirted from the ruptured jugular, and Hathor Maat completed the kill with a bolt round through the warrior's skull.

'I stand corrected,' said Ahriman, his thoughts drifting now that he had accepted the notion of his death. In what he knew would be his last moments, he wondered what had happened to Lemuel and his fellow remembrancers. Ahriman had not seen them since Kallista Eris's death, and he hoped they had somehow survived this horror, though he knew they were probably dead. The thought saddened him, but if this battle had taught him anything, it was that regret was pointless. Only the future mattered and only through the acquisition of knowledge could it be preserved. He lamented that he would never get the chance to replace all that had been lost on Prospero.

A screaming wolf leapt at him and Ahriman put a bolt through its skull. It landed in front of him and he recoiled in horror as he saw this was no wolf, but a monstrous beast clad in fragments of armour, as though a warrior's body had transformed into some hell-beast.

'What in the name of the Great Ocean!' cried Hathor Maat, as yet more of the hideous melds of man and wolf came at them.

Something Ohthere Wyrdmake had once said to Ahriman returned to him, and he watched as yet more of the howling man-wolf creatures leapt to the attack.

'Wulfen!' he shouted, unleashing torrents of bolter shells into the mass of charging beasts.

'And they say *we* are the monsters!' shouted Hathor Maat.

The Wulfen were once Astartes, but Astartes afflicted by a terrible curse. Their faces were bestial, but with the last glimmerings of intelligence in the yellowed depths of their sunken eyes. Matted fur covered their faces and hands, yet their jaws were not distended like a wolf's. Razor-sharp fangs and talons were their weapons, for the knowledge of technology was lost to these savage killers.

Only the most accurate shots would put them down, and they shrugged off wounds that would have killed even an Astartes. Their claws could tear through battle-plate with ease, and their teeth were as vicious as any energised blade. The single-minded savagery was unlike anything the

Thousand Sons had fought before, and they fell back from these newly unleashed terrors, horrified that the Space Wolves would dare employ such degenerate abominations.

The Wulfen punched a bloody hole in the Thousand Sons' line, tearing it wider with every second, and dozens of warriors fell beneath the tearing blades of their claws. Howls of triumph filled the air as the gap the Wulfen had opened was filled with Custodes and Space Wolf warriors. Bands of Thousand Sons were surrounded and hacked down by frost-bladed axes and glittering Guardian Spears.

Ahriman backed along the great basalt causeway over the water towards the Pyramid of Photep, their last refuge on Tizca. The best and bravest of the Legion, all that survived to sell their lives in sight of their primarch, went with him towards the bronze gates that led inside.

The howling of the Wulfen built to a deafening crescendo.

And high above, those howls were finally answered.

CHAPTER THIRTY-ONE

Prospero's Lament

PURPLE LIGHTNING SPLIT the sky and the heavens darkened with the sudden fall of night. A deluge of black rain fell, soaking everything in an instant and saturating the air with the bitter taste of sodden ashes. Ahriman looked up in shock to see a flaming giant descending from the highest reaches of the Pyramid of Photep. The crux ansata rippled with pellucid green fire, and kaleidoscopic bolts of lightning slammed into the ground, immolating dozens of the cursed Wulfen with every blazing strike.

Cracks split the ground and the waters surrounding the pyramid seethed and boiled with anger. Black waves crashed upon the shores, and the glass shards falling from the pyramid were caught in a surging, sentient whirlwind that hurled them like spears to impale enemy warriors and skewer them to the ground.

Ahriman felt an enormous build up of energy, and summoned all his strength to control his body, knowing the mutations within his flesh would seek to throw off the shackles of his form and unleash new and terrifying ones within him. Yet the painful surge of mutant growth never came, and he looked up at the radiant being of fire and light that drew ever closer.

Magnus the Red was a glorious sight, his golden armour and wild red hair ablaze with aetheric energy. His bladed staff threw off blinding arcs of lightning that destroyed armoured vehicles in thunderous explosions. Magnus swept his eye across the horrified Space Wolves, and all who met his gaze died in an instant as they were driven to madness by the stygian depths of infinite chaos they saw there.

Above Tizca, madness raged as the power of the Great Ocean pressed in and the sky became a transparent window into the realm beyond. Gibbous eyes the size of mountains, and amorphous monsters the likes of which only madmen could dream, leered down on the doomed world below. Hundreds died instantly at the sight of such blasphemous horrors.

No sane man could witness such vileness without recoiling, and the invading army paused in its slaughter, shocked by the sight of such dreadful things glaring hungrily at the world below. Even the Wulfen cowered before the sight of these abominable creatures, suddenly feeling the overwhelming insignificance of their existence.

Only Leman Russ and his wolf companions stood unfazed by this vision of Magnus, and Ahriman saw a gleam of anticipation in the Wolf King's eyes, as though he relished the idea of the coming conflict.

Magnus set foot on the causeway, and the normal tempo of time's passage slowed, each raindrop falling as though in slow motion, the zigzagging traceries of lightning moving with infinite slowness. The volcanic stone of the causeway rippled with transformative energies beneath Magnus's feet, and Ahriman dropped to his

knees before his primarch, centuries of ingrained obe-
dience making the motion unconscious.

The Primarch of the Thousand Sons was a divine, rapturous figure of light amid the darkness. The gold of his
armour had never been brighter, the red of his vast
mane never more vivid. His flesh burned with the touch
of immense power, greater than anything it had ever
contained before. His eye locked onto Ahriman, and the
depths of despair he saw in that haunted, glowing orb
froze the blood in his veins. In that moment, Ahriman
felt the horror Magnus had felt as his sons mutated into
monsters and the anguish, centuries later, as he watched
them butchered to serve a brother's lunatic ambition.

He understood the noble ideal that had stayed the
primarch's hand throughout the battle, recognising it
for what it was, not for what he had thought it to be. He
felt his father's forgiveness for doubting him, and heard
his voice in his head.

'This doom was always meant for me, not you,' said
Magnus, and Ahriman knew that every warrior of the
Thousand Sons was hearing the same thing. 'You are my
sons, and I have failed you.'

Ahriman wanted to weep at his primarch's words,
feeling the sorrow of a being who had beheld all of creation, but had fallen short in his reach to grasp it. When
Magnus spoke again, he alone heard the primarch's
voice.

'Ahzek, lead my sons within the pyramid.'

'No!' he cried, tears of grief mingling with the rain
falling in endless torrents.

'You must,' insisted Magnus, lifting his red arm and
pointing towards the bronze gates of the pyramid,
which now swung open. White light shone enticingly
from within. 'Amon awaits you, and he bears a priceless
gift you must bear away from this place. You must do
this, or all we have done here will have meant nothing.'

'What of you, my lord?' asked Ahriman. 'What will you do?'

'What I must,' said Magnus, looking over at the raging form of Leman Russ as he charged with a glacial lack of speed onto the causeway. The primarch reached down and touched the jade scarab in the centre of Ahriman's breast-plate. The crystal shone with a pale light, and Ahriman felt the immense power resting within it.

'This was cut from the Reflecting Caves,' said Magnus. 'Every warrior of my Legion bears one set in his armour. When the moment comes, and you will know it when it does, concentrate all your energies on the this crystal and those of your battle-brothers.'

'I don't understand,' pleaded Ahriman. 'What must I do?'

'What you have been destined to do since before you were born,' said Magnus. 'Now go!'

'I will stand with you,' vowed Ahriman.

'No,' said Magnus with an endless abyss of regret. 'You will not. Our fates are unravelling even now, and what happens here *has* to happen. Do this last thing for me, Ahzek.'

Though it broke his heart, Ahriman nodded, and the world swelled around him as the flow of time restored its integrity from the distortion Magnus's arrival had caused. The bellows of burning pyres and immaterial thunder rolled across the face of the world once more, and the deafening fire of weapons roared even louder than before.

The howl of the Wolf King blotted them all out.

Ahriman and the Thousand Sons turned and ran towards the Pyramid of Photep.

MASSES OF PEOPLE filled the pyramid, terrified civilians and exhausted Spireguard. The Thousand Sons poured inside, their armour black and dripping from the nightmarish deluge drowning the world beyond. At a conservative estimate, Ahriman guessed that just over a thousand warriors had escaped the attack of the Wulfen.

'A tenth of the Legion,' he said.

The horrifying scale of the loss staggered him.

Hathor Maat and Sobek came alongside him as he struggled to come to terms with what had become of their beloved Legion. Still numb from the sight of so few survivors, Ahriman sought out Amon, who stood in the centre of the vast chamber.

Amon was clad in his armour, but the plates were clean and unblemished. His weapons were sheathed and he carried a reinforced chest, sealed with a padlock of cold iron.

'He said you would live,' said Amon.

'The primarch?'

'Yes. Years ago as you lay dying in the midst of the flesh change he knew you would live to see this moment.'

'Spare me your tales,' stormed Ahriman. 'The primarch said you have something for me?'

'I do,' confirmed Amon, holding the chest up for Ahriman to open.

'It is locked.'

'To all others perhaps, but not to you.'

'We don't have time for this,' hissed Ahriman, looking over his shoulder as two gods of war clashed with the sound of worlds colliding. Blazing light filled the pyramid, and the howl of Leman Russ vied with the thunderous lightning of Magnus.

'You must *make* time,' snapped Amon, 'or all this will be for nothing.'

Ahriman reached up and took hold of the lock, which snapped open with a metallic click at his touch. He opened the lid and drew in a breath as he saw the book within, its cover red and cracked with age, as though it

were an archaeological find instead of a working grimoire.

'The Book of Magnus,' breathed Hathor Maat.

'Why me?' demanded Ahriman.

'Because you are its new bearer,' said Amon. 'You are
to keep it safe and ensure the knowledge contained
within its pages never falls into the wrong hands.'

Ahriman lifted the book from the iron chest, feeling
the weight of power and expectation contained within
its hallowed pages. The potency of the incantations and
formulae called to him, alluring and redolent with
promises of the great things he might achieve with the
secrets inscribed upon its pages.

He wanted to refuse, to place the book back in its
chest and secure the lock so that no one would ever gaze
upon its pages and crave the power it could grant. He
wanted Magnus to return and retrieve his grimoire, but
understood with sudden clarity that was never going to
happen.

Magnus had no expectation of surviving his duel with
Leman Russ.

Ahriman took the book and ran back to the bronze
gates of the pyramid, desperation lending his strides
greater speed. Brilliant flashes of light and thunderous
impacts came from the other side of the gate, as colossal forces beyond mortal comprehension were
unleashed.

Ahriman reached the mighty portal, and saw a battle
between two brothers that was unparalleled in its savagery, power and folly. Magnus and the Wolf King
struggled with the fate of a world balanced on the out-
come. Forking traceries of lightning shot upwards from
the ground, isolating them from the host of Wolves and
Custodes.

Russ rained blow after blow on Magnus, shattering
the horned breastplate, and in return Magnus struck his

brother with a searing blast of cold fire that cracked his armour and set light to his braided hair.

It seemed as though the combatants had swollen to enormous proportions, like the giants they were in the myths and legends. The Wolf King's frostblade struck at Magnus, but his golden axe turned the blow aside as they spun and twisted in an epic battle beneath the madness of a blazing storm of sheet lightning and pounding thunder. This was a battle fought on every level: physical, mental and spiritual, with each primarch bending every ounce of their almost limitless power to the other's destruction.

The waters around the pyramid broke upon the shores, black as oil, and churning as though an unseen tempest boiled beneath the surface. Space Wolves and Custodes ploughed through the water, wading through the crashing spray to reach the pyramid in lieu of aiding Leman Russ in his battle. Magnus swept his hands to the side, and the warriors on the water cried out in agony as it transformed into corrosive acid, burning through ceramite plates and rendering flesh and bone to jelly.

Thick rain fell, fit to drown the world, and the ground underfoot transformed into a stinking quagmire from which writhing shapes like grasping hands emerged. Wounded warriors were dragged down into the mud, struggling against their unseen attackers, but unable to resist being pulled under to their doom.

Prospero was breaking apart, the veil between worlds cracking, and the maddening gibbers and screams of the Great Ocean's denizens drove men to their knees in terror. The assault on the senses was total, and Ahriman could barely keep his feet as hurricane-force winds battered the pyramid, tearing glass panes from its structure and breaking the silver and gold towers from its corners. Thunder banged in the midnight sky, and heaving earthquakes ripped ever-widening cracks in the ground, toppling what few structures of Tizca remained standing.

The epicentre of this destruction was Magnus and Russ, and Ahriman watched the two titans wrestle with the bitter enmity reserved only for those who had once called each other friend. Such a contest of arms was the most desperate thing Ahriman had ever seen. He wanted to rush forward and remind them of their former kinship, but to intervene in such a planet-shaking conflict would be suicide.

Ahriman had cautioned his warriors not to wield their powers for fear of the flesh change, but Magnus showed no such restraint and battered Leman Russ with fists wreathed in fire and lightning. Russ was a primarch and such powers as could shatter armies had little effect on him save to drive him to higher fits of rage.

Magnus drove his fist into Russ's chest, the icy breastplate cracking open with a sound like planets colliding, and shards of ceramite stabbed the Wolf King's heart. In return, Russ snapped Magnus's arm back, and Ahriman heard it shatter into a thousand pieces. A blade of pure thought unsheathed from Magnus's other arm, and he drove it deep into Russ's chest through his shattered armour.

The blade burst from Russ's back and the Wolf King loosed a deafening bellow of pain. A chorus of the wolves that were not wolves added their howls to that of their master. The two enormous lupine monsters that accompanied Russ leapt upon Magnus, fastening their jaws upon his legs. Magnus slammed his fist into the black wolf's head, driving it to the ground with a strangled yelp, its skull surely shattered. With a bellow of anger, Magnus tore the white wolf from his leg with a thought and hurled it away over the heads of the milling army at Russ's back.

Ahriman felt hands dragging him away as the howling winds and driving rain tore through the gates. He tried to shake them off as someone shouted his name. Hathor Maat and Amon pulled him away from the entrance as the vast mechanisms slowly began hauling the enormous gates closed.

'No!' he shouted, his words snatched away by the screaming winds. 'We can't!'

'We must!' shouted Hathor Maat, pointing towards the crashing waters separating the Space Wolves from the pyramid. Using the stocks of their bolters as paddles, the enemy had jury-rigged concave shards of roof debris to use as makeshift boats, and were surging over the waves towards the gateway. The water had returned to its natural state, frothed patches of liquefied flesh and bone scumming its surface the only reminder of the men who had died there. Hordes of Wulfen plunged into the water, entire packs pushing towards the pyramid with hundreds more right behind them.

Ahriman looked past the approaching monsters to see Magnus and Russ locked in battle high above the causeway, the furious horror of their struggle obscured by ethereal fire and bursts of lightning. A flare of black light erupted and Russ cried out in agony. His blade lashed out blindly and struck a fateful blow against his foe's most dreaded weapon: his eye.

In an instant, the pyrotechnic cascade of light and fire was extinguished and a stunning silence swept outwards. All motion ceased, and the titans battling on the causeway were no more, each primarch now restored to his customary stature.

Ahriman cried out as he saw Magnus reel back from the Wolf King, one hand clutched to his eye as his shattered arm crackled with regenerative energies. As broken and bloodied as Leman Russ was, he was brawler enough to seize his opportunity. He barrelled into Magnus and gripped him around the waist like a wrestler, roaring as he lifted his brother's body high above his head.

All eyes turned to Russ as he brought Magnus down across his knee, and the sound of the Crimson King's back breaking tore through every warrior of the Thousand Sons' heart.

Ahriman fell to his knees, dropping the Book of Magnus as sympathetic pain, like a white-hot spear, stabbed through him. No pain in the world was worse, for this blow could unmake a primarch, and such wounds were a death-strike a hundred times over to any mortal warrior. He knelt against the closing gateway as the Wulfen packs reached the shoreline alongside warriors led by a bloody-fanged captain with burned hair and an ice-bladed axe.

The Wolf King howled his triumph to the blackened heavens, and a rain of blood replaced the oil-black downpour as Prospero wept for her fallen son. Ahriman's tears were bloody as Leman Russ dropped Magnus to the mud and brought the frostblade Mjalnar around to take the head of his defeated foe.

With the last of his strength, Magnus turned his head, and his ravaged eye found Ahriman.

This is my last gift to you.

Leman Russ's blade swept down, but before its lethal edge struck, Magnus whispered unnatural syllables unknown to Man since he had first raised his guttural chants to the nameless gods of the sky. Magnus's body underwent an instantaneous dissolution, its entire structure unmade with a word, and Ahriman gasped as vast and depthless power surged into his body.

It was too much for any mortal man to contain, but as it swept through him, he knew what he had to do.

Ahriman clasped his hands upon the jade scarab set in his breastplate, filling his mind with its every curve and nuance, its imperfections, the intricacies of its golden mounting and the exact dimensions of the black scarab worked into its substance.

He knew everything about that gem, and pictured the identical artefact on the chest of each warrior of the Thousand Sons. Even as he visualised them, the power in him spread to the entire Legion as Magnus gave the last of his strength to save his sons.

A terrific groaning shattered the stillness, like the spine of the world shearing out of true. The sound of madness tore through the mundane substance of reality as the dying breath of a god unleashed power of impossible magnitude.

The surface of Prospero *twisted*, and Ahriman felt a dreadful lurch of sickening vertigo. It felt like the bottom was falling out of the world, or like he was plunging down an endless shaft. The world vanished, replaced with the utter blackness at the end of the universe when all living things have been dust for billions of years.

It was not silent, this blackness, but filled with myriad howls, as though hunting packs of wolves stalked the unseen corners between worlds with them. Was there to be no escape from the Emperor's war dogs?

With savage suddenness the impenetrable, lightless void was replaced with a swirling maelstrom of light and colour, blistering visions of hellish despair and unbridled ecstasy. Everything and nothing came in and out of the bond in moments, stretching out to infinity as the nightmare continued.

Ahriman felt his grip on sanity slipping, the fragile notions of reality that mortals cling to snapping one by one as his mind was bombarded with a billion images at once.

Mercifully, his mind hurled itself into unconsciousness lest it be blasted to psychosis by this unceasing barrage of sensation.

Ahriman floated into the darkness, lost in space and time.

This is the end.

But it was not the end.

Ahriman opened his eyes and found himself face down on a slab of jagged black rock. Every portion of his body was in pain, from his bruised and battered body to the very sinews of his mind. Flickering embers of light reflected on the gleaming obsidian ground and he groaned as he tried to piece together the last remnants of his memory.

Thunder boomed overhead and crackling lightning threw strobing shadows out before him. Though his body protested with searing pain, Ahriman pushed himself into a kneeling position and looked around to see what had become of Prospero.

His first thought was that the last work of Magnus had wrought a dreadful change upon their home world, but it soon penetrated his fractured mind that the sky was not that of Prospero. It boiled with storms of a million colours, jagged forks of light and fire dancing in crackling columns that reached from the ground to the clouds.

He knelt upon the lower slope of an outcrop of black rock overlooking a broken volcanic plain ruptured with smoking fissures and threaded with glowing streams of lava. Gnarled fists of rock thrust up from the plain, their peaks topped with crooked silver towers that stood in mocking imitation of the graceful spires of Tizca. The leather-bound Book of Magnus lay beside him, and he tucked it protectively under his arm.

Jagged mountain peaks soared into the shimmering sky that bellowed with peals of thunder. The sky hazed and shimmered like the most magnificent Mechanicum Borealis, but this was no side effect of centuries of pollution and industry. This was raw aether saturating the air and raging with oceanic tides of power.

Warriors of the Thousand Sons wandered aimlessly across the broken rockscape in their hundreds, stunned at the desolation they found themselves in. Quaking discharges rumbled beneath the ground, as though an endless series of underground tremors constantly reshaped the planet's core.

Ahriman rose to his feet, surveying the nightmarish landscape of everlasting turmoil. A hunched figure shambled towards him, head down, and he recognised the battered form of Khaphed, one of the Lore-Keepers within the Corvidae library. In this hellish place, it was a blessed relief to see a familiar face.

'Khaphed? Is that you?' asked Ahriman, feeling his speech fill the air with potential for wonders and raptures, as though every breath was charged with power.

The warrior didn't answer and Ahriman felt a dreadful force within Khaphed's body. The Lore-Keeper's head came up and Ahriman took a backward step as he saw the mutant growths that transformed Khaphed. Distended eyes pushed their way from every surface on the warrior's face, such that there was no longer a mouth, nose or any other sense organ other than eyes.

Khaphed reached for him, his myriad eyes silently imploring him for help.

Ahriman thrust his hand towards Khaphed and unleashed a barrage of fire and lightning into the Lore-Keeper's body. Such powers were the provenance of the Raptora and Pavoni, but they leapt from Ahriman's fingers as naturally as though he had been trained by those cults since birth.

Khaphed's charred body collapsed and shattered into ashen fragments as it hit the ground.

Horrified, Ahriman ran down the slopes to rejoin the rest of his warriors.

* * *

HE FOUND HATHOR Maat, Amon and Sobek quickly enough, but it soon became clear that the Lore-Keeper of the Corvidae was not the only member of the Legion to have succumbed to the flesh change. Dozens more required to be put down, until at last all that remained appeared to be free of mutation.

All told, twelve hundred and forty-two warriors had survived the razing of Prospero.

'Where are we?' asked Sobek, raising the most obvious question.

No one had an answer, and for long days and nights, though it was impossible to gauge the passage of time since everyone's armour chrono had failed, the Thousand Sons explored the hideous desolation that was their new home.

The silver towers were discovered not to be parodies of those that had been raised on Tizca, but those self-same towers, broken and twisted by the strange alchemy that had brought them to this place. Beyond these relics of their lost home world, there was nothing to shed any light on the nature of the place.

No power of the Corvidae or any other cult could fathom its location or any hint of how they had come to be deposited upon its blasted surface.

All that changed on the day the Obsidian Tower rose from the depths.

IT BEGAN WITH yet another earthquake, a common enough occurrence that no one paid any mind at first. A sullen mood had fallen upon the Thousand Sons, which was wholly expected, for what manner of man would not keenly feel the loss of his home, father and brothers?

But this earthquake did not simply fade away after splitting yet another fissure in the endless volcanic plain while sealing another shut. Cracks spread from the centre of the plain in a radial pattern and a black diamond, like a thrusting basalt speartip, exploded upwards.

It rose into the sky, pushing higher and higher and growing wider and wider with every passing moment until a new mountain had been birthed. Towering and steep-sided, it rose higher than Olympus Mons and the Mountain of Aghoru combined. Broken rocks tumbled from its impossible height, falling from its angular sides to craft a fringe comprising shattered cyclopean stone and titanic blocks of strange angles and impossible perspectives.

When the rain of dust and debris had ended, the Thousand Sons gathered at the base of this stupendous creation, knowing that nothing natural could have created so magnificent an edifice. Glowing fire arced from the distant mountain's peak and a shimmering blue light suffused its entirety, as though lightning filled its tunnels like blood in a circulatory system.

A bright shape descended from the mountaintop, a wavering and indistinct form wreathed in the light of stars and the power of infinite possibility. Brilliant wings of shimmering aetheric fire unfolded from the figure's back, and the Thousand Sons fell to their knees as their father's light spread over them.

Magnus landed softly before his sons and they stared in amazement as his light illuminated the bleak darkness of the world. This was no corporeal shell of a subtle body as worn by the primarch when he had walked among them. This was a body of light that could exist beyond the confines of the Great Ocean. Magnus had sacrificed the flesh that had contained his essence, and in so doing had ascended to a more evolved form, one free from the constraints of mortality and the limits of reality.

'My sons,' said Magnus with weary resignation, 'welcome to the Planet of the Sorcerers.'

Time has passed.

Centuries or days, who can know?

It may be both and neither at the same time.

I cannot say how long has passed since we first came here, for I have come to appreciate that such concepts are an irrelevance here. All I know is that things have become immeasurably worse since the Obsidian Tower first reared its ugly immensity from the earth. Some say we could not have guessed that this world would have worked its evil upon us. I say: How could we not have known?

Hathor Maat fears it the worst, but I confess I too suffer the nightmarish dread that one day I will become less than nothing, a devolved creature with nothing left of the man I once was. Some even embrace their new forms, believing them to be marks of favour.

Fools.

It has become ever more rife amongst our number, and seventy-two warriors have succumbed to the flesh change since Magnus first spirited us away from Prospero.

Spirited… An old word, but an apt one perhaps, for we did not arrive on this desolate world by accident. This planet was waiting for us, prepared aeons ago by an intelligence greater than anyone, primarch or mortal, can possibly comprehend.

Magnus broods in his black tower, peering into the depths of the Great Ocean for validation, a sign that he was right to act as he did.

He will find nothing, for there is nothing to find.

His actions were never his own, for he forgot the first rule of the mysteries.

He let his ambition and hubris blind him to his flaws and the knowledge that there is always someone stronger and more powerful out there.

I will not make that mistake.

But we are still creatures of flesh and inclined to repeat our past mistakes, so I have been careful to surround myself with naysmiths to rein in my arrogance.

The bloodline of the Thousand Sons was born from the power that thrives all around us. We were given the chance to gather and pass on the knowledge of a hidden world, but we failed in that most golden of opportunities.

There are those among the remains of the Legion who do not believe the power of the Great Ocean can ever be mastered, that our accursed fate is clear evidence of that stark fact.

They are wrong.

This world is full of potential, but it is dangerous. Once I set foot on the path I believe will free us from our slow slide into degeneration there will be no leaving it. The Great Work I have begun will be the first step in proving how right we were, how loyal we were and how loyal we might yet be.

I promised to restore all that was lost when Prospero fell, and I intend to make good on that vow. This cabal will be the opening move in restoring the Thousand Sons to glory in the eyes of the Emperor.

I can feel them drawing near, the captains I must convince if I am to succeed.

Hathor Maat, I already know will join me, for he fears the ruin of his flesh more keenly than any. Sobek will follow my lead, as he has always done, but Amon?

Amon will resist, for he has served Magnus for longer than any of us can know.

He will be the key.

Win him over and this will work.

The Book of Magnus lies open before me, its pages filled with forbidden lore and knowledge from ancient, forgotten days. It holds the key to our salvation. In the labyrinthine collections of formulae, incantations and rites, I have found what I believe will be the beginnings of a mighty spell to undo all that has befallen us.

I call it the Rubric.

ABOUT THE AUTHOR

Hailing from Scotland, **Graham McNeill**
worked for over six years as a Games Developer
in Games Workshop's Design Studio before
taking the plunge to become a full-time writer. In
addition to sixteen previous novels, Graham's
written a host of SF and Fantasy stories and
comics, as well as a number of side projects that
keep him busy and (mostly) out of trouble.
Graham lives and works in Nottingham and you
can keep up to date with where he'll be and what
he's working on by visiting his website.

Join the ranks of the Fourth Company at
www.graham-mcneill.com

RYNN'S
WORLD

STEVE PARKER

The brand
new Space Marine
Battles series

UK ISBN 978-1-84416-802-6 US ISBN 978-1-84416-803-4